GALAXY RUN

THE COMPLETE FIRST SERIES

SAM RENNER

DEDICATION

For Gina.
For Ellie.
For Haddie.
For Liam.

CONTENTS

ACKNOWLEDGMENTS

Writing has been a thing that's always been there, something I've always done. But it wasn't something I pursued in earnest until I met the right person. This book wouldn't have become a reality if I wasn't encouraged by a pretty woman telling me she found writers attractive. Didn't matter if it was true or not, it's all I needed to make this hobby something more serious. So, thanks **Gina**, for the encouragement.

Thanks also to the rest of my family—**Ellie, Haddie, Liam, Mom, Dad,** and **Justin**—for either encouraging me to pursue a life of words when I was younger or tolerating that continued pursuit now that I'm older.

01: THE CASE

ONE

Blood drips in thin streams from the gash on his head. It comes in wider rivers from his nose. Which, he knows, is probably broken. The tears in his eyes—pain tears, not crying tears—make everything in front of him a blurry mess. But his ears, those still work, and he can hear Uzel growling something in Uzeki. He doesn't understand it—can't speak Uzeki—but he knows it's not good.

He also hears the two Uzeks that have his arms pinned to this alley wall breathing heavy from the chase he forced them to make.

He was close—so close—from making a turn out onto the street and losing them in the crowd milling about in front of the market. He could have donned the hood on his cloak, dropped his posture just so, and quickly looked like all of the people there buying ingredients for that night's dinner.

Would have if not for that busted little robot someone had tossed aside and that bent little antennae that caught his foot as he tried to jump over it. He landed on a knee, his shin catching a brick as he went down. And now that aches too.

He twists his wrists, trying to force a little circulation back into them, but it only causes the Uzeks to grunt and snort some kind of warning and clamp down harder.

The tears—pain tears, not crying tears—are almost gone now. He can see Uzel pacing in front of him. He's a squat little thing. Short arms and short legs and shaped like a garroway fruit that's gone soft—thin at the top and thick at the bottom, like Nixon could put a thumb in his guts if he were to push hard enough.

The shadows here make his light green skin look darker than it is, and the calluses on his forearms look more like armored plates. Uzel continues to grunt something then looks over at the translator he's brought with him. She's a young Uzek and begins to speak. Nixon hears her, but he's too lost in his own thoughts to actually comprehend what she's saying.

She's just a girl, and he hates that she's already gotten mixed up with Uzel the Uzek

"Where are the missing seeds? The twelve pounds?" she asks again.

Nixon tries to work up an answer, but he can't. He doesn't have a good one.

He'd told himself this wasn't a position he'd find himself in. He was better than this. He wasn't the same man his dad was, and he wasn't going to go out the same way—busted up and broken over a few pounds of seeds. But that's what he's done.

But this is what happens on Exte. You take work where you can get it. You hustle credits however you can. Work your angles. Find people who need regular work done and then put yourself in a position to do it. Maybe you're working for a day to help build one of those new towers going in over near the starport. Maybe, if you're lucky, you get to do that for a week or more. That's proud work. It's the kind that leaves you something to point to and say "See that balcony up there on the fiftieth floor? I installed that."

Most days, though, you weren't that lucky. The work wasn't something that made you proud. It was just something that earned you credits. You ran some deliveries. You helped organize something or clean something. Then, when that work dried up—or you did such a poor job of doing it that no one who needs it will hire you—you turn to the cartels. Like the Uzeks. They always had work. None of it legal. Like running seeds that they'll then use to make Cloud90.

You do that for a couple of months, reveling in the credits you're earning but also telling yourself that for the danger you're putting yourself in—running seeds means dealing with the kinds of people who see you as nothing more than a cog in a wheel, a piece in a broken process—you should be getting more. And if they won't give it to you then you'll have to take it.

So, you take the small ship they gave you and fly it out to the desert. You scoop out a bucket full of the seeds from the canvas bag they are in and cover the bucket before you bury the seeds three feet deep into the sand. Insurance policy, you tell yourself. You'll only get it if you need it. Find a fence for the seeds and restock your credits. Besides, it's 1,500 pounds of seed. Who will even know if a few pounds are gone.

Who will know? Apparently, Uzel will know.

"The seeds, Mr. Nixon." the girl says.

"Where are they?" It's Uzel. It's tough, but Nixon understands it. It's the first time he's ever heard Uzel speak in a language that's not Uzeki

"You steal my seeds."

Nixon shakes his head and clears his throat. He clears it again and then again. He's working something up from deep in his chest. Something that's not an answer to Uzel's questions.

He's being dramatic about it, dipping his shoulders then bringing himself back up to standing over and over again, looking and sounding like a skeen cat bringing up a hairball.

Then he stops, his mouth full of something phlegmy and loose. He turns to the Uzek that's pinned his right arm to the wall and spits this internal concoction in its face. When it hits the Uzek in the snout, and its grip on Nixon's arm changes. It loosens just enough for him to yank himself free.

He has control of his right arm again. He spins to his left and puts a fist into the other Uzek's throat. It lets out a gravelly grunt and struggles to breathe. Nixon brings both of his hands to the Uzek's neck, and it drops Nixon's other arm.

Nixon grabs the thing's shoulders and spins it around, putting the Uzek between him and Uzel. Blaster fire catches the Uzek in the back. Uzel is shooting.

The Uzek falls heavy against Nixon. This thing is dead or dying. Nixon grabs the blaster that's in the holster that hangs at the Uzek's side.

Nixon fires one shot at the other Uzek that had been holding him to the wall. It hits the thing in the gut, and deep green goo splatter-paints the wall where it stands. The thing makes a guttural cry and falls to its knees.

Another blast from Uzel digs a small crater into the stone wall at Nixon's feet. He fires a wild shot at Uzel that hits him in the shin. He falls immediately and raises the blaster from his back. Nixon fires a second shot at him that hits the blaster and blows off two of Uzel's three fingers.

"Graaaaaaaa!" Uzel screams and grabs at what's left of one hand with the other. "Nixon!"

Nixon pushes the Uzek off of him and slips the blaster into the waistband of his pants under his cloak.

The translator stares at him. He stares back, and for a moment doesn't know what to do, doesn't know what she'll do. But she doesn't do anything. Not for a long second then she drops to her knees to attend a still-groaning Uzel.

Nixon watches for a second. Uzel's breathing heavy. He's moaning without knowing he's doing it. Then, in between two of those moans, he looks at Nixon and squeezes out the words "Dead. Man."

Nixon turns and walks out of the alley.

"Dead. Man." Uzel says, louder this time, like he's used all of his energy to push it out.

Nixon gets to the end of the alley and looks to his left. There's his market. There's his crowd. He pulls the hood of his cloak up over his head and pulls his arms inside. He slips the Uzek blaster from his waistband. He keeps it pressed to his chest, a finger on the trigger. It's hidden but ready to fire. Then he stoops his body just so and disappears into the crowd.

TWO

Nixon sits at the bar of the Goodtimes Palace and wipes the sweat off the glass that sits in front of him. He wipes now-wet fingers on his pant leg and picks up his data pad. He opens it and pulls up his credit balance. It hasn't miraculously increased in the ten minutes since he'd checked it last, and it hasn't gone up from any of the other times he's checked it since he sat down.

He doesn't have enough credits for the drink that's going warm in front of him. He definitely doesn't have credits for the second one he's already ordered. And there's no way he can pay for the drink that Shaine just asked for.

"You look like a skeen cat got hold of you and you had to fight your way free." Shaine laughs at his joke.

"Just about." Nixon says. He fakes a laugh that jiggles his insides and a new wave of pain shoots to his toes. As bad as he looks on the outside, he feels ten times worse inside. That's what an Uzek beating will do to you. It was the beauty in their torture. Even on the receiving end of it, Nixon could appreciate that.

The bloody nose and the gashed forehead, those were Nixon's fault. Pay better attention during a footrace that he was going to win, and he doesn't go down into the ground face first. He doesn't slide a couple of feet on the hard-packed soil and go head first into the dried-mud alley walls.

He doesn't do that and Uzel and his friends aren't able to catch him and pull him off the ground and start putting their stun sticks hard into his middle. Adrenalin had covered the pain earlier. Now it's fading, and Nixon can feel where every stun stick hit him over and over and over.

He grimaces and puts his hand to his side.

"Gonna tell me what happened?

"Not tonight." Nixon finishes what's in his glass.

There's a bell over the door to the Goodtimes Palace, and it rings every time the door is opened. And every time that bell rings, Nixon flinches and shoots a look to the door. Uzeks don't come to places like this. They don't drink the kind of things served here. And even if they did, they wouldn't come to a place like the Goodtimes Palace.

Nixon and Shaine are sitting at a table slapped together with shipping materials and the soft pinkton wood that's used to make crates. Other patrons have picked at the edge of the table until the top is jagged on all sides.

Nixon looks down and catches a fingernail on a spot on the top and pulls. A thin peel of wood comes off in his hand. He drops it to the floor, and the bell rings again. He flinches hard. Waves of pain radiate out to his feet. Nixon checks the door. It's not an Uzek, of course. Just some other guy who looks like he's been up two days too long.

"You look like you've been dragged up and down the block, and every time that door opens you jump out of your seat. You're about snap your neck trying to see who's come in. Are you expecting company?

Nixon watches a Snapsit woman wave at a friend sitting in one of the tables behind him.

"Not expecting it. No."

"But if you see someone you recognize. Or if someone coming in recognizes you ..."

"Yeah. Maybe that.

There's a new drink in front of Nixon. The glass isn't sweating yet. He picks it up and takes a sip. The liquid stings a cut on his upper lip, but he drinks anyway.

"Had a seed job," he says to Shaine, "and it went a little sideways."

"A seed job?"

Nixon nods. "And it went a little ..."

Shaine doesn't let him finish. "The Uzeks?"

Suddenly his face explodes with recognition. "That was you? Uzel?"

Nixon lifts the bottom of his cloak and exposes the Uzek blaster he's been carrying with him since the fight.

"So, you've heard about ... it?"

"Your little fight? Everyone has heard about it, hot shot."

"Don't make fun."

"I'm not. But, man ... you've really ... wow."

"I know. I'm in a spot now. It's all I've been thinking about since it happened. That and I don't have the credits I need to pay for these drinks tonight." He checks his data pad again, still hoping for some kind of miracle. "I don't have the credits to hole myself up someplace that's not here and hope to just hide out for a while."

Shaine nurses what's left of his drink and asks, "You were desperate enough for a seed job? Are desperate enough?"

Nixon shrugs. "I've got to eat. I've got to earn credits. I didn't want to do it, but what choice did I have?"

"How many times have you run seed?"

"A few."

"How many?"

"Six. No, seven."

Shaine leans back on his stool. "Seven times? So you were becoming a regular. Why didn't you come to me?"

"And do what? Take a job that earns you credits? You need them too, maybe worse than I do. With Mira and the kids."

"I've got jobs. We have credits. Don't worry about me. But you don't need to be running seed again. And you can't really stay here, can you?"

Nixon shakes his head and takes another sip from his glass.

"I know a guy who needs some work. Pay's good because It's not exactly above board. But it's not running seed. The job is yours if you want it."

"What exactly are we talking about?"

"Courier job. He won't tell you more than that. Just give you an address and a name. If you are OK with that being all you know, it's pretty easy."

Nixon is hunched over, elbows on the edge of the bar and the weight of the world on his back. He blows a long breath into the bar top and begins to slowly nod.

"Yeah. I mean maybe. Let me think about it?"

Shaine calls the server over and shows him his datapad. The server scans the code on his screen.

"I'll get these tonight." He looks back at his pad and swipes a couple of fingers across the top then shows the screen to Nixon.

"Remember this address. Tomorrow morning. Early, just after first light. If you're there, job's yours. If not, I'll keep it for myself."

Nixon's home is a small mud-walled single room. There's a mat on the floor for sleeping, and a small fire-heated cooktop that vents smoke out through a hole in the wall.

Nixon lays on the mat and repeats the address Shaine had given him over and over in his head. He doesn't want to take this job. He doesn't mix friends and work. Not anymore. It's a standing policy, and one that's served him well. It keeps things from getting complicated if a job doesn't go well. And it keeps motivations clear. Friends are friends because they like each other. They aren't friends because one can provide work or the other can complete jobs. Just easier. SHaine taught him that.

A small fire crackles in the heat box next to Nixon, and he puts a hand above the hot plate that sits on top. It's warm. Nixon grabs a small container that sits up against the wall and pulls out the last two slices of Bowtan steer meat. He lays them on the hotplate. A few moments later their aroma fills the small space.

Shaine's been a friend for a long time, the longest of anyone that Nixon knows. The two boys grew up together, both being sent to the same forming school at the same time. The two new kids in class sticking together, fighting back bullies, establishing reputations as a couple of toughs. Then moving here to Exte after school was over and building lives for themselves.

Shaine had been more successful at establishing himself. Tonight, he's laying his head down on a real mat with a real pillow and blankets. He's eating real food cooked on a respectable cooktop. He's not here, eating tinned meat and checking his credit balance every 20 minutes hoping that it will somehow change.

He's not going to spend the entire night trying to sleep with an Uzek blaster laying heavy on his chest, a finger on the trigger and an eye on the door.

No, Nixon doesn't like to mix friends and business, but with Shaine it's different. He's not a friend; he's more than that. Still, sometimes you have to do what you don't want to do. You have to break your own rules. You have to take the work that will provide you credits.

THREE

The ceiling in Nixon's hole is low, and he has to stoop-stand to put on his cloak. He tucks the Uzek blaster back into his waistband and takes one last look around his little place. This is a courier job he's about to go accept, and if it pays what he hopes then he'll have enough credits to find some place in the new city—or, better, new planet—he's going to. He can lay low there for a bit. Let the Uzeks here get distracted by something or someone else. Then he can return. Maybe.

No matter what, though, this is the last time he'll see this place. He thinks for a moment about kicking the little heatbox until the mud sides crumble and the still-hot coals spill out onto the mat. Letting the mat catch fire and the flames get so hot that the straw inside the mud walls also goes up. Just watching the whole place burn. But, he doesn't, because he's not that guy. There's the Snapsit family that lives behind him, three of them jammed into a little room not much bigger than his. And the widow woman who lives in the unit around the corner who would set extra tins of Bowtan steer meat outside his door. He's not going to let their places go up too just because he hates his.

So, he settles for thinking about it. For mentally watching the flames from the mattress lick the ceiling. For mentally seeing the ceiling start to smoke and then glow red. Then the glow turns to flames. And eventually everything on this block is roaring and crackling.

He walks away, the mental fire burning bright behind him. He repeats the address Shaine showed him over and over in his head. Exte's first sun still isn't up, and the streets are darker than dark. Dangerous, he thinks, to be walking out in the open like this. But at least he has the black to cover him. He won't forever, though. The walk is across the city, and by the time he gets to where he's going, both suns should be up. He'll be vulnerable. He runs a thumb over the heavy handle of the Uzek blaster still tucked away.

At least I have that.

Nixon hates these moments, when it still feels too early for it to be tomorrow and it's too dark to think about it being anything other than night. Nothing good ever happens in these moments. There are people skulking in what would be shadows if there was enough light to create them. He hears them whispering as he passes. Talking to each other. Planning. Plotting. Plotting against him? He wouldn't doubt it.

He doesn't always understand the language. Is it Uzeki? Sometimes? Maybe.

He pulls the hood of his cloak over his head and makes sure its edge covers the top of his face.

He fakes a limp, falsely favoring his right leg. Anything to disguise himself. It's just a matter of time until the Uzeks start looking for him. Probably already have. He picks up his pace, the limp turning to more of a hop.

There was a time when he would have been one of those in the crook of a doorway or a couple of steps deep into an alleyway. He'd have been waiting and watching, looking for opportunity. Opportunity to do what wasn't as easily defined. Not necessarily to rob someone or rough someone up. Maybe it was an opportunity to take advantage of a situation. Someone drops something. Or they get distracted by something and quit paying as close of attention as they should to their belongings.

Maybe that thing they get distracted by is Shaine. The two of them always made great partners, especially when they were new to Exte.

Shaine: Big body. Big personality.

Nixon: Long and lean. Skinny fingers and a gentle touch.

One performs; the other picks.

Nixon is lost in his own memory, remembering days with Shaine and the schemes they pulled and the credits they took. He's lost in a time when it didn't hurt to get up in the morning because Uzeks couldn't catch him. He's lost in a time when there was more life ahead of him instead of behind him, and the world was exciting with possibility.

He's so lost in his own memory that he doesn't notice that the real world around him is getting brighter, that the rising sun is bringing everything to life. Not until a woman comes out of her small home and dumps a pot of something from the night before out into the street. Then he notices that it's past first light and that he's still not close to arriving at the address Shaine gave him.

A horn blares in the distance, and he steps to the side of the road. The horn goes again, three quick blasts. Nixon looks behind him and sees it—a people mover. He pulls out his datapad and checks his credit balance. Still small, but hopping a ride now saves him time, even if it costs him a little money.

The people-mover blows its horn again, and Nixon raises an arm to request that the vehicle stop. It pulls up next to Nixon. It slowly drops to the ground, and a small ramp unfolds from the side allowing him to step on.

He puts his pad in front of a small scanner. He watches five more credits disappear from his total then turns to find a seat. It's mostly folks who look like him. There is a Snapsit man who has folded himself into one of the seats, his knees pushing hard into the seat back in front of him. And there are three Uzeks in the back. There's a seat near them, but Nixon opts to stand near the front of the people-mover. No, not all Uzeks run seeds for Uzel and the cartel, but what's the point in testing these Uzeks out just in case they do.

He pulls the hood down farther over his face and slumps down lower in his seat. He listens to the automated driver announce stops. But he always has an ear on the Uzeks in the back. They grunt and snort in their very basic language.

He steals glances back there when he can. They aren't carrying anything. Nothing that indicates they are headed to some kind of work. But they don't try and sneak looks at him, either. Still ... he doesn't like sharing a mover with them.

He closes his eyes and crosses his arms and pretends to sleep again. Pretends and listens. A chime dings and an automated voice announces the next stop. He hears people get off. Then he hears how the ambient noise changes as the mover gets closer into the heart of Exte. The city shifts. The streets are no longer made of hard-packed mud. They become properly paved. There are no more mud walls on these buildings either. They are now made of metal and glass.

The mover stops, and Nixon sneaks a glance. A woman sitting near the door stands to get off. He looks behind him and the Snapsit man struggles to unfold himself out of his seat. The Uzeks haven't moved.

The mover starts again. There are only two others on board besides Nixon and the Uzeks. Seats are open, Nixon hears the Uzeks move to spots a few rows behind him. Their whispered chatter is getting louder. Nixon doesn't recognize any of it. Such an ugly language.

They aren't too many steps above animals.

Nixon pulls his right arm inside his cloak and rests his hand on the handle of the Uzek blaster tucked in his waistband. The automated voice calls out another stop and the mover slows. The woman sitting next to Nixon stands, and he steps to the side to let her pass. He looks behind him when he does and two of the Uzeks are looking at him.

Nixon grabs the rail above his head that runs the length of the car. The mover jerks to a start. It's moving out of the main part of Exte's business district now, and the only remaining person on-board other than the Uzeks stands. The mover calls for a stop and the gentleman steps toward the front of the car.

The ramp closes again, and the mover starts to move. The Uzeks are talking again. Nixon hears them step forward. The breath from their snouts tickles the back of his neck.

Nixon wraps his hand around the handle of the blaster. He puts two fingers around the trigger and pulls the gun from his waistband. He's ready to fire. He doesn't want to shoot. He doesn't want to fight here. Three of them and one of him. Close quarters. The blaster makes it more even, but they likely have them too. Plus, he doesn't want to have to shoot a hole into his cloak.

Then there it is, a meaty paw-hand on his shoulder. It pulls at him just slightly, and he turns. Face to face with an Uzek. The snout. The yellowing eyes. They jagged teeth.

"Excuse me," the thing says in its gravel voice and steps past, the other two right behind.

The mover announces another stop as the trio steps to the ramp. They wait for the mover ramp to open then step off.

Nixon drops into a seat. The blaster hangs at his side then slips from his fingers and clatters to the ground. His heart is racing so fast that he swears it'll make the mover fall over.

FOUR

The mover drops Nixon off outside of the glass and sparkle of Exte's central business district. Things here still aren't as rough-built as the part of the city that Nixon calls home--called home. The buildings here are lower and longer. The builders spread out. They gave themselves space. They didn't go vertical. But the walls aren't mud packed. The streets are still paved.

Nixon steps out and onto the street. Shaine's address is still a block or two away, but he can walk it from here. Even after the Uzeks exited, that mover felt too confining. He liked the streets better. They were open. He had visibility.

Exte's second sun is about to rise, and Nixon hotfoots it to Shaine's address, hoping that the job is still his to have. This is well past first light, and he knows Shaine well enough that if he said first light he meant first light.

The number Nixon is looking for is sloppily painted above an opening on the front of one of the buildings. He steps through cautiously and turns the corner into a wide courtyard. There in the middle is Shaine. He sits alone at a table, his head down and reading something on his datapad.

"Good morning," Nixon says.

Shaine looks up and smiles. "You're late." He's breathing heavy, and his cloak is sitting crooked on his shoulders.

"Rough commute." Nixon pulls out a chair across from Shaine and sits.

"Mira didn't think you'd show. She owes me a stack of hot griddle cakes with dinner tonight."

"You're so domesticated."

"It's not actually bad, You should try it."

Nixon shrugs.

Footsteps behind them and Nixon turns. It's a woman. She's also got her head in her datapad. There's a bag over her shoulder. She doesn't see either Nixon or Shaine, just heads toward one of the doors that open out into the courtyard.

"We waiting on someone else?" Nixon asks.

Shaine shakes no and says "This job is mine."

"So you just waited around to rub it in my face that I was late and you decided to take it?"

Shaine shakes no again. "That's not what I mean. I'm the one hiring out this job."

"I'm not following."

"I don't do these kinds of courier jobs anymore. People come to me looking to get goods from one place to another, and I find the people to do it."

"Oh, big boss man."

"It's not like that. I'm a small operation. Mira's idea. Said it'd keep me home with her and the kids more. And wasn't nearly as dangerous."

"And has it?"

"I am home more, and that's great."

"But..."

"You know the but."

"People need private courier service for a reason."

Shaine nods and reaches down beside him. He pulls a metal case off his seat and sits it on the tabletop.

"Still interested?"

Nixon nods. "I have no other options. I need credits, and I need off Exte. This gets me both. And it's not like I haven't been doing dangerous work before now."

Shaine smiles. "Good," he says. "Then here's the job."

He rubs his hand across the top of the metal case and begins to lay out the details: Get the case to Planet Azken within 45 days. Shaine can provide a ship. He pssses a small card with engine codes and a stall number where he's storing the ship. It's not much, but it'll fly straight.

"And what's all this pay?" Nixon asks.

"Five thousand."

Nixon hesitates. "Excuse me?"

"Five thousand. I'm getting fifteen thousand total. Keeping ten of it for me. You understand."

Nixon is still mostly speechless. "Five thousand," he finally says again. "So what's in the case that makes getting it somewhere else worth fifteen thousand credits to someone?"

"I don't know what's inside. It's pretty well sealed. It's not coming open without some kind of digital key."

Nixon doesn't understand. "You agreed to move this box for fifteen thousand credits and you didn't ask what's inside?"

"I don't ... I can't ... The people I tend to work with don't like a lot of questions."

"I get that, but still ... fifteen thousand credits."

Shaine leans forward and says in a whispered voice: "I need you to take this one. I need someone I can trust handling it. And I trust you."

"It's a lot of credits, but you aren't really selling it."

"It's a lot of credits, and I know we can get the box to Planet Azken on time. But if we don't, it's not just the credits that are lost."

"What are you saying?"

"It's Mira. And the girls." Shaine stands and paces a tight circle. "It's Mira and the girls. If the case isn't delivered, they've said they'll ..."

"Who's said they'll what, Shaine? Who are you working with?"

Shaine doesn't get the chance to answer. Blaster fire sizzles past Nixon's ear and hits Shaine in the shoulder. It spins him to the ground.

Nixon turns to see who's firing and pulls the Uzek blaster from his waistband. He gets off two wild shots that don't hit anything but do give him time to duck behind the table, putting it between himself and their new visitors.

"The case!" Shaine shouts. "Grab the case!"

A blaster shot hits the table and it explodes in a shower of splinters. The case flies a dozen feet away.

Nixon looks toward Shaine. "You have the address," Shaine says. "Get the case and go. For Mira. My girls."

The air crackles, and blaster fire peels the paver tiles from the ground in front of Nixon.

"Please," Shaine says.

Nixon sprints to the case and scoops it up in a single motion then heads for the opening that's opposite the one he came in. He fires wild over his shoulder and the fire from the other side stops momentarily.

He dives through the opening and finds a safe spot behind a wall. He pokes his head around the corner, ready to fire. Ready to set the case down and go help Shaine. Blasts from the other side of the courtyard blow apart huge chunks of the wall near him. He pulls his head back around the corner, but not before he sees blaster fire tear his friend in two.

FIVE

Nixon grabs the case off the ground again and sprints away from the courtyard. He doesn't know where he is. These are all tight alleys and small streets that he's never seen, so all of his turns are serving only to confuse him more. But, at least for now, he's not worried about confusion. He just doesn't want to hear any more blaster fire burn by his ears. He doesn't want to get hit in the back by a six-inch laser slug and look down just in time to see it burn its way out of his chest and through his cloak.

So he runs for a few minutes more until he gets to some deep-set doorway and stops.

This is the first time he's been able to think about what just happened. He doesn't know enough to think much. The one thing he does know is that the people on the other end of those blasters weren't Uzeks. They weren't Snapsits either. They were humans, like him and like Shaine.

"He's dead, right?" He asks no one.

Then he sees it again—three blasts hitting Shaine across the torso. His body bouncing as each shot ripped through him. Then the last shot tearing through flesh and bone and ... He doesn't want to think about it anymore.

He sets the case down and then finds a spot on the ground beside it. He's breathing heavy. He hasn't recovered from being chased by the Uzeks the day before, and everything hurts, especially his nose.

He thinks about leaving the case here. Catching his breath then getting up and walking away. Leave whatever trouble it's going to bring with it in that doorway.

"Sorry, Shaine," he says to himself. "Whatever trouble you're in Mira's going to have to find her own way out of it."

But he doesn't mean it. He's not going to do that to Mira. Mostly, he's not going to do that to Shaine.

He stands, still sucking air like someone is going to take it from him and racks his brain for the stall number at the starport that Shaine mentioned.

Six something.

Six ...

Six ...

"Come on, brain."

Twenty-eight.

Six twenty-eight.

"That's it."

Nixon steps from the protection of the doorway, blaster up and still inside his cloak. These streets are narrow and the buildings all look the same, one long and low profile structure after the other.

He knows he needs to get to the space port. He turns a circle in the middle of the street looking for the towers that are under construction. Their ragged tops reach above the rooftops behind him and he starts in that direction.

He keeps the Uzek blaster in his hand, two fingers resting lightly on the trigger. Shaine's case is in his other hand and tucked under his arm. First light has come and gone. Second light too. It's well into the day now. People are walking these streets. They are going between these buildings.

Nixon keeps his hood up and his head down, only raising it to make sure that the new towers are still in front of him. He walks what feels like a couple of blocks and starts to hear the sounds of engines. Then come the shadows of ships passing overhead.

A few blocks later the sounds of pilots and crews and mechanics gets added. Then Nixon looks up and his guideposts are now in front of him stretching tall into the sky. A block later and it's the Exte starport.

The outside is all metal with a pair of doors on the front. Nixon steps inside, and the place is packed. Crowded. Loud. The air full of the funk of a dozen or more species inside, either looking for a ship or looking to work on one.

Captains fly into Exte, put down at the port solo and leave a few hours later with a full crew. Plenty of the people Nixon knew from the Goodtimes Palace made their money crewing for those captains. It often didn't pay much, at least not what was expected. Those captains come up with creative ways to justify increasing their share of whatever job they were doing. So Nixon stuck to planetside work. At least that was honest. Mostly.

Nixon pushes through the crowd waiting in the lobby of the starport. It's full of filthy looking Uzeks. Spit-shined Snapsits. And at least a dozen other species looking for a few fast credits.

He repeats "Six twenty-eight" over and over as he makes his way toward the elevators. He waits for the doors to open then steps on. He keeps his hood up and head down and listens to the chimes for each floor. He counts his way to six then steps off.

The smell of burning oil and fried electrics hits him in the face as he steps off. Air recyclers woosh and a thin haze of smoke hangs in the air. Signs point the way to the slip he's looking for and the smoke gets thicker. He can smell the scent of fire-retardant foam, and the chatter of voices starts to rise over the air recyclers. Then it's footsteps. The people who belong to these voices are moving around.

Nixon raises his head, and the floor is full of people. All of them are holding blasters, and they are milling around what's left of a small hauler. Holes are punched in its side where holes shouldn't be. Scorch marks cover the sides, and everything looks like it's slightly warped. Everything near the ground is covered in the fire foam that's slowly dissipating.

Nixon looks up from the crowd to the slip number above the ship. Six twenty-eight.

"Shit," he says and keeps walking. These aren't Uzeks. It's more humans. "What the hell, Shaine?"

The case tucked under his arm starts to feel heavier, more like an anchor now and less like the opportunity it seemed it'd be last night. He pushes the button for the elevator and thinks again about just setting the case on the ground before he gets on. Just leave it there and walk away from this whole thing.

He can avoid the Uzeks. Go back out to that little spot in the sand and dig up the buried bucket of seeds that he stashed away. Take them to someplace other than Exte. Sure, it's the biggest city on the planet, but it's not the only one. There are other places where he can sell seed. There are other buyers, both nefarious and righteous.

The chime for the elevator sounds, and the chatter from the humans milling around slip 628 stops. Nixon waits for the doors to open. He hears footsteps. They are getting closer. The chime sounds again and the doors to the elevator begin to slide open, and Nixon steps inside before they are finished.

Footsteps turn the corner as the doors begin to close, and a face appears just on the other side as they finish.

"Hey!"

The man who'd been approaching jams an arm in the doors as they close and keeps the elevator from leaving. Nixon steps forward to push the arm back through and the guy grabs a handful of Nixon's cloak.

Nixon struggles to get himself free, and the man who's holding onto him calls others for help.

"It's him," he shouts. "I've got our courtyard man."

Nixon digs at the fingers that are clinging tight to his cloak, but they aren't moving. They are big meaty things, thick like the lower branches of a Gefta tree. The man takes his other hand and his Gefta fingers and pulls the elevator doors open. He looks at Nixon.

The whites of his eyes are yellow. The pupils are red. He smiles a big, wide smile at Nixon. He reaches with the other hand and tries to grab another handful of Nixon's cloak.

Nixon stops him then smiles back. He takes one of the man's fingers that he's got hold of and jams it in his mouth. He bites down hard and feels the skin snap under his teeth. He works his teeth through the meat of his finger and gets to bone.

The man is screaming and whatever bits of cloak he'd been able to get a hold of he's let go of now. Nixon works harder, bites with everything he has and feels the knuckle snap. There's the tip of a finger in his mouth. The tang of blood is on his tongue. He spits all of it out at the feet of the man who'd had hold of him.

The man pulls his hand back and holds it in front of his face, staring at the space where the end of his finger should be.

Nixon rapid-taps the button that will send the elevator to the first floor. The doors close as another of the men who were milling around Slip 628 rounds the corner. Nixon sees the man skid to a stop when he sees his friend with his own fingertip in the palm of his hand.

A bell signals the elevator's arrival on the first floor. Nixon pushes his way back through the crowd to the exit. It's all the same people who'd been there earlier. He's listening for the elevator to chime its arrival again on the top floor. He's waiting for a shouting mob to appear behind him and the burn of blaster fire to eventually catch him in the back. But it doesn't come. Maybe his little display of violence was enough to keep them away. For now.

Nixon has always had to be that guy, the one who has just a tiny bit of crazy behind the eyes. Usually, it was good enough just to keep it there. The crazy promised but not proven. Sometimes, though, you had to be ready to unjar the crazy and pour it out all over the table.

He's on the street and walking away from the starport with his hood down before he realizes that his cheek is smeared with blood. He swipes at it frantically with an open palm, and it only serves to solidify the image that he's someone who might be a little less than stable.

He looks behind him, and there's still not anyone following him. Not that he can tell anyway. But even if they aren't following him now, they'll be looking for him soon. And again, he thinks about dropping the case, just setting it down in some doorway and leaving it for someone to find.

Shaine's dead. Any ramifications of just walking away from this trouble for him are gone. Then he remembers one of the last things Shaine said to him: "Mira and the girls."

He never really liked Mira. And he's only met the girls a couple of times. Still. They meant something to Shaine. They shouldn't suffer for Shaine's bad business deals.

So fine. He'll keep the case. He'll get it to Planet Azken. He'll keep the family safe. He'll do it for Shaine.

But if he's going to do this, he needs a ship.

SIX

Before he can find a ship, he needs to get off the streets. Nothing good can happen here. He's a hunted man again.

He's been walking for close to half an hour. He's on the other side of Exte's main district now. The buildings are again long and low, and his stomach is suddenly reminding him that it's been nearly a day since he's had any real amount of food. He needs to find a place to eat.

There's nothing here, or not much. Neon signs color everything in a deep green, and they advertise just about everything other than food: blaster repair, ship modifications, combat gear that is designed to keep you safe but limits mobility as a byproduct. He walks at least two blocks before he sees something that sticks out like a bright star on a dark night.

It's a noodle bowl made of red and yellow neon. The red is the bowl. The yellow is the noodles. Alternating white squiggles are the steam coming from the bowl.

Nixon goes inside and asks to be seated near the back. There are only a couple of other patrons eating when he gets there. None of them look up as he's escorted to his table.

He pulls his datapad from a pocket in his cloak and sets it on the table. He picks up the menu in front of him, but before he orders he checks his credits. A few swipes of his fingers, and his balance is up in front of him. Nothing has changed.

A small part of him was hoping that Shaine had transferred the credits before they even met, his friend knowing that Nixon would take the job. But he's here, and he's seated, and he needs food.

Nixon looks at the menu, scanning the prices first and not the items. He finds something he can afford. It's a noodle dish that his mom used to make when dad was between paychecks.

The bowl is steaming when the waitress sets it in front of him, but Nixon doesn't care. He takes a big spoonful of the broth and puts it in his mouth. He lets it cool on his tongue before swallowing. He savors the flavor.

It's a hot meal, and, even if it's a cheap meal, he hasn't eaten like this in days.

The noodles are thick and ropy and resist slightly when he chews them. He tells himself to go slow, to take the time to enjoy every bite. But he can't. He tears through it, picking the dish up at the end and bringing it to his mouth to make sure he gets every drop of the broth.

He thanks the waitress and leaves. It's darker outside now. The first sun has gone down and everything is cast in long shadows. The day is nearly over, and he still needs a ship.

He also needs to know who's chasing him and who killed Shaine. The yellow eyes should be a giveaway, but he's not in this game. He doesn't play with these players. He's been working almost exclusively with the Uzeks and doing jobs for the cartels in Old Town for so long that he's not seen anyone outside that tight circle.

Then the threat to Mira and Shaine's girls. The cartels in Old Town didn't do that kind of thing either. Your job was your job. Those people around you didn't get pulled into things. This was a different kind of cartel he was dealing with.

That's when it hits him. Mira. The girls. Do they know what's happened? Are they even safe?

Shaine's place wasn't much, but it was miles better than where Nixon had called home. It was just outside of Old Town. A couple of bedrooms. A living space. Shaine had bought the land while he and Nixon were still regularly partnering on jobs, just after he'd met Mira.

He'd called the little plot his insurance policy. A girl like her didn't stick with a guy like him unless he gave her a reason. Shaine was betting hard on stability. It worked. They married a year later, and Shaine started building the home soon after.

Nixon stands in front of the door and knocks. "Mira!" he shouts. "It's me! It's Trevor!"

There's movement behind the door and then it opens. Mira's eyes are swollen. Her cheeks are red. She doesn't say anything. She leaves the door open and walks back to the table and takes a seat.

Nixon steps inside.

"So, you know?" he asks.

She nods and starts to cry again. Nixon takes a seat next to her and moves to put a hand on her shoulder. She dips and scoots away from him.

"What happened, Trevor? I know that you know."

"I don't."

"Bullshit. I know he was in touch with you."

"Not until recently. He offered me a job."

Nixon sets the case on the table. "Moving that."

Mira pulls the case to her and tries to open the top. Nixon watches her try to work the tips of her fingers in between the two halves and pry them apart. He watches as she adjusts her grip and tries again.

She slams the case down on the table and says: "You could have told me it was impossible, Trevor, instead of letting me look like an idiot."

"Sorry."

"So, what's inside?"

Nixon shrugs. "I haven't been able to get it open. And Shaine was ..." Nixon stops. He can't say the word killed. He doesn't want to hear the words come from his mouth. And he doesn't know what Mira will do if he does say it.

"Shaine never got a chance to tell me."

"You were with him?"

"When it happened?"

Mira nods

"I was."

Mira breaks down. Her arms are folded on the table top in front of her. She lays her forehead on her forearms and begins to sob. Nixon puts a hand on her shoulder, and Mira covers it with her own.

After a moment he says: "I'm really sorry. I loved him too."

She raises her head and takes a deep breath to gather herself. "I know you did. He loved you too. You were a brother."

"That's why I'm here. It all happened fast, but the last thing he told me was that this job was dangerous, and you and the girls aren't safe."

"What does that mean?"

"I don't know. But he told me about a ship at the starport…"

"Six twenty-eight?"

Nixon nods. "It's been damaged. Extremely unflyable. And the guys who did it … we had a moment. Chased me out of there."

Mira stands and begins to say something, but Nixon doesn't give her a chance to speak.

"You have to go," he says. "Take the girls and get away from here. It's not safe for you anymore."

She's walking the room now. She's pulling things off of shelves and digging them out of drawers. They are all going into a large canvas bag with a heavy locking clasp on the top that she pulled from the bottom of a built-in cabinet.

Nixon watches her for a moment before she says: "It's our disassembled go bag. It was Shaine's idea. I knew he was working with people …"

Her voice catches. She stops for a moment and leans onto the dining table next to the canvas bag. She breathes deep once. Twice. Then she starts again.

"He didn't give me a lot of details, but I wasn't oblivious. He said not everyone using his services was on the up and up. But I didn't know it was going to come to this. I always thought … if we had to leave, I thought he'd be the one getting this bag together."

Nixon continues to watch her work. She's methodical. There's no hesitation. She knows what goes in the bag, and she knows exactly where to find it. It's like she's practiced this one hundred times.

"Where are you going to go?"

"Shaine and I had a plan."

"And what was that?"

She drops the last of the items into the bag. She connects the clasp to close the top then sets the lock. She looks up to Nixon. "Nope," she says. "Where we go is just for us."

She pulls the bag off the table and the weight of it nearly knocks her to the floor.

"Fair enough," Nixon says.

Mira heads for the door then stops. She puts the bag on the floor and goes back over to the built-ins and pulls a vase off the shelf. It's painted a rainbow swirl of colors. She looks at it one last time then throws it to the ground.

"I've always hated that thing," she says and bends over. She stirs a hand through the shards of broken pottery and pulls out a card with codes written on one side. An address is on the other. She stands and hands the card to Nixon.

He takes it and flips it over, looking at both sides.

"Codes," Mira says. "To another ship. Kind of our escape hatch if we needed it. Shaine said it was just in case. This feels like just in case to me. Use it."

Nixon looks up from the card and back to Mira. "Are you sure?"

"I don't need it where I'm going. Me and the girls will be safe. You on the other hand …"

"I really appreciate it," he says. "Good luck."

She puts a hand on his shoulder. "You too. Deliver that box. Do it for Shaine."

SEVEN

Nixon studies the address printed on the back side of the card Mira gave him. It's familiar. Another starport, if he's thinking correctly. It's back near the main district, an evening's walk in the dark.

He goes to leave Shaine's place but stops. He goes and looks for food, anything that won't spoil. He doesn't find much. A couple of sleeves of crackers. A tin of dried meat. He grabs both and tucks them into the pockets on the inside of his cloak.

It's nearly black out, the only light is coming from the spaced out lamps hanging from wires high above the street. They cast wide pools of light, and Nixon hustles through the spots that aren't lit at all. In between is a special kind of black that he's never gotten used to. He doesn't like the mystery of the dark. There's too much unknown, and he's spent all his adult life trying to avoid what's out there when you can't see.

Out there. Where you can't see. That's where he's headed. He looks to the sky and the multitudes upon multitudes of stars.

How is there even room for a ship between all of them?

He hasn't piloted these kinds of ships in a long time. Hasn't been out among the stars where every direction is a possibility. Hasn't been jammed up with opportunity, so thoroughly confused by the fact that any direction is an option that you just fly straight and fly far.

He flips the card over and over in his fingers. He rubs a thumb across the raised lettering of the codes. He presses the hard edges into the flesh at bottom of his palm.

He's been walking a half hour now, and warehouses stretch out in front of him on either side of the street. These places are shut down. Empty. So he shouldn't hear voices, but he does. And these aren't human voices. These are grunts. Growls. These are Uzeks.

The hand that's resting on the blaster now has two fingers wrapped around the trigger.

Just because these are Uzeks doesn't mean they are associated with Uzel. Uzeks come in a variety of flavors, so there's not a reason to panic. Not yet.

More grunting and snorting coming from the shadowy spaces between the buildings. Nixon picks up his pace and he pulls the blaster free from his waistband. He pulls the cloak up from the ground with his other hand to keep it out from under his feet if he needs to run.

Footsteps crunch behind him, and, in front of him, the lights from the shipyard start to glow. He's still a mile away. Maybe it's more. The Uzeks are talking again. Whispers this time, as much as something that speaks a language based on grunts and snarls can whisper.

He doesn't speak Uzeki, but he has picked up a little and listens for the words he knows. He knows enough to know what he doesn't want to hear. There are two voices now, best he can tell, and they keep going back and forth. One grunts; the other groans.

He grips the blaster a little tighter. He eases the trigger back just a hair. He's careful not to pull it too much farther, but he doesn't want to be caught unprepared.

Then there's a third voice. These grunts are higher pitched, almost sounding female. The crunching of street gravel picks up. They are walking faster. Nixon's pace quickens. His followers double theirs.

He looks behind him. He doesn't recognize the two larger Uzeks, but the third—the one that belongs to those higher pitched grunts—he knows. It's the translator from the day before. She doesn't look so innocent out here. Especially with the blaster she's carrying across her chest.

Nixon gathers up more cloak in his hand and begins to run. All the pain from his Uzeki beating he'd been trying to ignore has his body screaming at him. His knees. His shins. His nose. His chest and sides. It's all there and singing a chorus of "What the hell are you doing now?"

He takes a fast glance behind and sees that the Uzeks are running too. Well, two of them. The translator isn't. She's standing still and pulling the blaster up to her shoulder. Nixon turns back around and begins to run in a zig zag, keeping his this ways and thats unpredictable—two steps this way then five steps in the other direction before going back seven toward the other side.

He's waiting for a shot to come, bracing for something to hit him in the back. He hears an initial shot, the deep *thunk* of a big blaster being fired. Then it's the sizzle of the air as a wide column of energy gets closer. Its crackle is nearly deafening as it passes by him and slams into a warehouse wall a few dozen feet ahead.

Stone and metal explode from the wall, and only fancy footwork keeps Nixon from stumbling to the ground.

A second thunk, and this time it's the ground in front of Nixon that disappears in a shower of dirt and rock. It's all too close for Nixon to avoid. His feet get caught up in the loose debris, and he goes down sideways.

A third shot passes over his head just as Nixon rolls onto his back. Heavy steps approach. It's the big Uzeks.

Nixon pushes himself up to standing and grabs the blaster that's fallen out of his hand. He takes off in a dead sprint for the entrance to an alley that's twenty feet away. He has his head down and fires a pair of blind shots up the street. They hit nothing but do allow him to make it to the alley.

There are still running steps behind him, but they stop just as Nixon gets into the deep darkest parts of the alley. They don't leave the alley. They just stop following him deeper. They are like Koona hounds on the scent of a Grindl cat until the translator grunts something loudly in Uzeki, and they return to her side.

"Well, Mr. Nixon," the woman says. "It seems we have ourselves something of a situation."

Nixon hesitates then decides not to say anything.

The translator goes on. "You killed my father. Now, I have to kill you. I don't like it. You've got a fight in you that I admire. But, this is how the business works."

Nixon still says nothing. It's blacker than black inside of this alley. He works his hand tighter around the grip of the blaster, and that's when he feels it. His other hand. It's empty. He's lost the card.

"So come out of that alley. Toss the blaster out in front of you, and we'll get this all settled."

Nixon inches toward the alley entrance. He has no intention of turning over the blaster or handing himself over to this girl and the memory of her father. He looks out to the street. There's something in the debris pile that doesn't look like it belongs, but he can't tell from here.

"C'mon, Mr. Nixon. I don't want to have to send someone in there to get you."

Nixon moves a couple of feet closer and looks again. There it is, the card that Mira gave him.

Shit.

"My father was patient, Mr. Nixon. It's not a trait I inherited. I'm going to give you to the count of ten and then I send someone to come get you."

Nixon moves back from the entrance and feels around in the dark for anything he can stack.

"Ten."

"Nine."

He's groping around and finds one crate. It's narrow and tall. Then there's a second. He puts one on top of the other and climbs up. He gropes for the top of the warehouse wall, but he hasn't stacked crates tall enough.

"Eight."

"Seven."

"Six."

He stoops and keeps a hand low, hoping to find anything else that will give him some kind of height. His hand catches something cool and smooth. It's a metal box. He picks it up and puts it on the other two boxes.

"Five."

"Four."

Nixon grabs Shaine's crate and tosses it onto the roof of the building. He tucks the blaster back into his waistband, then he climbs to the top of his stack of boxes and grabs for the edge of the roof. His fingertips catch the moulded concrete lip at the top of the wall, and his feet kick the stack of boxes over. They go down with a crash, and Nixon scrambles his feet up the wall just as the two big Uzeks round the corner.

"Oh, Mr. Nixon, there's that fight. But I'm afraid you're making a bad choice."

Nixon stands so he can see from his new position down into the alley. The Uzeks that rushed into the alley have stopped. Their eagerness superseded by their fear of what's in the dark. They start grunting something to one another, but neither of them moves.

Nixon quietly steps closer to the street and toward the edge of the roof. He's standing over them now. He's got a shot, but he can't fire this blaster accurately without both hands. He bends to set Shaine's case to the ground, but his fingers are slick with sweat and dirt and it slips. It bangs into the roof, and both Uzeks whip around. They bring their blasters up with them and both fire wild shots.

Nixon drops to the rooftop and hears the shots blister the air just above him. He goes to stand and three more blaster shots explode the brick and concrete at the edge of the building. A large chunk smashes Nixon in the forehead. He puts a hand to it and presses hard. He wipes, and his palm is covered in blood.

His head is light and he gives himself a moment before crawling back away from the edge of the building. He finds a large piece of mechanical equipment and crawls behind it.

"Gonna be harder than that to take me out."

"We can be here all night," the translator calls back. "Now that you're trapped like a dog."

Nixon looks around. He's safe here, for now. But he'd be safer if he could get off this roof. He puts a hand to his forehead and wipes away blood that was about to dribble into his eye.

It's all rooftop behind him, and that's the safest place to run, so he does. He's not more than a dozen steps away before he hears the Uzeks grunt their way onto the roof with him. One of them shout-grunts something that he ignores.

He's at a sprint. This pace can keep the Uzeks at bay, but that assumes there is endless road in front of him. This road ends abruptly. In about 20 yards.

Nixon tries to slow, but he's too late. He stutter steps until the very last second then leaps into what looks like a black hole.

From midair he looks down and makes out a pile of crates and boxes. He braces then crashes through them, back first. The case comes loose and falls out of his arms. It clangs against the ground, and Nixon hears it bounce away.

He picks himself up out of a pile of sticks and busted concrete, and there's a voice that starts speaking: "There you are, Mr. Nixon."

Grunts come from above him. Grunts and footsteps.

The translator, closer now: "Just come out and let's put an end to this. You owe us a debt, Mr. Nixon."

Blaster fire blows a hole into the wall next to him, and he rolls away then scrambles to his feet. One of the Uzeks is looking over the edge of the roof at him, a smaller blaster up and aimed at Nixon.

Nixon raises his blaster and fires a quick shot. It misses the Uzek standing at the edge of the roof, but there's a deep cry coming from behind that Uzek. The second one stumbles forward and into view. Nixon fires again and catches the thing in the shoulder. It spins around and toward the edge of the roof. It grabs at the air, trying to get hold of anything that can keep it from going over. It finds the forearm of the other Uzek. They struggle to stay up.

The other Uzek frantically works to free itself from the other's grip. It raises his blaster and points it at its friend, but it's too late. A misstep by the injured Uzek takes one leg off the roof, and its weight does the rest of the work. Both of them go over the edge, but there's nothing piled on the alley floor to break their falls.

They aren't high enough that the fall kills them, but Nixon's blaster does. A couple of shots into each, and the alley floor is shiny with Uzek black goo blood.

"It's just me and you now," he shouts.

"That's good," the translator says. "Fairer fight." She's not as close now. She's moved.

Nixon approaches the corner where the street meets the alley. He wipes at his eye, and peels away more blood. He has both hands holding the blaster. He sneaks a look out into the main street, but he can't find the translator.

She calls again: "Over here. I think I've found something that belongs to you."

Nixon pokes his head out again. She's out in the middle of the street bending over the pile of debris that Nixon tripped over earlier.

She stands up and Nixon sees it in her hand when it catches a spare bit of light. It's his card. She pinches two corners of the card and lets it spin between her fingers.

"Well now." She stops the card from spinning and holds it up above her head. "Looks like something important. How about you come out now?"

Nixon steps out from the alley and onto the sidewalk. He has the blaster raised and pointed at the translator.

"So that's how we're playing this?" She asks and raises the blaster rifle up to her side and points it toward Nixon.

"This is the game now," he says and takes three steps forward off the sidewalk. "And since I'm such a good sport, I'll give you first shot."

She laughs, casual. Then the rifle jumps in her hand. A shot goes well wide of Nixon, and he returns fire almost immediately. It's a well-aimed shot, and the translator screams when her raised hand disappears in a glow of light as the blaster beam hits her in the wrist.

Her big rifle clatters to the ground and she goes down with it. She's screaming and holding the nub that remains at the end of her right arm.

Nixon approaches slowly, keeping her in the center of his aim just in case she has some kind of plan for a situation like this.

She doesn't.

She's still screaming and rolling around on the ground when Nixon gets up next to her. He drops his blaster to his side and looks at the empty end of her arm. She doesn't fight.

"Now you and dad have something of a matched set."

He looks closer at it. Her hand came off just below the wrist, and her green skin has gone black. There's very little of the goo blood that he saw from the other two Uzeks he killed earlier.

"You're lucky," he tells her and drops her arm to the ground. She winces when the burned end hits the pavement. "Heat from that blaster bolt did a good job sealing up that wound. You should be fine walking back to wherever you go to after a fight like this."

She just looks at him and moans with the pain.

"I wanted to kill you. Still do, being honest. But you're going to go back with a message for me."

He pauses for her to at least acknowledge what he's said, but she doesn't. Not in anything that Nixon understands. She's muttering something in Uzeki under her breath and through the moans.

"This is finished. That's what I want you to tell whoever it is that's in charge now. We're even. I let you live. That squares our books."

She's shaking her head.

Nixon stands and looks around. It takes him a minute, but he finally sees it—a small bump in the road. And something in that bump that catches the light. It's her hand. It's his card. "Not. Finished," the translator says as Nixon walks away. "Not! Finished!"

EIGHT

Nixon picks up the translator's hand by its thick middle finger. It's pudgy and soft, like an overstuffed dumpling. He plucks Mira's card out of its grip and then drops the hand back to the ground. It slaps with a meaty whop.

He wipes the card across his cloak and cleans off her black goo blood then drops it into one of his interior cloak pockets. The crackers that were there are crushed to crumbs now. He pulls the pack out and rips open one end. He tips it up and the insides come out in a wave. Most miss his mouth and fall to the ground. The rest he chews quickly then swallows.

He balls up the packaging in his hand and lets it fall to the ground.

The spaceport is a glowing beacon in front of him. Bright lights become the only thing he can see. This kind of focus is dangerous. He recognizes that and tries to fight it off by looking away from the silhouettes of ships that continue to grow as he gets ever closer. He tries, but he doesn't succeed. Not for long anyway. He's drawn in by the spacecraft in front of him. He's swayed by the possibility they represent. They will let him put some distance between him and this place. Some distance between himself and the people here who want to pull him off these streets and get their pound of flesh. Or their pound of worse.

The first craft is a hauler. Boxy shaped. The kind of ugly pretty that you see when all that's left is the potential of what something could become. The second is a speeder. It's sitting so the cockpit points straight up. Big engines bulk up the backside of the ship. Two long arms reach out from the front.

There's another ship. A triangular cruiser with a pugged nose that's the best of both worlds. Plenty of room for gear but enough fire in the engines that it can get him where he needs to go and keep away from those he needs to keep away from. These are big ships, the kind of ships he hasn't flown in a while. Sure, the Uzeks have let him fly around little utility ships when he was doing work for them, but real piloting of real ships isn't something he's done in a long, long time.

He's missed the feel of a big engine pushing on you as you take off. Pressing you into your seat. A fire roaring beneath you. The rush of stars into your face and that feeling of possibility. Down here, he's trapped. This road tells him where to go. It's either this way, or it's that way. These low warehouses keep him from going any other direction. Even the alleys between the buildings don't offer much more in the way of choice.

But up there in the sky, controls in front of you and a ship all around you, everything is a possibility. Want to go higher? You can. Lower? Can do that too. Forward. Back. Left. Right. All of them, yes.

Nixon stares at the ships in front of him, even those ships in the second row that he can only see the tops of, but mentally he's behind the controls of one of them—doesn't matter which—and he's hitting the buttons needed to tell the engines that he's about to ask them to bring the big fire. He's talking to the guy in a tower that he can only see pieces of from here.

They go through the pre-flight checks. Nixon answers questions about his manifest. He gets the all-clear from his man in the tower and pushes the buttons needed to finally put life into the engines. They shake at first, all that potential energy capped and waiting. They won't actually get the ship off the ground without Nixon giving them permission. He reaches a hand out to push the button that tells the ship that it's OK to really rumble the rocks.

It's just then that in the real shipyard one of those real ships really does take off. It's the hauler, and its big engines make the ground shake and windows rattle.

Nixon smiles and watches. The noise from the engines, the rumble he can feel in his bones. The rattle that shakes his soul. It's all deafening, so much so that Nixon doesn't hear the first blaster shot. Doesn't hear the air sizzle as it passes him. Doesn't hear it crash into the alley wall across from him.

He sees the damage it does, though. An explosion of alley wall sprays down on him. Brick and mortar in his hair. He spins and another blast leaps out of the shadows.

A bloom of fire follows the blaster bolt leaving the barrel of the rifle, and it lights up the alley where the shooter has hidden. These aren't Uzeks. This is the gang from the spaceport earlier.

There's a thunk of a third shot, and Nixon falls flat to the ground as it screams through the air just above him.

He hears the whine of the big gun reloading and scrambles to his feet. He sprints toward one of the alleys on the opposite side of the street.

The whine stops, and all Nixon hears are his shoes slapping against the street pavers.

Thunk.

He dives into the dark of an alley, and the bolt from the blaster crashes into the wall above him. He slides across the pavers. His shoulder slams into a wall and bits of busted concrete smash his back.

Everything he hurt yesterday is screaming out again. He scrambles on his hands and heels deeper into the dark and begins to hear voices. There's more than just this gun man. The back of his head bumps into something. He feels behind him. It's some sort of metal barrel and feels big enough to give him some level of cover. He ducks behind it.

He pulls the blaster from his waistband and gets it ready to fire. The opening from the alley into the street is still clear, but the voices are getting louder. They are doing nothing to disguise that they are there.

One man appears. Then a second, and a third. They all stop a few feet away from the opening to the alley. None of them are holding the big blaster that was firing at Nixon.

"What are you waiting on?" calls a voice.

One of the men at the end of the alley takes a step forward then hesitates. He pulls a blaster from his waistband then takes another step into the dark.

Nixon aims his own blaster at this man. He wants to pull the trigger, lay a bolt of blaster energy square in the middle of this man's chest. He does that, though, and it's like shooting a flare. Sure, he'd eliminate one threat, but he'd signal his position to the other two. So, he drops his blaster and crouches behind the barrel he's been using for cover.

He listens to the man's steps. They get closer, and Nixon waits. Then, when the man is in front of Nixon he wraps his arms around the man's legs and pulls him to the ground. The man lands with a thud and reaches out for Nixon and grabs him by the shoulder. The man tries to raise the blaster, but Nixon grabs his wrist and tries to push the arm away.

They struggle. Nixon rakes his fingers across the man's eyes. The man screams and the hand with the blaster immediately grabs for his face. Nixon moves his hand up and grabs the man's hair. He pulls the man's head off the pavement then slams it back down. The smack echoes quickly down the alley, and Nixon does it again and then again and then again. The sound becomes wet then sticky and Nixon doesn't stop until it sounds like he's working a mop in a bucket.

It's all over in a matter of seconds. The man is still and not breathing. Nixon's never killed a man with his hands, but he doesn't have time to think about that now. He looks back down the alley, and the two remaining men are staring into the darkness calling their friend by his name.

He grabs the blaster out of the dead man's grip. He looks at it quickly. It's not as powerful as the Uzek blaster, but it'll get him out of this alley.

He pops up from behind his barrel and shoots once at the man leading the way. The man squeezes off a wild blast as he falls that winds up crushing a section of wall somewhere behind Nixon.

Nixon is back down behind his barrel and a shot from the second man pierces the top. A second shot rips a ragged chunk out of the wall above his head. A third hits the ground inches in front of him. He's pinned down.

"OK! OK!" he shouts and puts one hand above the barrel.

"Toss the blaster," the man shouts from the alley entrance.

Nixon tosses the Uzek blaster back into the dark of the alley. It clangs and clatters against the pavement.

"Now come up real slow."

Nixon does as he's told and stands slowly, one hand still raised above his head. Once his other hand, the one still holding the other blaster, clears the barrel he raises it quickly and fires a pair of shots in rapid succession.

The first: Hits the ground and tears up the paver stones there, the disintegrated tiles creating a cloud of dust.

The second: Hits the man in the neck, causing a fountain of blood to arc to the ground. The man grabs at his throat and falls to his knees then over on his side. He's not dead, but it won't be
long.

The world is suddenly quiet again. Quiet but for the whine of the big blaster charging. Nixon steps toward the street. He presses his back to the wall and takes small stuttering steps. He pokes his head out quickly but the street is empty. He pulls back.

He pokes his head out again, looking across the street to the alleys across from him. They all look empty, but he knows they can't be because the big blaster still whines.

He scans one more time, looking quickly from left to right and back again.

Then.

There.

A red light flashes. An indicator on the big blaster that it's ready to fire.

A bolt of blaster energy as thick as a tree trunk leaps from the alley and obliterates the wall next to him. Brick and concrete fall all around, and Nixon looks back to the alley opening where he'd seen the light before. It's dark now, but the whine has returned. He has time, but only a bit, and firing blind into an alley isn't going to do him any good.

He fires the blaster instead into the ground in front of the alley, and the shots start digging up and destroying the paver stones and creating a second cloud of pavers and dust.

It's cover. Not much, but enough.

Nixon breaks out of the alley. The blaster is in one hand. The case is in the other. The bottom of his cloak waves and pops behind him as he runs.

In front of him are the silhouettes of the ships in the spaceport. They are becoming a clearer picture as he sprints toward them. The little speeder doesn't look so little. The cruiser looks bigger and boxier the closer he gets.

Again, the big gun whines.

Then there's the concussive thunk of the big gun firing. The shot misses and digs a crater out of the ground in front of him. The impact knocks him to a knee and the case falls out of his hand. The metal box skips and skids away.

He scrambles on his hands and knees to get it, and he hears the sound of footfalls behind him. He looks, and coming up fast is the man who's been firing the blaster at him. The gun is whining again.

Nixon gets to his feet and picks up the case then turns back toward the spaceport. He runs an irregular path, trying to keep his next move unpredictable. The big gun fires again anyway, the shot smaller this time because whoever is operating it didn't let the gun get a full charge.

Nixon looks behind him, and the gunman is fiddling with the blaster, changing whatever kind of shot he's been firing. Nixon turns back around and tries to will more energy out of a body that's more than tired.

Has this only been two days? Was it really just yesterday morning that he was pinned against that alley wall, worrying what Uzel the Uzek was going to do to him? Just a day since he was sitting with Shaine at the Goodtimes Palace?

The air sizzles and a shot from the blaster passes over Nixon's shoulder. It bores its way through the wall of the spaceport that's still a hundred feet away. Nixon changes direction and hears another shot crackling its way toward him. This one is from a second gunman, and it catches the edge of his cloak.

He runs toward a wide opening in the wall in front of him. Above the opening is a sign: Exte North Spaceport. To the right of the text is Tychon's bisected triangle.

Nixon passes under the sign then stops and presses himself against the concrete wall. A shot from the blaster follows him in. The shot somehow misses hitting anything and drives a hole into the wall at the back of the spaceport.

Nixon looks back out the opening and fires a pair of shots at the gunmen who've been chasing him. They both miss, but these are moving targets. Still, they give him a moment. He starts running toward the ships and pulls out the card from Mira.

He's looking for slip 1112. A sign points him in the right direction, and he starts to run harder and faster, the possibility of imminent escape putting extra energy into his steps, an extra beat into his heart. A blaster shot comes from the entrance. It hits the ship in front of him, and Nixon changes course. He wants to put whatever he can between his back and these gunmen.

As big as these ships looked on the way here, they are ten times that large when running between them.

Slip 1108.

Slip 1109.

The air crackles with blaster energy, and a fat hauler absorbs a shot from the blaster. It leaves a scorched and jagged hole in the side of the ship.

Slip 1110.

Another shot. This one hits the bubbled pilot cover on the speeder and cracks it into a million spiderwebbed pieces.

Slip 1111.

Slip 1112.

There it is. Shaine's ship. The cruiser.

It's bigger than it looked from the street. Shaine didn't waste any credits on this ship. She's not a pretty bird, but she doesn't need to look pretty as long as she flies fast.

Nixon has been keeping something, anything, between him and the gunmen, and it's worked mostly. But now, he's going to have to step out into a clearing and expose himself.

Nixon counts down then sprints into the open.

Thunk.

Another thick and heavy blast from the big gun. It crushes the side of the speeder.

Nixon slips behind the side of the cruiser, and there's a ramp lowered to the ground. Nixon steps across and into the ship. It's all overwhelming—so many buttons and screens and switches. He looks at the card again. There are codes there that will get this cruiser started.

Thunk. And an instant later the sound of metal tearing, and the whole ship rocks to one side. Nixon hurries to the exit, and there's the gunman at the end of this row of ships. The blaster is up to his shoulder with the cruiser sited.

Another *thunk*, and the ship rocks again. This time alarms sound when it settles. An indicator on the board in front of the pilot's seat flashes. Nixon takes a seat, the card still out and in his hand.

The light says that one of the three engines is out. She should still fly if Nixon can get her started.

Nixon holds the card in front of him and starts punching the code written there into the keypad on the panel in front of him.

He enters the first few numbers and the ramp that had been open begins to close.

There's another *thunk*, and the ship rocks again—opposite direction this time. Another engine absorbing another shot.

Nixon continues with the code once he settles. He has to get it entered before the gunman fires again. He hits that second engine one more time and Nixon's not going anywhere.

He's staring at a series of three codes, each progressively longer. The first started the ramp closing.

He starts entering the second code and things inside the ship begins to ping and pop. Something liquid is moving behind these metal walls. Fuel, Nixon assumes.

He enters the last number on the card and the ship jostles. He can hear the fire in the engines waiting to be told that it's time to go.

Then there's a voice from outside. Barely audible but there.

"We know who you are, Mr. Nixon."

He keeps punching the final code, the longest of the three and the most complicated. While he's doing this he's waiting. Waiting for whoever is outside to continue their speech. Waiting on the gunman to …

THUNK

The ramp that had just closed crushes in on the ship, but the seal holds. Then there's more talking from outside the ship.

"We'll hit you again, Mr. Nixon. Maybe not here, but we'll find you. We're everywhere. You won't be able to outrun us no matter where you go."

THUNK

The gunman hits the door again as Nixon enters the last bits of the code. The ship shakes and Nixon is pushed back into his seat as the craft jumps from the surface and rushes into space.

The flight is uneven, off balance. It's the missing engine. The cruiser isn't sprinting out to space on a straight trajectory. It's going at an angle. Nixon is fighting to keep her from arching over and crashing into the ground somewhere outside of Exte. It's keeping him from thinking about the gunman. It's keeping him from thinking about whoever was shouting at him from outside the ship. It's keeping him from thinking about anything.

He fights the controls until the sky fades to black and the gravity has stopped trying to drag him back down into the dirt. He watches the screens to his left. He's expecting to see the indicator of another ship there, someone blasting away from the starport and giving chase, but he doesn't. The screens are empty except for ships and rocks and debris that was already out here.

With the screens clear, he settles into the pilot's seat. He lets his body sink into the cushions. He lets himself really exhale for the first time in two days. He knows he's not out of the woods. This is all just starting, especially if the warning that was being shouted from outside the ship is true.

"We'll hit you again, Mr. Nixon. Maybe not here, but we'll find you."

If whoever this is really is everywhere then nowhere is safe. He checks the monitors again. There's nothing suspicious there. Not yet. So, for now, this may be the safest place he can be.

He looks again at Shaine's card. There's another set of numbers on there. Nixon recognizes them as coordinates. He turns to the navigation console and inputs the numbers. The ship processes the coordinates for just a second then a plotted course to Planet Azken appears. It's going to be a long flight.

Nixon unbuckles from the pilot's seat and stands. He pulls off his cloak and empties the pockets. He puts all of it, the blaster and the case, on the top of the dash in front of him then folds his cloak over twice and sets it in the seat meant for the co-pilot.

He looks out the front of the ship, and it's nothing but the black of space. He sits again in the pilot's seat and grabs the case as he does. He rolls it over in his hand. It's smooth surface is reflecting the lights from the dash. The thin seam that runs around the case's middle catches the grooves of his fingers. Three buttons are slightly sunken into one side just above that seam.

He pushes the buttons, and they softly beep. He tries to work out the combination, but the case never comes open. Never even close.

He tosses it, and it tumbles across the dash.

"What have you gotten into, Shaine? What's in that case that can be causing this much trouble?"

02: UMEL

ONE

Nixon has drifted off twice. These modern ships don't need much in the way of pilot intervention to fly. Point them in the right direction and they'll find their way.

He'd entered coordinates into the navigation console a couple of days ago—It was just a couple of days ago, right?—and then spent almost all of his other time sitting in this pilot's seat. He gave himself a quick tour shortly after boarding, once he knew there wasn't someone taking off in another ship at the starport and giving chase.

The ship is mostly empty space, but that's what you get from this kind of craft. It's meant for hauling things. Not the kinds of things a full-size hauler would shuttle around, but smaller loads. The majority of loads, honestly. So, considering that, this ship had: Crew quarters big enough for two. A pair of small beds that were molded from the wall. A small side table sat in between and a small desk at the foot of each bed.

A tiny galley space is down the hall from the bedroom. It includes a small table that seats two and a small heating unit for food preparation. And across the hall and down from the galley is a small bathroom area. Big enough to stand in and clean yourself but not much more.

So, most often, Nixon finds himself spending the majority of his time here in this pilot seat. Watching things on his datapad and looking out into the black and tracking progress on the navigation console.

The ship calculated a nine day journey to Planet Azken. Nixon spent the first two days doing nothing and had no plans for the other seven. So he spent a lot of his time, when he wasn't staring out into the dark or watching something on his datapad, playing with the case.

He was trying to get it open, because he still couldn't imagine what was inside. What is so valuable that it cost Shaine his life and prompted Mira to completely uproot hers. He was nearly dead because of it, and now he's on a ship he'd never seen until he'd run up on it in the starport and riding it to some far off corner of the galaxy. All because a guy he hadn't seen in months—Or was it really a year?—asked him to.

So is this stupid? Is he trying to honor loyalties that only he feels? Before the night he called Shaine and met him in the Goodtimes Palace they hadn't spoken in months, and every time they did see each other, Nixon was the one who'd asked to meet.

Maybe Mira had gotten to him. Told him to cut all ties. She's the one who convinced him that he didn't need a partner in the first place. She's the one who'd forced Shaine and Trevor to have that tough conversation at the food cart in Old Town Exte. Shaine had said it was just him stepping back, but maybe Mira had wanted him to do more.

Shaine had gotten there first and had already bought a pair of hot meat sandwiches. The bread was toasted crisp. The meat inside was seasoned and grilled, and Nixon could smell it from two blocks away. By the time he arrived Shaine was already through one sandwich and was eating the second, wearing most of it.

He handed Trevor a sandwich as he approached, and the whole thing was over by the time he'd unwrapped the paper. Shaine needed to go in a new direction. Mira was pregnant, and he needed to find something that was stable. Something that was real. He'd hoped that Trevor understood.

He nodded his head that he did.

"You know I'd have loved to hear that from you." Trevor whipped around, and there he is. Shaine. Sitting in the navigator's seat. "I'd have loved to hear you say the words 'I understand,' "

Trevor stared.

"It wasn't my idea. It was Mira's."

"She was right," Trevor said. "You had her. You had the baby coming. I got it."

"But you never told me that. I felt awful. Like I was abandoning you."

Because you were, Trevor thought but didn't say.

"But look at this." Shaine gestures broadly to the ship. "This is pretty nice, right?"

Trevor looks around the flight deck. "Yeah, pretty nice."

"Well, you're welcome for that."

Trevor hadn't known until now just how stir crazy he'd gone. How much just a couple of days isolated like this would start playing tricks on his brain. His life is one that's lived alone, and he likes it. Alone never means entirely. No, he doesn't have a family to go home to like Shaine, but he still sees others. He still has interactions that stimulate those parts of the brain that crave relationships. But out here flying all alone, he's not getting any of that, so his brain is left to create it. That's all this is. This is Stir Crazy Shaine, and he likes to talk.

"So who were those guys who were chasing you at the end?"

"Shouldn't I be asking you?"

Stir Crazy Shaine stands up and starts walking the cabin. He runs his fingers over buttons. He grabs at locks. "Fair enough."

He continues to look at the ship like he's exploring some place new. "But I don't know who they were."

"Of course you don't," Nixon mutters to himself. "Because you're just me. You don't know anything I don't know."

"Doesn't mean you can't talk things out with me."

"You heard that?"

"Like you just said, I'm you. I hear everything you say. And the things you don't."

Nixon stares at Shaine but doesn't say anything.

"Yes," Shaine says. "Even that."

Nixon spins the pilot's seat to follow Shaine as he circles to the back of the room. "Then help me puzzle this out. What's in this box? Who are the people who seem to want it so badly? And why do they want it?"

"Well, I'm dead. You probably should be. So what's in the box isn't the usual stuff I'd been helping people get from one place to the next."

"And where were you supposed to take it?"

"You'll have to check your navcom for that."

Nixon does.

"Planet Azken. What do you know about Planet Azken?"

"I know what you know."

Nixon grabs his datapad. He taps the screen until he's pulled up a profile of the planet. He begins reading.

"Planet Azken is a mixed climate planet on the far eastern side of the galaxy. Three moons. Industrialized and … oh."

Stir Crazy Shaine turns and looks to Nixon on that last line. "Oh?"

"Tychon controls 60 percent of the economy there."

"Were you running for Tychon? After lecturing me about getting tangled up with the Uzeks?"

Shaine doesn't answer.

"Of course, you don't know if you were or not because I don't know if you were or not."

Nixon throws his datapad onto the deep dash in front of the pilot's seat. It tumbles into the case. Nixon grabs it next and runs a thumb along its smooth silver side. The bumps of its locks tickle his fingertips as he gently passes them over the top.

"No, you weren't. I know you. Even if you'd wanted to, Mira wouldn't have let you. She'd have let you do a lot of things. Would have encouraged some of them, actually. But not working for Tychon."

Tychon hadn't been able to establish itself much anywhere but Planet Azken and the planets nearest that one. A corporate power with a big footprint, it often comes in and stamps out any kind of competition both for customers and resources. Nixon and Shaine had heard things about Tychon, but it's creeping shadow hadn't made it to Exte in any real way, but it was coming. Just the small starport was the only kind of presence Tychon had on

Nixon continues to talk, but an alarm drowns out his next few words. Both Nixon and Shaine turn to look at the dash. A single red light flashes there—a warning. Code starts running across the screen in front of Nixon. There was a time when all these letters and numbers would have made some sense to him. Not anymore.

The same sequence scrolls past on a loop, and the alarm keeps blaring. The flashing red light in his periphery distracts.

The numbers begin to make some sense. It's coming back. Something about an engine. Only two of the ship's three are functioning—one completely shot through before leaving Exte and a second compromised by blaster fire in his fight to get off the planet. The ship's been pushing itself hard. It's bound to …

Another alarm joins the first one. Another flashing red light. Another line of code. Nixon looks for Shaine, but he's gone.

This scrolling string is just as confusing. He stares at it, trying to pry out any kind of information he can, but a third alarm sounding makes concentration impossible.

The codes become meaningless when a fourth and fifth alarm sound in quick order. The inside of the pilot's deck sounds like some kind of Rhummey bird sanctuary Nixon visited as a kid. The flashing lights bathe him in red.

He doesn't have time to try and decipher what's wrong. He taps the screen on the navcom console. He needs a place to put this ship down, and he needs it now.

TWO

By the time the navcom finds a place to land, two more alarms have gone off. Total of eight now. The ship is falling apart as it's flying.

Nixon straps himself into the pilot's seat. He tightens his belt down so tight that if the ship can't land gently he runs the risk of cutting himself in half.

He's helpless because of this modern ship. The whole thing falling apart around him and all he can do is sit here with his hands at his sides. He's buried his fingers under his leg to keep from grabbing the controls.

The ship jostles and shakes. All of the alarms are sounding, a wretched chorus of warning bells. The ship rolls hard to one side, and Nixon strains against the belt that's keeping him in the chair. Metal strains against metal. The whole ship creaks. It moans to keep itself together. The alarms continue to blare.

Then a ninth alarm sounds, one that screams louder than all of the others. Another light blinks red on the dash. Like the others, any label that may have been there has been worn off by whoever or whatever it was that flew this thing before Nixon.

He's trying to make sense of all the alarms and lights, but before he can figure any of it out the ship goes quiet. The screens go blank. This isn't back to normal. This is the opposite. The ship is another step—a giant step—closer to dying.

Nixon grabs the controls. He pushes them left and the ship responds. He asks the ship to go up, and she does.

"We're still alive then," Nixon says to an empty room.

"We are," the room says back.

Nixon drops the controls. He scans the room. There's no one else here, not even some stir crazy visitor from his past. Who just spoke?

"Hello?"

"Hello," the voice responds.

"Who is ..." Nixon can't finish asking the question.

"I am EHL 628. I am the craft."

"The ship?"

"I am."

"I didn't know this model could..." Nixon has never flown one of these responsive ships, the kind that could talk to you. The kind of ship that could puzzle out problems with you.

"I can."

"So, what's next?" Nixon asks.

"Please repeat."

Nixon shifts forward in his seat. "Help me find a place to put you down. You're in rough shape, and I don't want to die out here."

"I can't."

"That's not very cooperative."

"My systems are offline."

"Then how are you responding now?"

"My intelligence engines are on a different ..."

Nixon grabs the controls again and interrupts. "OK. OK. So, this is on me."

"What is on you?"

"The responsibility for flying the ship."

"It is."

Nixon tries to recall what he'd seen on the navcom screen earlier, but he was only making passing glances. He didn't need to know where they were headed. He just needed to make sure he'd be alive when they got there and that the case would be safe.

Nixon scans the narrow bit of space he can see in front of him. There's nothing there. He doesn't know where to go. That freedom that he was excited to experience again, the ability to go anywhere he wants—any direction—is suddenly paralyzing.

With just a single engine, Nixon fights the controls to keep the ship pointed straight. But straight at what? Who knows? There's nothing to point at.

There's a loud bang from the back of the ship and the one engine seems to stall. Then another bang and the engine fires back up. The ship lurches and Nixon struggles against the controls, but when he gets EHL back under his command he sees it. There's something in the corner of his view. Just a dot for now. A point of light. But it's a point of light that's in a fixed spot. It's something he can point the ship toward. It gives him a reference point for direction. This thing, this whatever it is—maybe it's a planet, or a starship, or just something big enough to reflect enough light to show up to the naked eye—is in front of him. That means this direction he's flying now is forward.

And as he flies forward this point of light becomes something more. It grows bigger in front of him until he knows what this is. It's a planet. It's still a long way off, but he knows this isn't something made by anyone's hands. This is natural.

As he flies closer, he can see the peaks of mountains. He sees the flat of the land. Mostly, though the place looks wet. There's a lot of sea. Everything is coastline.

He aims for pockets of population. What does he do, though, once he gets close? He has no idea how to land this thing. Even when he was younger, ships were able to take care of that part of flying. You turned over the controls to the internal systems and they brought you down easy. So smooth that you never felt when you were on the ground. It was like a Farrow bird feather settling.

Three cities come into view from this far out, and Nixon picks his favorite. It's a random decision, but it looks to be the most populous of the three. He sees small snakes of ship traffic flying above a city spread out wide along a coastline that looks to go on forever.

He points the nose of the ship at what looks to be the city's center then starts trying to bring EHL's systems back online. He punches buttons, hoping to see something spark. A monitor blink to life. A light on the dash flash. Something that says he isn't going to have to try and fly this thing nearer the ground, try to pass it through the traffic lanes above the city. Or bring it safely to the ground.

But nothing.

He looks back out at the planet, and it fills his entire view. The individual trees that grow on top of the mountains suddenly look like they're going to reach out and grab him. He banks the ship hard to the right and the mountains move out of view. Now, he sees the water and the city that stretches out along the coast. He brings the ship back level.

He turns back to the buttons inside the ship and again tries to bring everything back online. Nothing works. He lets out an "Arghhh" in frustration and closes his eyes. He's trying to summon up something, some kind of memory that can help. His earlier life flashes in a blurred mess of swirling colors.

Then it stops.

He sees nothing but hands, but he knows who they belong to. These are his father's hands. Nixon is a kid and suddenly this moment is coming back to him. He's not even 10, and he's in one of those beaten up ships his dad always seemed to bring home. He'd get infatuated with one, and they'd fly it everywhere until it literally fell apart. This one they'd been flying a while.

Alarms were screaming. Nixon was panicked. His dad, though, was calm. He was very deliberately pushing buttons, and, as he did, the alarms were shutting off. He watched his father's hands work. They found a button; they pushed that button. They found a switch; they flipped that switch. A quiet confidence that this ship wasn't going to crash. Not this day and not with this crew on board.

Nixon opens his eyes. He looks at the panels in front of him. Suddenly, they aren't just a bunch of plastic and metal without meaning. Do they make total sense? No, not yet. But they are no longer some confusing puzzle that isn't meant to be solved. He reads the labels that remain and presses the buttons controlling the systems he knows he'll need. Slowly things begin to come back online until:

"Shall I fly?" EHL asks.

Nixon collapses in the seat and watches as the ship breaks through a blue haze that hangs above the city. EHL dips itself in and out of a crowded cargo lane of traffic then shoots through a half-busy general traffic lane before emerging into the relative clear above ... where is this?

Nixon studies what he can see: Mostly low-slung buildings. One large, narrow tower shooting up in the middle of the city. Active coastline with several ports and docks.

The ship drops itself lower, and that's the first time Nixon notices the spaceport crowded with ships of every size.

"Not there," Nixon says. "Look for something just outside of the main district. Somewhere we might be able to put down ... for free."

"Yes, sir."

The ship lifts higher and banks left. It levels back out and Nixon sees where EHL is aiming. It's a wide expanse of mostly empty land. There are a handful of ships already landed there, but there is still plenty of space to add another.

"Perfect," Nixon says.

"Yes, sir."

EHL gives herself more speed, accelerating toward a nice wide patch of dirt at the front of the open field. The ground rushes at Nixon and, for a moment, he thinks about grabbing the controls, but he reminds himself that this was why he'd worked to get the ship's systems back up.

EHL pushes harder and the whole ship begins to shake.

"Whoa, whoa. This is why your systems went down before."

EHL decelerates hard, and her front end raises. Nixon feels the back end start to slide around. A moment later, she levels out and drops softly. Suddenly, they aren't moving. She's on the ground, coming down like a feather.

THREE

Nixon stands from the captain's seat and grabs his cloak off the back of the navigator's chair.

"Nice job," he says to the ship.

"Yes, sir."

Nixon slips the cloak over his head, and he suddenly feels better. He reaches onto the dash and grabs the case, dropping it into his cloak pocket. Next, he grabs the blaster he tossed up there when he left Exte. He slips it into the waistband of his pants. There, now he feels more than better. He feels complete.

"I'm going to get some fresh air. See if I can't figure out where we're at."

"Yes, sir."

Nixon steps across the deck and hits a button on the wall. A moment later the ramp is struggling to unfold. Metal grinds on metal. It hurks and jerks and all takes twice as long as it should. The blaster fire must have done a number to the outside of it, and Nixon is realizing how lucky he is to both be alive and to not be trapped inside this shop without a way off.

The ramp does finally fully unfold, and, when it does, natural light spills into the ship. The galaxy's two suns seem somehow brighter here.

The ramp locks into place, and Nixon walks down. The ground crunches as he steps off the ramp, and Nixon takes a knee. He pinches a bit of the surface between his thumb and forefinger and rubs them together. It's sandy. The heat from the suns reflects off the ground and warms his face. He shields his eyes with his hand and looks at the open field around him.

There are other ships here, ships that look like they haven't moved in a long time. Over there is another small hauler covered in a layer of sand. A speeder is opposite that. It still has a bit of shine, but only a bit. Then, as he walks closer he sees it. The whole back end is crumpled and crushed. And there, on the ground in front of the speeder is a gouge dug into the sand. Nixon looks away from the speeder, following this now-shallow indentation more than a hundred yards.

He looks back to his left and sees a … he doesn't know. It's some kind of piecemeal craft. A bit of this. Some of that. A little of something else. Smashed all together and everything held in place with some strategically placed welds. It's not a big ship, but it's in the best shape of any of them out here.

There's a woman sitting in a folding chair in front of it. Light blue skin. Darker blue hair pulled into a tight braid that hangs over her shoulder. She's on her datapad talking with someone. Again in a language that Nixon doesn't understand, but he watches her for a moment. Her voice gets louder, and she looks his way. He turns away quickly, suddenly feeling very conspicuous standing in the middle of this open field.

He turns to his own ship and sees that it's not in the best shape. He runs a hand along the side of the engine that died just after he took off from Exte. He puts a finger into one blaster hole and then another in the next. Whoever was firing at him was a heck of a shot. To hit this engine at that angle and at the speed the ship was going. This shot wasn't from some low-level criminal like him. This was a pro.

"Seriously, Shaine," he whispers. "What were you mixed up in?"

He steps to the back of the ship and looks at the other two engines. Both are burned to a deep black. He runs fingers through the ashy mess and comes away with a handful of carbon. He steps around to the other side of the ship and runs a finger along the seams where the engines join the rest of the craft, and there's a gap that's obviously wider than it should be. Not that he knows exactly what normal would necessarily look like, he just knows this isn't it.

He steps back, and all the seams are off. Too wide in some places. Too narrow in others. Then he sees the cracks in the metal and the missing rivets and screws and begins to wonder how he ever made it to this field at all.

The ship is in bad shape. Worse than bad. It's not flying again, not for a while.

He steps up the ramp and back inside. He sits back in the captain's seat.

"Welcome back, sir," the ship says.

Nixon reclines the seat slightly and says: "Thanks."

He sighs and looks to the ceiling. There are hairline cracks in the metal up there too, the stress of the flight even reaching inside the ship.

"Can I get a status update?"

"A status update, sir?"

"You. Your state. How are you doing? If we needed to fly …"

"Yes, sir." The ship goes quiet for a moment. "Two of my three systems are down."

"Three?" Nixon sits up and starts pushing random buttons on the dash for no real reason, it's just something to do.

"Flight, navigation, and environmental. I also have significant structural damage."

"I have visual confirmation of that last one."

"Yes, sir."

Nixon stands and goes back to the hatch. He looks out the opening and down the ramp. He sees the woman across the field sitting in front of the hand-made ship. She's not talking on her datapad anymore. He watches her stand and begin moving boxes and equipment back inside. The shadows are reaching long across the sandy field.

A breeze kicks up, and flutters the bottom of Nixon's cloak. The woman across the way pulls a kerchief that's been loose around her neck up so that it covers her nose and mouth. The wind catches the sand and starts blowing clouds of grit that ting against the side of the ship.

The woman picks up her pace, grabbing boxes two at a time and moving them inside. The clouds of sand whip across the ground, beginning to obscure everything. She's moving fast, but it's methodical. She's done this before.

These winds blow hard and straight. They keep the clouds of sand low, and now all he can see of the woman now is the top of her ship. One of the suns hits a spot on the hull. He hadn't noticed before. It's bright metal, new metal, and it catches in the light. That ship has had repairs.

There's someone here on this planet that can help him get his ship fixed, close the seams and patch the holes and get him flying again.

He steps back deeper into the ship and sits in the captain's seat. He pulls his datapad from his pocket and taps the screen to open it up. A few taps later and his credit balance is up in front of him. It hasn't changed. It's just as small as when he left Exte, and getting this ship fixed won't be cheap. He needs to find work.

FOUR

Nixon's hands ache. He'd been able to find work early today helping load one of the ships at the port just north of the city center. All day lifting boxes that weighed at least as much as he did. Not only did it kill his hands, but he could barely lift his arms.

The ramp locked into place with a thunk, and Nixon shuffled his feet into the ship. He collapsed into the captain's seat and pulled out his datapad. He opened up his credit balance, just to make sure he hadn't been conned by the guy who'd offered work. Something tickled Nixon wrong when the guy approached that morning. Nixon couldn't put a finger on it. Maybe he'd been the hustler so long that everything made him suspicious. Maybe this guy reminded him too much of himself.

There they are, the twelve credits he'd been promised. Nixon sucks in a breath then unleashes a scream. Twelve credits. Suns up to suns down picking up and putting down boxes. Arms that feel like they are about to drop off. All he got was twelve credits.

He screams again. The ship responds. "Sir?"

"It's nothing." Nixon sits back up. His stomach feels like an empty pit. Twelve credits and they didn't even give him time for lunch. He walks to the galley and opens the cabinet.

Two more packages of Bowtan meat and noodles to rehydrate. On top of repairing the ship, he needs credits to restock the ship with supplies.

He starts the noodles heating and goes back to the main deck. That's when he sees the case, and he thinks of Shaine. He sees his friend back in that courtyard on Exte, pushing the case toward him. Shouting at him about finishing the job. Then his vision cuts to a few moments later, like it's been edited by someone who puts together those shows he watches on his datapad. He's at the exit of the courtyard, blaster fire exploding all around him, trying to figure out how he can get back to help Shaine. His friend is lying on the ground after being hit in the shoulder. He's rolling over to his back when three shots catch him in the chest and split him open.

Nixon pulls the case off the dash and pulls at the seam where the top and bottom of the two sides come together. He tries to pry it open, but it doesn't budge.

The noodles beep from the galley. Nixon eats and tries to tabulate how much getting this ship restocked and repaired is going to cost him. He struggles, though, because he can't keep his mind off of Shaine. Nixon begins to build the back story in his head. If he can't ask Shaine what's happened then he can imagine.

He's tucked away again in his exit from the courtyard, and he sees Shaine sitting at the same table he was at when the two friends met that morning. He's waiting again, but for someone else. Two men come in together then go their separate ways once inside. Then a woman looking at her reader, the same one Nixon saw when he met Shaine. Then, after a few minutes of sitting in the quiet, two more men enter the courtyard. These are them. Nixon knows it. A pair of toughs.

They are in black. Long sleeves and long pants with light armor on the outside. They aren't openly carrying blasters, but their clothes are so bulky there's no doubt they have them tucked away somewhere.

One of the men says something. Shaine stands and responds. Nixon is too far away to understand the conversation, but he doesn't need to hear it to know that it's not good. The other man responds to Shaine, and Shaine says something back, something he shouldn't have. One of the men pushes Shaine in the chest, and he stumbles back.

Shaine catches himself then puts a shoulder down and charges the smaller of the two men. He drives through him and they both fall to the ground. Shaine rolls himself on top of the man and pulls back his arm, ready to drive his fist through the guy's nose and into the paver stones underneath him.

"Hey!" Nixon can hear that. It's the man who's still standing. He's pulled a blaster from somewhere and has it leveled at Shaine's back.

Shaine puts both hands up and stands. The other man, the smaller man, stands and dusts himself off. The conversation begins again. Shaine does most of the listening. Then it's over. The men leave, and Shaine sits back down at the table. He's still for a moment and then digs into the folds of his cloak and pulls out the case. He rolls it over and over in his hand then slips it back inside.

Nixon slurps the last of his noodles then crumples the paper container into a ball. He steps back out to the main deck. That's where he sees the case, the real one. He picks it up again and feels the cool metal on his palm. He runs a finger along the seam where the top and bottom of the box come together. He slides his thumb across the locking mechanism. Then he sees Shaine handing him the box. He tells Nixon that he's counting on him. That Mira is counting on him. Not just because of the credits they'll all earn, but because ... No.

He doesn't want to think about it.

He grabs his datapad from the dash and pulls up his credit balance. If it were this high at home—wait, where's home—he'd think he was almost rich. Almost two dozen total. But he'll need100 times that to get his ship fixed. More probably.

But tonight, he needs some of those credits so he can drink away these memories of Shaine.

Here's what Nixon has learned in the last few days:

He is on a planet called Umel. Learned that from the guy who gave him his first job here. Five credits to help him move a dozen boxes out of the back of one warehouse and into another. It took half the day, and at the end of it the gentleman gave Nixon a meal.

Umel was mostly uninhabited until someone found minerals just under the surface. Then the whole place was crushed by instant population. It was all people trying to find their little personal fortune, but it quickly fell into the hands of one of the cartels. Everyone who'd come here quickly left just as fast.

Judging from the crowd in this bar, most of those who were on Umel were Snapsits of one variety or another. That includes the female Snapsit sitting next to him. Her skin is a deep blue and her hair is cut short and close to her head. She's in short pants and a short-sleeved shirt with a floor-length vest that hangs over the back of her stool. It's made of a material that Nixon doesn't recognize. It's heavy and thick and tightly woven. The outside of it is covered in loops, and she mindlessly runs a finger around the inside of one while they talk.

"So tell it to me again," Nixon says.

She sets a sweating glass down on the bar top in front of her and wipes her hand dry on her vest. She then reaches that same hand into one of the pockets and pulls out a small pink rock that's been rubbed shiny. She lays it on the bar and says: "There. Smell that."

Nixon picks it up and puts it to his nose. His eyes go wide and his head jerks back on instinct. He drops the rock, and it bangs a divot into the thin wood of the bartop.

"Oh my ... what the ..."

The woman throws her head back and her laugh fills up the room. She scoops the rock back up and puts it in her pocket.

"It's Gee-Stat," she says. "It's awful like that. But you process it. Make it into a powder, and it's amazing on anything. It's rare, so it's expensive. But it makes everything you eat taste ... I don't know. It's just this amazing little thing. And Umel is crawling with the stuff. It's practically made of it."

"This is what all the fighting was about early on."

"Early on? It's been the source of every conflict on Umel for as long as the place has been populated. Even now."

"There's still trouble?"

She wipes a finger across the front of her glass, and it comes back slick. She licks off the wet. "There will always be trouble, but Umel is much too civilized for it to be out in the open now."

Nixon tips his head back and finishes what's left in the bottle he's been nursing for the last while. He sets it on the bar then sticks out the same hand and offers it to the Snapsit woman.

"I'm Trevor," he says.

"Oh my, we haven't done that yet? I'm Laana.

"So if this trouble isn't out in the open then ..."

"Then it's in the shadows," she says and grabs her glass again.

"And how much of that trouble is caused by Tychon?"

Laana shakes her head. "Gee-stat is too small-time for Tychon. Takes too much to get it out of the ground for the amount of pay off. But these littler operations make it work. It's on the back of cheap labor, but if you need the credits they have the work."

Nixon sits up a bit straighter. "Oh, yeah?"

Laana finishes what's in her glass and sets it back on the bar top. "Oh, yeah."

"Tell me more about that, because I can use the credits."

She points Nixon up and down. "They are guys like you. They have warehouses of mineral all along the coast. Right near the boats."

Like it was waiting on her cue, one of the big ships that takes the minerals out to the starport blows its horn.

She waits for it to finish and smiles. "There's plenty of work loading boats or moving crates of the stuff around the warehouses."

"Pay's good?"

She picks up and wiggles her empty glass. "Keeps me in this stuff. Keeps me fed."

"How can I find the people looking for this work?"

Laana pulls out her datapad and says: "If you're serious I can send you an address."

Nixon pulls out his own pad. "Dead serious," he says.

Laana begins tapping her screen. Nixon fills the silence. "I'm doing a courier job and am only here because my ship is busted up. I need money for supplies and repairs."

Laana grabs Nixon's pad and places it end to end with hers and flicks her finger across the screen, like she's tossing data from her pad to his. His screen blinks a moment later, and the address pops up. It means nothing to Nixon.

"You said this was near the docks?

"Yeah, short walk from here. I can show you."

Nixon stands and calls for the man who's been serving them drinks. He quickly checks his credit balance and then pays for both his drinks and Laana's.

They step out into the night, and the air feels heavy. It wants to rain. Distant thunder rumbles a hello. He hears activity coming from the docks. The general murmur of activity is punctuated with shouting voices and laughter. The ships never stop, Laana says.

"I stay up at night and watch it all. I've never been a great sleeper, so I got myself a spot up there." She points to the top floor of an unfinished tower that sits in roughly the center of the city's main district. Keep an eye on what's going on. Look through my scope if I see anything at all that seems interesting."

"Interesting?

They quickly cross the street, the pavers slick under their feet. The driver of a small truck loaded with crates blasts his horn and they pick up their pace. The driver shouts something Nixon doesn't understand and shakes a fleshy fist at them.

Nixon stops once they've crossed and looks back at Laana's tower. "How high up?" he asks.

She points to a spot near the very top. It's open to the air, some kind of industrial cave.

"Without the wall?"

"I like it that way. I get all messed up if I'm inside too long."

She turns and keeps walking. "Plus, put up a wall there and I miss this." She pauses and lets the music of the city wash over them.

"I like it. I like the noise. I spent too much time in a place where quiet was demanded."

Nixon follows her down the street and they make a turn toward the water and into a warehouse area.

"You said you looked down your scope earlier. Scope for what?"

Laana spreads her blue arms as wide as she can. The cloth from her vest snaps and pops in the breeze. "I've got me a rifle that's..." she stretches her arms even farther, as wide as they'll go. "Well, it's bigger than that. Got a really nice scope on the top that... helps."

"Long guns?"

"Oh, yeah."

Nixon lifts his cloak and shows off the handle of the blaster tucked into his pants. "Not one of these?"

"Naaah," she says. "I mean, a blaster is fine. It gets the job done, but where's the fun in one of those? Where's the challenge. You've got to be close to fire one. A long gun, though, you can be a ways away. There's margin for error there. Then if the target's moving, that's some real skill."

Nixon follows Laana around another corner, and she points down the block. It's all opened bay doors. Light pours out of most of them and illuminates the spaces out front like both suns are up.

"Come back in the morning. Just about anyone here could use some help."

She grabs his upper arm and squeezes. "You're a big, strong guy. They'll be happy to put you to work."

Nixon thanks her.

"Now, I'm going to go home and play spy. Find someone worth putting into my sites."

FIVE

Nixon wouldn't go as far as calling Laana a liar, but after days of still earning next to nothing for work that was twice as hard, he was close.

He was tired down to his core. He'd been offered ten credits for a day's effort reorganizing a warehouse.

"Can I get 20?" He'd asked the human offering the job.

"I know guys who'll do it for five."

"Fifteen?"

The man looked past Nixon to the other men roaming the street looking to find a job for the day then says "Never mind."

Nixon stepped back into the man's view. "Fine, fine. For ten."

The man turned and stepped back into the warehouse.

Nixon followed and spent the next 14 hours moving boxes on and off a hand truck that the man who hired him would push. He'd pass the time waiting for Nixon to finish a load by looking at his datapad.

Two hours into the day, Nixon wanted to crush the datapad to dust and drop a full load of boxes on the guy's head. Instead, he worked in silence then made a note of the place's name when he left. He wouldn't work for him again.

His feet kick up sand as he nears his ship. The night is dark, and the field is totally black except for a light out front of the piecemeal ship parked near Nixon's.

The woman who owns it is out front sitting in a chair with her feet up on a box and looking at her datapad

Her ship looks even more unique in this light. He can see what it used to be, the shape it left the factory floor with. In this light, the contrast between the old and the new, between what she bought and what she'd added, is even more striking.

The original ship looks to be a small economy thing, not a lot bigger than one of those little hauler ships that the Uzeks let Nixon fly back on Exte. But it is more than twice that size now. She's added two large cargo holds on the sides. She's expanded the cockpit to seat more than one. And that engine is definitely larger than anything Nixon has ever seen on the back of these ships on Exte.

He turns back to his ship, his busted wreck. He opens the ramp that's still crushed in from the escape off Exte, and the light from inside the ship is just enough to show him all the work that still needs to be done. He'd been spending so much time trying to earn credits that he'd not had any time to try and close up the wide seams, to fill the holes, or patch the cracks.

He runs a hand along the side of the ship. It's cool and damp. It leaves his palm slick. He wipes it dry on his cloak. He's lost most of the light from inside but keeps circling the ship anyway. He puts a finger inside one of the holes in the engine. Shoves it in as far as it'll go, down to the last knuckle. He wiggles it around and feels the loose ends of the engine wiring dance across his fingertip.

These holes are a reminder that there is someone after him. Someone who wants that case. Someone who will eventually find him here.

He goes back inside the ship and starts searching through bins and compartments until he finds a tool kit. It's small, just a few tools good for beating and screwing and prying and pulling, but it'll have to do.

Then he goes to work. He starts yanking and pulling at the metal that makes up the ship's exterior and closing up the open seams and healing the cracks. Yes, he is bone tired. And yes, he still doesn't know exactly what he's doing. But he needs to do this. To make progress. He works until the first of Umel's suns pokes its head over the horizon and casts bright spots of light across Nixon's open field.

He puts the tools down and steps back to look at his progress. It isn't much, but it's something. Enough to return the focus that had slipped. He's been so concentrated on figuring out how to earn credits that he's let why he needs them become secondary. Not again. Not anymore. He'll get this ship fixed and he'll get off this planet. Soon.

Another night after another long day of too little pay. Not as bad as he'd been finding. Twenty-five credits today. Back on Exte that would have been a good day. He'd spend the rest of his night praying to find another job like that. But here, there is no amount of money that's good enough. Every job could pay five credits more. Should pay five credits more considering the kind of work that he is being asked to do.

But don't sniff at twenty-five credits, the angel on his right shoulder reminds him, staring at the devil on his left.

The night is dark, and he listens to its sounds. There is still activity on the docks. There is always activity there. Men talk; they laugh. Machinery is in motion. All of that fades as the blocks between him and the water continue to add up. But that doesn't mean things are quiet, the noise just changes. The men on the docks are replaced by the men working deep into the night at the warehouses. The big machines out on the docks are replaced by the smaller more maneuverable machines scooting across the warehouse floor.

Nixon looks ahead of him. In front of him is the unfinished tower that rises up like a needle from the center of Umel. He looks up the length of the tower to its unfinished top and the open hole. He can't see her, but he assumes

Laana is there. Using her scope to scan the city and look for some entertainment.

Is she watching me? Has she been watching?

He waves to her, just in case.

Past the tower and out of Umel's central district, the night is nearly silent. That's where it becomes easier for Nixon to notice the footsteps behind him. The footsteps that speed up when he speeds up. That slow when he slows.

He walks another block then stops at a corner. The footsteps behind him stop. It's dark, and he wants to look behind him. Whoever this is, though, has probably already ducked into a shadow. It's what Nixon would have done.

He crosses the street and doesn't hear the steps. Then there's the blast of a horn and he looks back just in time to see whoever this is disappear behind a turning people mover.

Nixon picks up his pace, and a moment later there are the steps again. They aren't matching his pace. They are quicker—catching up. He turns a corner and heads down a street he doesn't recognize. There are lights coming from a building at the end of the block. There's laughter too. A crowd. He heads toward it.

A man emerges from the far-off door and pulls on a cloak. He shrugs it up tight around his shoulders and dons the hood. He turns Nixon's direction and walks with his head down.

Nixon watches him approach and keeps listening to the footsteps. They've slowed. Whoever this is is keeping his distance again.

The man in the cloak approaches and steals a glance at Nixon as he passes.

Perfect.

Nixon turns to watch him pass then shouts once he's a couple of steps by: "What did you say, friend? Did you threaten me?"

The man turns and looks up at Nixon confused. Nixon looks past him to the figure stopped on the sidewalk.

He's human, and he's huge. Nixon takes off. He sprints for the light at the end of the block. The footsteps follow.

He feels at his waistband for the blaster he knows isn't there. He runs through the light coming from what he can now tell is a data shack and turns the corner. He hears the feet of the man following him slapping the ground. He also hears the man fighting to catch his breath.

This new block is almost pitch black. Nixon runs a few hundred feet then turns into an alley and moves to the back where it's darker than dark, and he waits. He hears the man who's been chasing him slow to a walk.

"Hey!" the man shouts. It's breathy, and Nixon can tell it wasn't as loud or menacing as the man intended. He's struggling to catch his breath. Nixon understands; he is too.

He sits as quiet as possible and listens to the man slowly inspect the alleys all around him. It was just a matter of time before the man's faded silhouette would appear at the end of Nixon's alley, and there it is. He's as wide as the opening

"Hey!" That's a proper shout.

Nixon stands and approaches. It's either fight him here at the back of the alley where it's dark and the only way out is through this guy. Or he can fight him at the end of the alley where he has at least a chance to slip by him and away.

Nixon walks back toward the street, his hands held high above his head.

"What were you going to do?" he asks.

He watches the man slowly ball his fist. "What was I going to do?"

"If you caught me." Nixon continues to walk forward, one slow step after another. His arms are raised above his head, like he's being talked out of an alley by a security team that's discovered a bunch of people casting lots in an underground Garrate game.

"When I caught you."

Nixon is halfway down the alley and the man rocks in anticipation. His fists are tight knots now. He's coiling up his energy, becoming a spring that's primed to be sprung. Nixon sees it and recognizes that it isn't good. A man like that fighting in a space like this, the guy is going to pinball off the walls and be unpredictable. There's no way to win if Nixon keeps the fight fair.

He's close enough to see a gappy grin creep across the big man's face. To see his eyes narrow as the grin turns into a smile. Then to see his eyes widen and his mouth open into a wide O when Nixon kicks a foot hard in between the man's legs.

Kicks him so hard that he feels the man's pelvic bone with his foot. Kicks him so hard that he swears he feels things inside the other man pop.

The man doubles at the waist, and Nixon grabs two handfuls of hair on the back of the guy's head. He pulls down hard as he brings his knee up quickly. The man's face and Nixon's knee come together in a sickening crunch. Nixon feels the bones in the man's face crumble.

The man finally screams out, and Nixon lets him fall to the ground. Nixon stands over him, and the man rolls to his back. His legs are still curled up tight to his waist, and blood covers his mouth and chin.

"Was that what you'd hoped would happen? You wanted to get bloodied up like this? Unable to talk? Why? Because you wanted something I had? Well..." Nixon pulls his datapad from his pocket and pulls up his credit balance. "... joke would have been on you."

He turns the screen toward the man and the man tries to put on a broken smile. Blood crackles through what sounds to Nixon like a laugh.

Nixon stands and puts his datapad back into his pocket. He stares down into the man's face then spits. It lands just an inch from the man's cheek, and he laughs again.

SIX

Most nights Nixon collapses on the thin mattress in the crew quarters, too tired to care or notice that he's uncomfortable. A full day of working some back-breaking job then coming back to his ship and spending most of his night hours trying to get her back into flying shape.

She was close. Or he thought she was. The seams that had been wide weren't anymore. The cracks were now patched over with new metal that shines bright in the suns' light. It wasn't pretty—ugly, actually—but he wasn't trying to win any kind of awards for his work.

Tonight, though, he didn't work, and he didn't sleep. Instead, he dropped himself into the captain's seat and let his mind race. The fight, such as it was, had him amped. He felt like he could get out there and work his fingers under the ship, pick it up and press it over his head and throw it out of the Umellian atmosphere. Just watch it disappear into the dark of the night.

He grabbed the case off the dash and started pushing the buttons on the front, working combinations that he'd already tried hundreds of times. Tonight, it wasn't about getting this thing open. It was just something to keep his fidgety hands busy. They'd been shot so full of adrenaline that there wasn't a chance they'd be calm for hours yet.

Push one button. Push the next. Push a third. Try the top. Nothing.

Push a button. Then another. Then another. Try the top. Nothing.

Button. Button. Button. Nothing.

A new combination. Nothing.

Wait. Not nothing. Something. It budged.

But what was the combination? What did he push?

Nixon looks down at the case. Stares hard at the buttons, like looking at them more intently will somehow highlight the order in which he pushed them.

He starts pushing buttons again and checking the top. But none of them work. The top feels more solid than it ever has.

Nixon shouts, frustrated. He throws the case to the wall across from him. It hits corner first with a loud, metal clang. It leaves a small divot in the wall above the button that releases the ramp. It skitters across the floor and winds up under the navigator's chair.

"Sir?" The ship is responding to Nixon's outburst.

"What?" Nixon barks out a moment later.

"Did you need something?" EHL asks.

Nixon takes a moment. "What? Oh. No. Nothing. I'm fine. Just frustrated."

"Yes, sir."

Nixon stands and thinks about picking the case back up and taking it with him to the thin-mattressed bunk back in the crew quarters. Laying down and going through every combination there is to get this case open. But he doesn't. He lets it lie and goes back to his room.

He lays on that mattress, feeling every single seam left in the molded plastic shelf that's supposed to be a bed.

The heat from Umel's suns makes Nixon's patchwork fixes to the outside of his ship pop as the metal begins to warm in the heat of the day.

Snap.

Ping.

Nixon blinks his eyes open. He's still in his clothes from the day before, and he's sprawled across the mattress perpendicular. He crashed and crashed hard once the adrenaline from last evening's adventure wore off.

He drags his tongue across dry lips and sits up. He looks around the room and orients himself before standing. He does and exits the room. He runs his hands down the front of his clothes to try and get them something closer to straight.

He comes into the main deck and grabs the case off the floor beneath the navigator's chair. He tries the buttons one more time before tossing it back onto the dash. He pulls up his datapad and checks the time.

It's late. Too late. He's overslept any good paying jobs. But he needs to work. No, he needs the credits. So he goes back to the galley and finds something he can call breakfast, a tin of Bowtan steer meat that he bought a few days ago when he picked up a bit of food at one of the little shops on his way back here. He's sick of these little tins, but they are cheap and filling. He's already eaten through the packages of dehydrated fruit and containers of crackers.

He puts the tin of meat into the pocket inside his cloak then heads back to the main deck. He'll eat this tin of meat on the way to Umel's main district and look for work. He punches the button on the wall to release the ramp. It unfolds with a whoosh.

Nixon begins to exit the ship, but he can't. At the foot of the ramp is a man he hasn't seen before.

He's in a black cloak. His hair is wet and pulled back tight behind him. He's eating noodles from a cup, and they smell about one thousand times better than Nixon's tin of meat.

"Good morning. Well ..." the man takes a quick glance at his own datapad. "Yes, still morning."

"Can I help you with something?"

A sloppy forkful of noodles dangles down across his chin. He slurps them into his mouth in a noisy production.

The man puts the fork into his cup and extends a hand for Nixon to shake. Nixon lets the hand hang there for a moment then grabs it. They shake then the man pulls Nixon's hand up close to his face. He studies Nixon's fingers. Inspects his knuckles.

Nixon pulls his hand away. The man takes another bite of the noodles and offers some to Nixon. He shakes the man off.

"How can I help you, friend?" Nixon asks.

The man chews quicker then says with a mouth still half full: "The man you beat up last night was mine."

Nixon takes two quick steps back. "Was yours?"

The man crumples up the cup into a tight ball and tosses it to the ground then wipes his hands on the front of his cloak.

"I hired him. Asked him to follow you."

Nixon balls his fists, preparing for another fight. He looks beyond the man in front of him. Looks to the left and then the right.

"I'm alone," the man reassures Nixon. "Last night was a test."

"Excuse me?"

"I wanted to test you. See if you can spot someone trailing you."

"I'm still not ..."

"If I'm going to offer you work then I need to know you can handle it."

The man explains that he has a warehouse in the main district, a block or so off the water. That he saw Laana showing Nixon around one night. Had seen him come back almost every day since. He could tell that Nixon was a hard worker. But also that he was capable of more.

"What made you think that?"

The man points him up and down. "You don't look like the others who come out scrambling for credits."

He reaches over and grabs a handful of Nixon's cloak. "You've got proper clothing."

He reaches out and tries to grab Nixon's chin, but Nixon ducks away. "You keep up your appearance."

He pats his own belly. "I'm guessing you have food on you or have the shelves in your galley stocked up. You aren't like the other guys I see over there, and I have a job that needs not just another guy."

"How'd you find me?"

"I asked around. Like I said, you stand out."

That phrase sends chills rattling though Nixon. He doesn't want to stand out. Doesn't like being obvious. He hates that he's had to stay on Umel for as long as he has. Now he hears that he's being noticed. That his presence is being noted, that people are trying to mark where he's staying and monitoring his comings and goings.

The man begins again. "Again, I have work if you want it."

"I can find work," Nixon says.

"Not like this."

"I'm sure I'll be fine."

"Two thousand credits."

"What?"

"I'll pay you two thousand credits."

Nixon doesn't know what to say. Hearing that amount—two thousand credits—is deafening. He can't hear anything else. Can't think of anything else. It's enough to finish fixing his ship. It's enough to get him off of Umel and back on the route to getting this case delivered.

"What's the job?" he eventually asks.

"Delivery work."

Nixon pauses again. Thinks more.

"I like this," the man says. "You're deliberate."

"Delivering what?"

The man opens his mouth to speak then stops. He tries again then hesitates a second time. "You want the job?"

"Oh, it's like that?" Nixon looks back at his ship. He looks at all the work he's done to it. He looks at all the work that's left to do. He puts a hand on his datapad and remembers his still-too-low credit balance.

He looks back up the ramp and into the ship. He sees Shaine's case sitting on the dash. Delivery work, unknown and unspecified. It's what got him into this spot to begin with. He doesn't want to compound his problems by creating more enemies. He seems to have enough of those as it is. All he really has to do right now is get his ship in flying shape. Then he thinks about the lack of credits that's making that impossible right now.

Nixon turns back to the man. "Two thousand credits?"

The man nods. "Two thousand credits."

"OK. I'm in."

"One more thing, and it probably doesn't need to be said, but this work isn't exactly above board. If you get caught then I don't know you, and you don't know me."

"Yeah, yeah. I'm not worried about that. I've sold my scruples for a lot less."

SEVEN

"When do we start?" Nixon asks.

"We go now," the man says.

Nixon asks for a moment. He steps back into the ship and grabs the case off the dash then disappears into the back of the ship. He goes to the crew quarters and opens the drawer of the side table next to the bed that he's not using. This is where he's stored the blaster he'd picked up just before leaving Exte.

It feels appropriate to carry it again. New friends don't introduce themselves by waiting for you to step out of your front door. New friends don't offer you two thousand credits for a courier job either, so risk reward.

He feels the blaster's weight in his hand. Lets it pull on his arm. He feels it in his joints, and in the muscles that still hurt from last night.

"Everything OK?" The man's shout barely makes it to the back of the ship.

"Yeah!" Nixon shouts back. "Coming."

He looks at the blaster and almost puts it back into the drawer before sticking it into the waistband of his pants and pulling his cloak over top of it. He gives himself a quick once-over in the mirror on the wall. There's a small bump where the blaster's grip pokes away from his body, but it's barely noticeable.

He heads back out to the hall, through the main deck and down the ramp. The man is looking up to the sky. Umel's first sun is directly overhead. It's second is well above the horizon. The skies are clear and the day is humid. Nixon sees a bead of sweat streak down the man's nose then drop to the sand.

The keypad on the side of the ship beeps as Nixon enters the combination that initiates the ramp locking sequence. The two men wait as everything folds itself back inside the ship and the locking mechanisms set themselves.

Nixon turns and the man has already started walking away. A few quick steps, and Nixon has caught up.

"You worked my man over pretty good."

"What?"

"Last night. He came back bruised and busted. Like I've never seen him."

"He's not a great fighter."

"You don't think so?"

They pause at a corner as a larger hauler passes then cross the street.

"He left himself vulnerable."

"Oh, yeah?

"One kick ... down there. That's all it took. He was mine after that. He relies too much on his size to be threatening. But big often equals slow and out of practice. The size thing works more often than not. But sometimes they're ..."

The man turns a corner down a narrow street, maybe wide enough for a small hauler to pass through. Nixon thinks he could reach out and touch each of the walls if he wanted. He suddenly feels trapped, like he's being walked into a narrowing bottle neck. He and Shaine had run plenty of similar schemes. The goal is, at some point, to get him pinned in so tight that he won't have enough room to get himself out. He tucks his right arm inside his cloak and rests his hand on top of the blaster handle. He flicks the safety off.

The man shouts something over his shoulder that Nixon doesn't hear.

"My name's Roland," the man repeats.

"Nixon."

"Pleasure, Mr. Nixon."

"You too.

Nixon follows Roland around another corner. The street opens up again, and everything inside Nixon exhales. They walk another block. It's a quiet place, and not one that Nixon recognizes in the daylight.

There's another turn and then another, all the while Roland makes small talk. He's asking questions about how long Nixon has been on Umel. Where he was before. What kind of work he does best. What he prefers.

The conversation. The twisty turns through narrow streets and alleys. All of it has Nixon backward. Not that he knows Umel that well, but the mental map he'd been building is now a crumpled ball.

He follows Roland around one more corner and then Roland steps through an open bay door. They're here.

Nixon quickly scans the outside of the place. There's a 2401 sloppily painted in red above the door. This door is on the corner of a block. He turns around and sees the unfinished tower behind him. It's not much of a guidepost, but it's something.

Roland waits inside in the warehouse. There are stacks of crates and boxes all around him, narrow paths left between them for walking. Down one of those paths Nixon sees the bruised face of the man from the night before. Nixon nods, and the man looks away.

"This way," Roland says and disappears into one of the walkways. Nixon follows him again. They get to the back of the warehouse and pass through a door into a second room, this one smaller and with only one stack of crates on the floor. Nixon does some quick math. Nine crates on each layer. Four layers high. There are thirty-six crates here.

"This is it. Move these and you get two thousand credits."

The crates are unmarked. Either what's in these crates isn't exactly legal or it's so dangerous to move them that no one would want the job if they knew what was inside.

The man from the night before appears in the doorway to the room. He fills it and then some, and Nixon begins to regret the fight. At best it was foolish. The look on the guy's face tells him today that it could be fatal.

His cheek is bruised and his left eye won't open. He's carrying a crowbar. Nixon slips his arm back inside his cloak and puts his hand around the grip of the blaster.

Unmarked crates. Promise of credits. What if all of this was some kind of elaborate setup to get Nixon into a closed-off space and beat him so thoroughly that he was just a pile on the floor, lock the door and let him die.

The man steps into the room, Nixon and pulls the blaster half free from his waistband. He watches the man walk past him and wrench open one of the cases.

Nixon steps closer and looks inside the crate. It's glowing a light green.

"Are those …"

"Bastic fuel rods," Roland says. "Thirty-six crates of them."

Nixon exhales a long breath. "Each of the crates full?"

"Each of them."

Nixon pushes the blaster back into his waistband. He steps to the crate and pulls one of the rods out. His entire forearm is bathed in the green glow. He turns the rod over and over, looking at it from all sides and all angles.

Roland holds a hand out. "Be careful, you know those things aren't stable. You drop that and …"

"I know," Nixon says. "Big, big boom."

He places the rod back into the crate with the others and steps back next to Roland.

"I don't know that I've ever seen four or five of those things in one place at one time. But you have thirty-six crates."

"I do."

"And you clearly know how dangerous they are."

"I do," Roland says.

"Then you won't be surprised when I tell you the price has gone up."

EIGHT

Nixon walks around the stack of crates. He looks inside the open box and studies its contents for a second. He looks back up at Roland. The man from the night before is still there, glaring at Nixon through one swollen eye.

"How many does each of these crates hold? Twenty?"

"Twenty-five," Roland says.

"So that means ..." he does the mental math while he circles. "You have about one thousand of these rods."

"Nine hundred," Roland corrects.

"You want me to move all of these somewhere then I'm going to need a few of these rods.

"You are?"

"I think the credits and two crates of these rods.

Roland laughs a genuine laugh, one that comes from somewhere deep inside of him. "I like you, Nixon. You're funny."

"Thirty-six crates filled with the most unstable fuel source in the galaxy. And I'm taking them where?"

"A spot north of here. I'll give you an address once we get these loaded onto a mover."

Nixon steps back through the door and out into the warehouse's main floor. He makes a quick scan. There are three movers parked against a far wall. They're beaten.

They're worn. They have dents and scratches and mismatched body panels. All three are sitting on tires that are going bald.

Nixon returns to the back room and points over his shoulder and out the door. "One of those movers? Because if it's one of those then it's three cases."

Roland doesn't say anything.

"This address. How far away is it?"

"It's in the north docks."

Nixon shakes his head. "You know I'm new to Umel. That means nothing to me."

"It's about thirty klicks," the man behind Roland mumbles.

Nixon starts pacing the room again, walking half circles around the stack of crates. "And I suppose the roads there are smooth as glass and nothing like the rut-covered dirt and sand around here."

"No."

Nixon stops walking and sits on top of one of the unopened crates. He thinks for a moment

"And who is it that's thirty klicks away? Some legitimate businessman?" He pauses. "Of course not. You already said this work was something less than legal. And that's OK. But also something that needs to be factored into my calculation here."

He stands and starts walking again. He's making a show of doing some mental math. He looks to the ceiling. He counts imaginary numbers on his fingers.

He lets this go on for a moment then turns back to Roland.

"Four thousand credits," he says, "and a crate of rods."

Roland shakes no. "Three thousand credits and a rod."

"Twelve rods," Nixon counters.

"Three."

"Five."

Roland doesn't come back with another offer. He doesn't come back with anything for a long second, muffled waves crashing on the rocks a block away the only thing filling the silence.

"Three thousand and five rods." Roland says it like a question.

Nixon nods, and Roland is quiet again for another long second.

"Damn it. OK."

Roland turns to the man from the night before and tells him to go get one of the movers.

"Wait!" Nixon interrupts. "If I'm driving it with this stuff on the back then I want to be the one to pick it out."

"Whatever," Roland says. "Just be quick."

Nixon goes back out to the main floor of the warehouse and over to the movers that are parked on the wall. Someone has already loaded one of the movers with crates, so Nixon begins inspecting the first of the two that are left.

He drops to his back and slides underneath. He looks at the suspension system. He inspects the shocks. He looks closer at the tires, running a hand along a section of rubber that's as smooth as a cut gem.

He jumps up in the cab and looks at the steering column. He wiggles the wheel to see what kind of play is there.

He gets down and crawls under the second mover. On the outside, this one looks like it's been through a war zone—and who knows, maybe it has. There are large holes in some of the body panels. Half of others are just missing altogether.

But under here, it's not bad. Better than the first mover. Parts here are newer. The shocks look solid.

He jumps in the cab of the second mover and looks it over. He plays with the wheel. This is it. This is where he earns his three thousand credits.

He sees Roland watching him from the doorway to the back room. He points to the second mover then gives Roland a thumbs up.

"Keys are in the door!" Roland shouts. "Bring it around back."

The warehouse is quiet. Everyone stopped working when Roland shouted his instructions. Nixon looks around. There are more faces here than he'd realized before. There are Snapsits, but there seem to be Snapsits everywhere on Umel. There are Gomans, big things that are double tall and extra strong. And there are Uzeks. Far in the back and looking at him closely. On their toes to see around the Gomans.

Nixon looks away quickly and opens the door to his mover again. He reaches into the pocket and fishes out the keys. He starts the mover and pulls it away from the wall and out into the street in front of the warehouse.

The man from the night before is waiting around back near the now-open bay door. Nixon backs the mover in then jumps out. Roland is still in the doorway, and there's a small crowd standing behind him. The Uzeks are there.

He can't worry about that now. He's a new face. They don't recognize him. That's what he repeats over and over and over as he helps the man from the night before load these crates onto the back of the mover.

He grabs five rods from the open case and places them on the seat next to him before he closes and seals the top. Then he loads it, the last box, onto the back of the mover.

He helps get the crates strapped down tight then heads over to Roland, the Uzeks still watching him from a distance. They are talking now and looking right at him.

Nixon looks to Roland. "OK, boss. Where am I headed?"

NINE

Nixon climbs back into the cab and settles himself into the seat. Roland comes to the window and asks to see Nixon's datapad. He holds it up and Roland starts tapping the screen of his own. He swipes and gestures his way to a map. He shows the screen to Nixon.

There's a pair of flashing markers.

Roland points to the one at the bottom of the screen. "That's us."

He points to the marker at the top of the screen. "That's where you're going."

Roland turns his pad back so the screen is facing him and swipes up. A moment later Nixon's pad vibrates, and an indicator flashes that he has a new message. He accepts and the map is now up on his screen. He studies it closely. The drive should be easy once he gets out of Umel's main district.

"Who am I asking for once I get there?" He's still looking at the map, trying to remember street names and when to turn where. He doesn't want to be looking at the screen all the time considering what's sitting in the crates behind him.

"Ask for Daryl. He's expecting you. I told him you'd be there in a few hours, and that was about an hour ago."

Nixon looks up at Roland. A small crowd has gathered. There's the man from the night before. Then behind him are a couple of the other workers. And farther back, the Uzeks.

"Got it," Nixon says. Roland steps back and Nixon eases the mover out of the bay doors and onto the street.

Weighted down, the mover drives tougher than Nixon expected. He can feel the tires grabbing the road, and it's work to get it back to his own ship.

He looks in the space behind his seat and finds a handful of dirty rags. He pulls them up one after the other until he finds one that's big enough. He lays it out flat on the seat next to him and sets the fuel rods on top. He wraps them up like a package and takes them into the ship.

He searches quickly for a locking storage unit, but doesn't find one. He heads to the galley and pulls open one of the empty drawers there. They're long and shallow and will give the rods the tightest fit. He carefully places them inside then heads back for the mover.

It's spitting rain now, and he hustles back into the cab. He tries to pull away, and the mover struggles to find purchase on the now damp ground. The sand is getting wet. The dirt is turning muddy. It makes the whole drive more treacherous. The mover shifts and slides under Nixon as he turns through the city streets, and he can't help but picture some kind of disaster.

He tries to navigate a turn, traffic and pedestrians not minding that he's driving this loaded down beast of a machine. He has to make a quick adjustment and over-corrects. The mover slides away and out of control. It goes hard into the side of one of these buildings and all of it explodes in a ball of green fire. He burns up with it, and Shaine's case never makes it any farther than here—a damp, useless little planet.

He sits himself up straighter. He grips the wheel tighter and eases off the gas. This isn't a race with some kind of prize for the person who gets there first. He guides the mover slowly and carefully through the muddy rutty streets until he gets out of the main district and finds the road north.

They've taken the time to pave this road with large smooth stones. It's not the gentlest ride, so Nixon doesn't open up the throttle. But the tires do feel more solid under him, not like he'll go flinging off sideways if he jostles the wheel wrong.

There's nothing on his left side, just more sand like the field that he landed in a few days ago. On his right side is the water, a wide open sea that's crashing hard into the rocks and throwing spray up onto these stones. It's stopped raining, but the surface is still slick.

Wind howls outside, and it pushes water onto his windshield. He looks at his datapad. Twenty klicks left. He settles into the seat and focuses on the road ahead of him, trying to not let the winds from the water catch his stack of crates and push the mover into the sand. It's a fight all the way, but he finally sees buildings on the horizon. Like back in the main district, these are long and low.

Pulling closer he can see the bay doors, all open. One man steps outside. He's just a small smudgy shape against the tan wall at this distance. By the time Nixon has covered his last klick there's a small crowd outside to watch him pull up. He quickly scans the faces as he brings the mover to an easy stop.

There are Snapsits here. Uzeks. Humans. More species that Nixon has never seen. He doesn't recognize anyone who's watched him pull up until … . It's an Uzek, and not like the Uzeks back in the main district. This one is familiar. It's a face he knows. This mashed-in snout or these scarred and yellowing tusks, one slightly shorter than the other. He knows he's seen these heavy-lidded eyes before.

The Uzek cranes his neck, strains to see around the pair of Snapsits in front of him, and for a second he and Nixon lock eyes. Then a rapping on the driver's window pulls away Nixon's attention.

He cranks the window down and the man who was first out of the warehouse is looking up at him.

"Bring it 'round back," he says and points down the length of the warehouse with his hand and then indicates that Nixon will need to make a right turn once he's to the end.

Nixon pulls the mover back away from the doors and passes the crowd that's assembled. Everyone watches him drive past. He looks in the open bay doors as he drives by and sees workers inside stacking crates that are all organized into groups, loaded onto pallets and into containers. They are clearly shipments getting organized to go out. And when he makes the right, he sees where all of this material is headed.

There, just past the back of the warehouse is a small dock, and moored to its posts are a pair of ships. They are big, but Nixon has seen bigger. They are loaded, but Nixon has seen fuller. Men are walking the dock, wearing long cloaks that are dripping with water whipped up from the sea. All of their efforts are coordinated. This one pushing these crates to that one. These two loading a container on a lift that will take it up to two more men waiting on the ship. Men walking slowly up and down the docks supervising it all.

Nixon completes his turn and straightens up the mover. The man from the front of the warehouse waves Nixon forward. Nixon slows as he approaches and eases the mover to a stop. He jumps down out of the cab and sees that the crowd from the front has shown up again. At the back is the Uzek.

They lock eyes again, and the Uzek leans over and says something to the man standing next to him. He doesn't look away from Nixon. Nixon returns the stare, damned if this big, green thing is going to intimidate him.

Nixon steps to the mover and unlocks the straps holding the crates down. Each of the men gathered there starts pulling the crates down and loading them onto pallets with all the care of Hogun beast tearing into a fresh kill.

Nixon steps back and the man from the front joins him.

"You're Darryl, I assume," Nixon says.

"I am."

"They know what's inside those crates?"

"They don't."

Nixon winces as one of the boxes falls off the back of the mover and crashes to the ground. He hears the wood crack.

"Think you should tell them?"

Darryl shakes his head. "Wouldn't matter," he says. "They get paid by the load. The quicker they finish this one the faster they can get to another, and I have three more shipments due in a few."

Men are tossing boxes from the top of the stacks down to men waiting on the back of the mover and then down again to men waiting on the ground. They make quick work of thirty-six crates.

They have all of them loaded onto a hand mover. Nixon's Uzek is at the controls. He stands on a platform on the back and starts it moving toward the bay doors, staring at Nixon as he pulls it away.

TEN

Nixon gets a thank you from Daryl then climbs back up in the cab of the mover. He eases it away from the bay doors and back around to the front of the warehouse. He stops and takes one last look inside before he gets back on the road.

Everyone and everything inside is diligently working. All of them busy, heads down moving crates and boxes here and there, getting them ready to load onto the waiting ships.

Nixon turns and looks one more time at the dock. Everyone and everything there still working hard as well. Getting the ships loaded and then out to sea, moving their cargo to wherever Roland needs it to be. Nixon looks out to the water and sees the silhouettes of two more ships waiting there for their turn to get weighed down with boxes and crates.

The mover drives differently now. Without the weight on the back it gets moving quicker. It's actually fun to drive. And with the rain ending and the winds dying down, Nixon isn't having to white knuckle the wheel to keep the thing on the road.

That gives his mind a few moments to wander to things like the case sitting back on his ship and the reason he's out here at all. He replays that last conversation with Shaine. He sees them sitting back in that courtyard. He hears blaster fire and sees Shaine spin to the ground after being struck in the shoulder. He sees the case tumble end over end and the skitter across the paver stones. He hears Shaine scream for him to grab it and go. Then he sees Shaine's body tear and splatter when it's hit by blaster fire.

He closes his eyes quickly and shakes his head free of those memories. He looks out to the water and the waves rolling gently into the rocks. The angry sea that he'd seen and heard on his way to the distant warehouse is much calmer now.

He lets himself sink deeper into the seat and rests just one hand on the steering wheel. The road in front of him is straight and empty and long, the water on his left and nothing but sand on his right.

He feels the work of the day begin to take its toll. He's tired, and it's all he can do to fight off sleep. He cranks the window down and feels the light spray from the sea pepper his face. He hears the waves as they turn over.

He lets his mind wander again, and he starts rebuilding the face of the Uzek he saw back at the warehouse, the one who kept staring at him.

It's the eyes first, yellowed and veiny. Covered by thick, heavy lids dropped down low so they could focus on him.

The mouth is next. It's drawn tight and curled awkwardly around the two uneven tusks. One of them is shorter than the other and blunt at the tip. Broken, but Its jagged edges worn smooth by time.

After the tusks, it's the snout. It's shorter than the snout on other Uzeks, tighter to this one's face. It moves subtly, in and out. The wide nostrils flare every few seconds, and a scar drops from the bottom of the left one. Maybe there from whatever caused the tusk to break.

The rest of the thing's head fills in around the face. The skin a lighter shade of green than what was on Uzel before Nixon killed him. Then it's the rest of the body, all the way down to the feet. The callouses on this one's arms aren't as thick. It's skin not as worn. The belly isn't as pronounced.

Once he has the Uzek fully in his mind, the rest of the picture begins to appear. The surroundings start to fill in, but it's not the warehouse that Nixon just left. It's a street corner back on Exte. This Uzek is standing there with a few others, including Uzel. He's not saying anything, just a background man. Judging by appearances he's there to look tough and get tough if he needs to.

Was that a look of recognition? Did he know me? Or was he just trying to intimidate?

His mind again: The scene flashes from a street corner to a warehouse back on Exte. There's Uzel. And there, in the back, is his new Uzek friend. Another flash and another scene. Uzel standing next to one of the small ships that the Uzeks gave him to fly. And again, there is this new Uzek.

So long leisurely drive. If that Uzek knows what happened then he knows enough to say something to Roland. Especially since it wasn't just Uzel who Nixon killed. Got the daughter too, and a handful of others.

That makes him worth some kind of reward, right? One worth trying to get, or at least get a cut of. Maybe, though, he hasn't said anything else to anyone. Maybe he wants Nixon—and the reward—for himself.

It's what I'd do. I'd want the satisfaction of revenge. And I'd want the credits.

Nixon is so lost in his own thoughts that he barely recognizes that Umel's main district is quickly approaching. It's dark now. The day is gone, and the lights from the ships tied to the docks light up the water. The light coming from the warehouses' open bay doors light up the area around the docks. Workers run back and forth between the two.

Nixon slows the mover as he re-enters the streets of the main district. They are mostly empty, and their muddy surface is still slick. The mover, without the weight of the crates, dances more now than it did before. Nixon slows to almost a crawl. To be safe, he tells himself.

But even slow progress is progress, and he eventually makes that final turn toward Roland's warehouse. He sees a figure standing outside. As he gets closer, he recognizes the man from the night before. He puts up a big hand, gesturing for Nixon to stop.

Once the mover comes to a halt, the man waves Nixon down. He jumps out of the cab and comes around the front of the mover as Roland steps out of the bay door. The man from the night before steps behind Roland and positions himself next to a man who could be his twin. They are two towers and they do a good job of blocking any kind of light that comes from the door behind them.

"How'd it go?" Roland asks.

Nixon points back to the mover. "It's empty," he says.

Roland looks. "It is."

"So, are we …"

Roland starts shaking his head before Nixon can finish. "No, we're not."

"There something wrong?"

Roland shakes no. "Not with me." He pauses.

"But I hear that you…"

Damn, Uzek.

"I hear that you may have been in some trouble."

"What do you mean?"

"I know who you are, Mr. Nixon. Got a call. Asked around."

He reaches into his pocket and pulls out his datapad. He taps the screen. Nixon sees the light pop bright on Roland's face. Roland turns the screen to face Nixon.

"Seems that you're pretty valuable to some people."

On the screen is his face. It's a grab from some kind of security cam from a day that Nixon doesn't remember. Under his picture are a bunch of words that he doesn't bother reading. He's looking for the figures, trying to find his number. Roland clears the screen and pockets the reader before Nixon can see anything.

"Seems that you really made someone mad. I don't care what you did. I'm not one to judge someone for their actions. I gave up that privilege a long time ago."

Roland backs up a step, closer to the two hulks behind him.

"I am a business man, though. And I've got someone worth fifty-thousand credits standing in front of me ... well, you understand."

Roland looks back to one of his two men and nods. The man, the newer of the two, takes a few steps toward Nixon when ...

Thunk

The air crackles. A blaster shot hits the man in the forehead and splits him open from the eyes up. He drops to the ground.

Roland turns to the man from the night before. He takes a step forward and the air pops again. A moment later a blaster shot hits him in the chest, burning a fist-sized hole through his middle. He falls dead.

Nixon looks behind him, but doesn't see anyone.

Roland looks at both men then steps quickly back into the warehouse. He looks at Nixon, his face lit up with bright light now.

"Well, it looks like you have some kind of guardian angel. Count your blessings. I'd love fifty-thousand credits, but I'd like to see tomorrow more. Go. But don't stop looking back. I'll be there at some point."

Nixon hesitates for a moment, all of this impossible to process.

ELEVEN

Roland disappears back into the crowd of creatures still working in his warehouse. Two blasts from a big blaster and two dead colleagues have done nothing to dissuade them from their tasks.

Nixon still can't move.

He half expects Roland to come back with a blaster in his hand and put a shot right through his middle. But he doesn't.

Nixon can't get past the confusion. He turns around slowly. He looks to the buildings around him. Most behind him are shut down, closed up for the night. Those that aren't are at the wrong angle

He looks up and beyond the warehouses immediately behind him. There are a few buildings with second and third stories. He scans those windows and sees nothing.

He turns back around and sees the two bodies—big bodies—laying in crumpled piles. Large, wide pools of blood underneath them. He can smell it, the tang hitting the back of his throat. One more time, he looks into the warehouse doors. He doesn't see Roland. He doesn't see the Uzeks.

The walk back to his ship is in the dark. The winds are beginning to pick up again, and he can hear the rumblings of a storm building off the shore. He pulls his arms inside of his cloak to get them out of the chill and picks up his pace.

By the time his ship is visible in the far distance it's spitting rain. He starts to jog then hears someone shout.

"Would you hurry up already?"

He looks up and sees someone standing at his ship, but in the dark he can't make out who it is

The voice shouts again: "I thought you'd have a little more pep in you after what just happened."

It's a woman. Nixon squints. Laana.

He looks back behind him. In silhouette against what little light is coming from the docks is the unfinished spire shooting up from the middle of the main district. He smiles. He'd forgotten.

"Did you find something fun to watch tonight?" he says once he's close enough that he doesn't have to shout.

They shake hands.

"I did. Thought it was some creep easing a mover through the streets, casing my city. Then …" She stops making up some story.

"I'd heard that Roland had found someone to move his rods for him. Heard how much the job paid. Figured it might have been you. You're desperate enough."

"So you watched for me to return because.,.."

Thunder rattles and the rain starts in earnest. Nixon quickly opens the ship. The ramp descends and they both climb inside.

"I also saw a bunch of Uzeks arrive today. Came in on a pair of ships. Twenty of them. Maybe more."

They sit, Nixon in the captain's seat. Laana across from him as the navigator.

She continues. "Word quickly started getting around that they were here for a bounty, a reward.

"And you put two and two together …"

"Best guess. I knew enough of your story."

Nixon reaches on the dash and grab's Shaine's case. He mindlessly turns it over and over in his hands.

"I don't know what to say. Thanks. I wouldn't be here …"

She interrupts. "Oh, I don't know that I'd go that far. You seem like a scrappy guy. You've survived this far.

"No. This time I'm pretty sure. I was well out-numbered."

Neither of them says anything. They just listen to the rain outside. The ramp is still down, and the wind howls past the opening to the ship.

"What now?" Nixon asks. "Obviously, I can't stay here."

"No. And this ship…"

"What about it?

"Will it fly?"

"Not yet. But it shouldn't take much more work to get her back in the air and out of the atmosphere."

"Then you better get gone."

Nixon sighs. It's not like this is unexpected. He knew this was just the first stop on a trip he suspected would have many. But he hadn't planned on leaving like this, forced to go instead of choosing to.

"Thank you, again," he says to Laana as she stands. "You don't have to go just yet."

He looks down the ramp and into the still-raining night.

She just smiles at him and pulls the hood of her cloak over her head. "I'll be fine. It's just a little water, and this is Umel. If I wasn't prepared to get wet …"

He gives her a nod. "Take care of yourself," she says. "Stay alive."

"I will," he says. "I promise."

She smiles then turns and walks down the ramp, Nixon watches her step off the ship and into the night, and his mind immediately goes to all the ways he might not be able to keep that promise.

Uzek bounties with bands of the big green uglies already out searching for him. Guys like Roland are all over the galaxy wanting their own shot at fifty-thousand credits. And there's another shoe to drop with whoever it was that had chased him off Exte. He's sure of that.

He slides down into the captain's seat and begins to think. *First, get off Umel.*

03: IBILIA

ONE

Nixon is arms deep into his ship, and he has no idea what he's doing. The access panels on the sides of these engines are fine if you're trained as a mechanic, but he's not. His training is in running schemes and picking pockets, and while the dexterous fingers of a small-time crook could come in handy while dealing with small wires and tiny connections, they aren't much good when trying to do it all essentially blind.

His arms fill nearly all of the space these access panels give him. The openings on most ships are so small that only Geicans can get their skinny yellow arms in there and still have any kind of room to work. It's why so many of them make a fortune opening little repair shops all around the galaxy. If he had the credits, Nixon would have hired a whole crew of them to repair EHL. He doesn't though, so he's stuck fumbling with pieces and parts that he doesn't really know what to do with.

He drops one of the small wires for the third time, and shouts in frustration. He yanks his arms from the access panel and punches a fresh dent into the ship's side.

"Sounds like you could use a hand."

Nixon turns and sees the woman with the highly modified ship that's settled down across the field from him.

He's admired her ship for a while. At its core, it's a small jump ship, not good for much more than bouncing around a planet's surface. But she's done so much work to it that you have to look extra hard to see the original craft. Nixon has had plenty of time to do that kind of looking.

She sits outside of it most of the time, talking on her datapad or staring into it reading. But she's clearly taken the time to make the ship home. She's added larger cargo space. There's what look like extra crew cabins on the top. That big engine sticking off the back isn't standard as far as Nixon knows. He's certain that the two smaller ones bolted to the sides didn't come from the factory.

"I'm struggling," Nixon says. "Fat fingers and tiny spaces."

"What are you trying to do?"

Nixon makes up a story about buying this ship second hand and cheap figuring he could do what it took to fix it and get it flying efficiently again. The woman steps closer. She runs her fingers across seams that Nixon has already closed.

"Those aren't bad," she says. She turns to Nixon. "They aren't great, but they'll fly."

She looks closely at the blaster holes that Nixon has patched. "Rough."

Nixon shrugs.

"Show me what's got you so upset."

Nixon steps back to the open panel and points inside.

"That nest of wires in there. Can't see it when I've got my hands inside. Couldn't figure it out even if I could."

She kneels down and looks up at the ship.

"An Allain 1112. Cheap ship, but they never sold too many. Fine if you're wanting something to get around a planet. Looking for something to planet hop then you probably want something else."

"Sometimes you don't get a choice."

She shoves her arms into the panel, and they disappear below the elbows. "Even no ship is a choice."

Clearly, you've never made a decision with real consequences. "When I say this was my only decision it's what I mean."

She's concentrating, looking off into the suns and focusing on what she can feel in her fingers.

She pulls her arms out of the ship and wipes them off on her pants. "That whole panel is shot," she says, "but I think I have something back at my ship that can work as a fix."

She jogs off and Nixon watches her. She pulls a bin from the stack she's built next to her ship. She rummages through the contents, a tangle of wires and connectors. She settles on a small panel, looks it over, then runs it back across the field.

"This ought to do it," she says as she passes Nixon. She pushes her arms back inside the ship and begins to work. A couple minutes of small talk and she pulls her arms out and stands.

"There."

"I really appreciate ..." Nixon doesn't finish his sentence.

Blaster fire cracks the air, and a bolt of energy hits the ground in front of Nixon and the woman. It splatters mud onto the side of the ship. They both look up and see a man running toward them and firing. Two more shots hit the ground right at their feet.

The woman, panicked: "Who are you? What are you into?"

"Honestly, I don't know."

She sprints back to her ship, and Nixon runs back toward the ramp of his. He runs inside and grabs the blaster he'd laid on the navigator's seat. He runs back down the ramp and a blaster bolt just misses him, crashing into the ship above his head.

He whips around and fires a blind shot in the direction of the last blast. An Uzek ducks the blast, and Nixon fires two more shots. He's not looking to hit the thing, although he'd take it if it happened. He's looking to buy time to find cover.

He moves quickly behind a stabilizing fin, and another blaster shot hits the ground and creates a shower of mud and sand. Behind him, the man is still coming. Still firing.

He pushes himself tight to the ship and aims. Two quick shots. Both miss, but they stop the man from running. It's a brief pause, but even Nixon can hit a still target. He fires twice again, and a second later he hears the man scream out. The shooting from that direction stops.

Nixon stands. Back to the Uzek.

No. Uzeks. There are two of them.

One has a big blaster shouldered. He fires. Nixon drops to the ground, and the bolt passes over his head. He watches it disappear into the distance. He stands and turns. The Uzeks are coming now, in an awkward half-coordinated run. The big blaster is slung over the shoulder of the one Uzek. They are each aiming blasters that are swallowed by their massive hands.

Nixon fires. One shot goes well wide. The other splits the two of them and both duck away.

It's his chance. Nixon breaks for the ramp and up into the ship. He starts the ramp to closing and hears the Uzeks shouting something in their groaning and grunting language. He can't tell if they are talking to each other or to him.

While the ramp begins to close, Nixon starts the launch processes, hoping that whatever the woman across the field did has worked.

He gets to the end of the key sequence, pushes the last of the buttons and waits. But there's nothing. He goes through it again and nothing,

Someone is shouting from outside the ship, and blaster fire bangs hard against the ship's side. He can hear the whine of the big blaster charging. A shot form that gun will come clear through the ramp door. He only has a few seconds.

He goes through the sequence one more time. He hears the ship coming to life. Systems are setting themselves. Fuel begins moving to the engines. A moment later he feels the shake he felt back on Exte. The ship leaps from the ground. He's punched back into his captain's seat as the sky quickly goes to black.

TWO

Nixon is pinned to his seat. The ship is still roaring at full power even though he's well away from Umel.

The ship tried to slow once, but he overrode the auto pilot's instincts with the push of a couple buttons.

Nothing but black is in front of him, but it still feels unsafe. Feels too close. All of this feels wrong.

He looks to the navigator's seat next to him. The case. Shaine's little box is there, also pinned in place by the shear speed at which the ship is travelling. He stares at the box, tries to force all his mental energy on it. Hoping that somehow that will do something. But what? Heat up the box? Cause it to glow red, melt the plastic seat it's sitting in and fall to the ground? Eventually exploding?

Yes. That's what he wants. It's a trick he saw a street magician pull off ages ago on a dusty corner in an older part of Exte. Three boxes about the size and shape of Shaine's sat on a wooden platform. The small crowd gathered around watched the magician stare at the boxes. Watched him rub his mustache and concentrate intently on the boxes. Then they applauded as the middle one started to glow.

It glowed from the bottom up, color pushing its way slowly up the sides of the box, the whole thing eventually turning a bright and shimmering red. The magician concentrated harder. You could almost see the focus from his eyes baring down on the case. The box began to shake.

He squinted harder and the box shook more. Then, as if from out of nowhere, the box exploded. It broke into a dozen pieces that launched out into the crowd.

Nixon knew it was some kind of trick. This guy was just a street hustler, same as him. Something was rigged up between the box and the table it was sitting on that caused the whole thing to glow and shake and pop.

But what if it wasn't a trick?

So, Nixon stares at his case, squints his eyes and focuses his gaze. Shoots whatever mental energy he can muster like a blaster beam into this case so it will glow and explode. Because if that's what happens, then this is over. He's no longer getting shot at, no longer getting chased off planets by unseen thugs. At least when the Uzeks were chasing him around Exte he knew what he did to draw their ire. But these others, he doesn't. And it's the not knowing that makes this all unsustainable. He needs an enemy, because that's the game. Each side makes themselves known. Rules are established and may the best one win.

He concentrates hard on the case, pushing all his mental energy at it and waits for it to go red. To start shining and shaking and then pop like a little firecracker in the seat. He stares and wishes, but nothing happens.

His concentration is broken by another alarm. Nixon hadn't noticed that the ship was shaking, working loose all the work he'd done back on Umel, but it is. The alarm is a deep chime that's followed by the ship's voice.

"Sir?" It asks.

Nixon looks up from the case to the ship's dashboard and sees half a dozen red lights blinking for his attention. He begins shutting them off.

"Sir?" The ship says again.

"Go ahead," Nixon says as he turns off the last warning light.

"We are flying at an unsustainable speed. I'm afraid that a systems failure may be imminent."

"Which system?"

"Most of them, sir. All of them."

"Then get us to the maximum sustainable speed."

Nixon blinks his eyes quickly. They hurt now. Even if it's all fake, that kind of concentration can be draining.

"Sir, may I ask where we are going? I can plot us the quickest route."

"Depends on how long you can hold out," he says. He looks down to the control panel and takes in the numbers there. "Is this our sustainable speed?"

"For now, yes."

Nixon unbuckles and stands. He bends over and picks up the case and turns it over in his fingers. "What do you mean 'For now?' "

"We can run this fast for a while, but I'll slow us down if I detect any anomalies. Also, to preserve fuel once that becomes an issue."

"And when will that be?"

"I'll sound an alarm."

"Of course, you will."

Nixon runs his thumbs across the seams on the outside of Shaine's case. He tries to pull it open for the millionth time, forgetting the combination and just brute forcing his way in. For the millionth time nothing happens.

He tosses the case back up unto the dash and looks out at the front of the ship. It's all black and indistinguishable from any other time since they left Umel.

He asks the ship to bring up a galactic map on the display in front of him. A moment later it's there, pinpoints of light indicating moons and planets. He taps one of the planets that looks to be an impossible distance from where he is now.

"There," he says. "Get us there. Plot a course."

"Yes, sir."

Planet Azken is at the coordinates that Shaine gave Nixon just before he was killed. Nixon plotted it before, and the little indicator light didn't seem this far away. He sinks into his seat. Disappointed.

"Course plotted, sir. Permission to revert to a sustainable speed."

"Sure," Nixon says. He can feel the speed drain away. Everything inside the ship gets more comfortable, the pressure of high speeds not pushing him down into every surface.

Nixon stands again.

"I'm going to the crew quarters," he announces. "Signal if you need me."

"Yes, sir."

THREE

Nixon is back on his bunk. The thin mattress is doing little to separate him from the molded plastic he's laying on, and he rolls to his side to try and keep the seam off his back.

His mind has calmed somewhat. He's still questioning this whole endeavor, questioning this feeling of loyalty that he's for some reason a slave to.

He doubts that Shaine ever felt this. He always put Nixon in the tougher spot. Sure, Nixon was the smaller of the two men, so that meant that there were just some things that Shaine couldn't do. When they were committing petty little break-ins, Nixon got the job of climbing into raised windows when they were the only way in. Shaine would wait off somewhere else, buried unseen in the shadows until everything was clear.

Shaine had a way of explaining it all away that made sense to Nixon at the time. Now, he can't see it for anything other than the excuse that it really was. Shaine looking out for Shaine. Something happens, it's Nixon who gets pinched; Shaine skates free.

Running pick-pocket schemes in the streets, it was never Shaine that was the pick. He was always the distraction. Fat fingers, he tried to explain. Made sense then, bullshit now. Something goes wrong—a mark moves funny, a money pouch snags on a seam, anything not according to plan—and it's Nixon getting picked up, punched out. Whatever the consequences, they are his.

Damnit, Shaine. You can go to ...

Then enter Mira and everything changes. Decades of friendship unravel. Not completely and not quickly, but still different than it used to be. No sense of loyalty. No sense of responsibility. A girl coming between two friends who'd been inseparable. Shaine off living out the dream each of them had talked about: a house, a family, normalcy. Nixon left to work the streets alone, left to scramble together a life, seeing his friend—his brother—only sporadically.

He thinks about the case again, concentrating on the little square shape sitting on the main dash. Waiting, hoping— expecting?—to hear a muffled pop come from the main deck. Waiting to spring from the bed and go see little bits of metal scattered across the floor and whatever is so important inside sitting on the dash where the case had been.

But there is no pop. There's nothing but a headache caused by intense concentration.

He laughs through the pain, and remembers times—too many times—when he and Shaine would try something stupid like this, something that both of them knew wouldn't work. Neither would be angry when it didn't. They'd sit in some alley, breathing heavy after being chased by some security team, and recount their just-had misadventure.

Nixon smiles and rolls over to his other side. He grabs his datapad from the side table next to him and pulls up some show, a dumb thing that requires no extra thought. It's a game show where contestants are given some humiliating physical task to complete. Complete it, win an inconsequential prize. Fail and get covered in some kind of green goo that falls from the ceiling.

Nixon laughs his way through one episode and then a second. The third, though, is interrupted by a ringing alarm and the ship coming over its audio system.

"Sir, we have an issue."

FOUR

Nixon walks double-time down the skinny hall back to the ship's main cabin. The alarm continues to whalp. It's a warning he's not heard yet, and he thought this ship had given up all its tricks already.

"What's happening?" he asks as he steps into the main cabin and comes up behind the captain's chair.

"That's a proximity alarm. There's another ship nearby."

Nixon steps around the seat and sits. He looks at the displays in front of him. He doesn't see anything out of the ordinary. He turns off the alarm and the whole place goes silent.

"An alarm for something else being close seems excessive. Is this other ship aggressive?"

The ship doesn't respond. The alarm starts to sound again.

"The other ship is showing an offensive posture."

Finally, a blip appears on one of the monitors Nixon can see.

"Offensive posture? What's that mean?"

The alarm wails. There's a steady indicator light in the middle of the screen that Nixon is watching. It's the position of his ship. The blip he'd first seen a moment ago is closing the gap between them, and it's not appearing to do anything to vary its course.

"Many factors go toward determining an offensive posture."

"Secret math."

"If you want to call it that, sir."

Nixon watches the small indicator light get a little closer, and then, a moment later, closer still. He begins to say something when the ship dives, and Nixon's stomach winds up in his chest.

Another alarm sounds, this one high and shrill. It's screaming louder than all the others.

Nixon grabs the arms of the seat on the captain's chair to steady himself as the ship twists and turns in every direction. Out the front of the ship he sees two blasts shoot by, there a moment and gone the next.

The ship doesn't stop, but the loudest of the alarms does. It's only for a moment, and the ship starts winging through space again. Nixon does everything he can to keep himself steady in the chair. Two more blasts cross in front of the ship, and the ship suddenly goes straight up. It banks hard left and then there, in front of Nixon, is the ship that had been chasing them.

He hears the mechanical drop of something emerging from the ship and then, a second later, the roaring blast of guns firing. It's three shots, and the last two smash the back of the little speeder. It disappears into a shower of fire and debris, and EHL navigates this sudden field of a million little pieces that could take it down.

It all lasts just a few minutes, from that first proximity alarm to those last screaming warnings that Nixon can only assume means there is incoming fire. His heart is racing, and his breathing is fast.

"Are you OK, sir?" the ship asks.

Nixon nods.

"Sir?"

"Yes, I'm fine. I'm just…"

"I'm sorry. That was unexpected."

Nixon tries to stand, but his stomach is still out of place, and his knees tell him that maybe it's better to stay seated.

"Where did they come from?"

"Undetermined."

"What *could* you determine?"

"I don't understand the question, sir."

Nixon pauses to think how he can rephrase.

"You kind of shot that thing pretty quickly, but what were you able to ascertain? Once it was close enough, were you able to pull any data from the ship's manifest? Was it registered to anyone or carrying any kind of flight plan?"

"None of that. But we aren't either. I was never given an official manifest, crew record, or flight plan."

Nixon nods. "OK. Good to know."

He drops from the captain's chair and walks a small circle around the tight room. He stops at the navigator's chair and rests a hand on the left-side arm.

"So, it was a ghost. Did it get close enough for us to capture any images?"

A moment passes without any kind of response from the ship. Nixon is about to repeat his question when three images pop up onto the screens on the front of the dash.

"This was the best I could do. They are captures from the video that's constantly being recorded by the outside cameras."

The images are mostly smears of color on a black background. Like someone has tried to wipe paint off glass. There's a swipe of white crossing from corner to corner in one, red accents dotting across the middle. Another is mostly grey with a streak of blue cutting across one corner.

Nixon dismisses both of those images and pulls up the third. He sticks with this one. It's not exactly like the others. This one isn't clear; the ship was moving too fast for that. But it's better.

It was taken as the craft dropped in front of Nixon and EHL, just moments before the ship would become nothing more than grit and debris.

There's more here than just color. This ship was shaped like a lopsided pyramid. Its nose came to a point. Engines across the back, set in a triangular shape. The bigger engines sat at the points of the triangular and engines of varying sizes filled in the middle, all in patterns of threes. The body of the ship looks to have been grey and blue. White was on the underside.

Nixon leans into the screen and tries to force the picture into focus. He still can't make out specifics. He squints harder and focuses on the section of the image that created the blue streaks in the previous picture.

He leans back and points at the image. "Here," he says. "What's this?"

It's a small, broken-up section of blue. "Is it writing?" he asks. "Call numbers? Some kind of indicator?"

"One moment."

Nixon has something. He's sure of it. But this moment feels like two eternities. He stares at the screen and tries to will the image clearer. Tries to mentally force the pixels smaller and smaller and the image to become clearer and clearer until ... wait. There. It is clear now.

"I ran it through our enhancer systems, and this is what came back."

"Oh."

"Disappointed?"

"Not in what you were able to do. Looks great. Thanks."

Nixon turns his attention to the small jags and slashes of blue. These were definitely markings of some kind, but it wasn't any alphabet he recognized.

"Help me out again," he calls out and points back to the screen. "Help me determine what alphabet this is on the side." He points very specifically to the blue markings.

"Yes, sir. Another moment."

Nixon waits and looks harder at the image. He hadn't noticed when the image wasn't clear, but they caught the pilot, or at least part of him. Nixon gestures to enlarge the image and focuses on the cockpit. That little ship was a one-seater and the cockpit was one of those closed-in numbers that Nixon was sure would give him a heart attack.

There, though, in that tiny cockpit sitting in that tiny ship is someone with dark hair. Tight curls and messy. Nixon sees the back of the head, and there's a spot where the big mane is thinning, and he wonders if it was kept extra-long as some way to make up for the fact that soon most of it would be gone.

He can also see the pilot's right cheek. It's stubbled with salt and pepper growth, a few days at least. Maybe more, depending. Nixon instinctively reaches up and runs his hand across his own sandpaper face then pulls his fingers through his own tangle of hair.

This pilot was human. There's no doubt about it.

"Sir, that is the Cheshorian alphabet."

Cheshorian means nothing to Nixon.

"Show me a Cheshorian," he demands. He's never seen one, never even heard of them until now. The galaxy is a big place, and unless you have a lot of credits you don't get to see much of it. Nixon barely had enough credits to get himself to Exte. He for sure didn't have the credits it took to see any more than that.

After a moment, the ship throws up the image of a Cheshorian onto the screen in front of Nixon. Orange skin. Pronounced lips. Heavy lidded eyes. Bumpy skin, like just underneath were a thousand pebbles.

Whoever was behind the controls of that ship wasn't a Cheshorian. He knew a human when he saw one. But if he wasn't Cheshiorian, then how did he get behind the controls of a Cheshorian ship? And what did it mean that this pilot or the Cheshorians who hired him seemingly wanted to see Nixon dead?

"Show me Chesh or Cheshoria or wherever it is that ship was from." Nixon tells the ship.

"It's Chesh, sir. And you can find it ..."

The ship never puts up the image. Sounding alarms will interrupt any processes deemed non-essential, and another proximity alarm blares.

FIVE

Nixon looks at all the screens, but he doesn't see it. There's no threat indicated anywhere.

"Are you kidding me?" he asks no one.

"My systems detected something, sir, moving at ..."

At that moment something blurs past the front of the ship.

"Where did that come from? And why am I not seeing it hitting any of these screens?"

The ship doesn't respond. Nixon waits. The alarm whoops.

There's another roar and another blur in front of the ship.

"Is he circling us?"

Silence.

"Hello? Status please!"

Nixon grips the arms of the captain's chair until his knuckles go white. He studies the screens in front of him, still looking for any indication of what keeps passing in front of them. The ship never responds, not audibly.

Nixon leans forward and reaches for one of the buttons on the dash in front of him and is pushed back into his seat as the ship leaps forward, a full fire in its engines. There's a pressure in Nixon's chest that's pinning him to his seat. He tries to speak but can't. The gravity that this newfound velocity is creating makes it nearly impossible to speak. He can do nothing but wait for the ship to pull them out of this sudden rush. But it doesn't. It pushes harder. Faster. Nixon feels light headed, the blood slowly pooling in his feet.

The light around his eyes begins to tunnel. His brain should be prompting him with warnings. It should be feeding him ideas on how to get himself out of this, but it doesn't.

The proximity alarm never stops. It keeps sounding its staccato rhythm. And now it's joined by another alarm, a familiar one. One that Nixon heard earlier. He knows it. Doesn't he?

So hard to remember right now. So hard to think.

The pressure on his chest pushes harder. It forces him deeper into his seat, so far down that the gel cushions are starting to encircle his legs. They are starting to creep over his shoulders. His palms press harder into the moulded plastic arms, and his head finally gives up. The dark edges of his vision take over. It's all black now, and he's gone.

Nixon never feels the evasive maneuvers the ship makes. He never hears the warning alarms that indicate target lock or feels the impact as one of the blasts from the two ships that have found them skids across the length of EHL.

He never sees EHL get the other two ships turned around. Never sees one of them explode when a shot from the other slides past EHL and hits the other ship right in center mass. And he never sees the second of the two ships bug out when EHL achieves weapons lock.

He comes to when the alarms are quiet and EHL is flying normal again, like the last hours haven't been filled with dogfights and deliberate attacks.

Nixon blinks his eyes twice, then twice again and pushes himself to a more upright position. He wipes a small bit of drool from the corner of his mouth. He's awake, but he's not back. His head feels like a fog.

"I, uh..."

He looks around the main cabin.

"I, uh ..." he says again.

"I'm sorry, sir," the ship says.

"Sorry?"

"For the speed, sir. That's why you passed out."

Nixon opens his eyes wide and stretches his arms out in front of him, trying to force his head back to normal, blowing out the fog.

"It's OK," Nixon says. "You did what you had to do. But what happened?"

"Proximity alarm."

"I remember."

"Then a weapons alarm."

Nixon stands. He bends deep at the waist then stands back straight. He shakes one leg then the other.

The ship continues: "Two crafts. One eliminated. The second took itself out of the fight."

"Bugged out?"

"Yes, sir."

Nixon nods then mutters a distracted "OK. OK."

The cloud inside his head has lifted, and now his mind is working. They're moving slowly, but he can feel the wheels turning, the grit falling from the cogs.

He starts piecing this puzzle together, not that it's that complicated to solve.

Laana told him most of it. Roland proved it. There's a bounty out for him. People are willing to pay for him to be brought in. But who? The Uzeks are a good bet. Makes sense. Their leader is dead, and Nixon is the reason. But the Uzeks are also cheap. They aren't going to pay for him to be brought to them. They're going to do it themselves. Unless they just want him back so bad.... So, is that who this is? Maybe.

But ...

Nixon thinks back to Exte and that final chase off the planet that led him to this ship and a rocket ride out into deep space. Those weren't Uzeks pursuing him then. Those weren't Uzeks with the big blasters. Thunk. Thunk. Thunk.

Those were humans. And it was humans who took out Shaine. So, is that who this is? Yeah, maybe them too.

Then his mind goes back to the bounty. Yes, it could be the Uzeks. And, yes, it could be whoever those humans were on Exte. As for setting up a reward, that's who'd behind this. But those coming after him could be anything or anyone willing to turn him over to whoever is bankrolling the operation. It's good work if you have a ship and the ability to chase someone across the galaxy.

It's work Nixon would have done if he'd had a ship. It's actually something he considered talking to Shaine about more than once. He'd present it as a partnership, one where all the risk was on Nixon. Nixon would be the hunter, the one flying around and chasing down whoever it was that needed catching. Shaine would front the money for the ship and get a cut of each bounty. He could stay home with Mira and the girls and watch the money come in. But even in imagined conversations, things never seemed to work out like Nixon would have hoped.

"You say all the risk is on you," Shaine would say after hearing Nixon's proposal.

"Well, I'm out there trying to find these folks. I'm the one out there risking injury. Risking worse."

"Yeah, but you're out there in a ship that I bought."

"And for that you're getting a cut of the bounty."

"The smaller cut."

Nixon would look at him confused because they'd already established that he was at the highest risk, but he'd say it again to reiterate the point.

"It's different risk, but it's not less risk," Shaine would counter.

And it's in the middle of that sentence when Shaine's voice shifts to Mira's, because Nixon knows this isn't Shaine's argument. The Shaine before Mira would have loved this idea. The Shaine before Mira would have been sitting next to Nixon as part of some bounty hunting team.

But there was a Mira, and she'd convinced Shaine that he needed to do respectable work. Steady work that would support her and the girls. And Nixon knew she wasn't wrong.

If there wasn't a Mira, though, and Nixon was out flying around in Shaine's ship, what kind of bounty would a guy like him command? It was time to find out.

SIX

Nixon pulls up a keyboard and starts entering codes that will give him a directory to outside systems.

All around him the ship is rattling. He hears the soft ting of metal hitting metal. He hears plastic scraping against plastic. He can look up and see the interior of the ship shimmy as it flies him farther out into space, each of the large panels that were seamlessly connected before don't look as seamless now. The ship pushed itself too hard. It flew too fast and went past the edge of what it could take. Second time it had done that. All that work that Nixon put in back on Umel to get the ship flying again is rattled apart now.

The ship's condition sits in the back of his mind as he requests access to exterior systems. The screen in front of him blinks off for just a flash then reappears. It's blank now except for a blinking cursor in the upper left. He begins typing commands and a text menu soon fills his screen.

It's a series of choices that will send him off to different locations on a public message board. It's a place where Nixon had spent hours a night back on Exte. He'd lay in that cramped one-room hovel, his back nearly flattening the thin mat he called a bed.

His reader would be held above him—Not too far. His eyes weren't what they used to be—and he'd scroll through post after post. Looking at the jobs that people needed filled. But the threads he spent most of his time with weren't that at all. They were people detailing operations that had, more than likely, gone poorly. The people creating these posts took what was supposed to be an easy job, but it turned out not to be. Or maybe they'd so righteously screwed that job up they couldn't find their way out and now needed help.

Those were the threads he'd get lost in, picturing himself out there with these people, these bounty hunters. He'd play out their adventures in his head as he read their accounts.

All of it was in the hyper colors that he saw on the shows he'd watch on his reader. Impossibly beautiful women. Absurdly chiseled men. Landscapes he didn't recognize but that still felt familiar. Blaster battles and fist fights that went on for what seemed like hours. None of it perfectly real, but all of it engrossing and exciting.

Here he was now. Back on these boards and scrolling through message after message. Looking for what exactly? He didn't know, but he assumed he'd know it when he saw it.

He'd start by scrolling for familiar words one at a time, starting with Exte.

Message after message passes and nothing stands out. There are a couple that mention Exte, and he reads those. One is an older message about bargaining for a ride from the starport. The poster promises not to ask about what's in your hold if you didn't ask about what's in her bag. That sends Nixon's head going.

What's in the bag? How did it get there? Where is this woman going with it?

He continues to scroll while running out the details of each new scenario he comes up with for his female poster. There is another message that mentions Exte. This one even mentions the Uzeks, and Nixon is tempted to enter his own message in response telling whoever is asking to stay as far from them as possible. That getting involved with them is the kind of trouble from which you never unwind.

There are more messages that involve Exte farther down the board, but the timeline doesn't work. They are all from before Nixon connected with Shaine and got twisted up in whatever this is. Still, he reads the messages. They reference places he's familiar with—a couple of them very familiar—and suddenly this is like a little homecoming.

Nixon didn't realize how much he was going to miss that place and that life. It wasn't much—it wasn't anything—but it was his. He was in control of it. Unlike now, when everything feels like he's some kind of small particle in the universe and all these outside forces are acting on him—pushing him this way, forcing him that way, being made to make decisions that he wouldn't otherwise. No, that little hole of a home he had wasn't much, but it was safe. There was no one trying to kick him out of it. No one was trying to hunt him down.

Then he stops scrolling to remind himself that the way he's remembering things isn't true. He wasn't safe, not at the end. Far from it. That's why he's here. He'd even screwed up that little hoodlum life he'd built.

He begins scrolling through the messages again, looking for the word Umel this time. But there isn't anything that fits the dates. So, he changes boards and begins the process all over. He's looking for mentions of Umel, but he's also focusing on anything that accurately describes him—how he looks, his build, what he's done.

On the fourth board he finds it. It's nothing he was scanning for. He'd given up that tactic. He was checking all of the messages now, and in the middle of one more than halfway down that fourth board he sees an image embedded inside a bunch of text. It's the case.

He reads the message. He studies it. The poster describes a man, a man that sounds like he looks a lot like Shaine. The ask is for help locating him, identifying who he is, and then asking for the case to be brought to them. No questions asked.

Nixon scrolls through the responses. There are plenty of the typical nonsensical responses.

"On it."

"Done."

Lots of people who have more confidence in their bounty hunting skills than they probably should have.

But there are messages that ask questions, the kind that would lead to figuring out things like the name of the man being described and his location.

Then. There. A couple of dozen messages down is his name. Shaine. Someone knows him. Knows where to find him but warns that he won't come easy. Warns to be prepared for a fight, a fierce one.

Nixon scrolls quickly again through more inconsequential messages until he gets to one with a map and an image. It's an image of the courtyard where Nixon met Shaine. Shaine is sitting in the middle. He's fiddling with his reader. Nixon chooses to believe he's messaging Mira. That's how he wants to remember his friend. There's also a map with the location of the courtyard indicated.

The dozen of messages that follow all are some version of "I'm going after this man and this case."

But that's not where the messages end. Nixon keeps scrolling and reads accounts of what happened that day in the courtyard. All of them accurate, but none overly detailed. All secondhand, he assumes.

He scrolls down again and another message sends his stomach through the floor of the ship.

It's a picture. Looks like something caught on a camera at the starport. It's crystal clear, and it's him.

He's headed away from the camera. Looks like something mounted up near the ceiling. He's just exited the elevator and is looking back behind him to see if anyone is following him. The crowd is paying him no mind as he's pushing his way through.

He scrolls again, past that message, and finds another image. This one's not as clear, but it's obviously him. It's from farther away. He's at the starport and is about to climb inside the ship he's on now. Again, he's looking behind him.

This time it's at the man with the big blaster who can be seen in the bottom right corner of the image. It's just the back of his head and his shoulders. The end of the blaster's big barrel is extending out in front of him. Nixon can hear the whine of the gun charging. He can hear the concussive thunk of the gun firing.

He scrolls again, and there's another image from just a few moments later. It's of just the ship this time, it's only a second off the ground and just above the other ships around it. It's another crystal-clear shot. Every detail of the ship is visible, all of its distinguishing marks visible. It's everything someone would need to pick EHL out of a lineup of the dozen other ships that came off the line before and after it.

He sits back for a moment. This explains it. This is why it wasn't just the Uzeks who were pursuing him back on Umel. It explains these ships pursuing him off planet.

For good measure, he goes to a half dozen other bounty hunter boards. He finds some or all of the images there too.

That effectively puts his picture and the image of his ship in front of anyone in the galaxy who'd even consider tracking people for credits.

The ship still rattles and grinds. Everything sounds like it's shaken just a bit looser. It all feels more unstable.

Nixon knows there's not much he can do to disguise himself. He looks how he looks. He sounds how he sounds. He'll try to keep his cloak hood over him and pulled low. He'll wear a mask over his nose and mouth when he can. Doing that and he can be somewhat unrecognizable. As long as he doesn't stop and linger anywhere too long he might be able to get by.

But his ship. There isn't much he is going to be able to do about that beyond get a new one. But where do you go for a new ship when you're this far out?

He discards the bounty hunter boards and pulls up a star map of the galaxy.

"Is there something I can help with, sir?"

"Find me the nearest planet with a bit of population."

"Population, sir?"

"Yeah, we need to …" He hesitates. He doesn't want to tell the ship it's being replaced. "I need to make a transaction."

"Population, sure."

SEVEN

The ship offers Nixon three choices. All of them close. All of them small.

Nixon reads the brief descriptions of each then says "Give me more on this one."

He points to the second choice. "This one labeled Ibilia."

The screen in front of Nixon goes blank for a moment then is filled again. On the left is an image of a spinning planet. It's covered mostly in clouds, but what Nixon can see of the surface is mostly a light brown.

Not more sand and dirt.

A description of what he'll find if he lands there is on the right.

The planet is almost fully industrialized. There is no native population, but it's far from empty. Like Umel, things got crowded once it was discovered how rich in resources Ibilia was. And was it *rich*. Most of those clouds above its surface aren't clouds at all, but the result of mining operations.

"Tell me more about the population," Nixon asks. "How much of it's human? What percentage?"

"There's no official count."

"Any Uzeks?"

"Of course."

Nixon hesitates but looks again at the details the ship has been able to find. Other than the Uzeks—knowing now that he's being tracked on two fronts, he'd like to avoid them if he can—Ibilia has everything he's looking for. It's industrial. It's populated. He'll be able to find someone looking to off-load a ship for cheap.

"OK," he tells EHL. "Put us down there."

"Yes, sir."

The surface of Ibilia is crowded. Large groups gather around the bases of buildings that stretch impossibly tall and disappear into the smog-filled skies.

EHL fought its way through three different layers of sky traffic to get down this low, dodging haulers loaded with minerals and ore that were screaming out of the atmosphere, shooting up from the surface like darts toward a board.

Also dropping through the lanes of transport ships bringing new workers to the surface and taking old ones away. You didn't last long doing work on a planet like Ibilia. You came because of the promise of riches, and, technically, the promise was there. If you hit a good vein. And if you were working with someone reputable. And if you'd read the fine print on that agreement that was written specifically to limit your take home. If. If. If.

So those transport ships—big blocky things that were usually just retrofitted old haulers stripped of any interior comforts so they could hold as many fresh or broken bodies as possible—weren't flying anywhere other than to the big stations that Nixon and EHL had to avoid floating out at the edge of Ibilia's atmosphere.

They park just off planet and the transport ships shuttle up and drop off the worn and broken bodies packed tight inside. Then they pick up sets of fresh arms and legs.

Nixon's found a map of Ibilia on some public server somewhere and is trying to plot out where EHL can park itself, but this map is horribly out of date.

"The next left," he says to the ship. "Then down to the end of the block. Should be some open space where you can stowaway."

The ship turns, and Nixon struggles to see out the front windscreen. The block stretches out in front of him, all piecework construction stretching high. He's looking ahead as far as he can, waiting to see a gap in the glass and metal and brick, but there isn't one. This little gap he was expecting isn't there. He kicks a heel hard into the dash and the thump reverberates quickly through the cabin.

He turns off the map and tells the ship "I don't know if you can find something better than that map, but you're welcome to try."

"One moment, sir."

They circle the block and Nixon watches the city pass. Lighted signs hang in many of the windows advertising all kinds of services. Some reputable, most not. But all appreciated by the workers who are wearing themselves to nubs.

The ship suddenly turns upward ninety degrees and shoots high above the traffic at the ground level then slides itself sideways onto the top of a building five stories up. It settles gently, all four corners touching down in quick succession.

"Where have you put me?" Nixon asks.

"It was here or fly around the rest of the night. And you seem anxious."

Nixon nods. "Fair."

He pulls on his cloak. He tugs the hood down low over his head and covers his eyes. He goes into the medical cabinet in the galley and pulls out a mask that he can wear over his mouth while he's out. He looks at his reflection in one of the metal panels. Not bad. If you don't know exactly who you're looking for you won't recognize him. That's all he can ask for. And with the ship stored up this high, there's little chance anyone will see it and know he's here.

The ramp unfolds from the side of the ship, and Nixon steps off. The air is warm and thick and sticky, and he struggles to pull a breath through his mask. He crosses the roof and opens a small door that leads into a tiny room. In front of him are the sliding doors to an elevator. He hits the call button and waits. His ears fill with the sound of a whirring unit that's keeping this cramped space cool and the air inside dry.

The light above the elevator blinks off, and the doors slide open a moment later. Nixon steps on and uses the heel of his hand to push the button to take him to the first floor.

The elevator jerk-starts and sends a wave of pain up through Nixon's knees and into his chest, a reminder that it hasn't been that long since the Uzeks had him pinned to that alley wall back on Exte.

The elevator jerk-stops and Nixon winces. The doors open, and he steps off into a lobby that's much bigger than the small space up on the roof. It's all glass and tile. And it's clean. Cleaner than it should be, and cleaner than he expected considering what he saw while flying through the streets. There's a Snapsit man in a tight-fitting dark suit sitting on a stool near another bank of elevators. He's staring at something on his reader and doesn't look up at Nixon.

The door to the outside squeals as Nixon exits and steps into the crowd on the sidewalks. Traffic buzzes a few feet above Nixon's head and his cloak ripples in the jet wash coming from the ships' engines.

A mover blows its horn in the distance, and everyone walking in the street's crowds onto the sidewalk, all bumping shoulders as they make room. Voices grumble as the crowd gets tighter.

The horn blows again and a moment later the mover whooshes by. Nixon steps to his right and out of the flow of traffic. He takes a moment to read the lighted signs in the windows, and it all looks wrong. Everything here is too clean. The names of the shops in the window are too clever. Tychon's bisected T dots the windows of several buildings. But there, at the far, far end of the block, where the dust looks to be a little thicker and the people walking out of it a little dirtier, that's where he needs to be. That's where he'll find someone who's looking to off load a ship.

So, he walks. Head down. Weaving through the crowd, bumping shoulders and mumbling apologies. And as he walks he sees—emerging from the dust and debris in the air—a tall arch made with roughhewn stone. It marks the hard edge of this developed area.

There, Nixon thinks as he looks through the arch and into a part of Ibilia that he hadn't expected to see, *is where I'll find my people.*

His people. Those who understood work. Those who understood compromise. Those that were still rough like the stones on that arch. Tired from a full day's work for too little pay. There was where he needed to be.

He pulls his hood down a bit lower and stoops his walk. He rolls his shoulders a bit and tugs his mask up higher on his nose, trying to disguise himself just a bit more in case anyone has seen video of him somewhere. He doesn't know for sure if it exists, but if it does, through that arch are the people who'd pay attention to it. They'd be the ones looking to cash in a bounty. He knows that, because it's what he would do.

He passes through the arch, head down and looking to the ground. But eyes are on him. He can feel them, even through the cloak he's pulled up and gathered around his shoulders.

He doesn't stop for a block, but when he does he looks up and the buildings around him are all low and squat and mismatched. This is the part of the planet that was forgotten after Tychon and all of the big corporations caught wind of the opportunities and moved. Back when everyone on Ibilia was just a wildcatter betting all of their credits on gut feelings and speculation.

Everything is made out of whatever the people who needed shelter could find. Often, they were the containers they used to bring gear to the planet with them. Nixon recognizes wood from large shipping crates as the outside walls of several buildings. Others are made from cheap metal sides, likely pulled off the outside of cargo haulers that were abandoned by crews that no longer needed them.

Every building is different, but above every door in a dark red paint is a name. Some are clever and descriptive. Others are straightforward and functional, little more than a label— Mining Equipment, Sundries and Dry Goods. Nixon sees what he wants a few doors up on the left: Cold Drinks.

He's sitting at the counter. The place is mostly dark. Just a couple of bare bulbs hang on loose wires that drop from the ceiling and pools of light cover the middle of the floor. The place is narrow, and the lights leave small pockets of dark along the wall. Nixon looks at the others here with him. The place is moderately crowded. There are a pair of Snapsits sitting near the entrance. A lone Uzek nurses something in a tall glass at a table on the right. And there's a crowd of half a dozen Erealles making what Nixon has chosen to believe are deep belly laughs at a table nearest the counter.

Nixon is one of two humans in the place. The other one is sitting on another of three stools that face the counter.

Nixon pulls his reader from his pocket. He taps and swipes the screen until his credit balance is up in front of him. It's still too small, but he doesn't have a choice on spending a few of them here. He orders a drink from the long and tall Snapsit woman working behind the bar.

She reaches below the bartop and pulls out a small can. She opens the top with a tool she pulls from her pocket and sets it in front of Nixon.

She slides another glass of something frothy and slightly yellow in front of the man sitting two stools away.

Nixon makes eye contact. The man nods a hello then says: "You're new here. To Ibilia, I mean."

"Is it that obvious?"

The man lifts his arm and quickly shakes the sleeve of his jacket. A shower of dust falls into a little pile on the bartop. Then he points Nixon up and down. "You're too clean."

Nixon smiles and nods and takes a drink from his can. "Just got here."

"And this was your first stop?" He looks up at the bartender, and she looks back. He shrugs to ask for forgiveness. She turns and busies herself with work behind the bar.

Nixon lifts his can. "Was a long trip."

"And that's all you bought?"

"Was an expensive trip too."

The man chuckles. "Hey," he calls to the Snapsit woman. "Get my friend here a real drink."

He turns back to Nixon and points to his glass full of light yellow froth. "One of these?"

Nixon shrugs.

The man turns back to the Snapsit woman. "Two more of these. One for each of us."

She gets to work preparing the drinks and Nixon thanks the man.

"Did it more for myself than anything. I just finished five days in the hole surrounded by a bunch of creatures I couldn't communicate with. I'm dying to talk to someone, and with that little can you were going to finish up and be gone too fast."

The Snapsit woman slides the drinks in front of them. The froth from Nixon's sloshes over the edge of the glass and wets the bartop in front of him. He wipes it up with the sleeve of his cloak.

"With that," the man points to the drink that's still rocking back and forth in Nixon's glass, "I at least buy myself a bit of conversation."

"Whatever your motives, thank you."

Nixon knocks the can back and finishes what little was left inside then tastes the yellow froth. It starts sweet then turns sour on the back of his tongue. His mouth puckers, and his body shivers. Both the man and the Snapsit woman chuckle.

"Wow," Nixon says. "That's ..."

"You'll get used to it," the man says and takes a drink of his own. It doesn't affect him. "Then you'll say it's delicious."

"You said you were in the mines. Always do that for five days at a time?"

"Yow. You are new here. Yeah. We always do big blocks like that. Wears you out, but the credits. Those make it worth it."

"I'm no stranger to hard work, but I don't know, man. Five days?

The man rubs his hands together, and Nixon can see the calluses on his palms. "It is what it is."

"Ever think about doing something else? Something that won't leave you looking like that?" Nixon points to his palms.

"Those aren't from the mines. Most of that down there is automated." He holds his hands up, palms out. That's when Nixon sees that what he saw aren't calluses. They are scars, worn down and smooth.

"Caught in a fire a few years back. Better now." He puts his hands back down, one wrapped around his glass and the other in his lap.

Nixon doesn't know what to say, so he doesn't say anything. The men sit there quiet for a moment. Nixon needs to ask about finding a new ship, and he doesn't have time to do this chit-chat dance.

"Where does someone find a ship around here?"

The man was about to take another drink but puts the glass down. "A ship?"

Nixon nods and waits for an answer.

"Not a good bite to eat. Not a place to crash for the night. But a ship?"

He stops and pulls his shoulders up to his ears, scrunches his face, and does his best to copy Nixon's voice. "Do you know where I can find a ship?"

The man turns and tucks his knees under the bartop.

"You know, you guys come in here and you try to be nice. Sometimes we fall for it, like tonight. We're lonely, grab onto a bit of conversation. Then you go and do something like ask about a ship. Do you think I'm dumb?"

Nixon stays quiet. It was an odd question, sure. And he did ask it out of the blue. That much he'd grant the guy. But it wasn't a question that should make someone angry.

"So, do you?" He pauses again. "You think I'm dumb?"

Nixon shakes a vigorous no

"You guys from Tychon, kings of subtly. How many guys you got waiting outside to bring me in when I say yes? A couple in the front and a couple in the back, I'm guessing."

"I don't know what you're talking about."

"Oh, of course not. 'How dare you, sir, besmirch my reputation like that!' Give me a break. You're on this side of the arch. You're spotless. Those clothes look like they came out of the factory packaging this morning."

He grabs Nixon's hands and turns them over. He rubs the palms with his thumb. "I'm not sure these things have ever swung a pick, used a shovel, carried a box."

The man drops Nixon's hands and stands. He downs what's left of his drink then sets the empty glass on the bartop and pushes it away from him. He points to the half full glass of yellow froth sitting in front of Nixon.

"Enjoy that."

Nixon watches him leave and doesn't turn back to face the bar until the last trailing bits of sunlight disappear behind the closing front door.

The Snapsit woman doesn't turn away from her task, so Nixon continues to nurse the frothy yellow drink he's hoped would start to grow on him. It hasn't.

Tychon? Nixon rolls it over and over in his head. How would anyone think he was with Tychon?

He knew that most of the lines he said he'd never cross had been blurred by the hard choices you have to make in life. Things you say you'll never say, you wind up saying them. Those people you'll never work with? You make exceptions if there's enough mutual benefit. But Tychon? There is still one company on Nixon's list of "I would never…", and that is it.

He looks at his clothes. He holds a sleeve out and gives it a shake. A few motes of dust fall free and grab a bit of light coming through the windows that flank the front door.

He sits at the counter a bit longer. He finishes the frothy yellow thing the other gentleman ordered him. He pulls out his reader and checks his credit balance before ordering something else for himself, another of the low-credit brews in the can.

He begins nursing it when another Snapsit comes in and takes the stool that was abandoned. He orders something from the Snapsit woman behind the bar. They begin speaking. She's smiling. He says something and they both laugh. A few more minutes go by like that before the woman walks away.

It's quiet for a moment before Nixon says something. The Snapsit man responds in broken words that Nixon mostly understands. They struggle through a couple of minutes of a conversation that ends almost identically to the first one.

The Snapsit man stands up and says something that gets the woman's attention, and she rushes over from the opposite side of the counter where she'd been cleaning glasses. She begins hurriedly speaking, trying to stop this train before it starts running out of control and ends with Nixon in a mess on the floor or worse.

She slams a blue hand into the man's chest. He strains against it then calms. It's worked. He looks at Nixon, says one last thing then spits on the ground at Nixon's feet.

He leaves, and Nixon looks up at the woman. He tells her thank you.

"That's going to keep happening."

"Him?"

"Both of them."

Nixon takes a drink of the brew in the can. He sets it on the bartop before speaking. "But why?"

"Because you do look like one of them. We see them from time to time. They cross under the arch and come over here asking questions. Wanting to know information that will get people in trouble."

She clears the Snapsit man's glass and runs a wet rag around the lip of it.

"But ..." Nixon begins to protest.

She places the glass into a plastic bin somewhere below her. It lands with a hollow thud. She shakes her head to get Nixon to stop. "You don't get to protest this. It's how they see you. You can say all day that you aren't some Tychon plant sent over here to sniff out people running things in the grey market. But just looking at you ..."

"Is that what you think I am?"

The woman shakes her head. "I know you aren't. You keep checking that reader before you order anything. You're worried about something. Credits, I'm guessing. Someone with Tychon wouldn't do that."

"So, what do I do? I need a ship."

"You aren't going to get anywhere asking these guys who come in here anything. You'll get some conversation, but that's all."

Nixon finishes what's in his can then sits it on the bartop. "So, I'm stuck? That's what you're saying?"

The woman grabs the can and drops it behind the bar. She wipes his spot with the damp rag.

"That's not what I said."

She looks out at who's sitting out at the tables then leans in close. "My cousin knows a guy. You need a ship, he can help. He has a friend who has a yard. Salvage stuff that he can sell for parts. But he usually has a few that can fly. You want, I can arrange something."

Nixon sinks lower in his seat, like the only thing keeping him upright was the worry of finding another ship.

"Thank you," he says.

EIGHT

Nixon flips the card over and over in his hands. It's made of heavy stock, and it pops against his fingers as he spins it around.

Written in a black ink is a name and an address.

Keet
78 Bryan

He has no idea where he's headed, and none of the streets are laid out in any logical pattern. They intersect at odd angles, like someone dropped a handful of sticks and used the resulting pile as the basis for a whole city's street grid.

It is beginning to get dark, and that doesn't help his situation. Addresses, where they are painted at all, are done in a dark paint that barely contrasts with the walls.

Still, he searches. The Snapsit woman behind the counter had described the place he was looking for, so that's how he's searching.

A dead-end block, halfway down on the left. There should be lights on. And a crowd. There's always a crowd. He'll smell it before he sees it. And he'll hear it before that. She was right.

Nixon walks down a quiet block, but he can tell it won't be quiet for long. He can hear laughter, conversation, a crowd enjoying itself.

Then he smells it. There is some kind of meat grilling, and from the aroma it is being cooked by someone who knows what they are doing. Ahead is a cross street, and that's when he sees the glow. It is coming up over the tops of the buildings on his left, giving them all a halo that only gets brighter as he walks up the block. Then he comes to the intersection and that's when it all overwhelms his senses. The laughter. The noise. The music. He's missed music more than he's realized. And the meat. The place is still half a block away and he can see smoke rising in a tall column from a pit that is being worked by a tall, green-skinned something in a shirt without sleeves.

It is a two-story building with a large balcony that rings the second floor. The bottom is covered in bay doors. They are all open. People pass in and out. They fill the balcony on the second floor, but Nixon knows he's only seeing a portion of the crowd.

How is he ever going to find one man in that bunch?

Start by asking.

But these clothes. If they gave him away in the bar then they are sure to seal some lips here. He ducks in between a pair of buildings and pulls off his cloak. He holds it in front of him and still doesn't get it. All he can see is where he had to sloppily stitch a tear that came from getting snagged on a fence while he was running away from the security team of an executive he and Shaine had just taken for a few thousand credits.

He sees the series of holes down the side where a blaster shot from a different security team had passed so close it caught his cloak as it flapped behind him on a dead run. He puts a hand to his side and covers the spot where the shot had singed his skin.

This cloak isn't pristine. It's a document, telling the story of a man who's spent his life fighting for every day, fighting to make it to tomorrow. It tells the story of a man who is tired, who's seen too much, and has never been able to catch a winning hand.

Nixon tosses the cloak to the ground then stands on top of it and twists his feet, working the fabric into the dirt. He steps off the cloak then bends down and grabs handfuls of the dirt and works it into his pant legs with his hands.

He picks the cloak back up and looks at his work. No one can claim that it looks too clean now. He pulls it over his head and steps back out into the street and starts walking toward the crowd.

He meets the first of it milling about at the edges. Some are looking for a place to have a private conversation. Others are skeptical of the larger crowd. Out here feels safer.

He looks this group over and thinks back to his conversation with the Snapsit woman behind the bar. No one out here is Keet. She didn't say it, but Keet is a player. Keet is connected. Keet can get things done. Keet is in with the people. He's reveling in his status.

Nixon looks at the building from this angle. There are rooms on the second level that he didn't notice before. It's still dominated by the ringed balcony, but there's more to it. There's an interior he hasn't noticed until now, and that's where he's going to find Keet. He knows it.

He dips and ducks his way through a crowd that grows thicker with every step. Smoke from the pit where they are grilling meats stings his eyes. Murmurs of conversations surround him.

Not many here look like him. As a human, he's very much outnumbered. But there are also just as few Uzeks, and that gives him some level of comfort. He pushes deeper into the crowd until he comes to the first set of bay doors. They are each made of one solid sheet of some kind of brown-green wood, and when open like this they stick straight out from the side of the building, like some kind of extended shelf.

Nixon reaches up and runs his fingertips along the underside of one of the doors as he passes beneath. It's smooth and cool. He pauses once through the door and scans the room. He looks through the moving crowd and tries to get an idea of the space. There's a hallway off to his right, and a wall separates half of this room from the one to his left. And on the wall opposite the door, there's a set of stairs that lead to the landing.

People sit on nearly every step. It makes climbing to the second floor difficult, but the crowd is a bit thinner once he gets to the top. He pauses again and quickly takes everything in. Behind him is the balcony, and the night breeze coming in flutters the bottom of his cloak. He gathers it up in one hand and holds it tight. In front of him are only a few others. They all glance at him, the new guy coming off the steps and then coming to a stop.

Standing along the wall, leaning against it, is a Snapsit man. Tall and broad. His arms crossed at his waist in front of him. Every experience in Nixon's life tells him that this man isn't here for fun. This man is working.

Nixon makes eye contact and approaches.

"I'm looking for Keet."

The man looks Nixon over, up from the floor. Slow. Then says in broken words: "Lots look for him."

"I was told he was here."

"He is." The man gestures toward the door with his head. Nixon hears laughter coming from the other side, a high-pitched giggle from a woman and laughter from a voice that he assumes belongs to Keet. It's low and bouncy. Nixon makes a note: The man sounds happy.

"That's him, huh?"

The wide man doesn't respond.

"I was told he might be able to help me. I need to find a ship."

The wide man has stopped looking at Nixon. He is watching the people on the landing. A crowd of three Snapsit women had just finished the climb up the stairs. They are paying no mind to Nixon's new friend, but he is paying them all of his.

And then Nixon says what must have been the magic word. He mentions the name of the Snapsit woman back at the bar. Suddenly, his voice is audible again. His friend turns back to him. "Who did you say?"

He repeats it.

The man puts up a meaty hand and knocks on the door. It sounds thick, made of the same stuff as the bay doors.

All the noise coming from behind the door stops. A moment later a woman opens it. The wide man turns and looks past her to the man sprawled on the couch. He starts speaking in Snapsit

They exchange a few words then Keet looks at the woman and wags a finger toward the door. She spits a few words at him in Snapsit then goes, glaring at Nixon as she passes.

Keet looks at Nixon after she's gone. "Come in."

Keet sits himself up on the couch. He's shaped like most other Snapsits, tall and lean. But he doesn't look like most others. Scars run diagonal across his face, making him look almost like an animal.

"So how do you know my cousin?"

"She didn't tell me she was your cousin."

"My cousin. My bar. And if she sent you here then you must have made an impression."

Keet gestures for Nixon to sit in the chair that's angled toward the couch. "I think it's more pity than anything else."

"Knowing her ..." Keet doesn't finish his sentence. "What can I help you with?"

"I need a ship.

"And she sent you to me? That's a pretty big request."

Keet leans back into the couch and tips his head to the ceiling. He folds his hands together, thin fingers interweaving themselves in a complicated pattern that steals a moment of Nixon's focus.

"Honestly, I don't know who you are," Nixon says. "I'm in a spot. She said you could help. I came."

Keet continues to look to the ceiling.

153

"I can help," he says and then pauses. He looks back to Nixon. "But can you pay for a new ship?

"I have an old ship to give in trade."

Keet laughs that bouncy laugh Nixon heard through the door. It's deeper on this side, coming from his toes.

"That's funny." He gestures Nixon out of the room. "You can go.

"This is serious. I need a new ship."

Nixon's mind starts playing out all of the scenarios it can conjure up. Future battles where EHL is dipping and diving away from trailing ships piloted by bounty hunters looking to turn Nixon into space debris. They are all playing out at the same time, so Nixon is seeing dozens of these fights taking place all at once. Some end in wins, the other ships exploding in fantastic balls of blue light. Most, though, don't end that way. Most conclude with the bright white flash of a ship exploding all around him and then everything going black.

"You think I'm not serious?" Keet asks. "I don't have a ship to sell you, but I know people. That's why my cousin sent you here. She knows I can help you find someone who will sell you a ship. I go to them and tell them I have someone who wants to swap ships with them, like they are kids playing in the dirt and trading toys, they'll never talk to me again. That can't happen. So, if that's all you have then there's nothing I can do for you."

He gestures Nixon out of the room again with the wave of a couple of fingers. Nixon hears the door open behind him and the broad man steps into the room. Nixon's mind starts working again. He's mentally walking through the ship, looking for anything of value, and it takes only seconds to get to the only thing he has that anyone else would want. He blurts it out.

"Fuel rods," he says. The broad man hooks a hand under Nixon's arm and lifts him from the chair. "I've got fuel rods."

Keet looks back up at him and holds up a hand, palm out, telling the broad man to wait.

"What?"

"I've got fuel rods."

"OK. That's something. Not much, really, but it's a place to start. Unless they're …"

Nixon interrupts. "They're Bastic fuel rods."

"Put him down. Now we can talk."

NINE

The conversation didn't take long, but Nixon didn't expect it to. Mentioning Bastic fuel rods is like hitting fast forward. Keet's eyes got wide when Nixon told him he had some. They got wider still when he told him that he had more than just a few. It was a lie. Nixon only had the five, but that didn't feel like enough of a stash to keep Keet's interest. So five became a handful. And when Keet pressed, that handful became a case.

Once Nixon says he has a case Keet is eager, ready to start arranging a meeting with the gentleman he knows. So they quickly head out into the night. Back down the stairs. Back through the crowd and the bay doors. Back past the man still working the grill. Smoke disappears into the dark sky. The scent of the meat reminds Nixon how hungry he is, and the prospect of a meal that isn't rehydrated nearly causes Nixon's stomach to stop him dead there so he can shove sloppy fistfuls of meat in his mouth, grease slicking his hands, covering his cheeks, and dripping from his chin.

But they don't stop. He follows Keet past the stragglers standing at the edge of the crowd and out into the dark and empty streets.

Keet hasn't said much. He's mostly been typing into his datapad, sending messages back and forth with whoever it is they were going to meet, Nixon assumes.

The glow of the screen makes everything else around them seem extra dark, and Nixon keeps close to Keet. They turn a couple of corners, enough for Nixon to lose track of where they are. And without being able to clearly see any kind of landmarks, he realizes how bad of an idea this is. He doesn't know Keet. This guy clearly has some level of influence, and it doesn't seem like he uses it for the better. He could be walking him into some kind of ambush. Leading him into some dark alley with a team of more broad men waiting to lay into Nixon. Beat him into submission, get him to take them back to his ship, then lay into him again when that case of fuel rods isn't there waiting for them.

Keet puts his data pad in his pocket, and a few moments later Nixon's eyes have adjusted to the dark. He still can't see well, but he can see better. They walk in quiet for a few minutes more when Nixon speaks.

"I need you to do something for me," he says.

"I think I'm already doing something for you."

Nixon gives that statement a nod that Keet can't see.

"I need you to do something that's not going to have a lot of payback for you."

"I'm not really in the business of doing things that don't benefit me."

Nixon nods again and says "I need you to let me lead these discussions. Introduce me to your friend then let me do the talking."

Keet is quiet for a moment, the only noise is their breathing and the grinding of small gravel beneath their feet.

"So, I say 'This is …'. What's your name?"

"Trevor."

" 'This is Trevor' and then you want me to back away. Not knowing anything about this guy, who he is, or what he's done. Just leave everything up to you."

"Didn't think this would be a difficult concept, but yes. That's what I'm asking."

Keet has walked them back toward the downtown section of Ibilia where the lights are still shining bright and, from Nixon's experience, they probably will burn like that all night. They cast a glow over everything a couple of blocks this side of the arches.

Keet points to a tall building only a couple of windows wide. It shoots above all the other squat buildings, like a weed stretching to the suns.

"Top floor." Keet says, then leads the way down a narrow alley to a working door that opens to a small landing. It's lit by a pair of small lights mounted in the ceiling, and it takes a moment for Keet and Trevor's eyes to adjust to the sudden addition of direct light.

Nixon follows Keet up the stairs, staying a step or two behind. They get to the landing for the fifth floor, and Keet knocks twice on the door across from the top of the stairs.

There's a moment where Nixon wonders what he's asked to be brought into. There's nothing happening behind the door. Keet knocks again, and Nixon begins to fear again that this is all some kind of ruse, a scheme to take a sucker for whatever they have. It's the kind of thing that he and Shaine would have tried to pull off in a previous life.

Previous life? No, not for him. Earlier life, maybe. Previous for Shaine. But here Nixon was stuck in the same life. The same schemes being pulled, but he's on the rube end of them this time. Some sucker that looks like an easy mark.

Keet looks at Nixon and shrugs with his eyes, "I don't know what's going on." He knocks on the door a third time, and a moment later a voice comes from the other side. Locks disengage, clicking open. A Snapsit woman opens the door.

She sees Keet and her eyes narrow. He says something to her in Snapsit and she barks something back, anger dripping off every word. Nixon doesn't understand a thing either of them say, but he can tell that none of it's good. They trade barbs, voices raising. Nixon watches the other doors in the hall, waiting for one of them to crack open and a set of curious eyes to peer out from inside.

Then there's another voice from the other side of the door. It's bigger, louder than either Keet or this woman. Both of them stop arguing, and Nixon can hear footsteps approaching. The woman looks over her shoulder into the darkness behind her then steps away from the door.

Taking her place is a Snapsit man that is bigger and broader than any Snapsit Nixon has ever seen. He fills the door frame from edge to edge.

He starts talking to Keet, and Keet responds. His head is lowered. His voice more hushed, almost contrite.

After a couple moments conversation, the man turns to Nixon. "He says you have a ship you're looking to unload."

Nixon nods. "And I'd like to also acquire one."

"We might be able to work something out." He steps to the side and gives Keet and Nixon enough room to pass through the door. "Come inside. Let's talk."

Keet keeps his word. He lets Nixon lead.

The man introduces himself as Marko and tells Nixon to take a seat. There's a wide chair set against the wall diagonal from the door. Two other smaller chairs sit across from it. A table, long and low, sits in between.

Marko, after everyone is seated: "What kind of ship are you looking at?"

"I'm not particular. I'd love something fast. Nimble."

Marko listens and nods along, like he's doing a mental inventory of the ships he has access to.

"And how much do you have to spend?"

"I want a one-for-one trade."

Marko fails to stifle a laugh.

"I'm serious," Nixon says. "I have a ship. Good condition. Engines have been recently tuned up. Did it myself. It's a good ship. You'll be able to get something for it."

"That's not how this works."

Nixon knows that. He knows no one is looking to break even. No legit businessman will make this deal. But he's banking on the illegitimacy of Marko's business to make it work.

"Tell me more about your ship," Marko says.

Nixon begins describing EHL. He talks about her speed. He talks about her agility. Her internal intelligence. Her cargo holds. He spins up enough of a tale that for a brief moment he thinks he might be better off hanging onto her and taking his chances.

Marko nods along then stands. Nixon and Keet do too.

"I'll tell you what," Marko says and pulls his datapad from his pocket as he begins walking toward the door. "Pull out your datapad."

Nixon does and hands it to Marko. Marko taps his own device and gestures his way to a screen Nixon can't see. Marko places the devices back to back. He holds them there a moment until there's a chirp that fills the room. He hands Nixon back his device. Nixon looks at the screen.

"Come to that address in the morning and we can talk. You can look at what I have. I can look at your ship. We'll see if we can't work something out."

Nixon and Keet step back through the door. Marko says something to Keet in Snapsit and Keet nods.

"See you in the morning," Marko says and closes the door.

TEN

Nixon heads back to his ship just as the first of Ibilia's suns is starting to show signs of waking. He watches the glow on the horizon grow as he walks back past the bar and then back through the arch that leads him back into Ibilia's business center.

The streets aren't crowded, but they will be soon. For now, it is all young and eager businessmen hoping that the boss seeing them already at their desks when they arrive at the office will count for something down the road.

Tychon hasn't gotten it's claws fully into Ibilia, but its creeping shadow is starting to loom. Nixon counts a half dozen bisected Ts just in the few blocks since he's passed back through the arch. He counts a half dozen more by the time he gets back to his ship.

He steps off the elevator and back onto the roof where he'd left EHL. She is still there, light from the first sun bouncing off the metal of her engines and highlighting the seams that Nixon had to fix. The dull putty he used was supposed to blend in imperceptibly with the original surface. That was the promise on the canister. The canister lied.

He punches his access code into the panel near the ramp then steps back. The ramp unfolds, and Nixon steps on and looks around, taking a version of the tour he gave himself just after he left Exte. He gathers things as he goes.

On the main deck he grabs the card Mira gave him that night when she gifted him the ship. He grabs the case, of course.

In the mess, he quickly rinses a pair of mugs he used the last two days and throws them into the cabinet like they are actually clean. He wipes down the small counter top and the sink.

In the crew quarters he grabs, well, nothing. He's only slept in here, so he runs a hand across the thin mattress that was his bed. He smooths the wrinkles out then looks to the closet. It's empty. He only has one set of clothes. Something new to wear has to be the next on his list of things to acquire

He moves back to the main deck. He brushes some sand still left from Umel out of the ramp and then seals the ship back up.

"Take us up and head us west," he tells EHL.

"Good morning, sir."

"Up and west."

The ship lifts from the roof and Nixon looks back to the ground. It's more crowded now. The city is waking. EHL quickly finds the traffic lanes and forces its way into the flow.

"Where are we headed, sir?"

"West."

That's all Marko told him the night before as he and Keet left. He shouted the directions back down the stairs.

"Just west?" Nixon asked Keet.

Keet nodded. "Yeah," he said as they got back to the street. "You'll see it. Trust me."

They fly out of the main business district, but there is still plenty of city below them. It's all old Ibilia, like where he'd spent his day yesterday—mismatched and makeshift.

Then, even farther west, that disappears into a mess of mining operations. There's no order to most of it, just rigs working to pull and haul ore from under the surface of Ibilia.

It's all dotted with the large and professional looking rigs of Tychon. The company is coming.

Then, past all of that, Nixon sees it. It's a field of busted ships lined up in neat rows and ship parts gathered in tall piles. It is a ship junkyard, and it spreads on seemingly forever. The smaller ships, the little personal crafts that let you hop around a planet, are all at the front of the yard.

EHL begins to drop down out of the traffic lanes, but Nixon stops her.

"Higher," he said. "Let's get a good look at the place. And get me an external camera shot of what's below us."

The ship climbs higher and Nixon gets a better idea of the size of the yard. There are a dozen rows of those small ships. Then after those are the small haulers, a couple of dozen rows of ships that were like EHL. And beyond that is the big stuff, the military-class haulers that can carry a battalion of troops and all their gear.

In between each of the classes of ships are the piles of parts.

Nixon looks at the feed coming from EHL's external camera. It's all ships and parts rushing by. Then between two of the stacks Marko flashes by.

"Hold up," Nixon said. "Circle back. Slower. There's something I want to check out."

He begins slowly pushing the camera in closer on the stacks. There he is again: Marko, and he's not alone.

"Hang here for a second."

EHL begins to circle. Nixon locks the camera on this shot. The big man is definitely Marko. And Keet is there too. But there are also three others who Nixon doesn't recognize. They are standing in a circle listening to Marko talk. Two of them are Snapsits. They are big like Keet's man from the night before.

Marko is laying out points on his fingers. Nixon watches the conversation for a few moments more, and the feeling that something's wrong starts to build. It begins as a tickle in his gut. Just a little thing. A curiosity. A question from his subconscious. Then it becomes something more, a turning in his stomach. Something that makes him uneasy. From there it becomes a full-on topsy turvy-ness that's screaming at him to keep his attention sharp because none of this feels good or looks right.

He sits back in the captain's chair and tells EHL that it can turn off the feed from the camera. He breathes deep. Once. Twice. Then swallows hard, forcing all of these feelings down to his knees. He's made the note. Something may be up. Be aware. But he can't let that be the only thing he's thinking about when he steps off. It'll color everything. Each word. Each action. Each calculation. Marko will see it. Keet too. It'll put them off.

He swallows again pushing the feelings down to his toes this time. He exhales.

"OK, EHL," he says. "Get us to the ground."

ELEVEN

EHL circles the yard one more time then sets down in an open area near the gate that looks to Nixon like an entrance.

Nixon looks to the dash and the blaster he's tossed up there. He reaches for it then hesitates. Having it tucked into his waistband changes things. Yes, it makes him more confident in case that intuition he'd pushed to his toes is right. But it also puts him on edge. He listens differently to what's being said. He runs everyone's actions through a different filter. All of it ending with the question "Should I pull my blaster?"

He leaves it. Then, punching in the code to unfold the ramp, he pauses again.

"Don't be stupid, Trevor," he whispers to himself. He grabs the blaster off the dash and shoves it into the waistband of his pants and pulls his cloak over the top. He adjusts it so the blaster's grip isn't causing a lump in the fabric.

The keypad chirps as Nixon continues entering the code. The ramp unfolds, and the interior of EHL is filled with daylight. He takes one last look around. He half expects to feel something—a tug of some kind hitting him in the chest—but he doesn't. This ship hasn't served him well. It's been a burden, not the blessing that he thought it could be when he saw it standing in that starport on Exte.

He steps down the ramp, and Keet and Marko are there waiting for him. Both Snapsit men smile. They look different in the daylight. Keet seems longer and leaner. Marko is broader here.

"Good morning," Keet says.

Nixon gives a half wave and says hello.

Marko skips the pleasantries. "That's the ship you're trading?"

"That's the one. She flies well. Better than you might think by looking at her."

Marko steps next to EHL. He runs a hand along her engines. "Not too warm yet," he says. "That's good. Means they are efficient."

He stops and drags a thumb across the rough surface of one of the seams Nixon repaired.

"You do this?" he asks without looking back to Nixon. "They're clearly done by an amateur, but they're not bad. I won't be able to sell it like this, though. I'll have to get them redone. Something I'll have to consider if we try to work something out."

"Understood."

Marko looks back to Nixon and points up the ramp. "Mind?"

Nixon shakes no, and Marko steps inside the ship.

Keet and Nixon are alone outside, and Nixon thanks Keet. "You didn't have to help me. I appreciate it.

Keet watches the ramp. "Thank my cousin. But this is still just an introduction at this point. You haven't worked out any kind of deal yet."

Marko reappears. Nixon asks him what he thinks.

"It's a ship," he says as he steps down off the ramp. "But it looks positive so far. Follow me."

Marko passes and Nixon and Keet turn to follow. Each stay a step off his shoulder and keep up as he winds his way through the yard.

Nixon sees the tops of ships poking over a wide pile of parts. Most of them look like haulers from where he's at.

Blunt noses. Wide profiles. A couple, though, have the tapered fronts of speeders. Those catch his eye.

They round another pile of parts and Nixon can see the ships clearly now. There are three haulers. All of them look to be in worse shape than EHL. One looks to be held together with spit and hope.

Another looks like it could have been put together by the woman who'd helped him fix his engine back on Umel. It's all various parts welded together. None of it matches. He looks close at it and can make out—maybe—what looks to be a smaller hauler that serves as the base for this thing. But there's so much hanging off of it that Nixon can't be sure. Still, thinking back to the woman on and Umel and her ship, he's intrigued by it. He wants to fly it, to get it up into the sky and put it through its paces.

He knows better, though. Even if that ship flies like a dream, it won't work. There aren't any others like it. If people were recognizing EHL then he stands no chance in that one. No, he needs something that looks like everything else. Something that is the spaceship equivalent of beige. And that's exactly what the next ship is.

It's a Redbrook 2401. They've popped these out of a dozen factories all across the galaxies. They are feature free and cheap. Nixon could have likely built his own custom Redbrook just by digging though the stack of parts behind him.

He steps to the ship and runs a finger over a dent in the housing over one of the engines. He leans in and looks at the seams where everything comes together. That's when he sees them, two of the Snapsits that he'd seen before he landed. They'd been talking with Marko. Now, they were here looking at ships just a bit farther down the line from where Marko had led Nixon.

Nixon runs the scenarios. He lands on two, and they are exactly the opposite of each other.

The first: These are two Snapsits looking for a ship and they've come to another Snapsit to buy. What Nixon saw from the air was Marko giving them the sales pitch, counting out all the reasons they should buy from him.

The second: They are all working together, and Nixon is being set up. After some kind of cue these two Snapsits would be on Nixon quicker than he could blink.

He looks back to Marko then points to the inside of the ship. "You mind?"

"Go ahead. I'll be right ..." Marko takes a pair of steps toward the ship, ready to follow Nixon on.

Nixon stops him.

"No," he says. "I'll come out with questions if I have them."

Marko returns to where he'd been standing next to Keet.

Nixon walks up the ramp, his boots thumping as he climbs.

The ship is fine, if a little small. But he doesn't care about the ship. He needs a moment to sort out a plan, and this gives him that. He begins to think.

He goes back to running scams with Shaine and their extended crew. He thinks about how big some of those teams were. Five or six, even a dozen depending. Shaine in the role of Marko. Nixon as Keet.

It only got to a crew of twelve when things were complicated. If it was just some loner guy they were trying to pick clean then it was a handful of them. Five tops.

He pictures the scene from above in his head again, and recounts the bodies. Five for sure. Out on the yard he'd only seen four, but number five was likely hanging back out of site as insurance of some kind.

Marko shouts from outside: "Everything OK in there?"

"Yeah! Good!"

Nixon runs his hand over his cloak and lets it rest on the blaster.

Pull it out? If he does then he has to be ready to start shooting right away.

Leave it tucked and he can just see how all of this plays out. Run it to its natural end, which still could be him getting off this planet in a new ship. He walks back down the ramp and toward Marko and Keet with the blaster tucked away and hidden under his cloak.

For now.

TWELVE

"What did we think?" Marko asks.

Nixon steps back to the ground and gives Marko a shrug. "It's fine. I mean, it'll fly, and that's something."

He looks down the line of ships in front of him and points to one that's three away. It's a speeder. Older and showing some wear. But the three big engines on the back say that even at its age this ship should still be able to bring big fire.

"I was hoping to find something a little more ..." Nixon points a thumb at the speeder.

Marko smiles and nods. "Take a look."

Nixon turns and is facing the two men he'd seen talking with Marko earlier. They both look up at the small crowd now approaching. They both watch for a moment. Then Nixon sees one nod. Small, but it was there. Right? It was there.

Nixon turns quickly to look at Marko and Keet, hoping to catch them in the middle of some kind of unspoken communication. A wink. A returned nod. A gesture with the head. Something. Anything. But they only smile at him, and he says, "I'm going to climb inside."

He looks back to the other two just in time to see them walk away. Noted.

"Let me know if you have any questions," Marko shouts as Nixon disappears inside of the ship.

The wear on the inside is twice as bad as what is on the outside. There's only one seat in the cockpit, and it's been worn smooth by the pilots who've come before him. Crowded around that seat are banks of dated controls.

Nixon wiggles his way into the seat and starts pushing buttons, not that he knows how to fly something like this. Not that he knows anything at all without any of these panels lit up. But he can pretend. He can try to get a feel. He looks in front of him and pictures himself with everything turned on. The engine's low rumble behind him. He's going through some kind of pre-flight check, making sure that everything mechanical is doing what it's supposed to do. Making sure that all the atmospherics are operational.

Then he gives the ship the go, and he can feel inertia push him hard into his seat, a giant hand planted firmly on his chest. The speeder leaps from the surface of Ibilia and is through the atmosphere and into the deep black in a matter of seconds, shooting through the traffic lanes like they aren't even there.

The ship is into space and pushing hard. The engines are running as hot as they can, going full bore with no sign of slowing. They rumble deep and low behind Nixon, and he waits for eventual alarms to sound, but no warnings trigger. The ship is just fast.

Weaponry is light, though, Nixon notes. On the panel to his left, he assumes, are a couple of places to activate guns, but they would be purely defensive on a ship like this, meant more for distraction than damage. This ship's greatest defense is its speed. It doesn't get into trouble because it can outrun anyone who wants to start it.

This is it. This is the kind of ship he needs if he's going to deliver Shaine's damn case.

"What do you think?" Marko has poked his head into the ship and startles Nixon. Everything Nixon had been imagining suddenly disappears. The banks of screens are dark again. The engines are quiet.

"So?" Marko asks again.

Nixon begins to nod slowly. "I like it. I didn't think I would. It's kind of a junker. But I like it."

He stands, and Marko backs out of the ship. Nixon exits too and turns to get a better look at the back end of the ship. Marko follows.

Nixon runs a hand along the ship's metal side, his fingers catching on the seams in the metal. He gets to the back of the ship and steps away to get a closer look. It's three big engines set in a triangular pattern—one on top and two below. He reaches out and runs the palm of his hand along the exhaust cone of one of them and for a moment he swears it's warm.

"Those aren't standard. They are about twenty-five percent bigger than what you'd get if you bought this thing new."

"Factory upgrade or did someone do it on their own?"

Marko has his arms crossed across his chest. He shrugs. "I don't do business with folks who like to answer a lot of questions. That was just what the guy who traded her to me said. But I'd guess it was a custom job. The way he talked, he wanted me to assume it was his handiwork."

Nixon steps closer to get a better look at the engines. What he's looking for he doesn't really know. Obvious signs of shoddy work, maybe. Bad welds. Open gaps in the seams. Nothing stands out, though. It's competent work if not pretty.

"Want to go make this official?"

Nixon nods. He leans forward and touches the ship again. "Yeah," he says. "Let's do it."

THIRTEEN

Nixon follows Marko back through the twists and turns of the yard to where they'd left EHL earlier. Marko starts negotiations almost immediately.

"That little speeder you're looking at is a good ship. I know she's not pretty. And I don't know too many details, like I said. But I've got a couple of mechanics here who look at every trade before I take them in, and they really liked that one a lot."

Marko stops for a moment at one of the piles of parts and looks left then right. Bearings. Then begins walking again. And talking.

"Your ship is nice, but, as you saw, I have a lot of mid-sized haulers right now."

"I saw what you showed me."

"It's pretty representative."

Nixon doesn't say anything right away, but eventually settles for "OK."

"I'm not meaning anything by that. Just walking conversation."

"OK" again. "But stands to reason you'd have more haulers. That's what most ships are. Speeders are kind of rare."

Marko stops again and looks around, trying to see over and around the piles of parts. Keet follows but doesn't say anything.

"I mean, I think we'll still be able to work something out."

Nixon hangs back, a step off Marko's heel. "I never doubted that we could."

He brings a hand up in front of him and lets the heel of his palm brush the blaster handle sticking up under his cloak.

They come around a pile of parts, a sloppy stack of wired panels, and there's EHL. He sees his repairs again after spending time with the speeder and admires his work. For a guy who's lived off whatever work he can scramble up, maybe he missed his calling.

Marko walks up to EHL and gets a close look at her again. He runs a hand along her sides. He drops a finger into one of the blaster holes Nixon never had a chance to patch.

He shakes his head and looks over to Nixon. He looks concerned.

Both of Ibilia's suns have come up over the tops of the buildings now, and they are baking the yard. A bead of sweat forms on the top of Nixon's head, and he feels it drop slowly through his hair then streak across his forehead and down to the end of his nose. He wipes it away with the back of his hand, always watching Marko.

He takes a finger and starts picking at some of the patches that Nixon had put in place to seal up EHL. He digs a sharp Snapsit nail into the brittle putty and starts to pull it out in small chunks.

Keet steps forward and pulls a knife out from under his cloak. He flips the blade out and starts picking at another seam. His comes out in larger pieces, exposing large openings between the panels.

"Hey!" Nixon shouts.

"I don't think I got as good a look as I needed to earlier. Clearly this ship..." Marko kicks a big foot into the side panel behind him. His heel creates a new dent, the metal creasing in the middle. "... is in need of some serious repair."

"You Grascow's pet. What are you doing?"

But Nixon knows exactly what Marko is doing. He may own this big yard. He may have a place of his own to lay his head at night. And he may have a Snapsit woman who will be there in the middle of the night to open the door for him. But he isn't any different than Nixon. Not a bit. He is still running scams. He is still scheming for ways to get more.

Keet turns and punches a dent into the side panel he is standing nearest. He kicks a second dent into the panel with his heel.

"I don't know if, with a ship in this condition, I can do an even-up trade. I think I'm getting the short end of that one."

"Oh, yeah? Now that you've gotten a better look?"

Marko steps away from the ship and toward Nixon. Keet follows.

"You don't think I know who you are?" Nixon asks as they approach. "You're me, I'm you. We are the same people. Always trying to find an angle. Finding a way to get one credit more. I'm older than both of you, and it's how I've lived my whole life. What's available for the taking, and how can I get it?"

Marko smiles and nods. "And you think I don't know who you are?"

Nixon's heart beats double. *What does he know? Who does he think I am?*

"You're some low-level hustler. That's all you are. You come here trying to scam me. Telling me you're out of credits. You're not out of credits. Not a guy like you. You have resources. If nothing else, guys like you always have resources."

Nixon rocks on both feet. Left, then right. The blaster brushes across his stomach.

"You know what? You're right. I do have resources. Always something up my sleeve. I like to think about them as options. But not this time. This time I'm desperate. This time I'm playing this thing straight up."

"Nah," Marko says. "I don't believe it."

"It's true. This ship. This is all I've got, and I don't need it anymore. I need something else."

Keet looks to Marko. Marko nods. "Of course you do. Because that one's too recognizable now, isn't it?"

Keet pulls his datapad from his pocket and holds it face out so Nixon can see it. There on the screen are pictures of EHL from different angles. One is up close. One from far away. One from overhead.

"I got this yesterday morning," Keet says, turning the datapad back toward himself. He smiles. "I get a lot of them. Every time a ship with an untagged registration comes into our atmosphere it trips our alert system. Some days I get a dozen of these things. It's like I'm going to shake a hole in my leg with the alerts."

He holds the pad out for Marko to see it and then back to Nixon. "Yesterday, though, I just got the one. Just this one."

Keet laughs a little.

"Now," he continues, "the ship that tripped our atmospheric alarms is sitting here in front of us. I mean, what are the odds, right?"

Nixon begins to walk to the ramp leading up to EHL. "Look," he says. "Clearly, we aren't going to be making any kind of deal today…"

Marko whistles, and coming down the ramp the other direction out of the ship are the two guys who Nixon saw earlier. Both men have forced smiles that contort their faces and each are carrying Bastic fuel rods. Nixon looks down to see them pull their fingers tight around the rods, and their knuckles go white. Nixon looks close. Those knuckles are scarred, their blue Snapsit skin healing nearly black.

These are the mechanics.

FOURTEEN

"Look at that," Marko says, a smile in his voice if not on his face. "I wonder what other treasures we'll find on that ship."

Nixon turns from the mechanics and answers. "Nothing else. That's it. No secrets."

"Oh, I don't know about that," Keet says. He starts sliding his finger across the screen of his datapad. Everyone waits.

He finishes and shows the screen to the crowd. "It's not just that ship that has people's attention."

The image is of Nixon. He's back on Exte. He's standing in a crouch, his face twisted up in concentration. He's holding a blaster out in front of him, and everything around him is lit up by the bolt that's just left the barrel.

"Well, now," Marko says. "Now this is interesting. Seems that you've built a long list of enemies. Some of whom are willing to pay buckets of credits to see you again."

Nixon puts his hands out in front of him to say "Wait a minute" but it doesn't work. Marko reaches behind his own back and pulls a blaster. Keet reaches and grabs his own.

"Safe to say the deal's off," Marko says. "I think we are going to go...a different direction."

He looks to Keet and gestures toward Nixon with a toss of his head.

Everything slows down. Keet takes one slow step toward Nixon, his blaster pointed at Nixon's middle. The mechanics continue coming down the ramp from EHL, but it's like they're walking through mud.

Nixon feels his arm reach for the blaster tucked into his belt. He feels his fingers find the grip and slowly close around it. And he feels his arm draw the blaster out from under his cloak. He jab-points it at Keet.

He hears Marko laugh a deep laugh that seems to bounce off the dirt in between them. Then everything snaps to again. It's all running in normal time. "Well, now we've got ourselves a gun fight," Marko says.

"Doesn't have to be a gunfight," Nixon says. "It can end right here. We all go our own ways and forget we ever met each other. You can even keep the rods."

Marko keeps his blaster trained on Nixon. "That's not how this ends," he says. "Not anymore. All drawn like this, it has to end pretty badly for someone."

He looks aways from Nixon for a moment and toward the mechanics. "Over here, guys."

They both finish their walks down the ramp and off of EHL.

"Well, if you are telling me there's no other way that this ends ..."

He swings his blaster from Keet and shoots the first mechanic in the shin then goes right back to Keet. A large chunk of meat and bone scatter across the ground in front of Nixon. The Snapsit cries out, something that sounds like a pained animal calling for death.

The man tries to limp another step or two before falling to the ground. Instinct tells him to grab his wound, and when he does, he drops the Bastic fuel rod. Nixon's instincts kick in next.

He grabs for the fuel rod as it falls, not wanting it to hit the ground. When he does, he makes himself vulnerable. His head is down. His focus is gone. His blaster is pointed at the ground.

"Grab him!" Keet shouts to the second mechanic. The mechanic lay-drops the rods he's carrying to the ground and reaches for Nixon. Nixon tries to spin away and raise his blaster, but the mechanic snags him by the crook of the elbow.

He pulls Nixon to him. Nixon's blaster catches on something and is ripped from his hand. The mechanic gathers Nixon up in one quick motion. He's a tall and lean Snapsit. He has one wiry blue arm wrapped across Nixon's front. Nixon squirms and tries to wiggle free, but he can't. The Snapsit mechanic only grabs him tighter.

The other mechanic is still rolling on the ground, one blue hand grabbing at his lower leg. He's moaning.

Marko looks at Nixon and smiles. "Can I tell you something?"

Nixon doesn't respond, just tries harder to pull himself free.

"This is always how this was going to end. Keet came to me after you left last night. We worked all of this out."

Nixon struggles against the Snapsit's grip one more time then says "Why?"

Marko shrugs. "We don't get to have a lot of fun around here."

"So, I was entertainment for you?"

"You were, but I think the fun's over. Don't you?"

Keet shouts something that Nixon doesn't understand and three more Snapsit men step from behind the piles of parts.

That's five men and five blasters in front of Nixon. He's outnumbered. He's outgunned. And that's not counting the Snapsit mechanic who's got him wrapped up, that arm creeping higher. It's wrapped across his chin and neck now.

The Snapsit cranks his arm tighter, and Nixon struggles to breathe. He starts doing the calculations, figuring his odds. No matter how he does the math, it's not good. Too many of them with too many guns. And just one of him with his blaster on the ground out of reach.

He reaches up and grabs the Snapsit's arm and tries to pull himself free. The Snapsit leans back and lifts Nixon from the ground, his toes kicking the dust into clouds. He's lost his leverage, so all this pulling is only tiring him out.

Marko and Keet laugh while he struggles. Something inside of him catches fire.

I was just entertainment? And now you laugh? Laugh at this.

Nixon reverses his grip. He puts his hands underneath the Snapsit's arm and pushes it up to his mouth. He opens wide and then bites hard into the man's forearm, sinking his teeth deep into the flesh. His mouth fills, warm and wet, with Snapsit blood. He grinds his jaw and feels the muscles tear between his teeth. He shakes his head, like some kind of animal trying to rip flesh from bone. He can hear the muscle rip apart, and the Snapsit's grip on him goes soft.

One last pull and Nixon's through. He spits his mouth clean and lets go of the Snapsit's arm. The Snapsit falls to the ground and reaches for the blaster that Nixon had dropped earlier.

Nixon kicks it away from the Snapsit's grip then takes off, scooping up the blaster as he sprints in a wide circle.

Marko and Keet and the others are still for a moment. An animalistic display like that always stuns, and it's what Nixon had been counting on. He needed the time. He's firing wild shots as he runs. They hit nothing but buy him time.

Marko and Keet both drop to the ground and return fire. Their shots aren't any more accurate, and Nixon dives behind a pile of parts.

"You're insane!" Marko shouts."

"Not insane!" Nixon shouts back. "Just desperate."

Everything is quiet for a moment. Nixon counts an internal three then pops up, firing. He spreads three blasts— left, right, and center—in front of him. He drops back down without seeing if he hit anything, but there's a scream then moaning from the other side of the pile. He assumes he got lucky.

He counts another three and pops up again, but this time everyone is waiting for him. A volley of blaster shots come his way. He goes to drop back to the ground, but he's too late. One of the shots catches his blaster square and blows it from his hand.

He hits the ground, his hand stinging and hot from the heat of the blaster bolt passing so close. He tries to slow his breathing. He needs to think and if all he can focus on is sucking in another breath then he won't be able to come up with a plan.

His brain runs smoking hot trying to figure out what's next, and he can't come up with anything. Every scenario, no matter how far out he runs it, comes to the same end: Marko is turning him over to someone, either the Uzeks or whoever else is chasing him. Whoever it is, he doesn't see where it goes from there. Nowhere good, he assumes.

But it's his only option. He has to stand up. He has to place his hands above his head, palms out, and allow himself to be gathered up and hauled away. As much as it's going to go against every instinct he has, as much as he'll have to fight all of nature to stand still while Marko gestures one of his back up men to tie Nixon's arms behind his back and walk him through these piles of parts, he has to do it. Because something might happen. If this life of his has taught him anything it's that you always have the next day, the next hour, the next minute. Until those things are gone for good— you're dead or locked away—there's always a chance of something happening that flips everything to the unexpected.

So, he stands up, arms above his head and palms out. Marko smiles.

"Go get him, Keet."

But before Keet can take a step, the air roars with the sound of big guns firing and the three Snapsits behind Marko—the two still standing and the one on the ground— disappear in a cloud of dust and blood and fire.

Everyone turns to see EHL slipping closer to their little circle. As it moves it fires two more shots and both mechanics become nothing more than a memory.

Nixon stays planted behind his pile of parts. Marko and Keet aren't moving either. The three watch EHL rotate, putting Marko and Keet in its sights. EHL fires two more shots, and both men disappear. Dust and grit and bone and blood all hang in the air.

Nixon watches everything begin to settle then begins to move toward his ship. He walks slowly, waiting. Watching. Expecting for someone to get up. Waiting for someone to come around from behind one of these piles of parts that's still standing. They're beaten and bloody but ready to continue the fight. But no one does because no one can. Marko. Keet. The other Snapsits. They don't exist anymore, their bodies nothing more than a fine mist that's now part of the atmosphere.

He finds the blaster that was shot from his hand. It's damaged, but he thinks he can fix it. The Bastic fuel rods are singed, but they've also survived. Nixon picks them up as he passes and starts wiping them clean.

He climbs the ramp into the ship, and the inside of EHL has never felt more comfortable. It's never felt more like home.

The mechanics have ransacked the inside. All the storage cabinets are open. Some of the doors are bent and dented. Some have been ripped from their hinges and tossed to the ground, the cabinet contents scattered across the floor.

Nixon stores the fuel rods in one of the open cabinets and begins putting things back where they belong.

He works in silence, letting himself get lost in the monotony of the tasks, but eventually: "I suppose I should say thank you."

"Sir?"

"For saving me. Out there."

"Of course, sir. It's what we do."

Nixon continues to clear the floor.

"But, sir …"

Nixon stops. "Yes?"

"Never try to replace me again."

04: MAKURRA

ONE

Nixon white-knuckles the captain's seat and digs deep gouges into its arms while EHL shouts a warning.

"Brace for impact, sir. Our approach is too fast."

All Nixon can see out the ship's front window is the on-rush of green. He closes his eyes, bracing for the ship to clip the tops of these trees. He cinches the seat belt tighter on his waist then grabs the arm of the chair again, ready for the ship to ping pong through the trees then crash into the ground and roll who knows where.

He knows nothing about this planet, but judging from these treetops, he knows the surface isn't soft like some pillow. Hit it hard and fast, and it's going to split EHL right open. That will send him tumbling out across its unknown surface into the arms, or pincers, or tentacles of who knows what.

The trees are on them now, and Nixon hears the tops of them start to brush the ship's bottom.

"Brace, sir."

"I brace any harder I'm going to have handfuls of threads and cushion. Just get us down safe."

The trees start to swallow the ship, their topmost leaves now being pulled from their branches and obscuring Nixon's view out the front windshield. Their whish on the sides of the ship gets louder, and the snap of the first tree to break off echoes throughout the ship's interior.

EHL sinks lower into the canopy and the snapping trees become concussive, like Nixon is in some railgun shooting gallery. Pop! Pop! POP! He strains against his belt as the ship suddenly slows.

Then ...

Silence.

The leaves are gone. The branches are cleared. EHL is flying free.

Until...

The trunks on these trees are tight together, and the ship is still impossibly high. EHL attempts to navigate between, banking hard left, but it's too late. The ship clips a trunk and goes spinning. Everything outside the window is now a swirl. EHL is no longer in control. Nixon shouts for her to straighten them up, but there's no time. They clip another trunk, and it sends them spinning off in the opposite direction.

"Do something!" Nixon shouts again.

"There's nothing I can do, sir. We are at the mercy of the galaxy at the moment."

The galaxy—and physics—have them falling faster now. They hit one more tree before colliding with the ground. The impact sends Nixon bouncing out of his seat. His shoulders push hard against the restraints, but he doesn't slip free. EHL bounces once more and then again before sliding to a stop.

Nixon hangs upside down, the seat's restraints and his grip on the arms of the chair the only thing keeping him from falling into the ceiling of the ship.

"Are you okay, sir? EHL asks.

Nixon slips one shoulder out of still-clasped restraints. He pulls the second shoulder out next then grabs the belts and lets gravity do the rest of the work. It flips him around, and he drops feet first from the seat.

He puts a hand up on a weary shoulder and tries to rub away the pain. He can feel a bruise working its way to the surface.

"I'm okay," he says. "Or will be."

He kicks away items at his feet. It's all gear that's fallen from the cabinets and cases that jostled open as EHL pinballed through the trees and across the ground.

"How are you doing?" Nixon asks the ship.

"Assessing, sir." Then the ship goes quiet.

Nixon waits for more of an answer, but one doesn't come. "You let me know when you have something to report."

Nixon starts organizing the mess, pushing related bits of gear into piles. He gets most of the ceiling cleared and has begun putting things back into opened cabinets when the ship returns.

"Preliminarily, my environmental systems are operational. Somehow everything that needs to be working in mechanical is working. It's not perfect, but it's functional. I don't have any way of assessing my physical state. That's something…"

Nixon interrupts: "Yea, that's on me. Do you think you can get that ramp open at least enough for me to crawl out?"

Gears start to grind. They sound worse than normal, and Nixon's breathing quickens. Sweat begins to dampen his forehead. He wants to see light peak through that opening, even if it's just a bit. Otherwise, it means he's stuck in here, like a piece of Bowtan steer meat trapped in the tin.

The gears struggle. The motors that work them slip and whine, but eventually there is light. It's just a sliver, but it's there. Nixon's heart slows, and he waits. The ramp never opens fully, but it opens enough for Nixon to crawl out.

He grabs the opening and swings his legs above his head and forces himself out feet first. He twists and contorts his body so he's laying his front side across the side of EHL. The metal is cool against his belly. He lets himself hang there for a moment. He doesn't know what's below him. He assumes it's solid ground, but it doesn't have to be. He counts a mental three then lets his fingers loose. Gravity pulls him down the side of the ship, and he holds his breath until he feels dirt crunch beneath his feet.

He steps back and looks at EHL. She's in rough shape. Dents all over. A trail of ripped-off side panels litter the forest floor. Almost none of the putty that Nixon had worked so hard to apply to her sides has survived the crash.

This is going to be murder to fix.

But maybe this is a blessing. He needs to disguise her anyway. With her already in pieces, he can put her back together anyway he wants.

GALAXY RUN: THE COMPLETE FIRST SERIES

TWO

Nixon returns to the half-opened ramp and jumps, trying to hook his fingers over the narrow opening. He just misses the first time, and he slides down the metal sides of the ship. He just gets hold on his second jump and scrambles his feet up the ship's slick metal. He drops back through the opening and takes another look around the ship.

He knows there's work to do outside, but there's work to do in here too. Panels are separated from panels. Lights that should be on aren't. He knows that all the screens on the dash are likely irreparably busted. He starts making a mental list of everything he'll need to get EHL operational again, when the ship speaks.

"I have a detailed status report."

Nixon finishes picking up a tool set that's been scattered across the floor and putting it back into a storage bin. The lid closes with a loud snap and he says, "OK. Go.

"All of my systems are operational. We have problems with one of the engines. It's only showing to be operating at half its capability, but that doesn't preclude us from regular operations."

"So, you'll still fly."

"Well, my systems are operational. They are in flying shape. I can't speak to whether or not my condition is flight worthy."

"Surprise," Nixon says. "It's not."

Nixon pulls a loose bin over to him and sits.

"So, what happened?" he asks. "How did we end up here?"

"How far back should I go?"

Nixon thinks back through what he knows, saying out loud that he remembers the alarms sounding.

"Yes, sir. After our previous pair of visitors, I fine-tuned our indicators. I set them to pick up traffic earlier. This ship tripped those early warning systems."

Nixon says he remembers EHL picking up speed quickly but the alarm not going off.

"No, sir. This ship continued to gain on us no matter how fast we went."

Nixon's mind immediately goes back to Marko's speeder that he'd intended to leave Ibilia in. Could this have been that ship? Did someone Marko knew give them chase for a bit of revenge? No, he thinks. Marko and all of his little goons were left worse than dead.

Nixon says he remembers the evasive maneuvers. He remembers EHL beginning to dip and dive again, twisting one way and then another, throwing Nixon and his equilibrium upside down. He says it nearly caused him to pass out. Then he remembers a second alarm.

"Yes, sir. Incoming fire warning. The ship started shooting."

"Several shots, right?

"Yes, sir. We were able to successfully avoid those shots, but as the ship got closer it was going to be harder to keep them off of us. Harder to keep them from getting one of those shots to land."

Nixon nods. "So, you ..."

"I saw this planet coming up and hoped that I'd be able to use whatever was on the surface as some kind of cover."

"And the reckless drop into the trees ..."

"Again, a defensive decision. I was hoping that whoever was the pilot would see how recklessly we were flying and wouldn't follow us in.

"At least you recognize how reckless it was."

Nixon moves to one of EHL's displays and asks the ship to bring up video. He's hoping to be able to find any kind of identifying marks on whoever or whatever it was that had chased them.

"One moment."

Nixon stares at the black screen and taps a rhythm with his fingers on the display's frame. A moment later footage from EHL's rear camera appears.

"I'm afraid there won't be much there," the ship says.

Nixon doesn't respond, just watches the images play out in front of him. EHL isn't wrong. The other ship never gets close. It doesn't become much more than a dot on the display. It does fire. Three shots jump from that pinpoint on the display. Blasts of deep green scream by the camera, Nixon recognizing now just how close he'd come to becoming a tangled ball of burning space debris. The decision to take a chance at crashing through the trees looks like the right one now.

The video stops, and EHL turns the screen black again.

"Do we know what happened to that ship?

EHL doesn't respond for a moment then: "According to my data it followed us into atmosphere, but I don't know any more than that. I lost the signal pretty quickly."

"And you lost that signal when we crashed onto ...

"One more moment."

"It looks like we are on Makurra."

"Makurra," Nixon repeats.

"Yes, sir. Mostly uninhabited."

That's not good. Nixon needs supplies. He needs to fix this ship, to give it a new look and a new identity. Some of that he can do without new gear. There's metal scattered across the ground outside the ship that he can beat back into usable shape. But he can't do that with all of it. He needs someone or something who can sell him those tools and materials.

"How uninhabited?" he asks, hoping that EHL will come back that there's at least a couple of population centers here.

"One more moment.

Nixon paces what should be the ceiling of the ship. It's quiet while EHL digs for Nixon's answer, the only sound his feet shuffling across the metal. He makes one circle and then another.

The displays in front of Nixon light up, and EHL begins talking again. It's a map of the northern hemisphere of a planet that looks to be mostly lush and green. An indicator appears on one side of the map.

"This," she says as it begins to blink, "is our current location."

A second light begins to blink. "That is the nearest place with any significant population."

Nixon studies the distance, and, no matter how he looks at it, it's far.

"Two days walk," EHL says, like it knows what Nixon is thinking. "Two full days.

Nixon doesn't say anything. He looks at one blinking light and then to the other then takes out his datapad. He starts taking inventory and making a list of things he needs. If he's going to make that walk, he only wants to make it once.

THREE

Nixon keeps repeating the name of the planet, putting the accent on a different syllable every time.

Ma-KUR-ra.

MA-kur-ra.

Ma-kur-RA.

The last one makes him chuckle, and his laugh fills the forest. He left EHL hours ago with a map displayed on his reader, but the route isn't complicated. Head east.

When he first left, all of this was interesting, trees stretching so high that the tops of them disappeared into the suns-brightened sky. Now it's just monotonous and frustrating.

The trees grow together so tightly that Nixon has to walk a twisting path through them, and it's making his progress slow. He runs his fingers across the smooth trunks as he passes them. He pulls off long curls of thin bark and ties them into knots that he then throws to the ground.

Earlier, the forest had been alive. Animals had scurried at his feet. Wild Farrow birds sang from the trees' high branches. Now, though, the suns are beginning to disappear and casting slashing shadows across everything. The birds have gone quiet. The animals are all calm, and, except for his steps, everything is silent.

Nixon stops for a moment and begins to consider whether or not this should be the end of the first day's walk. He has no plan for this little journey beyond "Walk as long as you can." He assumed that would be until it became too dark to go any farther, but he can see now that dark is going to come on quickly.

He looks, for what he doesn't know. All of this appears the same. Tree after tree after tree as far as he can see in any direction. He has nothing on him but his cloak, the case, the blaster and two Bastic fuel rods.

The case he's keeping in a pocket inside his cloak. The blaster is tucked into the waistband of his pants. And the fuel rods are wrapped in an old oily blanket he found on the floor after it fell out of a busted cabinet he never knew existed.

He begins walking again. If it's all the same, then he might as well make as much progress as he can before stopping. The forest floor is covered in a thick layer of leaves and branches, and he pushes them into deep piles as he shuffle-steps his way through the trees. The winds begin to pick up, blowing cold. They rustle the leaves above him and push his piles back out flat.

It's nearly a full dark now, and he activates the screen on his reader. He holds it out in front of him to give himself enough light to keep going.

"Would you just stop?"

Nixon quick-turns, his reader still extended out in front of him, and the light shines bright on Shaine's face. Stir Crazy Shaine. He's back.

Nixon drops the reader, and Shaine stays lit with a soft glow. It does nothing to help light Nixon's way, but it does make Shaine visible in the dark forest.

"Hey, Shaine."

Shaine steps in front of Nixon and around the next tree. He's looking into the black sky. "Where are we?"

"Ma-kur-RA." Nixon laughs again.

"Never heard of it."

Nixon has his reader back out in front of him and steps around the next tree and then the one after that. "Me either."

"Well, if you had and I hadn't then I'd be surprised."

Nixon follows Shaine through a few more trees before Shaine stops. Nixon stops too, and Shaine turns to him.

"Seriously. This is ridiculous. You need to stop."

Nixon knows Shaine's right. It's late. His already-slow progress is even slower now. And his body is starting to feel the effects of this walk and the crash earlier.

He turns a slow circle, holding his reader out in front of him as far as he can. Everything looks the same. Trees. Trees. Trees. So he sits where he stands.

He pushes the leaves and branches into tall piles behind him until he sees the bare dirt of the forest floor. He pulls his cloak over his head and the blaster from his waistband. He lays the cloak on the ground in front of him and lays the blaster in the middle. He folds the cloak around the blaster and into a neat square. He places the cloak behind him and lays his head on it like a pillow. Shaine is still standing and watches Nixon make himself comfortable.

"So, what's your plan?" Shaine asks.

Nixon thinks for a moment then pushes himself up on his elbows. "My plan?"

He finishes pushing himself up until he's sitting upright again. He scoots until his back is leaning against a tree.

Nixon continues: "My plan is to finish this walk tomorrow and use whatever I can get for these fuel rods to buy whatever I need to build a machine that will take me back to that alley on Exte so I can let the Uzeks do whatever it is they were going to do to me. Let them get their pound of flesh. That way we'd be even. I don't throw those punches, I don't shoot Uzel, and I'm not here. I don't have to meet you. I don't take that damned case. Life is back to normal."

Shaine sits. "That really what you wish?"

Nixon thinks for a moment then says "No.

He pauses again. "What I really wish is that I could build that machine and go back farther. Back to when we were kids. To whatever day we met so I could avoid you. We don't meet then who knows how my life goes. Better than this. Fighting. Escaping. Running away. Sleeping on the floor of some forest."

"Hurtful," Shaine says.

"Don't get all twisted up. You aren't real. Remember.

Shaine stands back up and turns away from Nixon, looking out into the dark of the forest. "Want to know what I think?" he asks.

"About?"

"About you. About all of it.

Nixon stands to join Shaine. The forest's night animals are starting to wake.

"If I say …" Nixon begins but doesn't get to finish.

"I think even if you don't meet me, nothing changes. You are who you are. I was who I was. And we weren't all that different. So, even without me, you end up here, or somewhere a lot like it."

Nixon doesn't say anything in return. They just stand in the quiet and listen to the patter of little feet on hard dirt.

"Yeah," Nixon says. "You're probably right."

He sits back down and leans against his tree. He reaches his hand up behind him and digs a nail into the soft bark and starts pulling off thin strips. He ties the end of one to the end of the next, making a long uneven chain.

He works in silence for a moment before Shaine sits and leans against the tree across from Nixon.

"You do have a plan, though, right?"

Nixon tightens one of his knots then pulls on the two pieces of bark to check that the connection is secure.

"I'm going to finish this walk tomorrow and get supplies to disguise the ship. There's pictures of it all over the boards the bounty hunters use. I have to make her unrecognizable."

"Physically unrecognizable."

"What?"

"You're making her physically unrecognizable. No matter what it looks like on the outside, the transponder will still give up her actual identity."

Shaine's right. He hasn't planned for the transponder. He hasn't made it there yet, but he's nearly certain that no one in the little bit of civilization EHL found is going to have anything technical like that.

"So what does that mean?" Nixon asks. "Is all of this pointless? Am I wasting my time trying to disguise this ship?"

"No, it's not a waste of time," Shaine says. "But you do have a problem you need to figure out."

Stir Crazy Shaine is just a creation of Nixon's bored and worried mind, only knowing what Nixon knows. He's Nixon's thoughts manifested in the body of his dead friend, and Nixon knows that. Even Shaine knows it. Still, that hasn't kept him from talking all night.

When Shaine finally gets quiet, Nixon asks him a question. "Did you know this would happen? All this trouble?"

Shaine takes a deep breath. He looks up into the dark canopy above them then out into the dark of the forest.

"Did I know?"

Shaine goes quiet again, and Nixon waits out his answer.

"I mean, we don't really know what I knew, so I can't give you a definitive answer. But if we think it out. … I knew more than you did, for sure. I knew who I was working with. Or at least in theory, I did. I probably knew there was at least some level of danger, right?"

Nixon has his fingers interlaced behind his neck. He's pulling his head off the ground and looking at Shaine as he talks, and he's realizing that their relationship had never changed. Even now, with their little partnership just a memory, Shaine is putting Nixon in the hard spot. He's shoving him out front, walking the point, putting him in the crosshairs. Literally this time.

Seriously, Shaine. Gutu Inkoa. Gutu Inkoa

And as he thinks that, Shaine and his faint light blink off. Nixon is alone in the forest. Well, not alone. He puts his head down on his folded cloak. He drifts off listening to the distant mewing of some nocturnal creature that he hopes doesn't see him as dinner.

It doesn't, and he wakes when the heat of the suns warm his face. The mewing from the night before is gone, and the birds have returned. He pulls his cloak back over his head and secures the blaster back into his waistband. The case is still in the pocket from yesterday. He grabs the fuel rods and picks up his journey.

He walks for half the day when the forest starts to thin out. The trees aren't as tightly packed, and he nearly trips over the stumps that are poking up from the ground. The tops of these stumps have been worn smooth by time, but they're even. They aren't jagged. Someone or something has cut these trees down, and there are only a couple of reasons you do that. To build with it or burn it. Either way, it means he's close to something.

He picks up his pace, and the forest continues to thin. The number of stumps continues to grow. He smells it first: smoke from a fire.

Then he hears it: voices.

Then he sees it: It's a three-quarter circle of buildings. Behind these are more buildings, built here and there in no discernible pattern.

This isn't a city. It's not a town either. It's just a collection of structures. Like something you'd find if you were among the first settlers on a new planet, everyone getting off the big ship and building a home wherever they can find space. And even though you'd just spent months or years on the big ship living in tight quarters, no one wants to get too far from anyone else just in case this new planet is full of big, green meanies. So, the first settlement is a clump of structures, thrown up haphazard but with a purpose—protection.

The voices Nixon hears are coming from a handful of people in front of an arc of buildings. They are gathered around a waist-high fire pit. Smoke is rolling out of the top, and the conversation has turned animated. Nixon watches for a moment before he hears: "See something interesting, friend?"

FOUR

"You've been standing here staring at my real friends for a bit of time now."

The big man behind this deep voice has his arms raised to his chest and is working a grubby fist into the palm of his other hand.

"You're carrying something wrapped in those rags that looks long and stiff. You've got a blaster of some kind tucked into your pants under that cloak. You'll excuse me if I'm a little suspicious."

Nixon puts his hands up, palms out. The galactic signal that he means the man or his friends no harm.

He starts to explain: "I've had a ..."

Then he hesitates and begins doing mental calculations while he looks the guy over. Head shaved smooth. Stained shirt tucked into some kind of heavy-fabric work pant. A rubber apron around his neck. Combine that with threatening language and a threatening posture, and Nixon changes course.

"I'm no threat," he starts over. "I have a blaster in my belt. I'll let you hold it if that makes you more comfortable. I need some gear to fix a ship. In the rags is what I was hoping I might be able to trade for that gear. If you'll let me, I can open it and show you."

The man gives Nixon permission with the quick nod of his head.

Nixon lays the rods on the ground and begins to carefully untangle them from the old rags.

Their tell-tale green glow creeps out of the folds of the rags and Nixon's new friend can't help himself. He kneels next to Nixon, his scarred and scratched hands twitching, doing everything they can not to reach out and grab the rods.

"Are those …" he starts to ask but never finishes his question.

Nixon is already nodding. "Bastic fuel rods."

"Where did you …" He doesn't finish this question either.

"Traded for them. The rods for a little work."

The man looks up to Nixon, looks him up and down.

"What kind of work does a guy like you do for payment like that?"

"The hard kind." The work wasn't that hard. Dangerous, sure. But driving a flat truck full of these rods for mile after mile could have had disastrous consequences for Nixon, but this new friend doesn't know that. If he thinks rods means Nixon is somehow dangerous or unpredictable then Nixon isn't going to correct him.

Nixon wraps the rods back up in the rags and stands. The other man does too.

"You said you needed ship parts?" the man says, still looking at the oily ragged package lying on the ground.

"I have a list. You have someone who can help?

The man finally looks back to Nixon. "I might. Follow me."

The man turns and walks into the heart of the arc of buildings. Nixon scoops up the rag-wrapped rods and follows. They aren't more than a few steps into their walk and Nixon already feels eyes on him. Watching from door ways. Watching through windows. He's new here, and new always gets attention in a place like this, a place where things don't often change.

Most everyone watching him is human, and something about that feels better. It shouldn't. He knows that. It was humans who killed Shaine. It's humans who chased him off one planet and across two others. He won't hesitate to pull a blaster on any of them. Won't hesitate to burn a few holes in their chests if he has to. And he knows the feeling is mutual. Still, he's human. They're human. He knows how they think, how they reason and react.

They pass the clutch of men having a discussion in the middle of the arc. All the talking stops. They look to Nixon's new friend, and it's clear he's trying to tell them something without saying a word. Nixon sees their eyes narrow. They aren't understanding. Then they go wide with recognition. Message received.

Nixon and his friend pass and a few steps later the other men start to follow. Nixon takes tighter hold of the rods. He puts his free hand inside of his cloak and rests it on the blaster—ready to pull, ready to fire.

They pass the halfway point of the arc, and Nixon's new friend points to a building a little farther down the line. This walking trip takes twice the time it would have taken if this man had walked Nixon straight there, and Nixon is now realizing that the walk was to put him on display. It was so everyone could get a good look at him. "Look everyone. New guy. Size him up. Measure him out."

Nixon looks back up to the door of the building his friend pointed to and a man steps into the doorway and leans on the jamb. He's wiping his hands on a rag. He's wearing a rubber apron, just like Nixon's friend, and tucks the rag into the tied belt that's keeping the apron cinched around his waist.

Nixon's friend waves and the man standing in the door shouts "Did you tell him that we don't take too kindly to strangers?"

Nixon's friend shouts back: "I think this is someone you'll want to meet."

The man comes down the steps that drop from the narrow porch that extends the length of the building.

"Why's that?" he shouts.

"Just trust me."

All this man's boldness and bluster disappears at the sight of the Bastic fuel rods.

"Yeah, I think we can help you find some things to fix that ship," he says through a goofy grin.

"Told you," Nixon's friend says.

The inside of this building is a disorganized mess. Small bits of this and that are pushed into piles on the floor. Larger items are leaned against the wall.

There's an open door leading to the back, where things that don't fit inside are sitting on the ground.

This isn't a shop. It's not organized like that. It's more of a storage space, just somewhere that the members of this commune can bring things they don't need or get things that they do.

Nixon pulls out his reader and taps his way to the list he created earlier. He begins reading the items off one at a time. Nixon's friend and the man who organizes the space start picking through piles for the parts Nixon needs. And if they don't have something that matches his request exactly they offer options that might work.

Nixon, while the two men scramble around: "You mind if I ask you guys some questions?"

"You can ask," the shop owner says, "but no promises that we're going to answer. Makurra isn't the kind of place people come to if they want to answer a bunch of questions."

Nixon notes and asks anyway.

How many people are here? A couple hundred.

All human? So far.

How'd they get here? Silence.

How long have they been here? Long enough.

Is there someone who can get Nixon food and supplies for the ship? Let them finish here.

It takes just more than an hour, but most of the items are checked off Nixon's list. All the small parts—the fasteners and catches and hooks—are in a couple of boxes at Nixon's feet. The larger items are stacked near the door or have been brought out the front of the shop from the back.

"I think that's the best we can do," the organizer says.

Nixon looks at the gear by his feet then the gear out the door and gives a nod. "I'm appreciative."

He lays the oily rag-wrapped rods on the counter he's been leaning against. "And these are yours."

Both men look to each other and smile. Nixon's original friend then turns to Nixon.

"You've got a lot of gear here." Nixon nods that he does. "Where's your ship. Maybe we can help you get it back there."

Nixon almost tells them that it's two days' walk through the forest, but he doesn't. Something inside of him pricks something else. A warning. Share only what you have to with these guys. No more than that. Maybe it's the looks they've been giving each other. Maybe it's that they've made it clear they don't much like strangers. Maybe it's that he sees too much of himself in each of these men, a schemer always looking for a leg up or another score. He doesn't know what it is in the moment, he just knows that the years have taught him to listen to his instinct once it starts singing.

"I'll have to make multiple trips."

"Maybe not," the organizer says then disappears out the back door and around the corner. He comes back a moment later with a float cart. It's long and flat and just fits through the doorway. The man picks up the two boxes at Nixon's feet and drops them onto the cart. The cart bounces and tips to one side with the new weight, but a moment later levels itself.

"You can have this. We've got two others and don't use this one."

The man kicks the back of the cart and it floats out the front door and down the steps. It stops near the stack of larger parts. Nixon and the two men load the cart. It takes a moment for Nixon to get used to the cart shifting and dancing every time he puts another metal panel or sprayer of paint onto it, but eventually he does.

Once everything is loaded, he and the other men step back and look at their work. If he can keep the cart level—and that's not his job; the cart will do that for him—then everything should be fine.

He gives the cart a nudge and it begins moving slowly away from him. He gives both men a wave and thanks them for doing business.

"No," the organizer says. "Thank you."

Nixon turns and begins to head across the center of the arc and back toward the forest that he walked through to get here. He gets a couple of dozen steps away then stops and turns back. The two men are furiously talking. Nixon watches for a moment and all of his alarm bells are ringing again. That bad feeling he'd had since he found the arc is doubled now. These men aren't the kind to be happy with a little. They always want more. And in this case, they want more fuel rods.

FIVE

The two men stop talking once they notice Nixon watching them.

"Food?" Nixon asks. "Anyone here have some they'll trade for credits?"

The shop owner points to a building still ahead of Nixon. A woman is standing in the doorway, and she waves at Nixon when he spots her.

The cabinets in EHL's galley aren't nearly as full as they were when he was back on Umel. He stops the cart and pulls his reader from his pocket. He taps and swipes his way to his credit balance. It's not much, but it should be able to buy him a box of something dried out and packed tight, as long as he can charm the woman into giving him a discount.

"Come in," the woman says then turns and disappears into the dark of her shop. "But leave the cart out there."

His goal of charming her just got much harder.

"What can I get you?" she asks Nixon as he climbs the steps and crosses through the door.

"I need to get ..." he begins to answer then stops. He was going to ask for a case of noodles to rehydrate. Planet like this, that's the best he figures he can get. But, no. This building is packed to the point of bursting with food he hasn't seen in years. Things he'd only see through restaurant windows on Exte. Or on the plates of people eating on a patio.

"You need to get what?" the woman asks.

"Food," Nixon says, still taking all of it in.

"Well …" she says and gestures broadly to the room.

Nixon doesn't know where to start. All of it is tantalizing. He wants to grab armfuls of everything and take them back to the float cart and load it down so heavy that it overwhelms all of the cart's internal technology and just lays on the ground.

But he realizes he doesn't have enough room on the cart or enough storage space on the ship to handle that much food. So he's as judicious as his hungry mind will let him be. He starts picking out things he hasn't eaten in years. He grabs ingredients for dishes his mom made. He doesn't know these recipes, but he doesn't care. He'll figure them out. And even if all he can figure out is a close approximation, it'll be better than eating another container of noodles.

But his judicious mind tells him that all of this other food is fine, but he also needs to be practical. He grabs a case of the noodles that he's come to hate. No, they don't taste good, and no, they offer very little nutritional value. But they are easy to make and easy to store, and that accounts for quite a lot out here.

He thanks the woman after he gets the last of the boxes loaded onto his cart then begins the long walk back to his ship. This cart makes his walk easier, no doubt. But it also makes it longer. He learns quickly that he can't walk through the forest the same way he came. The cart sits too low to navigate its way over the stumps, and it'll be too wide to fit between the trees once he gets closer to EHL. So he's walking around the forest, and he's not nearly halfway back to his ship by the time the suns start to set behind the mountains and everything in the valley gets quickly dark.

Finding a place to camp isn't nearly as easy this time. Without the protection of the trees, he feels very exposed. The mewling he heard the previous morning is back. And it's louder. And there's definitely more than one of them this time.

He turns the light on from his reader and pulls boxes off the float cart and stacks them like bricks one on top of the other. He tips the float card up on its side and makes for himself a bunker. It's not much protection, but at least it makes him feel more confident.

He lays his head down and hopes that sleep will come. He begins thinking of the day and then thinking more specifically of the food in the boxes all around him.

He gets excited about the meals in the coming days. He thinks again about dishes his mother used to make. About their small, cramped apartment outside the city. About the stories she used to tell him when dad still hadn't come home after he'd been expected days earlier. Thinks about how even though dad was more than a week late arriving from whatever questionable job he'd taken, she'd explain it away with a story for Nixon that seemed plausible at the time. Then he thinks about the smells that came from the kitchen and the food on the plates in front of him. About how mom used food as a salve, as medicine to calm a young boy's worried mind.

He's thinking about one specific meal—it was the meal she always made the night before dad would come back home. It was a signal to Nixon that everything was going to be alright. He finally falls asleep thinking about the food in the boxes that he's hoping to use to recreate that feeling.

He wakes the next morning and reloads the cart, putting everything back on in the same order that he took it off. It's easy work, but it takes time. When he's finished, the suns are well above the mountain tops, and Nixon has worked up a sweat. He takes off his cloak and drapes it across the top of the boxes on the cart.

He gives the cart a push and it slides and bounces forward. He stays a couple steps behind. This is the pattern the entire day. He gives the cart a gentle push and it slides a little bit forward. He walks to catch up. He gives a push again. Over and over and over until it's dark. Finally using the light from his reader to guide his path back to EHL.

He unloads the float cart in the dark, stacking the food boxes on top of the ship near the busted ramp. He puts all of the repair gear in neat piles close to the ship. He covers the smaller bits with the large metal panels. He knows there's no one out here to see his gear, but life has taught him but it's better to be safe than sorry.

He tries to jump on legs that are tired from a full day's walk, and he can barely do it. He needs to hook his fingers on the opening of the busted ramp and scramble his way inside of the ship. He tries and misses. He leans a hand on the ship and tries to will a bit of energy in his muscles. He gives it one more shot, and the fingertips of one hand just catch. He swings the other hand up to grab the opening. He works his feet up the side of the ship and swings his legs up and into the hole left by the ramp. He drops inside.

He'd dropped the food in before him. He looks at the boxes. He's hungry. No, he's starving. It's been two full days since he's eaten anything at all, and that was just noodles.

He thinks long and hard about digging into the new food, the good food. Making one of those meals he spent the entire day thinking about. But he doesn't. It's late; he's tired, and he just needs to eat. So, he unpacks noodles—more noodles—and eats them cold.

SIX

It's a grunt. Or a snort. Nixon can't tell. He hasn't heard another, but one was enough to wake him from a fitful night of sleep. His mind sprints hard and fast to the Uzeks.

Nixon reaches all around him, looking for his blaster. He peeled off the cloak last night once he was inside the ship. He tossed it aside, pulled the blaster from his waistband and tossed it too.

He finds the cloak first, his hand landing with a dull thump on crumpled fabric. He hits the case next, his hand knocking it across the floor when it connects. But there's still no blaster. He spins, slapping around faster, frantic.

Another grunt comes from outside. He looks to the opening that the ramp can't close up. He's feeling around behind him and watching and waiting. Any moment now he's expecting to see fat, green fingers wrap themselves around that edge.

And if I had this damn blaster, I'd be able to turn them into a pulpy mess.

But there are no fingers, and Nixon has finally had enough of this blind searching. He looks away from the opening and quickly scans the room—he'd slept in the main cabin on what should be the wall since EHL was still resting on its side. There's the blaster, far behind him—an impossible reach if he was still groping around. He scrambles on his hands and heels and grabs the blaster. He aims it at the opening. He waits a moment and then another, still expecting to see something look down on him.

And when it does

He fakes a shot.

But after a third and fourth moment, the opening is still empty. He approaches cautiously then tucks the blaster into his waistband when he gets directly underneath. He jumps and grabs hold of the edge of the opening and pulls himself up quickly. If someone is out there, this is when he'll be most vulnerable. He'll do what he can to limit that

He sticks his head out and scans the area around his ship quickly. He can't see anything, but he does hear a third grunt. It's coming from right below him. He slips his body almost imperceptibly closer to the edge of the ship and looks down.

A Fison hog. That's all it is. Rooting around the ship and the gear stacked outside.

He laughs at himself. The Fison hog looks up once it hears him then scampers off.

Another one appears from the other side of the ship and runs off after its companion, snorting as it heads for the opening that leads from the trees out into the open field.

Nixon watches these two rejoin a group of five or six gathered there then drops back into the ship. He tears into one of the boxes of new food and pulls out a package of bread that he'd eagerly picked up yesterday. He grabs a knife from the galley and cuts himself a thick slice. He eats it slowly, savoring the sweet and spice on his tongue. He wraps up the remains of the loaf and puts it and the rest of the food into the cabinets and bins in the galley.

He goes through the rest of the ship securing anything loose. With EHL still on its side, his first task, before he can begin any of the real work, is going to be getting the ship back upright.

He jumps back up through the ramp and slides down the side of the ship. He looks back out to the clearing. More

Fison hogs have joined the others that were already there. They all have their heads down, digging through the dirt with their snouts.

Across the field is a hill, and beyond that are mountains. Everything is bright and green. It's all calm and quiet. And it's all things that Nixon has missed. He's spent so much of his adult life around others, trapped inside of civilization, he forgets that not everything is like that. Most things aren't like that. Places like Makurra still exist, and being here doesn't seem like such a bad life.

One day, I'll get back. Bring buckets of credits and buy supplies and another float cart from someone and build myself a little place here where I can listen to the sounds of nothing and just enjoy the peace.

He turns to EHL and puts a hand on her side. The metal is cool. He gives the ship a push and she doesn't move. He steps closer and leans a shoulder into the ship and digs his feet into the dirt. He pushes hard, and she rocks. It's slight, but it's something. He leans in hard again and digs his feet a little deeper into the dirt. He pushes harder, and it moves again. He'll never get her over on his own, but she will go over. He just needs some help.

He steps back and looks around the forest floor. He needs a rock, a good-sized rock, something vaguely triangular if he can find it. EHL's crash landing into the forest floor left a deep trench dug deep into the dirt. It's snapped smaller trees and scattered their branches and trunks all over. It's also helped to uncover rocks that Nixon would have never found on his own.

It doesn't take long for him to find what he needs. It's a rock with a broad flat side. And rising from that flat side, the rest of the rock narrows. It's perfect.

Nixon doesn't know much about science. He quit going to school long before they ever got to the tough stuff. But he did learn about simple machines. Ramps and pulleys. Levers and ... he holds the rock out in front of him. Fulcrums.

He looks at the ship and places the rock in approximately the center of her mass a couple of feet away.

Next, he needs something for leverage. He needs a pole, something long and heavy. Luckily, the crash landing helped there too. The tops of the trees EHL snapped off are scattered among the limbs and trunks of the smaller ones.

Nixon quickly finds a pair of thick and sturdy trunks. He drags them closer to the ship and begins pulling off the small limbs and branches that survived the fall to the forest floor.

He grabs one of the branches and tests its weight in his hand. He looks close for any kind of breaks or cracks. Then he heads to the opposite side of EHL, the direction he wants to roll her, and starts to dig at the dirt she's laying on. He's pulling it out in large piles. Hopefully, this is going to make it easier to get her to roll back upright. Once the dirt is moved—she looks like she's perched on a precarious ledge—he goes back around to the other side, tossing the digging stick back out into the brush.

Cleaned, he shoves the end of one of the trunks underneath EHL and sets what looks like roughly the center of the trunk on the smaller, smoother side of the rock. The free end is angled to the sky, and it's higher than he anticipated. He jumps, trying to grab the trunk, but it's too high. His fingertips brush the underside of the trunk, but he can't get a steady hold in it.

He finds another rock and sets it on the ground then climbs on top. He jumps from there and grabs the end of the branch, but EHL doesn't budge. He just hangs a few feet off the ground.

He drops. He needs more weight, and he has an idea. He climbs back inside of the ship. He pulls out a couple of the deeper drawers from the cabinets in the main cabin. He goes to another cabinet and fights it open, the cabinet's frame twisted in the crash. He pulls out two long lengths of rope. He tosses it all back through the opening from the ramp and listens to it land on the dirt outside with a thump. He climbs back out and starts securing the rope to the drawers then loops the rope over the top of the tree trunk so both drawers are now hanging there like baskets.

He steps back and starts looking for rocks again. He grabs the biggest he can and starts putting them into the drawers/baskets. He loads the first and then the second. EHL rocks, but only slightly. He climbs back onto the second rock he found and jumps for the trunk. He hangs there for a second before he feels himself start to drop.

It's not the quick and violent flip that he'd played out in his head during his walk back from the little arc of shops. It's slower. More graceful, but only to a point. There's a moment when gravity overtakes grace. And when it does, EHL resettles with a rumble and a crash that echoes through the forest. Nixon pauses, half expecting to see someone come running from somewhere in the trees shouting "What was that?"

But when the echoing stops, there's no one else there. It's quiet. He's alone. He starts digging through the pile of gear he bought the day before. His first step to getting EHL flying again is to patch her holes, so he gets busy cutting metal to fit, he starts slapping it on the ship's sides. It's not easy work, but a few hours later, EHL looks whole again. She's ugly as all get out, looking like one of those long quilts Nixon's mom made for their bed when he was a boy. But that will soon be taken care of.

He walks back to the busted ramp and into the ship. He opens the food he bought yesterday and pushes past the containers of noodles and pulls out a tin of hen meat and peels off the top. He dumps the container into a bowl and begins mixing this and that into it, trying to copy a memory that's playing in his head. It's his mom making him the same thing for lunch when he was a boy. He's sitting at the kitchen table and she's working over at the counter, singing a song to herself.

He puts the bowl to the side and picks out a package of crackers from his food stash then moves everything over to the small table in the galley. It's a booth moulded out of plastic. The cushion covering the seats are identical to the thin mattress on top of his bed.

He piles a large spoonful of the hen mixture on top of a cracker and takes a bite. It's sweet and tangy, just as he remembers. He closes his eyes and he's back at that table with his mother. She's listening to him tell one of those hard-to-follow stories children tell parents. She's smiling and watching him eat but without a plate of her own, something she did often. It never registered with Nixon as a boy, but it's something he now thinks about regularly often—mostly when his own stomach is begging for food.

"That looks delicious."

It's Shaine.

Nixon opens his eyes. "It is."

Nixon takes another bite. "What's in it?"

Nixon runs down the list of ingredients then says: "I've been thinking about it. Something you told me the other night. That whether or not I'd met you, my life would have turned out the same."

Nixon takes another bite then continues through a mouthful of food: "You're wrong."

"I'm not wrong. I was who I was. You are who you are. The galaxy assigns us roles. There's no shame in it. But it's better to embrace it."

Nixon shakes his head and takes the last bite of his mixture-topped cracker. He takes his bowl over to the counter and wipes it out with a towel that's lying there.

"I don't believe that anymore," he says as he leaves the galley. He heads back through the opening and outside. Shaine is there waiting.

"It's not something that's up to you to believe or not believe. It's a fact. You and I weren't made for fancy dress and jobs in those glass towers. We're lower than that. And I don't mean that as an insult. It's just the truth."

Nixon is working as Shaine talks. He's pulling the large sprayers of paint from the stack of gear he'd bought. He's hooking them up to the large compressor units he'd also bought.

Shaine continues: "You weren't unhappy when we were working together. We laughed. We had fun."

Nixon gives the sprayer unit a light squeeze and a fine mist shoots from the end.

"We were. And then you left. The last ten years for me has been brutal. It's been day-to-day. No planning for anything other than how I get to the next sunrise. You were off making the life we'd both dreamed about. You had Mira and a home and a family."

Nixon turns his back on Shaine and begins putting a first coat of paint onto EHL. He's envisioned a two-toned look with red on the bottom and a muddy green on the top. The red is going on first. He concentrates on applying an even coat, and Shaine defends himself.

"Don't put your disappointments on me. You said you were happy for me. Happy that I'd found someone."

Nixon continues to work. "I was happy for you. For you. But for me, it was the worst thing that could have happened. I relied on you. I depended on you. My future was tied to yours. And for the last ten years I've just been floating out there, like a ship that's lost its engines. Things pushing me this way or that, but me never getting to go the direction that I want to go. Never getting to live my life."

"I'm sorry to hear that, friend," Shaine says. "But your inability to make a decision about what you want to do isn't my fault."

Nixon stops painting for a second. He stands and looks to Shaine. This vision of Shaine looks back.

"Goodbye, Shaine."

And he disappears.

SEVEN

The second of Makurra's suns is still behind the mountains when Nixon makes his way outside the next morning. He picks up the first green sprayer of paint and attaches it to the compressor then gets to work.

The green isn't going on as easy as the red, and he can tell right away that he's going to need a second coat to get the look he wants to make sure EHL is unrecognizable. He doesn't mind, though. He's enjoying himself. He's stretching a creative side of his brain, something that doesn't always get used like this unless some con has gone wrong. Then it's creativity all the time just to figure out how to survive the next few minutes.

This, though, is scratching that creator side, that maker side. It's taking a steady hand to get the paint to go on even. Even paint means a professional probably did it. Even paint doesn't look like you're some small-time crook trying to slap fake glasses or a funny nose on your ship. So it's slow and methodical, back and forth.

The sprayer of green sputters then stops. He unscrews it from the compressor then steps back to look at his work. His conversation with Stir Crazy Shaine from the night before has been rolling around his head all morning. He keeps replaying one exchange over and over. The idea that Shaine keeps putting forward that they are bound by some kind of galactic force that predetermines who they can be.

He admires his work. "This, Shaine. I could have done this."

And he really believes it. If his life had taken another turn, he could see himself with a little shop on some crowded planet where he'd have a crew that did nothing but fix busted ships. He'd step out of the office a few times a week to still get his hands dirty. But mostly he'd watch through a window as his team moved ships in and out and the credits accumulated in his bank account.

He attaches the second sprayer and gets back to work. It doesn't take long before he's lost again in the work, the rhythm of the painting. He starts to hear those voices in that imaginary shop. He hears the crowds passing on the streets. The laughter of his team. He sees the smiles of happy customers.

He gets so wrapped up in his own mind and lost in the task in front of him—applying this second coat of green paint—that he doesn't eat. He just works until this sprayer of paint also sputters and stops.

He steps back again and looks at EHL. He's happy. This new paint gives her personality. She looks mean. She looks like the ship of someone serious. But most importantly, she looks completely different, completely unrecognizable.

His stomach reminds him that he hasn't eaten since this morning. He sets down the sprayer and heads back into the ship. He thinks about making a stew from his childhood but doesn't want to wait that long. So, instead, he grabs what's left of the loaf of bread from yesterday morning. He takes it back outside with him, tearing big bites with his teeth.

He sits in the opening where the ramp should be closed up and relaxes into the feelings of a job well done. He works on an extra-large bite of the bread, and again savors the flavor he hasn't had since he was a boy

He looks out through the forest at the field that's just beyond. It's filled with knee-high grass and tiny yellowpetalled flowers. Beyond that the foothills of the mountains begin. They rise gently from the meadow. The grass follows about a quarter of the way up. It stops growing about where the trees start. They aren't gefta trees like the forest that Nixon and EHL crashed into. These trees don't grow together as tightly. Their trunks are thicker, but they aren't nearly as tall. And replacing the grass are large stones, some half the size of EHL.

"We'll set up with our backs to one of these larger rocks." That's what his dad would have told him if they'd come to a place like Makkurra on one of those adventures they'd go on after his dad had been gone for a longer than expected long time.

Dad liked to reduce what he called "attack vectors," he never seemed to realize that while he was eliminating threats from the back he was opening them up to threats from the top. Still, those trips were fun. Any time with dad was fun, until ...

No, stop thinking about this.

His mind switches channels. Shaine is the star of this new show, and Nixon smiles. He'd only partially meant what he said to Shaine before. Yes, there are times—most of the time, if he's being honest—that he wishes he'd never met Shaine. That he thinks about how things might have gone. But you can't live in "might haves." A life that involved Shaine was his history. It was the reality, and the reality was that it wasn't all bad. It wasn't even mostly bad. There were a lot of good times, and being out here in the quiet and the calm reminds him of some of the best.

The two friends got in hot water. A lot. And most of the time it was trouble they could talk their way out of. And, if they couldn't, they could just go hole up somewhere for a few days and whatever it was would pass. But sometimes, they got into the deep stuff, the kind of hot water that couldn't be waited out. When they did, they fled. Shaine would somehow get a ship and they'd take off. They'd fly who knew where, but a lot of the time it was somewhere like Makurra. Land the ship somewhere remote on an already remote planet and spend a couple of weeks eating noodles and doing a whole lot of nothing.

They are Nixon's favorite memories with Shaine, and they are playing on a loop in his head. He smiles around another big bite of the bread. He needs to fix this ramp. No matter how pretty EHL looks now, and no matter what her system checks tell her, she's not going anywhere if this ramp isn't functional. But it's getting dark, and he can't focus. He's too happily distracted by his mental yesterdays.

EIGHT

Nixon wakes the next morning. He's rested and relaxed and happy. He didn't think a mental trip a bunch of years back would do that, but here he is.

He makes himself breakfast, something his dad had called "Glop". It's a mixture of grains and dried berries soaked overnight in Bowtan milk. He's sures there's a real name for it, but he never heard it. It was always just Glop, and it's what they'd make when they went out on their little adventures.

He takes his bowl to the broken ramp and sits. He looks out through the forest to the open field. A fog hangs just above the tall grass and stretches to the trees. A breeze starts blowing and pushes the fog farther up the foothill.

He hears a snort and sees the grass start to ripple. The Fison hogs are back. Only two this time, and they are small. Babies. They chase each other through the grass and then up into the forest. They run right past the ship, no more than a dozen feet from where Nixon sits, but they don't pay him any attention. Just run by him and then off.

He smiles and takes his last bite of Glop. He starts to wonder if this is it. Is this what he wants? He hasn't thought about the case in a few days. But it's still there. Literally in one of the cabinets in his quarters. And it's still there in the back of his mind. Always looming. Always coloring everything he's doing. It's why he's here on Makurra at all. But maybe this was the blessing the case was supposed to show him. The life he was meant to have, one of quiet and of solitude.

He looks back out to the opening and imagines if this was every morning. Up with the first sun. Out on some kind of patio or porch on the small house he's built from these trees that are all around him. It's a rough-sided place. Small. Just the one room. But it's just him. He doesn't need much space.

He'd need some kind of hot box to prepare food. This imagined life doesn't come with rehydrated noodles. But he's sure that someone back in that little town could help him secure what he needed.

He'd watch the animals early in the morning. He'd wait until the second sun was up to go into the hills and check if the traps he'd set the evening before had found anything. Finding his own food and foraging would mean he never needed many credits. That payment for delivering the case should set him up well. But he'd keep EHL stored next to his little cabin in the woods just in case he needed to run off somewhere and find work to restock his credit balance.

When the suns had both set he'd spend nights eating meals his mother made, watching shows on his reader, and listen to the mewling of whatever animals those were he'd heard the first night here.

He looks away from his imagined cabin and back down at his ship. She's still broken, still unflyable. And if he's going to have any shot at even part of this imagined life he has to deliver this case. That means fixing the ramp.

He stands and takes his bowl back to the galley then gathers his tools. Back at the ramp he removes body panels and tries to puzzle out what he's seeing.

This can't be that complicated, can it?

No, it can't. It all looks pretty simple, and it doesn't appear that any of the triggering mechanisms are broken. When Nixon initiates the ramp to unfold or retract and the gears and inner workings of the ramp itself bind up and grind.

He begins to work, and again convinces himself that this could have been it. This could have been his life. He could have fixed ships. Then, mentally, the cabin is back, but this time it's not alone. There's another building there. This one is bigger and more permanent. He sees himself stepping out of it, wiping his hands clean on a rag that he's hung from the belt of his coveralls. He's waving at someone. Nixon mentally swings his attention that direction and sees the back end of a ship as it accelerates out and away from Makurra.

Nixon works on the ramp most of the day, skipping lunch—dad wasn't wrong when he said Glop will stick with you. But being crouched over this busted ramp for this long has done a number on his back.

He stands. He stretches. He tries to twist some life back into sore muscles.

He interlocks his fingers; he closes his eyes and pushes his arms high above his head. He breathes in deep then lets it out slowly.

THUNK

His eyes pop open, and a blaster shot sizzles past his ear.

NINE

The blaster bolt tears a fresh hole into the newly painted side of EHL. Nixon feels the heat from the shot burn his cheek and dives back inside the ship.

The air crackles behind him as another shot follows him into the ship. It rips into EHL's main deck, and Nixon swears he hears the ship moan.

He grabs the blaster from the dash. He waits for another shot to come, but one doesn't.

No target.

He takes a deep breath then looks quickly out the ramp opening, across the forest and open field, then up the hill.

THUNK

Another shot. He ducks back inside and the bolt of energy takes out an empty storage bin

His mind races. Blaster fire? From who? From where? The men from town? But why?

A deep breath and then another. He pushes his head out into the opening again, looking higher up the hill this time.

THUNK

He drops flat to the floor and the shot passes just above his head. He can smell his own singed hair, and the shot tears a deep gash into the floor of the main deck.

He still doesn't know where these shots are coming from, but he does know he can't stay here. Even if he did survive this, he's not sure his ship can.

He crouches by the ramp opening, his back pressed hard to the wall. He counts a mental three then takes off running out of the ship.

THUNKTHUNKTHUNK

Shots explode into clouds of dirt just off his heels. He dives for a spot behind one of the larger trees. It doesn't offer much cover, but this trunk along with all the others in between him and whoever is shooting means that hitting him is going to require a next level of expertise.

That doesn't keep whoever this is from trying. Shots splinter three of the trees around him. They don't offer much in the way of a threat, but they do allow Nixon to narrow in on where the shots are coming from. Up the hill, he knew that. But now it looks like it's even above the trees.

He focuses his attention there, but he sees nothing. It's all a landscape of tans and browns. Nothing jumps out … wait.

There.

A flash. Small and quick, but it's something. The setting sun has caught some…

There. Again

Behind one of the large rocks. May be nothing. But it may be…

Nixon raises the blaster and squeezes of a volley of shots. He doesn't count, just keeps shooting until his finger can't shoot anymore.

He's only hit rock, but he's pelted it with so much blaster energy that he's created a storm of dirt and dust big enough to let him move from behind this tree.

He runs, his head down and shoulders pushed up to his ears, to another tree—a bigger one with a wider trunk—that's closer to the forest's edge near the open field. He looks back up to the hill. His cloud of dust has nearly settled. He sits, back pressed against the tree trunk, and he waits.

And he waits.

He turns his head and leans out, trying to find his shooter.
THUNK

A blaster shot catches the tree beside him and splinters of the thin Gefta wood sting his face. He looks out from around the tree again, and there's movement. His shooter is shifting position.

Nixon wants to run. Make a mad dash. But where? The ship took out too many trees as it came crashing down. There's no cover there. And, here, where the trees are still standing, they are doing it so close together that he won't be able to build up any kind of speed to even be considered a moving target.

THUNK

Another shot. A new direction. His shooter has established a new position.

They were moving to the right. That puts them more behind me now.

He looks out to the field and has two thoughts.

First: He needs to be moving.

Second: This person is keeping their distance for a reason. So, let's take the fight to them.

He stands, and he sprints. The blaster is swinging at his side, and the tops of the tall grass in the open field slap at his knees. He's aiming for a large rock that sits at the edge of the field just before it starts climbing to become the hill.

THUNKTHUNK

Both shots end up somewhere behind him in the grass, but he feels their heat through his boots. Confirmed: Moving is better than stationary. His rock is coming up fast, and he dives behind it.

The day is fading. Makurra's first sun is beginning to disappear behind the hill tops, and the valley is being cut up by shadows. He's harder to see now, and that's good for him. But the tops of the hill, where his shooter is camping out are still lit bright with the light of the second stronger sun. But even that's going down and it's going to soon be shining right in the shooter's eyes. If they can't take Nixon out soon, they are going to lose their chance.

So, let's make them work for it.

Nixon stands, and another shot screams past him. Nixon starts running a zig-zagged path toward another large rock that's rolled down the hill and ended up in the open field. He's watching the hill and waiting for …

THUNK

Perfect.

He cuts hard to the right and the shot winds up in the grass somewhere behind him. He slides behind the rock he was aiming for and waits a moment. He doesn't want to. He's seen the shooter's position. He wants to stand and aim and fire, but he'd miss. He's breathing too hard. He needs this moment to gather himself, but he knows that every moment here is a moment the shooter could be moving.

He stays low and sticks his head around the far side of the rock and looks up to where he'd seen the shooter before, but he doesn't see anything. He gives himself another moment, then sprints from behind his rock. He's moving up the hill now. His blaster trained on the spot where he'd seen the shooter. He zigs and fires one shot. He zags and fires another. Then he finds a spot behind a tree.

THUNK

A limb above him crashes to the ground, one end charred and black by the blaster bolt. He doesn't wait this time. He spins out from behind the tree, blaster firing red hot. The shooter runs higher up the hill. Nixon tries to follow and can't tell if any of his shots connect. The shooter drops behind another rock, and Nixon finds a spot of his own.

His heart is about to beat through his cloak. He's struggling to get a good breath. He sneaks a look back up the hill. The setting sun catches something on the shooter's gun, and he sees another flash. This one just before another shot is fired. He curls up and makes himself small. The shot passes just above him.

He uncurls onto his belly and spies the shooter again. They are so close now. The fight feels somehow fair at this point. He can look at the shooter. The shooter can see him. Let the better one win. If, for some reason, he dies here he's OK with that. But there's something, he doesn't know, shameful about being taken out from a distance. It's too easy?

The shooter isn't visible, ducked back behind their rock, he assumes; he hopes. So, he aims, and he waits. It doesn't take long. The shooter pops up, long gun pressed to their shoulder. There's little more than that visible when Nixon fires.

It's four shots in rapid succession. Two of them connect.

TEN

The impact of the blasts spins the shooter back to the ground and behind the rock. Nixon steps out, his own blaster drawn and trained on anything that might step out in front of him.

He takes cautious steps forward. He knows that two of his shots hit the shooter, but he doesn't know what kind of armor whoever this is might be wearing. Because if they are armored then the blasts will have stunned but not wounded. And that means this battle is paused; it's not over.

Nixon cuts a wide path around the rock where the shooter is positioned, and that's when he sees the gun. It's been blown from the shooter's hands and up the hill out of immediate reach. It's a long gun; he knew that. But it's a gun he knows. It's one he's seen before. It's Laana's gun.

He's suddenly back on Umel. He's standing outside his ship the night she saved him, taking out two goons who'd been hoping for a chance to make him a mess in the street. She's leaning on the gun, the barrel still warm, and she's smiling at him. He thanks her, and she tells him it's not safe for him there. She helped. She was a friend. So why is she here?

He calls out: "Hello?"

Only a moan returns.

Nixon continues to circle the rock. His blaster still drawn, his brain still working out all of the possible outcomes here. That's Laana's gun, but is that Laana? Whoever this is, do they have a small blaster, just waiting for enough of him to come into view? If they do, is he fast enough on the trigger to defend himself? Can he shoot someone who's injured, even when they clearly wanted him dead?

"Hello?" he says again.

Nothing for a moment then "Hey, Trevor."

It's her. It's Laana.

"That your only gun?" he asks, able to see her legs now, stretched out in front of her.

She moans before saying "You know I don't like those small things."

"Doesn't mean you don't have one on you as protection."

He finally comes around and can see her face. It's grimaced, but she tries to smile through it. Her hands are empty. She's leaned her back against the rock, and her whole left side is bloody.

"You got me," she says and wipes a hand across her shoulder and upper arm. Blood smears and reveals two ragged holes where Nixon's blaster bolts have blown through her. New blood quickly covers them, and pain wrinkles Laana's face.

Nixon keeps the blaster aimed, unshaking, at her chest. He doesn't say anything, just stares at her.

Her breath catches, and she coughs before saying "How have you been?"

Nixon doesn't laugh.

"I don't understand." His finger wants to squeeze the trigger. All the small muscles in his hand want to contract, paint this big rock with Snapsit blood. Leave her slowly dying with a hole in her chest. Just tuck the blaster in his waistband and walk cooly back to his ship. She's left him with a lot of work to do inside.

He doesn't though. He fights it, and the urge is gone after a moment. She's clearly no longer a threat. Still, he takes a few steps to her gun and kicks it so it starts tumbling down the side of the hill. It rolls a few dozen feet before coming to rest against a rock that's half the size of the one holding Laana up. He turns back to her and she's staring at her gun, barely visible now in the near dark of another Makurra night.

"I don't understand," he says again.

"My bag." She looks to the sling bag sitting on her chest. "Look inside."

Nixon begins to bend down then stops.

She sees his hesitation. "It's just my reader. Pull it out."

He reaches inside and grabs her reader. The screen is still lit bright. On it is his image. Below it is a number: 100,000 credits.

Wow.

"That number sets me up for life. I quit living in half-finished towers. I quit having to chase bounties. This wasn't personal."

Nixon is still looking at the reader. The image is the one he'd seen on the boards, him leaving the spaceport on Exte. Looking behind him. Nice clear shot of his face.

"It's personal to me."

He tosses the reader back toward her and it lands on her stomach. She struggles to get it back in her bag.

"How'd you …"

"How'd I find you?"

Nixon nods yes and puts the blaster at his side. In his hand but at his side.

"I've been playing this game a while now. I'm not stupid." She pauses and catches her breath. "I can tell when someone's an easy mark and when someone's not. I can tell when to stalk and wait for someone to get more valuable."

"That's kind of ruthless."

"It's a business. But I could tell by watching you back on Umel that you were going to be tough to bring in. If you could …"

Light bulbs start going off for Nixon. "If I could survive Roland."

He's back in the dark alley. The water is crashing against the docks on the other side of the warehouse. He's looking at a grinning Roland as he sends two mountainous goons toward him, ready to bring him in. Then both of those goons get burned through by a blaster bolt from a gunman he couldn't see at the time. Roland backs away and somehow he's safe.

"Yep," she says and adjusts, pushing herself up with her elbows. "He takes you in then ..."

"You lose this opportunity."

She nods.

They sit in the dark for a moment. The wind comes down the hill and ripples Nixon's cloak. "I thought you liked me. I thought we were friends. Or friendly."

"We were. We are. You haven't shot me yet. Well ..." she looks at her shoulder and runs a finger over one of the wounds. She grimaces with the pain. "You haven't shot me again."

Nixon raises the blaster again, and once again it takes everything inside of him to keep from squeezing that trigger and walking away from her and from this. But he can't. So, instead he stands and begins walking a small circle in front of her.

"But how'd you find me?"

"That night when I met you at your ship, I stuck a tracker in one of the engines. I hadn't planned on seeing you at all, but it took me too long to find a good spot on that dumb ship to place the tracker so you wouldn't find it when you were trying to get it flight-worthy."

Nixon slowly nods. That makes sense.

"You've been tracking me ever since. And you were the one that followed me into atmo here."

"But I like you. Part of me is glad I missed."

Nixon starts walking a slow circle again. The next step is his, and he doesn't know what to do.

"I should kill you. Right here. Right now."

He circles in front of her again.

"That's what I should do. So, why is it so hard to just do it?"

She doesn't respond. Nixon stops and lifts the blaster. He aims it at the center of her chest. He lets it hang there a moment. She's not looking at him. She's looking at his hand, at his finger on the trigger. She isn't breathing; she's waiting.

He stares down at the blaster and stands stock still in front of her. He closes his eyes, pinches them shut tight, then drops his hand.

He screams, and it echoes up and down the hillside.

"Why can't I do this? You want me dead. Why can't I kill you?"

She gives him a look that says, "I don't know."

He drops to a knee in front of her.

"So, if I can't kill you, what should I do?"

She thinks for a moment then says: "Cut me in. Whatever this is that you're doing, let me help."

05: OTANZIA

ONE

EHL's cooking unit sounds a chime, letting Nixon know that whatever he'd put inside is sufficiently warm. Truth is that he doesn't care if it's as hot as one of the galaxy's suns or cold as an ice cap on one of the far, far off planets where heat is only a rumor. It's noodles and they aren't for him.

They are for Laana. He pulls the container from the unit and drops it on the table in front of her. The liquid inside slops over the side and lands partly in her lap.

Must not be that warm.

"I don't have anything to eat with."

"You have two hands."

She tugs at the restraint that has her right arm bound to the table. "Only one technically," she says. "And I'm not a lefty."

"Make do."

Nixon turns from her and starts putting together his own food. Truth is he's not hungry. Adrenaline kills his appetite, and right now, after his little shootout with Laana, he's pulsing with the stuff. It's running through his veins so fast that he's surprised he's not shaking.

He starts piling a plate so high with meats and breads, enough to make even a rich man wonder how he could afford all of it. Then he stops. He puts everything back where he got it then sits.

Laana is bringing the noodle container to her face with her left hand and drinking them like they are coming from a cup. The broth runs down her chin and gathers in little pools on the table.

"Not hungry?" she asks, her mouth half full.

Nixon shakes his head no.

"You'll sleep here tonight."

Laana puts the noodle container back on the small table. "Here?"

Nixon nods.

"Like a prisoner?"

"You're not a prisoner."

Laana tugs again at the restraints. Smears the broth on her chin across the rest of the bottom of her face. "Sure feels like it."

Nixon stands. "I can't help the way you feel."

He picks up the noodles from the table and throws them away as he walks to the door.

"Hey …" Laana protests.

He doesn't respond and turns off the light as he exits.

He turns the light back on the next morning, and Laana is just staring at the door when he arrives. He opens up a cabinet and pulls out a medic kit. He sits it on the table in front of Laana and pulls out a spray can of antiseptic and a sterile cloth.

"This is going to sting," he says just before he liberally applies the spray to her blaster wounds from the day before. She winces, and some of the spray wets the back of the seat behind her.

"Hold still. This is going to be worse."

She closes her eyes and breaths while Nixon wipes the wounds with a rag, digging a finger into each hole.

Laana shouts something in Snapsit that Nixon doesn't understand but doesn't really need any translation. "You enjoying this?"

"I'm not. But if you're going to help me—and you are—then I need you better. This hurts, but it's how you heal."

She watches him remove the last of the dirt and dust from her wounds. "So you're a medic now?"

"I know enough."

Nixon grabs two absorbent pads and places them above each of the wounds then takes a cloth bandage and wraps it around the pads and her shoulder, tucking the loose end back into a fold in the fabric to close the bandage off.

"And why didn't you do this last night?"

"You didn't deserve it last night."

"You're sure I'm not a prisoner?"

Nixon puts the medical kit away and comes back to the table. He unlocks the restraint.

"See," he says. "Not a prisoner. Now stand."

She does, and he spins her around. He puts her arm up in a sling to immobilize her shoulder as best he can

"But we do have work to do."

She follows him as he leaves the galley and heads toward the main deck. The ramp is still open, and the cool morning has made its way into the ship.

"EHL," Nixon says as he comes into the room.

"Sir?" the ship responds.

"This is Laana. She's with us now."

"Yes, sir."

"You are never to take an order from her. Is that understood?"

"Yes, sir."

Laana sighs. "You're welcoming committee is top notch."

Nixon ignores her. "Repeat that back to me, EHL."

"This is Laana. I'm not to take orders from her."

"Never."

"Yes, sir."

"Ever."

"Your point is made," Laana says.

Nixon gathers the tools that were scattered the afternoon before in their gun fight, and Laana gets a closer look at the long gashes ripped in the floor and walls by her blaster bolts.

"You're a bad shot," Nixon says.

She starts working the floor back into place as best she can with one free hand. "I wasn't trying to kill you," she says.

Nixon pulls a panel off of the ramp and sets it to the side. "That's not what it felt like from this side."

"You're worth 100,000 credits alive. I had to bring you in breathing. Looks like someone wanted to see you squirm under their thumb. Can't say I blame them at this point."

Nixon doesn't respond; he just continues to work on the ramp. He watches Laana struggle to make any kind of progress. Most of the day passes, and he thinks about what she said. He's more valuable to her and to whoever put the credits on him if he's alive. So, was this foolish? Was keeping her around going to be that last and final decision that he'll regret as he transitions into whatever kind of existence comes next?

The first of the galaxy's suns is disappearing behind the tops of the hills. Shadows from the trees are beginning to reach into the ship like long fingers. A cool breeze whips in through the open ramp and across the floor of the ship. It spins up leaves that have found their way inside.

Nixon secures a few final fasteners then stands. He moves to the panel on the wall that controls the ramp and punches the button that will activate it. A moment's pause then it starts to close. Nixon smiles.

Laana: "Look at you, Mr Fix-It."

The ramp seals itself shut, and Nixon looks down at Laana. She's proud of her joke, a little barb meant to sting. But Nixon won't let it. He's fixed the ramp. He's proud of himself, and he's thinking again about different directions, about how if life had taken another turn here or a twist there this could have been what he did. Not running mystery cases to mystery places, dodging blaster fire and mixing with people who had to think about whether or not they wanted him alive or dead.

"Get up," he tells Laana. She is still struggling to make more than minimal progress on her project. She puts down the mallet she'd been using and stands.

She grabs at her bandaged shoulder and rubs it gently.

"How's it feel?"

She tries to shrug but winces.

"We can put more spray on it after we eat. Should make it feel better and heal it faster."

He turns and heads down the hall to the galley. Laana follows.

It's noodles for both, because they sound good to Nixon. Sometimes the simple things are the most appealing. He gives Laana a spoon this time, but she still struggles with her left hand. Maybe more tonight than she did the night before. The broth has slicked her chin. Loose noodles lay curled on the table in pools of liquid.

Nixon laughs.

"When this is healed," she says, "I'll shoot you twice in your good arm since it seems to be good for a laugh."

Nixon takes his container to the trash and drops it in. "Calm down."

He tosses her one of the cloth napkins that sits folded on a shelf above the sink. She wipes her face dry and then the table.

"Check the seat, too," Nixon says. "You're sleeping here again tonight."

"Restrained?"

Nixon shakes no. "Not tonight. Just don't kill me in my sleep."

"I told you. You're more valuable if you're breathing."

TWO

Nixon wakes with a start. Laana's cried out. He grabs the
blaster as he rushes out of the crew quarters and to the galley.
In the hall, he hears her mumbling something in between
muffled cries of pain.

Please? Please? Is she begging? Pleading?

He steps before turning the corner into the galley. The
blaster is raised. He's primed to fire. He just needs a clear
shot at whoever this is that's broken into his ship. But it's no
one. Laana is alone. She's laying on the floor. Tears have
tracked her cheeks. The canister of antiseptic spray is in her
hand and the bandage is off her wound.

Nixon sighs, relieved. "You scared me."

He bends and hooks one of his arms under her only good
one and helps her to her feet.

"I haven't slept at all." She puts a hand to her shoulder
and rubs hard. "This thing won't let me. I was just trying ..."

Nixon takes the canister of spray from her and tells her to
go sit back down. She picks a spot on one of the stools.
Nixon grabs the rest of the medic kit and stands next to her.
He sprays her shoulder liberally, and he sees the muscles
physically relax.

"Thank you," she says, but Nixon doesn't respond. He
just continues to work. He digs through the kit for a tube of

ointment. He squeezes out an amount that nearly covers his palm and begins rubbing it into the wounds, the white ointment extra bright against her blue skin.

Laana screams.

"Give it a minute. This is good stuff. It'll numb the whole thing."

She breathes heavy and deep, but soon that returns to normal.

"Better?" Nixon asks.

She nods. He rewraps the bandages then tells her to sit at the table. She does, and he takes the seat across from her.

It's early. Too early. Nixon had barely been asleep when Laana cried out, but he knows that returning to sleep now is going to be impossible. His mind is running too fast.

He hadn't been able to sleep because he'd been regretting his decision. He should have shot Laana out on that hill when she was leaning against that rock. Closed his eyes and put a blaster bolt through her forehead. Turned around, opened his eyes, and walked away. Wouldn't have been the first time he'd killed someone. He'd killed Uzel the Uzek. He'd killed one of the men Uzel sent after him. Killed Uzel's daughter just days later. He was familiar with death. Intimate even.

But those were all different. Each of the others were all capable of fighting back. It was him, or it was them. But not her. Not that day at least. She was unarmed, and she was injured. He couldn't kill her. He didn't know that he had a code, but, apparently, he does. Is that code going to come back and bite him once she's better? Maybe. But for now, she's mostly harmless down one arm.

"So, what are you doing out here? Middle of the forest on a backwater planet in the middle of the galaxy."

"You chased me here. I had no intention of landing here."

"Then where were you going to land?"

Nixon begins to speak then pauses. How much of this does he tell her? "I was heading to Azken."

"Planet Tychon?"

"Azken."

She laughs then winces when her shoulder bounces. "No, I know. We call it Planet Tychon."

"We?"

"Anyone who doesn't work for Tychon."

"Oh," Nixon says. "I didn't realize we called it that."

"What's on Azken?"

"I'm making a delivery."

"What kind of delivery?"

"A case."

"You're a courier?"

"A reluctant one. For now."

"Reluctant?"

Nixon hesitates again then begins to explain. Whether she knows the story or not doesn't matter. She's here. She's part of it now. So he tells her about Shaine and Exte and watching his friend get torn apart by blaster fire. He tells her about the escape from Exte, being chased by the Uzeks, and the humans who are after him. Then he gets up and steps into the main cabin. He grabs the case and takes it back to the galley. He hands it to her.

She rolls it around in her hand. She runs fingers along the corners. She traces a finger along the thin grooves that have been carved in its sides.

"It's pretty." She starts punching the buttons on the locking mechanism.

"I suppose. I hate the thing."

"Why?" She starts pulling it from either end, but it doesn't open. Doesn't even separate.

"It's not worth everything it's cost."

He takes the case back and returns it to the main cabin.

"The faster I can get that thing off this ship and out of my life the better."

She shakes her head. "I'd want to know what's inside before I gave it up. Find out what was worth all of this. You're worth a lot of credits to someone. I'd want to know why."

Nixon considers it and nods. If this were a few days and a couple of planets ago he'd have agreed. Just off Exte, all he wanted was to know what was in that case and what Shaine had gotten himself into. But since then he's been more concerned with staying alive. With making this delivery. With getting on with his life.

"How much do you think your friend knew about what was in that case?"

Nixon stands and pulls food from the cabinet. He grabs a loaf of nut and berry bread and cuts two thick slices. He puts one in front of Laana and sits back down across from her with his own. He takes a big bite.

"So ..." Laana says.

"Honestly," Nixon says and swallows, "I don't know. I've thought about it. I don't think he'd put me in a situation to get ..."

Laana is shaking her head as he speaks, and he doesn't finish his thought.

"He knew. He absolutely knew."

"But he knew what?"

"He knew it was dangerous. He knew this would happen. It's why he asked you to deliver the case."

Nixon is shaking his head now. "I contacted him. He hadn't approached me."

"He would have. And if not you, someone else. He knew the dangers and was pawning them off on someone else, keeping most of the spoils as his own."

It's like all of the things Nixon has been thinking now have an actual voice, and hearing those thoughts spoken out loud by someone else helps them make sense. He stands and tells Laana to stay here. She needs to rest. He's going to go keep working on repairs to the main deck.

He gathers tools on his way and sets to getting these fixes complete today. He's getting an early start and the work is easy. So easy that his mind wanders back to his childhood and the schemes he started running with Shaine. Then when they are a little older. Then older still. Most of the time it's

Shaine giving orders. It's Shaine overseeing. It's Shaine picking out a crew, everyone putting themselves at some kind of risk. Everyone but Shaine.

Nixon is getting mad all over again. He can feel it. His face is flushed. His movements are more violent. His chest begins to ache. He stops for a moment and stands. Laana is in the hall watching him

He tries to shake these feelings. Tries to throw them off his back and onto the floor.

"I was thinking," she says, "that even when we get these repairs made we still need to change out the transponder. It's trackable too."

Nixon nods as she speaks. "On my list of things to do."

"All right," she says, and they just look at each other for a moment. "You OK?"

Nixon looks at the work he's completed. He looks at the ship. His ship now. He's made too many repairs, made it too much his own for him to think about it as anything else. This isn't Shaine's ship any more. It's not the ship that Mira let him borrow. It's the ship that he's earned.

He starts to nod as he takes it all in: "I'm gonna be."

THREE

"Come on," Nixon says. "We are going to get that transponder."

"You mind if I stay?"

Nixon thinks for a moment then repeats himself. "Come on."

"I'm serious. I'd love to try and rest."

"If you have anything you want to take with us, grab it. It's two days walk where we're headed."

Laana's nice enough. He likes her company, although he likes any company that's not just some kind of complicated programming at this point. She's smart. Knows people that he doesn't know, and that could be handy. Still, only a few days ago she was winging blaster bolts by his head, hoping to earn a ship full of credits. He's not letting her hang around his ship unattended.

The truth was he hadn't slept well in the two nights since he brought her onto the ship. It was thin sleep, every small sound waking him. And that's if he got to sleep at all. Something still pricks his insides whenever he doesn't have something else to occupy his mind.

"I don't have anything. Unless you want to give me back my gun."

"You won't need it."

Nixon steps around Laana and pulls a bag from a cabinet. He takes it to the galley and fills it with food. He grabs the case and puts it in the pocket inside his cloak then tucks the blaster inside his waistband. Laana watches him walk around the ship then follows him out the ramp.

The suns are just coming up, their light sneaking over the tops of the hills and pouring down into the valley. It's just now beginning to push its way through the trees of the forest, and the air is hanging onto the chill of the night.

Laana crosses her arms, hugging her chest. Nixon heads out ahead of her and his long steps put quick distance between them. They walk most of the first day separated like this. They say very little to each other, and Nixon stops walking just as the first of the suns drops behind the hills and the light changes.

"We'll lose that second sun sooner than we realize. Better find a place to bed down for the night."

Laana waits for Nixon to find a spot to settle. It takes him a moment, but he finally finds a gap between the trees that's wide enough for both of them to lay down. He drops the bag off his shoulder and sits. Laana follows.

Nixon opens the bag and pulls out a couple of tins of meat and a sleeve of crackers. He opens the tins and sets them on the ground between them then opens the crackers and does the same. He pulls a cracker from the sleeve and drags it through the meat. It's the consistency of a paste, and it mounds up on the cracker as he pulls it. He pops it in his mouth then grabs for another cracker. Laana watches him go through the process again.

"This is all I brought, so if you want to eat then grab a cracker. You don't want it, suit yourself. I'm sure you could trap something small out here, but I didn't bring anyway to clean it or start a fire to cook it on."

Laana grabs a cracker and picks up her tin of meat. She copies Nixon's move and drags a heavy pile of the paste onto her cracker. She takes a hesitant bite, and her eyes pinch narrow and her mouth puckers into an O.

Nixon laughs.

"Yeah, it's kind of an acquired taste."

"Salty."

"I've been eating it since I was a kid. Shaine and I practically lived off the stuff when we first got to Exte. It's cheap. Crackers are too. When our big schemes weren't paying off we could hustle up enough credits to buy a few tins and sleeves."

Laana picks up another cracker and is less aggressive with the paste this time.

"Well, if you can't taste good at least be cheap."

She pops the cracker into her mouth.

They eat the rest of the tins in silence, the only sounds come from the forest's nighttime creatures waking up. Nixon puts the empty tins and what's left of the crackers back into his bag then lays down, resting his head on his arm.

"Get some sleep," he says. "We've got another day ahead of us tomorrow."

Nixon doesn't sleep. His mind can't stop thinking about the blaster in his waistband. He rests an arm across it when he lays down and keeps it pinned there. He has his eyes closed, and he's waiting for Laana to try something. Waiting for her to gently try to shift his hand, to move a finger. Free the blaster so she can free herself.

Each time she turns over in the night he sneaks an eye open to make sure she isn't creeping just a little closer to him. Each time one of the forest's night creatures pads by on little paws he does the same thing. Paranoid? Maybe. He prefers to think of it as cautious.

When the first of the suns begins to come up, he's already sitting with his back against one of the trees watching Laana sleep. He gives her a few extra minutes then pushes her shoulder with the toe of his boot. She jostles awake and tries to slide her tongue across dry lips. She sits up, and he opens his bag. He tosses her another thick slice of the bread he gave her the morning before.

She eats it eagerly. He stands and watches her. A piece of the dried fruit falls from the corner of her mouth and to the ground. She plucks it from the dirt and pops in her mouth. She puts the last bite of the bread in her mouth a second later then brushes her hands together to get rid of the crumbs.

She stands and says: "Lead the way."

Nixon heads out, and Laana follows. It's quiet for a bit then Nixon tells her more about where they are headed.

Small settlement. Looks to be a fairly closed group. Most of them here for a reason.

She asks what he means by that last point.

"I didn't get the feeling these people had a lot of other options. They are here because they don't have any place else they can go. It's safer to live with your head down in a place where people won't ask you any questions if you promise not to ask them any either."

Laana nods. "Kind of sounds like Heaven.

Nixon chuckles then agrees.

The trees start to thin out. More and more stumps poke up from the forest floor. Again, Nixon hears it before he sees it. Multiple voices. They have to be coming from people standing outside of the buildings. He gestures for Laana to stop. They listen. The conversation is heated, but it doesn't sound angry. Just passionate.

Nixon steps out of the forest, through the trees, and into the clearing. The man he met emerging from the woods just a couple of days ago is at the center of the conversation. Again, they are gathered at the fire pit. Nixon can't tell what the discussion is about, but he knows that it stops once he's been spotted.

He raises a hand, a wave to look friendly. "Hello," he says. "Do you remember me?"

They all look at him for a moment before the man from the previous day gives a slight nod then says "I remember you. Don't remember your friend, though."

Two others were part of the discussion that Nixon and Laana walked up on, but Nixon doesn't recognize either one. He quickly scans the buildings in the circle. The woman who sold him the food has her door open, and he can see her moving boxes here and there inside.

Behind the group in the middle of the circle is the man who sold him the ship parts. He's leaning in the doorway of his building, his arms crossed across his chest.

"Didn't bring her last time," Nixon says.

"Maybe shouldn't have brought her this time."

"Ship's almost ready to go, just need one more part."

No one is looking at Nixon. All of them, the three in the middle and the woman in the doorway, are all looking at Laana.

"I'm afraid we're all sold out."

"I haven't even told you …"

A new man has stepped into one of the doorways. He shouts down to Nixon, interrupting him: "Yeah, we're all out."

"I think we all know that's not true. The other day you all kept making ship parts appear from nowhere."

"That was the other day," the man from the middle says. "Things have changed."

He reaches behind his back and leaves his hand there. "Now it's probably time you two head on back.

The others in the circle nod. The man in the doorway isn't quite as subtle. He pulls a blaster from his waistband and lets it hang loose at his side.

"Come on," Laana says. "It's not worth it. We're outnumbered."

She pulls at his arm, trying to get him to turn around, but Nixon resists. He rests his hand on the blaster in his own waist band.

"Just a couple of days ago, you were eager to take my credits. Today, I come to ask about a transponder and you want to go to blasters. I don't get it."

The man in the middle's face brightens. "A transponder? You only ask about one of those if yours is busted ..."

The man in the doorway finishes the thought. "... or you're trying to hide something or someone. That what's going on here? What kind of trouble are you into?"

Nixon doesn't answer that question. "Do you have a transponder you can sell me?"

"Fresh out," the man from the middle says.

"I don't believe you. I saw crates of ship parts the other day. You're saying in all of that..."

The man from the doorway: "Things have changed."

"What's changed? You still want credits. I still have them."

Laana grabs Nixon's arm again and pulls him around to her. "It's me, Nixon. I'm the change. Let's just go."

He looks at her for a moment then back to the crowd. The other two in the middle have also pulled blasters. Nixon turns and walks away, Laana at his side. He's waiting to feel the heat from a blaster bolt suddenly warm his back and burn its way through his front. It'd all go so fast that it'd take a moment for his body and brain to register what had just happened. He'd take a few stumbling steps forward before he fell over, dead by the time he hit the ground.

But nothing happens. They make it back to the thin cluster of trees. Then they make it to where the forest thickens. Then they are back to where the trees are so tightly packed hat they have to take a winding course just to get through them.

Neither one has said anything since they turned and started walking, but Laana breaks the silence with an apology

"I'm sorry," she says. "I know that was your plan, and it didn't work out."

"Not your fault" he says. "I just wasn't expecting that."

They are walking single file now, Nixon leading the way. "Didn't surprise me."

"I'm not sure what we do now, though. If they won't sell us a transponder..."

"Actually," Laana interrupts. "I know where we can get one."

FOUR

Laana takes a moment to orient herself then hesitantly points over a distant hill.

"I put my ship down over there. Let's take my transponder."

"We can't."

"Why not?"

"What are you flying?"

"A little speeder.

Nixon nods like he was expecting that answer. "Ship data won't match."

Laana chuckles. "You ever deal with a gate agent? Ever try to check into a space port?"

Nixon shakes no.

"There isn't one of those workers getting enough credits to worry that the type of ship they're talking to doesn't match the type of ship the transponder says it should be."

Laana starts walking toward her distant hill. "It's not the gate agents you need to be worried about. It's other hunters like me. They'll be running scanners waiting for a code to ping. And when it does they'll be on you so fast you won't know what happened. And there will be so many of them that you won't be able to breathe. Suddenly, it's all over."

Laana pulls her hair back and ties it into a loose knot. Nixon follows. The suns are up, and the walking is hot.

"How do you like your speeder?" Nixon asks.

He's thinking back to Ibilia and the shipyard where he got to sit inside of an older model speeder. All of the instrumentation was aged and worn. And he doubted the engines could bring as much speed as he imagined they did. But the push of force that pinned him to the seat. The rush of space coming on as he blasted out of the atmosphere. It all still appealed. Not that he wanted to replace EHL. Not that he could if he wanted to. He owed that ship everything. It's the only reason he made it off of Ibilia in the first place. Still, something that could jump off a planet's surface and speed you through space ... wow.

"You mean Ruimy?"

"What's Ruimy stand for?"

"What do you mean?"

"Like EHL. That's my ship. I could call her El. I don't, but if I wanted to. So, what does Ruimy stand for?"

"Doesn't stand for anything. It's her name. Like mine's Laana."

"Oh," Nixon hesitates. "Then I guess you like her well enough to give her a name."

Laana slips on the loose rocks under her feet. They are still climbing the hills—above the trees now—and all of the ground here is less than friendly. Laana puts a hand down to catch her fall.

"She's everything," she says, dusting the dirt off her palm. "But I don't have to tell you how our head can go a little crazy out here when you're on your own. She's a good ship. Saved my hide more than once when a bounty's gone sideways."

"Sideways?"

"Well, yours didn't go as planned."

They come to the top of the hill, and Laana scans everything in front of them. It's all flat ground. Nixon expected that the other side of these hills would slope gently down, but they don't. What he's been looking at aren't hills but a plateau of sorts.

Laana points. She sees her ship. She sees Ruimy.

There's not a lot to it. Big engines. A little cockpit. Not much room for anything extra. Any paint that was on her sides has worn off, beaten free by space debris and blaster fire. Now she's just a dull grey. Laana opens the small port on the side and climbs in.

She throws out a personal bag, and that's quickly followed by a smaller bag that clangs when it hits the ground. She pops back out and grabs that smaller bag. She opens it and dumps the contents on the ground. It's a handful of tools. She pushes the pile around until she finds what she's looking for. She steps to the back of the ship to a panel between the engines and begins undoing the fasteners that hold it closed.

It's all wires and unmarked parts inside. None of it makes sense to Nixon, but Laana works with confidence. She pushes her arms deep inside the ship.

"So, you're probably wondering what's happening," she says. She's talking to the ship. "This is my friend Nixon, and we need to borrow something. Not forever. Just for a bit."

Laana's hands are buried inside the nest of wires, but Nixon can see the muscles in her forearms flexing and moving. She's working hard and fast. She pulls the freed transponder out from inside the ship.

"I'm going to leave you here for now. Again, it's not forever. Just for a bit. But I'll be back. I promise."

It's just a small, unmarked box. Smaller than Nixon was expecting for something that's such a critical piece. She hands it to Nixon and puts the tools back in the bag. She grabs her personal bag and throws it over her shoulder.

Nixon doesn't want to tell her, but he knows he has to. Still, his desire to avoid a scene overwhelms his need to make sure she understands that they aren't coming back here. That they can't. If they leave his transponder here then it's going to be a magnet for anyone looking for him. It's going to become a galactic hotspot, and a place he's going to have to steer well wide of from here out.

Gone are his visions of a little place back in those woods where he can sit in peace and quiet and let the whole day wash over him in a wave.

They walk in silence for a few moments, negotiating their way through the rocky upper part of the hill. When they get to a point in their trip down where the side of the hill is more grass than rocks, Nixon speaks up.

"Heard you talking to your ship. Told her you'd come back for her. You know you won't be doing that with me."

Laana doesn't respond, just continues to walk down the hill.

"Because when we swap out these transponders this place is burnt. My old signal sitting stationary, it's going to be a sounding beacon…."

She doesn't let him finish. "I know. I knew when I suggested the swap."

"It's just that you said …"

"I know what I said. It was for Ruimy's benefit."

Nixon is still a couple of steps behind Laana. She's looking over her shoulder to speak.

"This is me telling you I'm in. I'm giving up my ship to finish this with you. But we still haven't talked about terms."

"Terms?"

"What I get for my effort. I'm not doing this for …"

She stops mid-sentence and holds up a hand.

Nixon stops next to her, and she points down the hill and into the trees where EHL is sitting.

"Look," she says. "Movement. Somebody's down there."

FIVE

They quickly hide themselves behind a tree then watch.

Looks to be two men, but the trees are bunched so tightly together that they can't see faces.

"Recognize them?" Laana asks.

Nixon shakes no. "The only people I know here are you and two of the men from …"

Nixon stops talking and concentrates on the action down by his ship. One of the men continues to walk around out front while the other is exiting the ramp, something in his arms. They've somehow gotten the ramp open. Nixon feels blindly through his cloak until he finds the case.

Good. It's here.

"Wait."

Laana concentrates on the two men. She chuckles.

"Yep," she says.

"It's …"

"Yep."

Nixon stands. "I don't guess we should be surprised." It's the men Nixon knows, the ones Laana met earlier. They've found his ship. They were hoping to find him.

"Nope," Laana says. "But do we have a plan?"

Nixon pulls the blaster from his waistband. "Nope," he says and holds the blaster up, a finger resting on the trigger guard, "but I do have this."

Laana looks back down in between the trees. The man working on the ramp has a medium-sized blaster thrown across his back. The other one who's pacing a shallow trench to the side of EHL is holding a bigger blaster pointed to the ground.

Laana rocks her head from side to side, likes she's considering things. Then she says "At least is a fairer fight. And if that still doesn't matter, it's a beautiful day. Nothing wrong with spending it dying."

"You're not going to die." Nixon starts down the hill. He picks up speed as he goes, and when he gets to the tall grass he's shouting

Shouting and shooting.

"Hey!" Two shots. Both of the men dive to the ground. The one exiting the ramp drops whatever's in his arms. It glows green, the Bastic fuel rods. Everything inside Nixon tenses, waiting for the rods to go fully unstable and send both men and his ship up in an explosion of fire. But they don't. They just hit the ground and roll away.

Neither of Nixon's shots is a threat. Both hit a tree before they come anywhere close to EHL or either of the men. Hitting the ground is instinct. But if you've been in a gunfight before, so is getting up. Laying on the ground, belly first, just makes you a nice widening target for someone who's approaching.

Both of these men are up fast, and Nixon fires another pair of shots. Again, they burn holes into tree trunks but have no chance of hitting anything.

"What are you doing?" Laana shouts, but Nixon doesn't respond. He sprints into the trees. Luckily, he's just as hard to hit as his two targets are. Both men fire off a volley of shots. Only one comes close to hitting Nixon, passing over his head as he slides to a stop behind a tree.

Nixon looks behind him. Laana is sitting on the ground at the edge of the forest. She's made herself small and is putting as much of a tree between her and Nixon and the two men as she can. He turns back to see one of them poke his head around the side of EHL. Nixon lets off a wild shot in the man's direction. It goes well wide of anything.

"What are you doing?" Laana shouts. "If you're going to fire, do it expecting to hit. Quit firing right away."

Nixon keeps an eye on the ship, but she's right. He's fighting from anger. He's mad that these guys have found his ship. He doesn't know what they want, but they broke into EHL so he assumes it isn't good. And he's mad that he started shouting at them from the grass. He let his emotion overwhelm his better sense, and now he's in a gunfight as opposed to approaching them with a plan and limiting the action.

Think, Nixon. Think.

Scenarios run through his head. All of them end up with him dead and Laana being marched back to their camp. And they all involve him sneaking around the side of the ship to try and surprise at least one of them. If not surprise them, at least catch them flat footed.

So that's it. The plan that makes the most sense. Mostly because that's the only plan. He turns to Laana.

"I'm going around," he says and gestures a wide path with his hand.

He stands, and she says no. He can't hear her, though, because at that moment blaster fire erupts from both guns. Bolt after bolt leap from behind EHL and rocket skyward. They are tearing through the canopy above Nixon and bringing down a rain of large limbs and branches. They are falling from hundreds of feet up, and landing all around him. It sounds like explosions when they hit the ground.

BOOM! BOOM!

Nixon is weaving through trees, trying to get to the back side of EHL. The blaster bolts continue to tear apart the branches above him. He comes around the front side of EHL with his blaster drawn.

"Be careful, you're about to be fully exposed," Laana shouts. She's following him.

BOOM!

His weapon is out in front of him ready to fire. Both men are looking up, not paying attention. He squares up one of the men in his sites and squeezes off a shot.

CRACK!

One of the falling limbs lands across his shoulders. It knocks him to the ground and the blaster from his hands. The shot goes well wide.

He looks up and sees both men turn to him, a look of surprise on their faces. Then they smile. They bring their blasters toward him, but before they can get trained on him a blaster bolt catches one in the chest. He spins to the ground.

BOOM!

Another limb lands and shakes the ground. Nixon's vision is going soft, everything beginning to dim. He barely sees Laana jump over him and into his view. She has his blaster, and the next bolt she fires momentarily lights up everything. She's put a second shot into the man already down, and quickly fires another at the second gentleman before he can get his blaster up and aimed.

Darkness is collapsing in from the sides. Everything is becoming a mess of colors. Two more blaster shots fire off bright, and he can see Laana turn from the second man, who's now falling to the ground.

The last thing he sees as the darkness overwhelms is her face tensed up in determination, her mouth open and teeth bared. The blaster jammed out in front her on arms that are tight with tension. It's pointed right at him.

Then ... black.

SIX

Nixon's shoulders and back more than ache. This is pain he's not felt in a long time, and it pulses through his whole body when he tries to push himself up to a sitting position.

"Whoa, whoa," says Laana and offers him a hand.

Nixon's head is foggy, and that confusion is painted on his face

"Nothing's broken," Laana says. "Not the best I can tell. But you took a pretty good shot."

Things are fuzzy. A pretty good shot? Nothing's broken?

He takes Laana's hand and she pulls him up to a sitting position. She gives him a tin of Bowtan steer meat and some crackers.

"Eat this. You've been out a while."

Nixon doesn't say anything, just takes the tin from her and drags a cracker across the top. He puts it in his mouth, and she continues to talk.

"I went ahead and swapped out the transponders. Anyone scanning codes will think we're a cute little speeder. Until they see us, of course."

That makes some sense. He's remembering transponders. Conversations that didn't go well. He's remembering a fire fight. And tree limbs landing like explosions.

Falling limbs.

Across his back and shoulders. Limbs pinning him to the ground. Laana leaping over his back and firing his blaster, a look of anger on her face and a touch of crazy in her eyes. Then, finally, staring at the wrong end of his own blaster just before everything going dark.

"Thank you," he tells her.

"For what?"

"For not killing me."

"I wasn't going to kill you."

"That's not necessarily what it looked like."

"You don't have to worry about me. I'm in this. I'm committed." She gets up and moves to look at Nixon's back. He reaches an arm behind him and feels bandages.

"Besides," she says. I can't kill you. I don't know how to fly this ship."

Nixon laughs and a new wave of pain runs through him.

"How long was I down?

Laana thinks about it. "A day. Long enough for me to change out the transponder and make preparations to bury the bodies."

"Bury the bodies?"

She stands and heads out to the main deck. Nixon follows her and sees on the floor a box holding gathered leaves and a tub filled with some kind of brown paste.

"When we take a life, we need to show respect to the universe. Show that we understand that the thing we've done has ripples and that we can't see what those ripples affect. We can't know. So we give her an offering and return these spirits to her intact."

"When we take a life?"

"Snapsits. It's just something I have to do."

"Did you do it on Umel when you shot Roland's two men?"

Laana shakes her head no. "And look where it got me. This fight you're preparing for is bigger than me chasing you around the galaxy. I don't want the universe still upset with me, so I'm doing this."

Nixon doesn't argue with her, just watches her gather the things she's already put together. He follows her to the ramp and stays in the ship while she walks out to the bodies.

She's pulled them closer to the ship and placed them side by side. Torn open by blaster fire. Features missing. She kneels next to the first one and brings her hands to her face. She begins to gently rock back and forth while chanting something in Snapsit that Nixon doesn't understand. This goes on for a moment then she drops her hands and dips them into the paste that she's made. She pulls out heavy handfuls and smears it across the wounds while continuing to say something under her breath.

She stops and looks up to the sky, stretching her arms up to the canopy that was so full just days before. Sun now pours through and lights up her face.

She stands over the first body and bows then turns her attention to body number two. She begins repeating the ritual: covering her face, spreading the paste, standing, bowing.

She hooks her arms under the shoulders of the first man and begins to drag him to one of the shallow holes she's dug a few feet away

"You can help me with this part," she shouts to Nixon, never looking at him.

He hustles out the ramp and begins pulling the second body toward the second grave. Laana rolls her body into its final resting place and kicks dirt piled on the sides back on top of the body. She then goes and gets the piles of branches she'd gathered and places half of them on top of the fresh dirt.

She waits for Nixon to finish filling his hole then places the rest of the branches on top. She steps back and puts her hands back in front of her face and begins again chanting something that Nixon doesn't understand. He watches until she brings her hands back down.

She looks at him. "OK. Done."

"Great," he says and turns to head back to EHL, "because we need to get out of here. Let's start getting the ship ready to go. Secure anything that's not already locked down or put away. I want to get us back in the air before these suns start to go down."

Back on the ship they both get to work. Neither of them are at 100 percent, although Nixon notes that Laana seems to be mostly healed.

That healing ointment is a miracle

He sits back in the captain's seat and starts the process of getting EHL's engines to fire.

It takes a long minute—one longer than he's comfortable with—but that familiar rumble returns, that gentle vibration in his feet that tells him his ship is just waiting for instructions on where to head.

"You never told me about the Bastic fuel rods," Laana says, now standing behind him.

"Everything secured?"

"You never told me."

Nixon is looking at the panels in front of him, these buttons and switches that all felt new just a few days ago. It's a few days that feel like a few years now.

"I was under no obligations to tell you about the fuel rods."

"Feels like those obligations may have changed. You kind of owe me. What else should I know about?"

"Owe you? I figure that, at best, we're even. But those rods are it. No secrets."

"I put them in the cabinet down by the galley. I didn't know where you kept them."

Nixon nods his thank you.

"So, where are we headed, captain?"

"Not sure," Nixon says. "Not here."

"That's not much of a plan."

"Best I've got for now."

"Then let me out."

Nixon turns to her, expecting to see a smile. He doesn't.

260

"I'm serious," Laana says. "If you don't have a plan then I don't want to be part of this. I won't follow you or come after you. Like you said, we're even. But I'm not interested in running from perpetual trouble until you figure something out.

"Then what do you suggest?"

"Get off this planet. Put down some place where you can be safe and figure something out."

"Where would we find a place like that?"

"Actually, I know somewhere."

SEVEN

Nixon has never been a bounce-around-the-galaxy guy. He prefers his feet on the ground somewhere. His boots getting dirty. But now, up here in the dark of space, he's kind of growing fond of it.

There is something about the freedom that's appealing. Not being bound by gravity or some city planner's idea of where you can go. This is the life of the pilots and bounty hunters and odd-job takers he read about on those boards. This is the life he dreamed about at night in his little hole on Exte. It may not have been how he thought he'd find it. And it's always something he thought he'd do with Shaine. But here he is. And, in a way, it's because of Shaine that he's doing it at all.

"Tell me again about this place," he says to Laana. She's sitting next to him in the navigator's chair. She's looking at something on her reader.

"It's called Otanzia. It's a civilization-class ship. A flying planet."

"And we'll be safe there?"

"Safer than we would finding a planet that's organic. There's enough population there that we can hide easily. We can buy plenty of supplies to get everything on this ship stocked up. And there are people there who can help us with that case."

"Help us with the case?

"To get it open. See what's inside."

"I don't want to get it open.

"Liar."

"I did. Before." He pauses. "I'm not sure I want to now."

"Whatever. It's a good place to lay low for a day or two and create a plan."

They fly in silence. Laana sticks her head back into her reader. Nixon stares out the front of the ship into the all-consuming black and gets lost in thought.

Does he really not care about the case?

No, I don't. Right? Tell yourself that again.

I don't care about the case. Not anymore. The only thing I want with that case is to turn it over to whoever it is that wants it. It's cost me too much already.

He grabs it off the dash and rolls it over and over in his hands. He plays with the buttons on the top. He pushes them in a random order. He pulls at the two halves of it almost out of habit. It doesn't move.

He tosses it back to the dash and sinks his body lower into the pilot's seat.

"Mmm hmm," Laana says.

The ship Otanzia is a growing spot in front of them. Nixon has heard of these civilization-class ships. Galactic way stations with mostly transient populations of travelers looking for a place to stop and restock. Rooms to rent for those crew members who want some place to sleep that isn't a thin mattress on top of a molded platform. Restaurants where you can get food that isn't rehydrated in some kind of heating unit.

Honestly, it sounds great.

Otanzia is shaped like a brick, wide from this angle and tall. Light from windows dot most of the side, and at the bottom a series of wide openings.

"Point us to one of those gaps," Laana says. "We'll put down in there."

"Did you hear that, EHL?"

"Yes, sir."

"Then do that."

"Yes, sir."

The ship drops and sets a course for one of the openings. As they approach, it gets almost impossibly wide, and the size of Otanzia makes Nixon feel impossibly small. All of the galaxy around him, and this is what makes him feel tiny.

It takes up all of his vision. He looks left. He looks right. He can see nothing else. This wide opening swallows up the ship as it moves inside.

"Hello, captain. This is Officer Markum, gate agent for the ship Otanzia. Please state your reason for boarding."

Nixon turns to Laana.

"Rest and restock," she whispers.

"Rest and restock," Nixon repeats.

"Thank you."

Officer Markum is silent for a moment.

"Space 1112. We'll push directions to your ship's systems. Enjoy your stay."

"Thank you. You too."

EHL moves deeper into the Otanzia, following the directions that the ship sent.

"You too?" Laana says and smiles

"Shut up."

EHL finds space 1112 and sets down. Nixon and Laana go about securing the ship

"Told you there wasn't anything to worry about with the new transponder."

"Still makes me nervous, but this time you were right. What now? You're familiar with places like this."

"Food? I have credits. My treat.

Nixon agrees. He grabs his cloak and slips it over his head. He drops his reader into one pocket and the case in another. He pulls his blaster off the dash and shows it to Laana.

She nods. "Wouldn't hurt to have it."

He tucks it into his waistband and then hits the button to open the ramp. The relative silence of EHL is replaced by the hustle of activity. Voices talking, shouting. Ships firing up, winding down. Equipment moving here, there. It's a noisy energy that Nixon hasn't felt in a while. Even on Ibilia, it wasn't like this. There was a quietness there, everyone drawn into themselves moving on some kind of invisible path to wherever it was that they were going. All together on those streets but all still somehow alone.

Not here.

With all of these pilots and all of these crews, the whole space is energized. It's lit bright with huge lights hanging from ceilings that feel exceptionally high. Adding to the cacophony are the fans that keep the air moving, the exhaust and the fumes down, and make everything cold.

Laana steps ahead of Nixon and says, "This way."

She weaves herself through the crowd toward a sign indicating a bank of elevators. It's less crowded here.

Laana hits the call button, and they wait for the next elevator up. "So," she says, "what are you hungry for?"

EIGHT

Nixon sits back in the seat. His belly is full. He's happy. Laana smiles at him. "Enjoy that?"

He exhales then grabs a crust of bread left on his plate. He bites off half of it and says "I did. Very much. Thank you."

"My pleasure. Partner."

The crowd in the restaurant—a little place that roasts meats and serves them on silver trays with assorted vegetables—is clearing out. The staff is pulling dishes from tables. Wiping down left-behind messes.

"How about a drink? I know a place that's a couple of floors up and a good distance away." Laana points out a window in the front of the restaurant and toward the opposite end of the ship.

"I can show you more of Otanzia while we walk."

Nixon agrees and stands. The energy in the ship itself isn't as intense as it is down in the hold. The sheer size of the space helps to dissipate much of that. But there's still a buzz. Nixon feels it as he walks these corridors, following Laana close. She's pointing out places and objects. Nixon is sure that what she's telling him is important stuff, all will be critical to know at some point, but he's having a hard time listening to her. He's distracted by his own presence here. It's dawning on him how outlandish all of this is, that he's been given this case and this mission. That he accepted it at all, and that the galaxy paired him up with a Snapsit woman. That it put him on one of these civilization-class ships.

All the stuff that makes a civilization a civilization is on the ship's edges. There are restaurants like the one Nixon and Laana just left. There are places to get a drink, like where they are headed now.

There's also every kind of store you need. Ship supplies, ship parts, And every kind of store you most definitely don't need. Blue neon clouds hang in the windows of some of the shops. Nixon recognizes the little icons from Exte. The shop owner is saying that if you know how to ask for it, he can sell you Cloud 90. Let a couple tabs of the blue powder dissolve under your tongue and you'd forget entirely where you are. A third tab and you'll lose and entire week. Add a fourth and ... well, Nixon had never heard about anyone surviving a fourth. But he'd also never heard of a shop owner-dealer deny someone who wanted to try.

"Just don't take it here." Dead bodies are bad advertisements.

Of course, a second tab made with the wrong stuff could be just as fatal as four of the good kind.

These little glowing icons are mostly just a reminder to Nixon that he left a bucket of seeds buried in the sands on Exte. He'd kill for those credits right now. His balance is running low, and he was hoping he'd not have to sell the remaining Bastic fuel rods.

The inside of the Otanzia is a dull grey and everything that Laana is pointing out looks vaguely the same, but she hasn't stopped talking since they left the restaurant. It's clear that she likes this place. Clear that she's spent more than a night or two here.

"And then if you follow that hallway down there," she points down a passageway that disappears around a curve, "you'll get to…"

Nixon puts up a hand to stop her.

"What?"

He puts a finger to his mouth to signal quiet
He concentrates.

Yes, he did hear it. Grunts. Snorts

He sniffs the air. Whatever scent Otanzia pipes in is now mixed with sweat and dirt and that very specific scent of ...

"Uzeks," Nixon says.

"Yeah?"

"You didn't say there'd be Uzeks here."

"There could be anything or anyone here. It's an open ship. No restrictions on who or what shows up."

"Yeah, but..."

Laana starts walking again. Nixon follows, keeping his head turning and his eyes open.

"Besides, you think it's the same Uzeks? This far out?"

Nixon considers that. "No. Maybe not. It's a long way to go, but..."

"No," Laana interrupts. "It's not the same Uzeks. I chase bounties. They haven't come out this far."

"You came out this far."

"Nah," she points to a place just ahead of them. It has a neon sign hanging above a double-wide entrance. There are tables out front of the door. "I stumbled across you. I was already out here. Technically, you came to me."

"Maybe you're right."

They take seats outside of the bar. Nixon sits with his back to the wall. A Snapsit woman comes to the table to take their orders and speaks to Laana. Nixon doesn't understand any of it, but it's not where his attention is. He's watching the long walkway they're sitting in the middle of. It stretches out for a hundred feet on either side. At one end of those walks it turns in the direction that Nixon and Laana just came from, and he can see down that walk until it almost disappears into the distance.

But the other end of the walk also turns the other direction, and that's what worries Nixon. He can't see around that corner. He hasn't just come from that direction. He's blind to whatever is over there.

The Snapsit woman returns with two drinks on a tray. It's the frothy yellow thing that he'd been given back on Ibilia.

His face sinks when the waitress puts his glass in front of him.

"What?" Laana says.

"I've had these before."

"And you didn't like it?"

He shrugs and looks past Laana to the end of the walkway. Then he turns his head and looks to the opposite end.

"Sorry. You can get the next round."

She picks up her glass and takes a long drink then puts it down. Yellow froth clings to her upper lip. It looks a pale green against her blue skin.

Nixon picks up the glass and raises it to Laana as a thank you. He takes a drink and smiles.

"Good."

"Better than what I had on Ibilia. That was bitter. This isn't."

He looks back past Laana to the end of the walk then back up the path they took to get here. It's not empty, but there's nothing there that's concerning. He turns his head and checks the opposite direction.

Laana takes another drink then puts her glass down. "Would you relax?"

"How far back to the ship?"

"How far?"

"We need to get back. How long will it take?"

She takes another drink. "You walked it like I did. We are a good way from where we came in, but you don't have to worry about that."

She tries to make more conversation, but Nixon isn't listening to her. He's nodding and offering one-word responses.

"Don't take this the wrong way," she says. "But you've turned into an awful date."

He begins to tell her that he's sorry. That this place is so big it's disorienting. That he's OK with new planets. That doesn't freak him out. But here, this ship. It's all walls. Even if those ultimate walls are so far apart that you could fit a million EHLs inside this place, he'll never stop feeling claustrophobic here. That he'd just as soon they kept flying to Azken without a plan because at least there he'd have a sky above him. And if he's got a sky he's got a way out.

But he doesn't say any of those things, because just as the words were forming in his head, an Uzek turns the corner. Then another two turn the corner behind the first.

Laana sees him and follows his gaze.

"It's OK," she whispers. "There's lot of Uzeks."

"There aren't that many Uzeks.

Nixon locks eyes with the one who turned the corner first. He stops walking and grunt-snorts something to the other two. He points. They all grunt-snort something to each other. It's all just noise to Nixon, but he doesn't need to be able to speak the language to know what they're saying.

He stands.

"Come on," he says to Laana. "We've got to go. They know me."

NINE

Laana jumps up and follows Nixon. They knock two other tables over in their rush. The Uzeks are close behind them chattering things to each other.

Nixon sprints to the end of the walk and turns left heading back the way he and Laana came. He's regretting that he didn't pay attention to her little tour now, because he has no plan. She's not armed. He has his blaster, but there are three of them. One man's blaster is only going to do so much good for so long.

"Where to?" he shouts over his shoulder.

The path he's on is nice and wide, but they keep passing narrower walks that look more twisty, more turny, and more advantageous for someone trying to make a foot chase more difficult. Especially if those people are being chased by big and lumbering creatures that are known for their anger but not their agility.

Laana begins to answer, but a blaster bolt passes between them and the sizzle from the shot drowns out anything she says.

They both look behind them in time to see one of the Uzeks approaching quickly. He's on a motorized float cart, some kind of rigged up contraption created to make moving items around this big ship easier. Nixon has no idea where this thing got the cart from, but it's standing up and holding a medium-sized blaster pressed to its shoulder with one hand. It isn't aiming the gun, it's just firing wild shots with one hand while steering the cart with the other. Two more bolts scream toward them but miss.

Nixon pulls his own blaster and turns to fire at the Uzek on the cart. He only takes one shot, but it's a good one. It connects with a front corner of the cart and spins it out from under the Uzek. The creature goes flying one direction, the damaged cart flies off in the other. The Uzek hits the ground behind Laana and Nixon and slides across the floor. The blaster is knocked from its hands and slides toward Laana. She stops running and picks it up then shouts for Nixon to stop too.

"Down here," she says. She's stopped by an entrance to one of the skinnier passageways. She gestures for Nixon to head down it.

She puts her back to a wall and brings the blaster to her shoulder. The other two Uzeks are still giving chase, grunting and snorting amongst themselves. Laana fires three shots hoping to make quick work of most of the Uzeks, but this blaster fires a wide bolt. It's noisy and it's powerful. More powerful than she expects, and she lets out a moan each time the blaster rocks her shoulder.

She lets the gun fall from her hand. It lands with a heavy thud on the ground, and she steps over it to follow Nixon down the hall. The grunting and snorting is still behind them.

"I don't know where I'm going," Nixon shouts without slowing down.

"Honestly," she says, "I don't know either."

Nixon keeps running, and a blaster bolt crashes into the wall behind him. Laana screams.

Nixon stops and turns.

"Are you OK?"

She runs past him. He follows.

There's another blaster shot.

"We've got to be faster than this," Nixon shouts.

Laana moves quicker. He can see it. She's separating from him. He steps up his pace, and the grunting and snorting behind him becomes more distant. Neither of them stop running, though. They keep the faster pace, making this left and that right. And at some point, Nixon follows Laana around another right turn and it dumps them back out into a walkway.

He's sure all of this makes sense to someone who calls the Otanzia home, but it's only turned him around more than he already was. Laana too.

"Hmmm," she says, looking up and around. "Never seen this before."

The whole area feels abandoned and is only lit with half light. What should be open shop doors are closed. There's a bit of grit and grime on all the surfaces. Nixon doesn't like it. He hasn't liked anything about this place since they put down here. He let Laana lead. He let her determine where they'd lay up while they came up with a plan. Even after she said where she wanted them to go, he didn't like it. Not for all of the reasons he'd thought through before. Not for all the new ones that are coming to him right now.

"Get us back to the ship," he tells Laana.

She turns to him and starts to make a joke then stops. Her face gets serious.

"OK. Will do."

It's not a "yes, sir" but it's close. Nixon kind of likes it.

TEN

Laana is still sleeping in the galley when Nixon gets up for the day. He barely slept. He listened to Laana and gotten too confident, too comfortable. But nowhere is safe. There's not a spot in the galaxy where he can go that the Uzeks can't find him. No spot he can go where a bounty hunter won't be able to track him down. This case is a curse. No more dallying. He wants it off his ship. He wants it out of his life. And he wants all of that yesterday.

He takes a seat in the pilot's chair and pulls out his reader. He checks his credit balance. It's still painfully low, and there's no way to wish it fuller. But he needs funds. He's not going to rely on Laana's credits to get him anywhere. This is his mission. He'll take her help, and it's been life-saving so far, but he's not counting on it. Not anymore.

He knows what he has to do. He stands and takes a deep breath. The Bastic fuel rods.

He opens a cabinet and pulls out a bundle of rags, mostly clean, and lays them out on the floor into a somewhat square. He takes the rods out of a second cabinet and places them on the square of rags and wraps them up tightly to disguise their glow.

He pulls on his cloak and pulls up the hood before opening the ramp. He steps off the ship into surprising quiet.

He was expecting the noise and activity of the night before, but it's not here. Everything seems to be just waking up.

The ships are all lined up in organized rows, every one parked in its space. There are the put-together captains out working on their ships, getting ready for the day. And there are the less-put-together crew members struggling to find their home ships after late nights exploring everything Otanzia has to offer. All of the bigger ship's life-support systems create a dull hum that's the background for the random conversations Nixon hears bits of as he passes.

The fuel rods are tucked under his arm that's pulled inside of his cloak. His blaster is in his other hand. Last night doesn't have him spooked. It would have back on Exte, but this is reality now. The walk back to the ship made with Laana made him realize that. He's a guy who carries a blaster. He must be. And not just carry it hidden away as some kind of security blanket. He's a guy who carries a blaster and is ready to use it. That's the life he leads now.

He looks at the ships as he passes.

How many of these are just small-time captains looking for loads to haul? Or, more importantly, how many of these ships are bounty hunters keeping their eyes peeled for familiar faces? He pulls the hood of his cloak down lower. He suddenly feels very conspicuous. He's looking for a big ship because in his head that's how the math works. The captain of a bigger ship is likely to have more credits. He knows that a bigger ship is no guarantee of anything. The captain of a bigger ship could just as easily have bigger debts. But there are hundreds of ships in this bay, and he needs some kind of criteria that will speed up this process, so big ships it is.

Also, bigger ships are less likely to be bounty hunters. It's not a business that can support a lot of expenses, and big ships have a lot of expenses.

He finds a ship quickly. It's huge and can easily carry a crew of a couple dozen. Part of its team are already out and working in one of the panels on the side. They have it swung open and are all busy pulling wires loose, cleaning off connections. It looks like typical maintenance to Nixon, and it reminds him that his own ship could probably use a little of that more often.

The woman who seems to be the captain is standing off to the side watching her teamwork.

"Excuse me," Nixon says, pulling off his hood.

The woman doesn't look to him but says "Not taking on new crew."

"No, that's not what I was asking about. I have a ship of my own …" he turns and points toward EHL.

"Don't need a security team either. We're covered."

"No, no," Nixon says.

"Look," the woman finally turns to Nixon, "whatever it is you are looking for. Work, whatever. We don't need it. We can't give it you. We aren't interested."

Nixon nods and apologizes.

There are other big ships here, but that was the biggest, and her little scolding stings. But he keeps searching and finds a second ship a few minutes later.

This captain is also outside his ship. Just him this time. No crew. He's in a chair with his head in his reader.

Nixon pulls off his hood again and brings the roll of rags out from under his cloak.

"Excuse me," he says.

The man finishes something on his reader then places it in his lap.

"Help you?"

"Right away, just so you know, I'm not looking to crew for you. Not looking to pair up in some kind of mutually agreeable relationship. Just looking to offer you a deal."

"Well, I don't need crew. And I don't partner with any other ship. Burned too many times."

"How are you on fuel?"

"Oh, one of those?"

Nixon doesn't understand, and that fact is written all over his face.

The man explains: "Some kind of recurring fuel thing. You have some places across the galaxy. I give you credits and you give me access to some exclusive fuel stops scattered here and there. Except you don't. It's all a lie to scam me out of a few hundred credits. No thanks."

Nixon shakes his head as the captain talks. He puts the rods in one hand and starts to unwrap the rags. The green glow is there before the rods are actually visible.

"Just looking to unload these. No questions."

"Those Bastic?"

"Of course."

"Been burned there too. Can I hold them?"

Nixon passes the bundle across.

The man takes the rods and begins to unwrap them. The rods' green glow creeps up his arms as he pulls the rags open. His breath catches when he sees the rods.

"You weren't kidding," he tells Nixon. "These are real."

"One hundred percent."

"And you can document ownership."

Nixon hesitates.

"That's what I thought," the captain says and begins to wrap the rods back up.

"They're mine. I moved a load of them for someone else, and I took payment in rods instead of credits. I don't have paperwork documenting any kind of transfer of ownership, but these aren't stolen off some other sucker captain who's going to come tracking them down. Believe me."

The man hands the rods back to Nixon and thanks him for the offer but says he's going to pass.

So, it can't just be a big ship. It also needs to look a little … what? Off? Dirty? Broken? Something. Nixon will know it when he sees it, because it's going to look familiar. Its captain is going to look like someone Nixon already recognizes. Not because he knows whoever that is. He's too far from home for that. But he's still going to be able to tell this person's story. Broken life. Struggle to survive. Worry about tomorrow

tomorrow, let's just get through today. He's going to be dealing with someone who's a lot like him.

Adding that extra layer of qualification actually makes this process easier. He skips easily past those big, pretty ships flown by some up-and-up captain. Soon he's not seeing those ships at all, like he's had some mech added to his own eyes and he's turned on some kind of filter.

Now all he sees are those bigger ships piloted by the questionable captains. These ships are a little dirty. They are a little worn. They aren't pretty in the traditional sense. They don't gleam or shine, but they tell much more interesting stories.

He approaches a captain of one of these ships. It's a mid-sized hauler, bigger than EHL but a similar build. It's sides are potmarked by blaster fire and space debris. The captain is a human man. His unkempt beard brushes his chest when he talks. And when he talks, he's doing it around what's left of a thick cigar.

"You want how much for these?" he asks. But that's all he asks. He isn't worried about documentation or certificates of ownership. That's because after he pays Nixon the five-thousand credits he asks for the rods, this captain is going to put them straight into his engines. He's putting them to use, burning up any evidence that he'd bought them in the first place.

Nixon watches his reader. Once his credit balance updates with the transfer from this captain, Nixon thanks him and walks away. He's now headed inside of Otanzia, the retail district this time. He's not worried about entertainment. He has supplies to buy.

More food. Feeding two mouths, it's all getting eaten faster. What he'd bought on Makurra is almost gone now.

More medical supplies. He and Laana can't seem to keep themselves from getting hurt. If they want to be able to dress those wounds he needs more bandages, ointment, and spray.

Otanzia feels different today. The lights are brighter now, the ship's attempt to simulate day and night cycles. Nixon likes that better already. But the crowd, at least here by all the shops meant to serve the come-and-go visitors of the ship, is much more professional. These are the captains of all those polished ships out there in the hold. They aren't looking to kill time. They are checking items off to-do lists before they can get flying again. Their ships are mostly haulers. If they aren't hauling then they aren't earning. Otanzia is a stopping point on a longer journey, it's not a final destination for these captains or their ships. Nixon likes that thought. Motion. Movement. No standing still.

What was that rule he was taught as a kid? Something about objects in motion ... Whatever it is, he knows it's harder to hit a moving target, so after he gets rid of this case then maybe life is better with that little ship always moving.

He gets back to EHL and Laana is sitting in the navigator's seat playing with the case.

Nixon asks her to help load the food and medical supplies into the cabinets.

"I figured something out about your case," she says as they load the last of the items.

"What's that?"

She leaves the galley to go back to the main deck. Nixon follows. The case looks normal, but Laana picks it up and says "Watch."

She starts pushing the lock buttons.

"It's a nine-push combination."

Nixon had assumed it was a single three-button combo.

Laana pushes the last button then pulls the two halves of the case apart. They separate but don't open. On the case, the small etched lines deepen once the two halves are separated.

"This is a Tychon case," she says.

"Yeah, I figured. Tychon makes everything. Almost all that stuff we just loaded has a Tychon T on it."

Laana shakes her head. "No, not just made by them. This is a Tychon case. They didn't make it to sell. It's something they made to use. If your friend had this case then he was working for Tychon."

ELEVEN

"You're wrong."

"I'm not. Maybe he wasn't employed full time by Tychon, but to get this case he was definitely tied up with them in some way."

"Couldn't just be a case that someone had laying around?"

Laana shakes her head and hands the still-separated case to Nixon.

He takes it and looks at it closer.

"See those holes?" Small pin holes at the end of the etched lines that have appeared on the case.

Nixon turns the case over in his hands. The little holes are on each of the surfaces.

"To get the case open you need a set of keys that fit inside. You can't get those keys if you aren't Tychon."

"That's what you wanted to show me. A case that I still can't get into."

"Well ..." she hesitates. "I know a guy."

"Of course you do." Nixon pushes the two halves back together. The lock resets. The etched lines disappear.

"He's here. On Otanzia."

"Of course he is."

Nixon places the case back on the dash.

"Want to meet him? See if he can get inside?"

"I don't know," Nixon says. He thinks for a moment. He doesn't want to know what's inside. It doesn't matter. The job was to get the case to Azken. Deliver it. Be done.

The job was supposed to be easy. It wasn't supposed to cost Shaine his life. It wasn't supposed to cause Mira to uproot hers. It wasn't supposed to leave Nixon scrambling his way across the galaxy. And it definitely wasn't supposed to involve Tychon.

But here he is. A job that's gone all directions of sideways and working for an organization that he never wanted to tangle with. Why not find out what's cost so much and been deemed so valuable? Why not at least know?

"Sure," Nixon says. "Contact him."

The main hallways of Otanzia are lit like it's early afternoon, but here, inside of this bar, everything looks like it's deep night. Nixon and Laana are sitting in a booth that's shadowed even more. A small bit of light comes from a fake candle sitting in a glass holder on the table.

Laana watches the main door and taps her fingers on the tabletop. Nixon fidgets with the case. It's sitting in his lap underneath his cloak.

"Why were you hesitant?" Laana asks.

"Hesitant?"

"This morning. When I said I knew a guy who could get the case open, you didn't jump on it. Had to think about it."

Nixon shrugs.

"You still seem unsure."

"Because I am," Nixon says.

"You don't want to know what's inside that case?"

"End of the day, yes. That's why we're here."

Laana turns back to the door. A pair of humans who look like they just stepped off a ship for the first time in months walk through. They look worn down and tired, but they aren't going to miss the opportunity to take a real walk and get a real drink.

"They'll be drunk within an hour," Laana says.

"I'll give them half that."

The crowd in the bar starts to grow as the afternoon wears on and more and more captains bring their ships into Otanzia's hold. Nixon and Laana size up each of the people walking through the door until she waves at a new entrant.

It's a big thing. Tall. Arms as thick as tree trunks. It's skin is orange, and its bald head is covered by a field of small blue horns.

It raises a meaty hand to Laana as it approaches.

"Aldius," she says. "It's good to see you."

"You too, Laana." It's a voice that rattles everything inside Nixon, all the way down to his toes.

Aldius takes a seat at the table with them and Laana makes introductions. Nixon wastes no time diving into their situation. He runs his thumb across the locking mechanism as he explains that Shaine was a friend and that he was killed while he briefed Nixon on the job. Small case. Needs to get to Azken. Doesn't know who it needs to get to. Doesn't know exactly where it needs to be delivered. Not yet.

The whole time "He was working for Tychon" is running on a loop in the back of his head. Nixon finishes his explanation, and Laana says "That's why I contacted you. Best cracker I know. If anyone can get into this case ..."

"I appreciate the confidence. But if your friend is giving you a case and is asking you to get it to Azken then you're delivering to Tychon."

Laana jabs him with an elbow.

"I don't think I am," Nixon says. "I knew Shaine a long time. I know the kinds of people he'd work with. I'm sure there are plenty of people who aren't Tychon on Azken. He was working with one of them."

"Could be. I suppose," Aldius says. "But I prefer to play the odds."

Nixon doesn't respond, and the table sits in silence for a moment.

"So, let me take a look at this case."

Nixon pulls the case out from under his cloak. He places it on the table and slides it across to Aldius.

Nixon removes his hand and Aldius' eyes go wide, and his horns stand on end.

"Whoa."

TWELVE

"What?" Nixon and Laana say it in unison.

Aldius inspects it. He turns it over and over. He plays with the locking mechanism.

"I've heard of these, but I've never seen one."

"A Tychon case?" Laana asks. "I've been talking you up and now you're saying that you've never seen a Tychon case before?"

Aldius continues to stare at the case. He rubs gentle fingers against the metal sides.

"Yes, I've seen Tychon cases before. Hundreds of them. Thousands." He pauses and continues to admire Nixon's case. "But not one of these Tychon cases."

"What do you mean?" Nixon asks.

Aldius slowly moves the case around in small circles.

"This case is special. It's Tychon. There's no doubt." He points out some of the work done by whoever put it together.

Aldius inspects the locking mechanism closer. He brings the case up to his face and gets a good look at the lock.

"This is good work."

"Glad you're impressed," Nixon says.

Aldius puts the case on the table and starts talking, but he never looks up, like what he's saying is meant for the case and not his tablemates.

"This isn't a standard Tychon box. This isn't one that they sell anywhere. You only get one of these boxes if you're part of a Tychon security team. These are internal only. I've heard about them. I knew they existed, but I'd never seen one. Not until today."

He finally looks back up at them. "So thank you."

"Yeah, sure," Nixon says. "Can you get it open?"

Aldius looks back to the case.

"Three-button mechanism, so it'll be a six- or nine-push combination."

Laana sits up straighter and blurts "It's a nine-push. I got that much on the ship."

She's smiling a proud smile.

Aldius nods. "OK, so nine-push. Then we'll need…"

He doesn't finish his sentence. He picks up the case instead and rubs the tips of his thick fingers all along the surface. It's slow and deliberate.

He puts the case back down and reaches into a pocket. He pulls out a canvas pouch. He undoes the tie keeping it closed, and a mess of pins and keys spill out onto the table.

He picks up the case again. He begins working on the locking mechanism. He pushes the buttons with his eyes closed, his face frozen in concentration.

He tries a first set of nine pushes then pulls the two halves of the case. Nothing.

He tries the second set of nine pushes. Again, nothing, but he smiles.

The third set of pushes he's more confident. It doesn't separate, but there's more movement this time. He begins to nod then rushes through his fourth attempt. He pulls the two halves confidently and the case separates. The etched lines appear. The keyholes open.

He puts the case back on the table and wades a finger through the keys and pins laying across the table.

He puts pins into each of the holes. Picking up one. Considering it. Looking at the case then inserting the pin into what looks like the right hole. He keeps repeating the process—Considering a pin. Inserting a pin.—until all of the holes are filled. He then tries to open the box, but it won't.

He pulls all of the pins out and begins the process over. He tries the box again. It doesn't open, doesn't seem any different to Nixon than the first time. But it is different to Aldius. He pulls the pins again then hurriedly adds them back in a new combination this time. He tries to open the case. Now Nixon sees it. It's small, but it's movement.

Aldius only removes some of the pins. He digs through the pile of other keys and pins on the table. He inserts new ones and tries the case again. Even more movement. He pulls even fewer pins out this time and rearranges the pins that he's left in.

Nixon watches him try the case again, and it's nearly there. It's nearly open. Nixon is about to see what's been so important that it cost Shaine his life. About to see what has turned Nixon's life upside down.

The excitement starts to build in his toes. It bounces his heels. He pushes his hands hard into his knees to try and keep the energy from rocketing him out of his seat.

Aldius holds the case out in front of him and focuses his attention on it, concentrating like he can force the pins and holes to show him which goes where. He mutters something to himself, then his face lights up like it all finally makes sense. He pulls pins out of holes and places them in others and tries the case one more time. It opens.

There's no hiss. There's no pop. The halves just separate. Aldius looks inside. His eyes go wide. "I don't believe it." He puts the two halves of the box on the table.

"What?" Nixon asks. "What is it?"

"They did it," Adlius says. "They actually did it."

"What?" Nixon asks again. "What's in the case."

"It's the whole galaxy."

Nixon and Laana look at each other. Laana shrugs, because this makes just as little sense to her. Nixon opens his mouth to ask for an explanation, but before he's able to get anything out an alarm sounds from inside the case.

06: AZKEN

ONE

Nixon sits at the galley table on EHL trying to catch his breath. Sweat beads on his forehead, and everything covered by his cloak is sweltering. He pulls the cloak off and tosses it on the ground over his shoulder.

Laana sits next to him and also struggles to catch her breath. Running full sprint out of a bar and across most of a civilization-class ship, an alarmed Tychon case shouting its presence, will do that. Her friend Aldius sits across the table from them, and he's the most settled of the three.

"How many people do you think saw us?" Nixon asks.

"All of them?" Laana says.

"Nobody," Aldius says. "People here tend to keep to themselves. They mind their own."

"I don't believe that," Nixon says. "You can not see a lot of things, but the three of us—you," he jams his thumb at Aldius, the gigantic orange creature that Nixon has only just met, "you notice that, no matter how much you are wanting to keep to yourself."

The alarm still sounds from the case that Nixon has been carrying with him since Exte. He'd turned to Aldius to get the thing open. He was Laana's suggestion after she'd halfway convinced Nixon that he wanted to see what was inside, what has caused so much trouble.

He did want to know what was inside. He did want to see what was so important that it's caused all these ripples in Nixon's life.

Ripples? Waves are more like it.

Aldius seemed duly impressed by whatever is in the box, but Nixon hasn't had a chance to ask him what that was. The alarm made sure of that. Once it sounded, the three of them were up from their seats at the back of the bar where they'd met and sprinting out the door.

Laana led the way with Nixon shouting for her to just go back to the ship.

Aldius has the case unfolded on the table in front of him. He's focused on nothing else, his head down and leaned in close to the case. His hands are so big that they make it impossible for Nixon to see what Aldius is doing.

A moment later the alarm stops, and the inside of EHL is quiet. Aldius sits back for just a second then leans back over the case. His elbows straddle, and he looks like a victorious giant staring down another defeated villager.

Laana asks the question that Nixon has been wanting to ask since they ran from the bar. Aldius had told them that the case held the whole galaxy, but he'd never explained what that meant.

Aldius smiles and sticks a finger into the top of the case. He hooks a meaty knuckle around something that Laana and Nixon can't see yet. He pulls it out and tosses it to Nixon. He reaches in for another then two more after that. He hands those to Nixon as well.

"Toss them," he says.

"Toss them?"

"Just out in front of you, gentle." Aldius makes a tossing gesture wanting Nixon to copy it, and he does.

The orbs that Aldius handed to him immediately scatter and create the four points of a horizontal rectangle. They all bounce slightly for just a moment then the space in the center of all of them fills with a shimmering black surface.

"Oh my …" Laana doesn't finish.

"Right?" Aldius says. "I've heard … but I never thought they'd actually be able do it."

"Somebody tell me what I'm supposed to be impressed by," Nixon says. "What am I looking at?"

"It's a portal," Aldius says.

"A portal?"

"Wiggle some fingers in there."

Nixon hesitates a moment then pushes a hand into the void. It disappears. He pushes his arm up to the elbow, and everything below that is just gone.

"Careful," Aldius says. "Pull your arm back out."

Nixon does, and he's whole again.

Laana steps up next to him and brushes her hand against the shimmering blackness. "I'd always heard …" she says but doesn't finish. "I just assumed those were rumors. Stuff that hunters told each other about while waiting for work. But look …"

She takes another swipe at the portal, and her fingers briefly disappear.

"They did it," Aldius says. "They've been working on it for years. But they did it. This changes everything."

Nixon listens to this conversation, but he's not understanding. "Changes things how?"

Aldius: "This opens the galaxy to Tychon. These portals allow them to be anywhere at any time."

Laana picks up the narrative. "No more taking turf. You hadn't seen much of Tychon back on Exte because it was just too far from Azken. They haven't made it out there yet."

"With this," Aldius continues, "that's not a factor anymore."

He spins the now unfolded case to face Nixon.

"Coordinates go in here," Aldius says pointing to a small keyboard. "That tells the portal where to open to. Toss the orbs and step through."

He wipes a hand in a wide circle and gathers up the orbs and the portal disappears. "Toss them again."

He does. They scatter and float in a horizontal rectangle again. "Ready to come back? Step through from the other side."

"At least you assume that's how it works," Nixon says and looks closer at the case's new configuration.

Aldius shrugs. "Sure. I assume. But it's the technology that's complicated, not the concept."

"And that's why you say it was the whole galaxy in the case."

Laana gets up from the table and pulls a cup from the cupboard. She's making something for herself, a cup of java drink. She offers a cup to the other two. They both wave her off.

She talks as she makes her own cup. She's not speaking to either Aldius or Nixon, just reasoning things out loud.

"If Tychon can now get anywhere in the galaxy just by stepping through one of these portals then they need a much smaller security team. A smaller team made up of better agents. Beating Tychon just got a lot harder."

Aldius stands, and the galley suddenly feels smaller. Nixon pulls the unfolded case closer and begins to study it.

The keyboard is small, just enough keys to enter in galactic coordinates. There's a small screen, again just big enough to display the coordinates entered. This case is a one function tool.

But, man, that one function ...

"And what's this indicate?" Nixon asks, pointing to a small green light that's just started blinking a pattern near the corner of the display. "It wasn't doing that a second ago."

Aldius looks over Nixon's shoulder.

"Oh ... gorotza."

"Gorotza?"

Aldius has the unfolded case back in his hands. He's looking at the back. Then he spins it around and looks at the bottom. He runs a finger in a very distinct path along the outside of the case back to where the green light is quietly blinking.

'Gorotza," he says again.

"Why do you keep saying that?" Nixon asks.

"If the audible alarm wasn't enough to scare us away from this case, then this could."

"Because…" Laana says, waiting in expectation for Aldius to finish her sentence.

"It might be a warning signal back to Azken. Back to Tychon."

"Might be?"

"Yeah. Might also be just some light. I don't know enough about the actual workings of the case. Could just indicate some sort of benign network connection. Or it could indicate …"

Nixon interrupts. "Yeah, we just don't know."

The room goes quiet. Aldius and Laana look to Nixon. He looks at them. Things hang in this awful limbo for a few moments when Laana finally asks: "What now, boss?"

Boss.

Boss?

Nixon's never had anyone call him boss before and actually mean it. He's always been the one looking to others for direction. He's looked to them for next steps, for marching orders. And now he has two faces looking to him.

He thinks. What would Shaine do? That's the person he's seen model this kind of role most often. He's the person who sat himself at the head of the table and started giving out assignments. The person who laid out the plan, the always complicated plan and all its steps. A person in every role and a role for every person. So, what would Shaine do here?

Someone who may have spied out your position? Someone who might know when you're coming? Someone who may have stolen the element of surprise and is looking to strike? Shaine would take the fight to them. So that's what Nixon is going to do here.

He's been in enough fights to know that if you see someone getting ready to lay the haymaker on you then you step into the punch. You shorten the blow. You lessen the impact. You reduce the force with which the punch lands. Then you counter.

"We go to Azken. Today. Now. We leave, and don't give them a chance to surprise us."

TWO

"Laana, let's get everything secured. Get things cleaned up in here. I'll get the engines started."

Laana begins clearing java drink trash from the counter. She puts mugs and tools back into the cupboards and engages the locks on the doors.

"Aldius, it's going to be tight, but we'll figure out a place where you can sleep. It's not going to be much, but ..."

Aldius interrupts.

"Don't bother. I'm not going."

Both Laana and Nixon stop what they are doing.

"Not going?" Nixon asks.

Aldius grabs his rolled package of pins and keys and heads back to the main cabin. Both Nixon and Laana follow.

"Everyone here saw you with that case. They saw you with us."

"Not everyone," Alduis says as he gets to the ramp. "Fewer than you think probably. I'm not at the kind of risk you think I am. Besides, when you two put distance between me and that case, things will be fine."

Laana: "That thing was howling. Screaming as we ran down the hall. And you're big and orange. You think someone didn't make note of that interesting trio?"

"I've been here a long time. People keep their heads down most of the time. And a good majority of the people aren't here long. Even if they did see us, they won't be on the ship by tomorrow."

Nixon is about to interrupt with his own protest, but Aldius continues.

"I can go back to my place and hole up for a bit. Let all of this pass. Let the crowd here cycle off. I'll be fine."

Nixon looks to the now-empty dash. He's so used to seeing the case sitting there. Closed. Taunting him. Now it's in the galley. Opened. All of its secrets revealed. All of its possibilities known. He owes that to this big orange thing.

"You're right," Nixon says. "You probably can just hole up in your space here for a bit and all of this will pass. Wait until our little mad dash becomes just a funny 'Did you hear about that time' tale that people who live here tell to those just passing through. All the details will be so twisted up by then that no one will know that's you in the story. You'll probably tell it yourself."

Aldius is smiling.

"But," Nixon says, "that's a lot riding on a probably. That's probably what will happen. But ..."

Aldius nods.

"What if you came with us for now. Get to Azken. See how this all plays out. Then we can bring you back here after."

"Probably," Aldius says.

"What?"

"You can probably bring me back here. If everything works out on Azken."

Nixon smiles. He nods.

"Yeah. Probably."

"I appreciate the concern. Honestly. But I've spent a lot of time getting myself setup here. Getting myself established. I'm not ready to walk away from all of it. Not going to give it all up for a probably."

Laana begins to protest again, but Nixon puts a hand up and stops her.

"It's fair," he says. He's thinking back to that courtyard with Shaine and how he made his choice. How it's a choice that changed everything and how it's one he made in a heated moment. He didn't think. He just acted. And now look where it has him—squarely in the sights of Tychon and its security team.

"I wish you we're making a different choice. We could use you ..."

"I'm a cracker. What you're doing, you don't need a cracker."

"A cracker is what you do. A fighter is what you are. We'll always have room for another fighter. So if you change your mind ..."

Aldius smiles and nods. "And if you ever need help ..."

"We'll reach out."

Aldius thanks Lana and Nixon for letting him see an internal Tychon case that close up. They both thank him for the help. Then he turns and is gone.

Laana and Nixon watch him go then Laana begins to speak. "I just can't believe ..."

Nixon interrupts her.

"No time for that," he says. "Aldius made his choice, agree with it or not. We've made ours. Let's get the ship ready to fly."

Laana responds with only a nod.

There's not a lot to do. Laana goes back to the galley and continues working there while Nixon jumps into the captain's seat.

He begins running through his personal checklist in his head. First, he presses the button on the dash that starts pushing fuel to the engines and gets them ready to fire. It's all done in the back of the ship, but when it's quiet you can hear the chemicals beginning to mix in the lines that will carry the fuel to the fire.

Today is not quiet, though. Laana continues to talk about Aldius' decision. She's shouting to be heard, and she's literally the only noise in the entire ship that Nixon can hear.

About halfway through Nixon's list, the engines begin to rumble beneath them. Nixon smiles. It still feels good to have that constrained power all to himself. It's just waiting to be told what to do, to be told where to go. EHL is just like Laana. EHL is just like Nixon used to be.

Now, though, he's in the pilot's seat. He's the one leading this mission.

Laana joins him in the main cabin a few minutes later. She slides into the navigator's chair and buckles in.

"That mean we are ready to go?" Nixon asks.

"Everything is secure and tucked away. We need to do anything evasive, there shouldn't be anything bouncing around the ship to hurt us."

Nixon nods and smiles. "You said that like you think evasive maneuvers are something that's going to be optional."

"A girl can dream."

Nixon laughs and lifts EHL off the ground. He signals to the Otanzia control team in charge of getting them out of here.

Overhead speakers crackle and a thin and anxious voice fills the cabin. "Request acknowledged, captain. Our pattern is currently full. We will send signal when your position becomes available."

Nixon grunts a response. He looks to the screen in front of him. There are a dozen ships ahead of him in the departure pattern. It's going to take more than an hour for his position to come up. Then, after it does come up, it'll be another hour before his turn comes up to depart.

"EHL," he says. "Let's get out of here."

"Sir?" The ship asks.

"Sir?" Laana says just after the ship.

"I said get us out of here."

"Yes, sir," the ship says.

Nixon sits a little higher. His first in-the-moment decision. Feels good. Feels smart.

"Are you stupid?" Laana asks.

EHL spins slowly so it's facing out of the slip. Ships lining up to depart are above them. The wide openings that Nixon and EHL came in through sits what feels like an extra long distance in front of them.

"What do you mean?"

"You jump the line like this, go out of pattern, and you get flagged. You won't be able to come back here or to any of the other civilization ships that the Uhartea Corporation operates. You jump that line and the first thing you do with that new transponder is burn it on a stunt."

Nixon wants to say that he doesn't care. He wants to tell Laana that her opinion isn't important. He's made his decision. They are jumping the line and getting off the Otanzia. That he'll instruct EHL to put so much into the engines that they'll be nothing more than a blur of color and smoke.

But he knows Laana's right. No matter how fast EHL gets going, they will trip alarms. They will burn that transponder. They will create trouble behind them when they already have plenty ahead of them.

"Stop, EHL," Nixon says. "Put us back down. Wait for the signal that our spot in the pattern is up."

THREE

EHL is on auto pilot. It's flying to Azken, and Nixon sits in the pilot's seat barely paying attention to where he's headed. He is too distracted by the now-open case.

He holds the orbs in one hand and rotates them around each other in his palm. With the other hand he's entering coordinates into the case. They are random combinations of numbers, but he doesn't care. He tosses the orbs out in front of him and watches them spread into a rectangle and the shimmering black film fill the space between them.

He stares into the gap trying to pick out what's on the other side. It all looks like a screen to him, like he's watching something on a busted reader. He'll stare into the black until he determines that he can't see anything in there then gathers up the orbs in a wide, sweeping motion.

He programs more random coordinates into the case and tosses the orbs again. Every third toss, he sticks his arm into the black and it disappears to his elbow.

"You know that's dumb," Laana says as she sits in the navigator's seat. She begins checking coordinates and settings, confirming that EHL still has them on the right course.

After hurrying to get off Otanzia, the whole trip to Aken has been quiet. They've seen no signs of Tychon security coming for the case.

"What's dumb?" Nixon gathers all of the orbs.

"That," Laana says. She enters a few final commands into EHL's system then turns. She looks at him. "Everything you're doing there is dumb."

Nixon punches more numbers into the case then tosses the orbs again.

"I'm not sure," Laana says, "that you should be playing with portal tech on a moving ship. Seems like you're playing with fire with some of the physics. More importantly, though, you're jamming your arm into the black up to your elbow without knowing what's on the other side. There could be someone waiting to cut it off or some big hungry beast looking for some kind of snack."

He sticks his arm back into the black once Laana finishes speaking. "You'll never know what's on the other side. That's what makes this kind of exciting."

Laana pulls something up on her reader and begins to watch. "Suit yourself," she says. "But when you pull your arm back and you're missing your thumb, don't say I didn't warn you."

Nixon gathers up the orbs but doesn't enter new coordinates into the case. Instead, he packs it all back up. He refolds the case and sticks the orbs inside. The only thing he doesn't do is set the locking mechanism. He carries the case back to the crew quarters and sets it at the foot of his bunk then climbs on himself.

He stretches out and starts to think about everything that's happened in the span of just a few weeks. It wasn't that long ago he was in that courtyard with Shaine seeing the case for the first time. He thinks about all the chaos that followed that moment. The spaceport on Exte. Mira. The Uzeks. Finding EHL in that shipyard and dodging blaster fire just to get her engines started and fire off the planet.

Carting a mover full of Bastic fuels rods to earn credits on Umel. Learning everything he has so far about repairing a ship. Outgunned on Ibilia. A stop in the Otanzia that was supposed to be a breather but turned out to be anything but.

And picking up a partner on Makurra, someone to do all of this with. It's more adventure than he's ever had, and he survived in ways that he never thought he could. It's been tiring. It's been dangerous. It's been deadly. But damn if it also hasn't been fun.

Nixon tries to think father back. Think to his previous life on Exte. To his little hole of a place, ceilings so short that he couldn't stand up straight once he was inside. He tries to think about meals cooked on a hot box in the corner. He tries to think about watching his credit balance, just hoping that it would somehow miraculously increase by a credit or two. He tries to think about all of that, but his mind has made so much of it a blur. It's like it's all been wiped with a wet rag and now it's just a swirl of colors. He can recall bits and pieces of things. He can see moments. Little snippets of time. Enough, that he knows he doesn't want to go back to that after this case is delivered.

He pulls his own reader from the side table next to him and pulls up the boards he used to look at back on Exte, dreaming of a different life than the one he'd had. Back then, the messages left there by those rogue captains all mentioned places he never thought he'd see. Now, they include names of planets that he recognizes. They include names of cities that he's been to.

He scrolls through the messages from captains asking for help. He scrolls through the messages that offer bounties. He scrolls through the messages that offer delivery work. All of it pulls at him. All of it feels like opportunity now. Real opportunity. Things that he legitimately could do. These offers don't feel like the impossible opportunity they were back on Exte. There they were something to dream about.

Tonight, though, these messages have him more than dreaming. He opens one message and reads it. There's a space for the request. There's a space for whatever the job pays. Then there are the coordinates pointing to wherever in the galaxy this job is taking place.

301

He opens another message, and the format is the same: Request. Price. Coordinates.

Another message: Request. Price. Coordinates.

And another: Request. Price. Coordinates.

Coordinates.

Coordinates.

He remembers what Aldius said just a few days ago. He'd just cracked the case and was looking inside for the first time.

What did he see? His answer "The whole universe."

Suddenly, Nixon feels like he's been slapped. He has the coordinates for every worthwhile job in this galaxy. And now, with this case, he has the ability to jump to any of those coordinates he wants to.

That previous plan–to deliver the case and move on—it's out the window. He now has an idea that will be much more lucrative.

FOUR

Nixon stands and sticks his head out into the hall and shouts for Laana.

"What is it?" she asks a few moments later when she's standing in the doorway to the crew quarters. Nixon is standing too, and he's smiling. He hands her his reader.

"Look at this," he says, "and tell me what you see."

She looks at the screen for a moment then drags a finger along the screen, scrolling the lists of messages there.

Nixon waits for her to have the same observation he did. He waits for her to come to the same realization.

"Job boards? I knew about these."

"Yeah, I did too." Nixon takes back his reader. He taps on one of the listings.

He hands the reader back to her. "There. Now look."

She again runs her finger up and down the screen. "I mean, it looks like a good job. Seems like something I could, I mean, we could, pursue after we get the case delivered. Doesn't look like it pays …"

Nixon snatches the reader from her hands before she can finish her sentence. He quickly scrolls the screen to the bottom of the post then hands it back to Laana.

"Now," he says.

"The coordinates," she says, and he smiles. He waits for her to now make the connection. She doesn't.

"Every job ends with coordinates," he says.

"Yeah?" She's still not getting it.

"You've done this. You've chased jobs on these boards. What's the most important element to catching one of them?"

She steps through the door and sits on his bunk. "Time," she says.

Nixon nods. "Faster you can get there the better chance you have to get any job, right?"

"Sure."

"And what do we have now?"

She thinks for a moment.

"The case," Nixon says, his patience for this little game worn away. "We have the case. And like Aldius said, it's not really a case. It's the whole galaxy."

"Are you saying you want ..."

Nixon sits down and doesn't let her finish. "I want to take that case and what's inside of it and use it to be first to every significant bounty job and courier job in the galaxy. Anything where there's a pilot or someone willing to pay ten thousand credits or more, I want to be there. I want us first in line. We can make a fortune."

"Sure," Laana says, "assuming we can avoid Tychon. You think they are going to just not come looking for their case?"

It's the part of the plan that Nixon hadn't figured out yet.

"Probably," he says, then he switches. "Yes. They're going to come looking for it. But think about how much we can make before they catch us?"

"So, you expect them to catch us?"

"Yes. ... No. ... I don't know. They are going to come looking. I know that. But if we got distant enough. Go somewhere in the galaxy where there's nothing. No planets. No ships. Just stray asteroid fields and other space junk. Just park ourselves out there and use the orbs in that case to jump in and out of all the good jobs. We get enough time to collect enough credits we could even turn the case in ourselves and both head our separate ways and retire."

Laana picks at a stitch on Nixon's bed cover. She pops a thread loose and spins it between her fingers. "I don't hate the idea," she says. "But I hate the plan. Come up with something more concrete, something that accounts for Tychon, and something that defines how all of this will actually work then I'm in."

Nixon smiles and claps his hands together. "OK," he says. "Go back up front. I've got some thinking to do."

Laana leaves and Nixon sits back on his bunk. He pulls the case from the side table and unpacks all of its parts again. He lays the keyboard in front of him and keeps the orbs in one hand. He picks up his reader, and the last job listing he showed to Laana is still there on the screen. It's specifically showing the coordinates.

He looks to the keyboard and hesitates for a moment then turns back to his reader. He memorizes the coordinates then enters them into the keyboard. He tosses the orbs out in front of him before he can think too long or too hard about what he's doing.

The orbs split and bounce and the shimmering black barrier forms between them. Nixon jumps down from his bunk and lifts a leg to put it through the barrier but hesitates again. He drops his leg back to the ground.

Is this dumb? Probably so. But ...

He steps through the barrier before he can talk himself out of doing this.

On the other side it's green and lush, and he's immediately met with the sound of fire from three different blasters. There's yelling in a language that he doesn't understand. He drops to the ground as he watches the big leaves of whatever plants these are rip and shred as the fight that he's stepped into ramps up.

There's more yelling and more fire. The tail of a ship pokes over the tops of small trees to his right. On his left is some kind of rock face. He follows the rock face up and sees a dozen men firing big balsters down onto the ship. He reaches for his own blaster, but it's not tucked into his waistband. It's still on the dash back on EHL.

His heart begins to race. The yelling gets louder, and the leaves on the trees in front of him begin to rattle and shake. Something bigger than Nixon has ever seen suddenly bursts through and is charging right at him. Its teeth are wet and bared. Its eyes are yellow and narrowed. Its arms, all four of them, are extended out in front of it, the claws sharp and stained with blood.

The ground shakes with every quick step this thing takes. Blaster fire screams out through the plants and slams into this thing's back, but it's unaffected.

Nixon scrambles back to his feet and jumps back through the barrier. He quickly swipes the orbs, two into each hand, once he's back through to kill whatever connection these things create.

He's still on the floor. His heart is racing, but he's smiling.

This idea can work. No, he didn't expect to see whatever that was, but he could have been. He grabs his reader and scrolls back through that last posting. He reads what the captain wrote about the kind of work he was looking to have done. It's vague but was clearly a defense job. And the pay—just 500 credits—isn't worth that kind of risk. But if Nixon can be more discerning about the jobs he takes and strict about the amounts of credits he'll work for then this idea can work. It can work really well.

FIVE

The thought of buckets of credits has Nixon excited. He wants them. He wants all of them. He wants so many that his reader gets physically heavy because the number on his balance is so high. This plan can get him that.

But if he's being selfish and greedy—and he is—then he doesn't just want credits from new jobs. He wants the credits he's supposed to get from this job. All of those credits that Shaine was promised, he wants them in his account. He wants to be able to see them on his screen.

But how? How does he keep the case but also get the credits for turning it in? He doesn't know. Not yet, but he will. He just needs time to think this through.

He heads to the galley. All this excitement, the energy of what's possible, has left him hungry. He digs into the cabinets and pulls out the tins of meat and crackers.

He sits at the table and starts to think about that heavy reader and all the things he could do with an account overflowing with credits. His mind dances and bounces between a few scenarios before it lands on the one that sticks. It's his vision from Makurra. Not the vision of himself running some kind of galactic repair shop, although that does come to mind. The vision that sticks is the one he had of a little house on a quiet piece of land. EHL parked off to the side and a comfortable chair out front where he could spend his days watching whatever world this is pass by him. He sees that solitary life. It's doubly appealing now as he and Laana speed toward Azken.

He finishes the meat from one tin and starts picking at the off-white label that wraps it. It comes apart easily, and Nixon rolls the paper off the metal and looks at it. That's when it hits him. This Bowtan meat isn't the good stuff. He didn't buy that this time. This is the stuff you buy when your funds are low and you want to get the most you can for whatever credits you have left. Most people call it fake meat. It's not that, Nixon knows, but it's not far from it. It's a trace of Bowtan meat, but it's mostly filler. Other animals and grains. But if you're hungry enough, it'll do.

What if he created a case that looked like the real thing from the outside? What if he created something with a wrapper that said "orb case"? And what if even when you opened it up it looked like the real deal?

If he controlled the meeting where he turned over the case could he make them think this is the real case? Maybe? Probably? Was he willing to try it? Yes.

Nixon has opened and emptied three more tins of the cheap Bowtan meat. He's dumped their contents out onto a plate that he's left near the galley's heating unit. He's found a hammer in a repair kit that's stored in one of the cabinets and he's beating one of the tins flat with it. Every blow is reverberating throughout the ship, and it's enough to get Laana's attention.

"What are you doing?" she asks a moment after she appears in the doorway to the galley.

Nixon's been at this for more than an hour, and Laana kicks one of his previous attempts as she enters the room. It's made of soft metal and one end is smashed flat from where it hit the wall after Nixon threw it in frustration.

"Trying to make a fake case." Nixon says through gritted teeth.

"A fake case?"

He explains his plan.

Laana considers what he's said.

"I like it," she says.

Nixon, genuinely surprised: "You do? I'm not so sure it's a good idea anymore."

"Why not?"

"Because I'm not sure it's possible to create a passable fake. I can't get past the very basics, and we are running out of raw materials on the ship."

Laana grabs the plate of Bowtan meat then takes a seat at the galley table across from Nixon. She puts a pinch of the meat in her mouth and says to Nixon: "Let me try."

She pulls the tin that Nixon has flattened in front of her and begins to work. She's quiet and concentrating, and Nixon watches as she bends the metal. She gets up and looks for more tools. She's using a ruler to measure lengths and to force clean seams and distinct folds in the metal.

She works and reworks certain sections, leaning close to work out finer details. Nixon admires her precision, and it's easy to get lost in her concentration. An hour passes quickly, then a second hour. And by the time she lifts her head and pushes her creation to the middle of the table it's been nearly three hours since she'd come back to the galley.

She's smiling and staring at her case. Nixon looks at it too.

She looks up to him. "Well?"

Nixon hesitates then says, "It's good."

"You think so?"

"Considering what we had to work with and that, I assume, you've never made one of these before, yeah. It's good."

Her shoulders slump. "That's some qualified praise."

Nixon bends and grabs one of his crumpled attempts that landed at his feet after he threw it across the galley. He shows it to Laana. "You did infinitely better than I did, and on one attempt."

He squeezes his case into a ball of thin, malleable metal and tosses it toward the trash bin. He misses.

"Problem is we can't just do a good job. We have to do a perfect job. It has to be able to pass an up-close inspection. At least for a moment or two."

Laana nods. "Fair."

Nixon picks up Laana's case. She's included a lot of the details from the original case. She's tried to replicate the etched lines. "Look," he says, pointing to the lines she's drawn and the small dots she's added to indicate the pinholes on the original case. "That's good stuff, but it's all facade. Run a finger across that, and it's all smooth. We can't have smooth."

"We'll never make a perfect copy."

Nixon shakes his head. "Doesn't have to be perfect. But it has to feel like it just long enough that I can pass it across, get the credits, then get out of there."

Laana nods along as he speaks. "OK, then. What do you suggest?"

"I think we need help. I think we need Aldius."

SIX

Laana's reader connects after the second attempt, and Aldius' large, orange head fills her screen.

"Trouble already?" Aldius asks through a laugh.

"Not trouble," Laana says.

Nixon finishes the sentence: "But we could use your help."

"This isn't just you guys wanting to check how I'm doing?"

Aldius sits back in his seat and his image on Laana's screen jiggles as he sets his reader on a desktop stand.

He props his feet up on the desk, and now they are about all either Laana or Nixon can see.

"If you weren't wanting to know how I was doing …"

Nixon interrupts him. "We have a plan we need a little help with."

"A new plan? Already?"

"We aren't giving them the case," Nixon says.

Aldius pulls his feet off the desktop and sits straighter in his chair. "Interesting new direction."

"We're keeping it and all its potential for ourselves. We'll use it to make as many credits as possible until they find us and make us give it back."

"Oh, they won't make you give it back. They'll kill you and take it."

That stops Nixon for a moment. It wasn't how he ever saw this ending. He didn't know what the end looked like specifically, but it wasn't with him or Laana dead. It just ended with them leaving the case behind somewhere. They make an agreed upon number of credits, shake hands, congratulate each other on a good run, then go their separate ways, the case sitting on top of some empty table somewhere just waiting for someone else to pick it up and discover its secrets.

That, or they crush it and the orbs under some big rock somewhere then call the partnership agreeably dissolved.

"So, what did you need me for?" Aldius asks.

"We need you to make us a fake case," Laana says.

"Why do you need a fake case?"

"Because we are still going to try and get the credits for this job. I have to give them something to do that."

Nixon stands and steps toward the wall. He picks up one of his failed attempts and also grabs Laana's version. He holds them up to the camera.

"We thought this wouldn't be that hard. Clearly, we were mistaken."

Aldius laughs. "Points for effort."

"Can you help us?" Laana asks.

Aldius considers the question and asks Laana to show him the original case. She holds it up to her camera. He leans in close and his face again fills her view. His eyes narrow in concentration.

"Turn it?" he asks, and she does.

He asks her to turn it again and then to open it. The light from inside the case makes Laana's reader glow green.

Alduis leans back again and says "Yeah, I can make you a copy."

Nixon lets out a breath that he's been holding since this conversation started. "Fantastic. Thank you. Thank you."

"For a third of whatever it is you guys are getting," Aldius says.

Nixon stops his internal celebration. "What?"

"Whatever it is that's been worked out as payment with Tychon, I want a third of it."

"For building a case?" Nixon says.

"I'm not building a case," Aldius says. "I'm building a working replica of a private internal Tychon case. I'm building you a replica that your whole plan hinges on passing muster at the exchange. And your whole plan wouldn't even be your plan if you didn't know what was inside that original case. You owe me for that too. Only asking for a third almost feels like I'm cheating myself."

Nixon doesn't like it. It's selfish, but it's been his life on the line this entire trip. He's the one who's been chased. He's been shot at more than anyone else. He's been the one trying to outrun trouble. Why does he have to share a third of his take with Aldius? Just as quickly, he realizes that he's not in the power position here. He needs a case. That means he needs Aldius. He reluctantly agrees.

"Give me a few days to get this together. The details might be a little tricky to figure out.

"We are a few days out from Azken," Nixon says. "We'll connect again once we're there and settled."

"Sounds good," Aldius says. "I'll get to work."

His connection blinks closed.

"Well," Lanna says. "Looks like we've got a case."

"Yeah," Nixon says. "A damn expensive one."

SEVEN

Nixon is in the crew quarters, the case open in front of him. He's keying in coordinates again, places he knows this time. There's the numbers for his old hole on Exte. There's Shaine's house. The Goodtimes Palace.

He doesn't toss the orbs, although he wants to. As he gets closer to Azken the more this plan seems like a bad idea. He's talking about running a scam on one of the biggest powers in the galaxy. This is a company that could make him and his ship a ball of hot, galactic slag without even lifting a finger. And it wouldn't think twice about doing it.

Key in any of those familiar coordinates, toss the orbs and step through back onto Exte. Let EHL and Laana continue the trip to Azken. He'd just go back and find his old life again. Get a small place. Scramble up work every day. Small stuff, here and there. A little construction. A little courier work. Just enough to keep the credits flowing. And now that he's had this little taste of adventure, he's not going to live that life wondering what else is out there. This ship and this trip has stamped out that little spark of curiosity for more, that expectation that it has to be better than this. Maybe that life was the better one. He didn't have people chasing him. He didn't have the threat of a blaster bolt appearing from nowhere and for unknown reasons.

Except he knows none of that is true. That life that he's remembering now didn't have that golden glow he's recalling. It did have looming threats. It had Uzeks. It had desperation and bad deals. It had back alley beatings and mad dashes through crowded streets.

Those things, though, were things he knew. Those were things he was familiar with, enemies he knew how to fight. This, though, this is picking a fight with the biggest of the baddest. This is turning the volume up well past its top levels.

He grabs the orbs from the case, and he rolls them in his palm. They make a dull pulsing sound as they go around and around each other. They start to warm his skin. He thinks hard about tossing them out in front of him. The muscles in his arm twitch, just waiting for his head to give them the instructions to do it. And he almost does, but …

"Hey," Laana says.

She snaps him from his spiraling daydream. He shakes his head and places the orbs on his bed.

"How are we looking?" he asks. "Everything OK up front?"

She steps into the room and takes a seat on her own bunk. "No change. Everything is running fine. We'll be at Azken soon."

Nixon folds the case back up and drops the orbs inside before closing the top.

"Playing with that thing again?"

"Just … making sure I'm comfortable with how it works."

"I figured you'd have it cold by now."

"Getting there."

It's quiet in the room for a moment, neither of them speaking. Laana breaks the silence.

"You know," she says, "the more I think about this plan of yours, the more I like it."

"You do?"

"Not the part about trying to fool Tychon. I give that a fifty-fifty chance at succeeding. But, if it does, that second part is smart. Time is critical to landing these big-credit jobs, and this gives us a big advantage. We could really set ourselves up well pretty quickly."

"She's right." It's a new voice. It's Shaine. He's standing in the doorway now, leaning on the jamb. Arms crossed. "Get past that risky first part and you guys can make some quick credits. You need to do this."

"I don't know. I'm starting to think ..."

"Stop," Laana says. "Don't overthink this. You've already thought it through. There are things that could go wrong, sure. But there's also a lot that can go right. We just have to be smart."

Shaine: "Be judicious with the jobs you pursue. Don't go after everything. Look for the things where there's likely to be success. The things where you aren't putting yourselves at risk. If you don't let greed start making your decisions ..."

Laana starts reminding Nixon that she does have experience looking at these boards. She knows all those secret codewords that these captains use when they don't want to be exactly clear about what the job entails.

"Great opportunity for someone who's self-drvien" means that the captain isn't looking to help you at all. It's going to be lots of work, and it's going to be all on you.

"A chance to build your legend" means this job is hard, and I don't have many credits to pay for it. But you'll definitely earn some reputation points.

Be aware of anyone offering a mound of credits and still calls the job easy, because it never is.

Shaine stands behind her nodding along.

Nixon looks back to the folded case, and he can feel the orbs in his palm. He can feel their smooth surface sliding across his skin. He can feel their heat. He can see their possibility again.

"You're right," he tells Laana. And Shaine. "It's a good plan if we're smart. We just have to make the first part work."

He looks specifically to Laana. "How do we get you more confident that it will work? You put our odds at fifty-fifty, and I don't like those."

Laana shrugs. "That's all riding on Aldius and what his case looks like. I'll let you know more once we see his work in person."

A chime from EHL sounds from the main cabin.

"Please find a secure seat, sir. We are preparing to enter Azken's atmosphere."

EIGHT

Nixon buckles himself into the captain's seat in the main cabin. Laana secures herself into the navigator's seat next to him. EHL shimmies slightly as it enters with the growing atmosphere around Planet Azken.

The thick clouds out the front windscreen make everything look soupy. EHL cuts through them quickly and springs out into a briefly clear bit of sky, but in front of them Nixon and Laana can see the dark clouds that hang over most of the planet. Lightning ripples through them, and Nixon grabs the seat as EHL dives inside. The ship twists and turns and fights the winds that are pushing these clouds across the Azken sky.

EHL breaks through the clouds, and Nixon winces. This planet is all industry. The buildings are all made of grey steel, and their jagged tops are practically reaching out to grab EHL from the sky. The ship bucks and twists to avoid the metal spires.

Even up here the traffic is thick. Nixon looks to Laana, and she has her eyes closed. She's missing EHL jumping it's way through the haulers that are carrying the gear and equipment that feed the industry that makes this planet run, feeds the machine that is Tychon.

"You OK?" Nixon asks, looking back out of the front of the ship and everything happening there. Below the clouds, rain is peppering EHL's windscreen and peeling off in thin streaks, blurring what Nixon can see into smears of greys and blacks.

EHL suddenly drops out of the traffic lanes full of heavy haulers and into more open sky. A second traffic lane is rushing like a river below them. These ships are more EHL's size. These are the small haulers full of cargo that keep the day-to-day businesses working and running.

Laana's eyes are open now. Ships rush by on either side of EHL, and the ship is in constant motion as it adjusts to their washes.

"This doesn't bother you?" Nixon asks.

She doesn't say anything, just grips the arms of her chair tighter.

A blast of air from a passing ship clears EHL's windscreen, and the ship drops out of this traffic lane back into clear sky. It's flying by the upper floors of the planet's tallest buildings now, the ground still feels impossibly far away. But it's visible now, and with a clear windscreen Nixon can see the little pools of bright neon lighting everything down by the streets.

"Where to now, sir?" the ship asks.

"Find us a place to put down. Not Tychon if possible."

"One moment." The ship goes quiet again.

EHL returns. "Not Tychon is going to be difficult, sir. I've scanned all of the public ports. THere are only two that don't belong to Tychon and those are showing full."

"Just find us something."

"Yes, sir."

EHL drops into the lower traffic lanes. The ducking and diving it was doing earlier in the upper atmo is over now. This is a different kind of travel. Slower. Stop and go.

"We need a plan," Laana says. "We are trying to pull off something pretty impossible. We don't do this right, and that's it. Tychon doesn't play around. They don't offer much mercy or grace, not in my experience. We have to get this right."

Nixon knows she's right, and how they pull this off has been on his mind. He's been thinking, when EHL hasn't given him reasons to panic, about earlier days when he and Shaine were still working together and about the schemes they pulled and the people they took as marks.

He tries to think of schemes that were similar and modifying the plan to make it work for two people. It's not easy, though, because Shaine was always in charge of figuring out a plan and he loved nothing more than a complicated scheme. He liked involving lots of players and lots of moving parts. This piece reliant on that piece, all of it building to success. At least in his head.

The reality was that so many of his schemes failed because something didn't go right. Either someone forgot a piece of the plan or something didn't work exactly like Shaine had laid out. So that left everyone scrambling, and Nixon hated scrambling. Scrambling required you to anticipate, to know what the others were going to do, and Shaine's schemes often involved so many new players that you couldn't anticipate. Nixon didn't know any better when he was younger. He followed Shaine's lead. But Shaine's not here. This is his team. This is his operation. He knows how he's going to play it. Fewer people. Fewer parts. Eliminate the points of failure.

"Here's what I want to do," Nixon says.

He then lays out his idea. He contacts Tychon. He arranges a meeting in a moderately public location. He goes, just him. Laana waits back here on the ship.

"What if something goes wrong? You don't want someone there as backup?"

"No," Nixon says, "because I'll have the original case in my cloak. EHL's coordinates will be already programmed and waiting. I make the swap. I get the credits. And before they can realize they've been given a fake case, I toss the orbs and disappear."

Laana looks off into the middle distance, her mind lost in thought. She considers Nixon's plan.

"It's simple," she says. "I'll give you that."

"It's how I like it. Overly complex schemes have too many places where something can go wrong."

Laana nods while Nixon speaks. "There's a reason I work solo. Seems like you only have two places where this could go sideways."

"And what are those?"

Nixon is looking out EHL's windscreen. The ship is still trying to find a place to put down, and is giving Laana and Nixon a tour of Azken. It's all looking the same. Neon lights advertising every kind of store and shop imaginable. All of the buildings made from glass and steel, and their fronts slicked with rain.

Laana: "If your contact at Tychon doesn't come alone."

"Fair," Nixon says. "And the second?"

"If Aldius' case doesn't pass the test."

NINE

Laana's face is bathed in a rainbow of neon, and she's holding her reader out in front of her. Azken rises up all around. The tops of the buildings disappear into thick clouds, and, on the ground, hucksters stand out in front of every shop, doing everything they can—shouting, grabbing, cajoling—to try and get the people passing by to come in and part with their credits.

Laana wipes rain drops from the reader's screen and the indicator blinking there is clearer. It's noting Aldius' location.

Trash swirls at their feet, food wrappers dancing in the breeze. This food is all served from carts parked on the sides of the street. Their owners are shouting for any passer's attention. The mix of cuisines gives the air a vague but delicious aroma, and Nixon's stomach reminds him that he's hungry.

Large red banners hang from wires that stretch between the buildings and across the street. They snap and pop in the wind. The messages written on them long faded in the Azken skies, a combination of harsh conditions and pollution erasing whatever it is the people who'd placed them there wanted to say.

Nixon's reader vibrates in the pocket of his cloak with another notification from another of these shops, pushed to

GALAXY RUN: THE COMPLETE FIRST SERIES

him as he and Laana pass. Most of them are announcing sales
and specials, all of these shop owners desperate for some
kind of attention.

"Are we close?" Nixon asks.

Laana wipes her screen again. "Getting there. A few
blocks ahead we'll take a ..."

She's interrupted by one of the cheap store hucksters
throwing his arms around both of their shoulders and
pushing his face between theirs.

"You two look hungry, and I've got a solution for that.
Come over here to ..."

Nixon pulls his cloak aside just enough for the man to see
the handle of the blaster. He lets go of their shoulders.

"So not hungry? OK. I get it," the man says as he
backtracks to his previous location. "But next time. We'll get
you next time."

Nixon says just loud enough for Laana to hear "I don't
like it here.

He pulls the hood of his cloak over his head and tugs it
down to cover his eyes. It doesn't do a great job of blocking
the blinking and pulsing of the neon signs that hang above
the doors to each of the shops.

"You never been to the big city before?" Laana asks.

"Exte is a pretty big place, but this is ... "

"Yeah, it's something different."

Nixon peaks from under the hem of his hood at those
distracting signs, and in the bottom left corner of almost all
of them is a small black circle. And inside that small circle is
Tychon's bisected T. Eventually, even with all the built-in
distractions, it's just about all that he sees. The place is
practically polka dotted with them. All of this a reminder of
where he's at and who's in charge.

"Over here," Laana says and points down a new street
with her reader. Nixon looks at her screen and sees the
indicator. They're close.

He follows her down a different street that's just as
crowded, just as loud, just as distracting.

323

"A block up and on the right."

Nixon lifts his head and looks at the signs in front of him. None of them look like an ideal place to make this swap. Hucksters are dancing out in front of every shop. Nixon's reader continues to buzz in his cloak pocket.

"There," Laana says and points.

It's the door to a bar. It's just a skinny space between two larger businesses. The sign out front says The In-Between in a gentle script with a dim red glow behind it, lit but not obnoxious. Most importantly, though, there's no black dot underneath. There's no bisected T. This should be a safe space. Should be, but this is still Azken, Nixon won't take his chances. Laana opens the door, and Nixon pulls his arm inside his cloak and places his hand on the blaster tucked in his waistband.

The whole place is dark and glows faintly red like the sign out front. Aldius' big body is folded into a booth just to the left of the door, and the horns on his head are a slight purple. He gives Laana and Nixon a subtle wave as they enter.

Laana slides in the booth opposite Aldius, and Nixon follows.

"Thank you again for your help," Nixon says. "I know we called you last minute. This project couldn't have been…"

Aldius pulls the case he's made out from under the table. He places it in front of Nixon and Laana, and Nixon doesn't finish his sentence.

"Gorotza," Laana says.

Nixon doesn't say anything. He grabs the case instead. He rolls it over in his hands. He runs a finger across it. He feels the etched lines pass under his fingertips. The marks are light and thin, just like on the original case.

"I mean, like, for real, … gorotza," Laana says. She leans in toward Nixon to get a closer look.

Nixon passes the case to her, and she takes a closer look. Her eyes go even wider. She puts it right to her face. She looks at the seams. She studies the corners.

"Just …"

Nixon interrupts. "Safe to say we are both impressed."

"Thank you," Aldius says and holds a hand out palm up in front of him. "Let me show you something."

Laana hands him back the case. He works the locking mechanism on the top then pulls his canvas pouch of keys from under the table. He inserts the right series of small pins into the case and it opens all the way. It glows from the inside and provides a near-spotlight on everything happening at their table.

Inside the new case are even orbs. "You can pull these out, but if you throw them you aren't going to create a portal to anywhere. They'll just land a roll away. So, you know, it's not a perfect replica."

"It's more than perfect," Nixon says. "We really do appreciate it."

"I'm glad you're saying that. Because things are … different now."

"Different how?"

"I was burned on Otanzia. It didn't happen immediately, but soon enough. Things started getting tough, and I couldn't stay. So, now …"

"Sorry to hear that," Nixon says. "What's that mean for us?"

"Means I'm here. Means I can help if you need me to. Figured a bit of extra muscle might come in handy."

Nixon picks the case back up off the tabletop. Extra muscle isn't a bad idea. Especially here. Especially now. This is Tychon they are trying to scam. No, he doesn't want a big team, but this is just one more moving part. One more is fine, especially if he can keep Aldius close, and Nixon's already working through how to do that.

TEN

The spaceport EHL found is small. It's a fenced-in space with a control tower on the farside from where EHL put down. Nixon, Laana, and Aldius have to walk the length of the yard to get back to the ship.

Nixon jumps as steam vents from a grate a few feet away, a column of vapor shooting dozens of feet high and making the air stickier and thicker with moisture.

The three of them pass ship after ship after ship. They are all well-used. Their paint is beaten and scarred where it exists at all. Most of them are mid-sized. Captains and their crews wander outside of several of them. Nixon puts one hand on the blaster tucked into his waistband. He grips the new fake case tighter with the other.

"I see you guys didn't spare any expense here," Aldius says.

"Options are limited," Nixon says.

A crew from across the yard watches the three of them walking and talking. Nixon points them out to Laana, and she nods that she's seen them.

"Besides," Nixon continues, "it's better than the alternative. I'm not going to try escaping from a Tychon-owned spaceport. That feels like adding a layer of difficulty we don't need."

Nixon opens the ramp to EHL and follows Laana and Aldius onboard once they can go inside.

"What now, boss?" Laana asks.

Nixon doesn't answer. He scratches and scrambles through the small bits of paper that have collected on the dash since this whole adventure started. It never seemed like a lot until he had to go through all of it. He's picking up individual pieces then putting them down almost as quickly.

"Tell me what you're looking for and maybe ..."

What he's looking for is the card he got from Shaine when he gave Nixon the case in that courtyard.

Nixon had been avoiding thinking about that moment, but, right now, there's no getting around it. As he looks for this card, the one that has the name of the person he's supposed to contact about the case, he pictures those last minutes with Shaine.

Shaine waiting for him in the courtyard. Talking before the whole situation flipped over. The men coming in. The fire fight that left Nixon scrambling to safety. The same one that left Shaine dead.

He sees his friend's body being pummeled by blaster fire. He sees it bounce on the paver stones as bolt after bolt rip it apart.

It's not here. The card is in the crew quarters.

"Seriously," Laana says as Nixon pushes past her and down the hall. "Let me help."

Nixon knocks over a pile of papers he's stacked on the table next to his bed.

"Ha ha!" he shouts and pulls the card from the near-bottom of the stack.

"Found it! Found it!" he says as he heads back to the main cabin.

"Found it," he repeats once he can see Laana and Aldius again.

It's not much. It's just a card and a reader address. He doesn't have a name or a real location. He's at the mercy of whoever it is that answers this message. That makes him pause. He's suddenly wondering if the small team is the smartest play. This is Tychon, after all. They'll have a whole squad of people. People with uniforms and ranks and chains of command. His whole team is now just three people.

His mind rushes to try and find a plan that includes finding a team here on Azken. He thinks for a moment about going out to the crews and captains in this spaceport and trying to recruit more members. They are parked in an independent space port. Nixon has to assume that's for a reason. Once he has a few more people willing to help and he knows the size of his team Nixon can build out a new plan.

No. It's a momentary thought and a bad one. He has his plan. He has his team. Adding more hands just complicates things. It also adds more hands waiting to be paid at the end, assuming things go well.

Nope. What he needs, instead of a different plan, is a better idea of when he's going to pull the plug, when he's going to abandon this whole thing because it's suddenly turned too dangerous. That is something he can define with his team. But before he even needs to worry about that he needs to set up a meeting.

He pulls out his reader and types a message to the address written on the card.

"I have your case."

He sends it then the three of them wait. Laana, Nixon, and Aldius all look at each other, but none of them say anything. A moment later Nixon's reader chimes. He looks at it, and it's coordinates and a time: Mid-day tomorrow.

ELEVEN

"We have our meeting," he tells the other two then begins laying out his plan. After all of that thinking, it's still simple.

He looks to Aldius: "I'm going to show them your case and ask for half of the fifteen thousand credits before I give it to them. That way we are sure to get something for all of this trouble."

"And what if they refuse?" Aldius asks.

"I figured you'd be standing to the side looking, you know, big and orange. They'd be intimidated."

Laana climbs into the navigator's seat. Nixon continues.

"They'll open the case, check it out. Before they get too deep into that inspection I'll ask for the other half of the payment. Once we have it, I throw the orbs and you and I disappear through the portal. That puts us back here, and Laana gets us off this planet."

Aldius: "Sounds a little ... simple."

"Exactly," Nixon says.

Aldius lets out a long breath and then says, "This is your show. If you want simple, then well do simple. I just don't want your simple plan to simply get me killed."

"We'll be fine. I've got a blaster. I assume you've got some kind of protection you plan on bringing."

Aldius shrugs a yes.

Nixon continues. "Every time I've been part of a complicated plan or scheme something goes wrong. Too many contingencies. Too many parts relying on the other parts to go right. This plan has one contingency: your case. If that hadn't been done well then the whole thing would fall apart. But you made us something amazing. Now, if I can get whoever this is we're meeting to not try to toss your orbs ..."

Laana snickers. Nixon gives her a look and continues.

"... then we'll be fine. And I'm confident I can do that. So, I feel good. I feel like this will work. Are you two comfortable with it?"

"If you're good then I'm good," Laana says.

"Sure," Aldius says, "you're back here watching and waiting."

"Then trade me places."

Aldius shakes no. "No offense, but you aren't all that scary."

"You've never been on the wrong end of my scope."

Aldius says to Nixon, "I'm good with it. I was just expecting something that was more ..."

"I don't do complicated," Nixon says. "Not anymore. If you're good with it, be back here tomorrow morning."

"I'll be back here light of the first sun."

Nixon activates the ramp, and it opens with a hiss. He shakes Aldius' hand before Aldius steps off.

"Again, thank you. None of this works if you hadn't made that case."

"You paid for my best work. Or you will."

A breeze from the still-open ramp ripples the bottom of Nixon's cloak as he pulls it over his head. He grabs the blaster from the dash and puts it in the waistband of his pants.

"Where are you headed?" Laana asks.

"Out," he says. "For some air. I want to try and clear my head before tomorrow. Too many thoughts dancing around up there. I'll never be able to sleep. A walk will do me good."

"Want some company?"

"Not this time."

"All right," she says. "I'm going to get EHL ready. Be careful."

Nixon gives her a small wave as he steps down the ramp and back into the night.

More crews are outside of their ships. Some are gathered around small fires built to thwart the coming chill. There's an industry here, a hum of business and commerce and creation, that seems to keep the city warm during the day. But now, out on the streets everything is mostly empty. The crowds are gone. The noises from earlier are now silent. That rainbow of neon has vanished as most of the businesses close once night sets in and the population goes home. Only a spot of blue or a shock of pink are left, those businesses still open that cater to the small crowd of people who like the night, prefer life lived in the relative dark.

Nixon pulls out his reader. He taps a finger on the address his mysterious Tychon friend sent earlier. A moment later a map appears in front of him. An indicator blinks blocks and blocks away. Nixon studies the location and the rest of the map for a moment then puts the reader back in the pocket of his cloak. He walks.

The street is mostly empty and quiet except for the banners that pop in the night breeze. It also blows through Nixon's hair and he pulls the hood of his cloak up to keep out of the cold. His stomach grumbles, and he reminds himself that he needs to at least eat something before they head out for the meeting in the morning.

There he is again: Shaine. Nixon can hear him. He can see him. He's stepping into Nixon's little hole back on Exte, bent at the waist because the low roof means he can't stand up straight. He's carrying a paper cup and a spoon. He hands both to Nixon and tells him to eat.

"I don't need you distracted by a growling stomach."

Nixon would pop the lid off the cup and eat whatever was inside without any kind of hesitation. It was likely the first real meal he'd had that week. He didn't care what it was as long as it was thick and warm, and it usually was. He'd crush the cup in his fist when he was finished and they'd head out. Shaine would remind him of all the things the plan needed him to do that day.

Shaine never needed to eat, but he always made feeding Nixon part of the plan, because success was paramount. For Shaine, it was the plan above everything. Everything in service to the plan.

Nixon got it then. He doesn't now. Not since he's in charge. His team is admittedly smaller, but all of them coming out of this alive and ready to fight again means more to him than anything. Yes, he wants them to also come out of this with each of them five thousand credits richer, but that was a bonus to coming out of it at all.

He stops and pulls his reader back out. He looks around to orient himself then starts walking again. He's only a few blocks away from tomorrow's destination now and, even though the real thing won't happen for hours still, the little flutters in his stomach have already started. It's the rush of excitement that proceeds running a scheme.

This part of Azken doesn't look all that different from where his walk started. The buildings all look like they've been popped out of the same mold. They are wide and tall, their tops disappearing into the dark night sky. Lights shine through random windows, blinking on and off like bubbles popping. Almost all of the doorways are dark now. Those occasional shops don't operate over here. Also, Tychon's presence is much less subtle now. Those small black circles are bigger, displayed proudly over every door. This is clearly a Tychon neighborhood.

Nixon checks his reader again and turns left at the next corner. This street is narrower than those he's just walked. The buildings on either side are just as tall, and, in the dark, Nixon can feel their looming presence. The indicator blinks on his reader, and he keeps walking toward it.

The street opens up to a wide landing that's about half a block wide. A set of three steps lead up to a wide flat space. A bit further back the space narrows to three more more steps and another flat space. Then a bit further back the space narrows again to three more steps that lead to a bank of eight doors that lead inside one of Azken's biggest buildings. It's glass all the way up, and about 20 feet above these doors is a bisected T logo that's a story high and a story wide. His meeting is happening on Tychon's front porch.

He looks left. He looks right. Up and down both sides of the road, and there's nothing there. There are no doorways. There are no streets that connect somewhere in the middle of the block. It's just flat building front all the way down. There's no place to hide. There's no place to run to if things go south. He doesn't imagine that's by accident.

Running was always his fallback. Did something go wrong? Run. Did someone seem to get suspicious? Run. Did the whole plan collapse in the middle of the execution? Run. There's no running here if he thinks it's going poorly because there's no place to hide.

So don't let it go wrong.

He takes one more look around, takes a mental picture, then begins his walk back to EHL.

Laana is waiting for him when the ramp opens. She's still sitting in the navigator's chair but stands up when he steps on board.

"I don't like your plan," she says.

"I don't like it much right now either," he says. "But we're sticking with it."

"What do you mean you don't like it?" she asks following him down the hall to the galley.

Nixon opens the cabinets. He pulls out two bowls and a pair of grain packets. He stirs water into them and places them in the heater. While he does all of this he describes what he found.

"We are meeting right out front of Tychon headquarters. Literally on the steps that lead up to the front door. And that's not ideal, but whatever. I can work with that. What worries me more is across the street."

"What's across the street?"

"Nothing," Nixon says. "I mean, it's a building a block long. But there are no doorways into this building. There are no planters. There's no kind of decoration. It's just smooth wall from one end of the block to the other."

"That's not good."

The heater chimes, and Nixon pulls out the two bowls of grain. He keeps one and hands the second bowl to Laana. He sits at the table.

"Eat that," he tells her as she sits across from him. "I don't need you distracted by an empty stomach tomorrow. We'll have another bowl before things get started."

"About tomorrow."

"And the plan you don't like?"

"You aren't using me," she says around a bite of mush from the bowl.

"I am."

"Not well. You have me waiting here."

"I have you flying us out of here. You're handling the getaway. I've given you arguably the most important job."

"Only if you succeed is my job important. If they kill you on those steps then I'm just a girl in someone else's ship."

Nixon chokes down a bite of the bland grains. "You think they're going to kill me?"

"I hope they don't, but is it possible? Yes. Is it probable?"

Nixon waits, but she doesn't answer.

"You think I'm probably going to die?"

She shrugs.

"Thanks for the vote of confidence."

She shoves a half-eaten bowl of grains to the middle of the table. "I understand the need to eat, but if you want me to finish a meal in the morning then you need to give me something better than that."

Nixon pushes his partially eaten bowl to the middle of the table too and Laana picks up the conversation.

"I wouldn't be here if I didn't have confidence you could pull it off. But I've known too many others who were caught off guard by something unforeseen. So, yes, there's a chance that you don't come back tomorrow. I just want to be able to help you increase your odds, and I can't do that from this ship."

Nixon leans back in the stool and thinks about her argument.

"No," he says after a moment. "I want you here. I need you here. I need EHL ready to jump to deep space as soon as the exchange is done. That's the only way this works, and if you're out there with me then there's too many steps that need to happen before we can leave."

Nixon takes the bowls from the table. He empties their contents into a compactor and drops them empty into the sink.

"I do appreciate the argument. And you make a good point. But I want you here."

Laana lets out a long breath and slips lower into her seat.

"Don't pout," Nixon tells her. "It's my decision, and that's the one I've made. Now get to sleep. Big day tomorrow."

"For you," she says.

TWELVE

Nixon doesn't need the blinking indicator on his reader's screen, but he has it out anyway. Aldius is glancing at it every dozen feet, and Nixon figures he needs to keep the big guy as comfortable as possible.

The streets are crowded, just like they were yesterday, but everything feels … more. The people seem more amped up. The conversations happening all around them feel louder. The blasts of the movers' horns echo longer. The lights above each of the doors are brighter, their colors more intense. Nixon pulls a hand inside of his cloak and presses it to his chest. His heart is pounding hard. He can feel its power through bone and tissue and skin.

These aren't nerves. This is anticipation. He's ready. All of this—Exte, Umel, Ibilia, Makurra—all of this that's happened has been pushing him here to this moment. To this now, and he's ready. He has his plan. He has confidence in it. And, if nothing else, everything that's happened since he picked up this stupid case has taught him that he needs to have confidence in himself. He's a scrambler. He's a fighter. He's a survivor. Even if something happens and he has to scrap his plan, he'll fight his way to safety somehow.

Aldius glances over to Nixon's reader one more time, and Nixon clears the screen. He puts the device back in the pocket inside his cloak.

He points to the corner they are approaching. He tells Aldius they're turning right once they get there, but he's surprised that Aldius can hear him at all. His breathing is quick, and it's shallow.

"You OK?" Nixon asks. "We need to loop the block to give you a moment to gather yourself?"

"What do you mean?"

"You're about to make yourself sick. You need to take a few deep breaths and calm down. I need you able to focus."

The pair stops at the corner. Traffic rushes by them on the street. A mover blows its horn and Aldius jumps.

Traffic clears, and Nixon crosses the street. Aldius follows saying, "I thought we were turning there."

"Not right now."

Nixon slows his pace, and Aldius matches it.

"If you need to beg off this that's fine."

"I'm fine," Aldius says. "I promise."

"Seriously, I'll pay you your cut. No hard feelings. The case you made is more than enough to earn you your share."

Nixon stops in front of a bench and sits. Aldius joins him, his breathing slower now but only slightly.

"Quit." The word comes out short and clipped. "I'm fine. I'm just mostly a behind-the-scenes guy, so I'm not as used to this kind of work as you are."

"Take a second then let's go."

Aldius rests his elbows on his knees and bends deep at the waist, his broad back exposed. He's nearly sweat through his shirt.

Nixon stands and gives Aldius a moment. That's when Nixon looks up and realizes where they've stopped. A few dozen feet ahead is an entryway, a bank of at least ten doors. And above those doors hangs a bisected Tychon T that's twice the size of the one just a block over. Behind it is a blue glow, and below it are the words "Shop Tychon." This is a Tychon storefront, and it's a block long.

This makes it even more curious that there are no doors in and out on the back. There's no way to move new product in and out through the rear of the store.

A few moments later Aldius stands and lets out a long breath. "OK," he says. "Let's go."

Both Nixon and Aldius stop before heading down the street that will lead them to Tychon's entrance. Nixon looks to his left and that flat, blank wall.

This place isn't like it was last night. Then, it was empty. Today, it's filled with workers. Some are guiding float carts piled with boxes out of Tychon headquarters. Others are hurrying down the sidewalk with bundles of documents tucked under their arms. All of them, Nixon assumes, making a life by working for Tychon. For some reason Nixon had pictured this swap happening with no one else around. Just him and a Tychon agent. And Aldius now. All of them alone, voices echoing down the street, the shadows making everything feel dark and ominous.

Nixon looks to Aldius, and Aldius gives him a nod. Nixon takes the first step down the street. This walk didn't feel as long last night, but today it looks like it will take forever. All of those feelings of anticipation that felt so intense earlier are double that now. Triple. His heart is so loud in his ears that he can barely hear any of the people around him. Light from both of the suns seems to wash everything out.

He has both hands pulled into his cloak. One is squeezing the handle of his blaster so tight a small part of him expects the whole thing to snap in half. The other is holding the case Aldius made, and he isn't certain that when he pulls it out to pass it across the case won't be crushed into something unrecognizable.

He's watching the steps in front of them. It's all motion, people moving in and out of the Tychon building, but he's looking for someone waiting, standing still. But there's no one.

He looks to Aldius. The big man seems better. Not that it matters at this point. They are committed. Can't turn back, and he's not going to let them just keep walking past the steps. If no one comes out, then he's going to go in. He's pulling this off, and he's doing it today. He's not wasting all of this work and a full day's anticipation.

Then he sees it. Someone comes to the steps and stops. They are waiting. As they get closer he sees it's a woman. A human woman. She's looking down one side of the street then down the other. It doesn't take her long to spot the mismatched pair. Nixon hadn't considered how much they'd stand out. He's tall and thin and wearing an oversized cloak. He's walking next to an orange-skinned something even taller than he is and wider than a door. They look nothing like the workers around them who are all in jumpsuits or put-together workwear.

She begins to come down the steps and right toward them.

She smiles. It's not a welcoming smile. It's not one of warmth. It's one of obligation. It's her attempt to start this process on a friendly note.

"Gentlemen," she says once she's close enough. "I believe you have a case of mine."

"We do," Nixon says.

The woman has stopped short. She's keeping distance between them. It's at least an arms length from Aldius. It's more from Nixon.

They are on the sidewalk. Workers keep walking past, unfazed. Across from them is the smooth wall of the Tychon storefront.

"You got here just under the wire," the woman says. "That forty-five day clock was really starting to tick pretty loudly."

Nixon had forgotten about the deadline. Shaine had mentioned it, but forty five days seemed to be impossibly far off when that conversation happened. Then, with how that exchange ended, things like deadlines all fell away. He just wanted to get this case delivered.

"Now," she says, "which one of you is Shaine?"

Nixon can feel Aldius giving him a look then says: "I am."

"Well, Mr. Shaine, can I see the case?"

Nixon pulls the case from his cloak and begins to hand it across to the woman then hesitates. He pulls it back.

"First," he says, "we had a deal. Fifteen thousand credits for the safe delivery of the case. I want half of that now."

The woman considers then agrees. She pulls a reader from a pocket. She navigates through a few screens then puts the reader away. Nixon feels his own reader vibrate a notification that the credits have been transferred.

"Thank you," he says and pulls Aldius' case out from inside his cloak. He hands it to the woman then pulls his hand back inside of his cloak.

She runs her fingers across the grooves. She plays a thumb across the locking mechanism. She enters the code that unlocks the box, inserting a set of pins that she'd also been carrying in her pocket. She opens the case, and, even in the direct light of the Azken suns, her face takes on a green tint.

She smiles. "You know, you were right, Mr. Aldius. You do very nice work."

THIRTEEN

Nixon turns to Aldius. A million thoughts start to align.
"How much of this was fake?"
Aldius considers the question.
"Depends. The case was fake for sure."
"You know what I mean. Were you burned on Otanzia?"
"That was true. Like you all said, running through the halls
carrying a wailing case tends to attract some attention."
Nixon begins to walk a tight circle. Head down. Thinking.
"But I don't ... we told you to come with us."
"And I told you that I had a nice set up there. I've done all
of this." He swings his arm in a wide circle. "I've drawn
blasters and run scams, splitting a paltry amount of credits
between too many players. I'm done with it. I have been for a
long time. And on Otanzia I had a place where I wasn't asked
a lot of questions. I could live my simple, small life."
Nixon's head immediately spins up the cabin he's been
dreaming of. Simple. Small. Remote. Tucked into a bed at
night that's safe, sleeping soundly. Not with one eye open.
Not wondering what the next day will bring. Not wondering
where your next credits or your next meal are coming from.
It sounds ... perfect.
Aldius: "You took that from me."
"You agreed to help."

"I saw an opportunity."

"To get your old life back."

"You burned me. I burned you. Besides, they pay more."

Nixon turns back to the Tychon woman. She has a blaster drawn.

"Now, Mr. Shaine, let's see those hands. Bring them out. Slowly."

Nixon wraps his hand around the blaster and runs the next few moments through in his head. Once he draws the blaster, he can get one shot off for sure. Right now, that's the Tychon woman since she has the blaster already on him. Maybe he can get two shots off if all that time laying low has slowed Aldius' instincts.

He turns to Aldius, and now he's drawn too, a blaster stretched in front of him, holding stock still and trained on Nixon's chest.

New information, new scenarios. Nixon runs them double time, and no matter how they start, they all end the same way. One shot is all he gets off before a blaster bolt—from either Aldius or the woman—is burning its way through his middle.

He lets the blaster go and grabs something else instead— the orbs for the real case.

He pulls his hands from his cloak slow and easy like he'd been instructed. His right hand is open, fingers extended. His left is closed tight.

The woman from Tychon points to it with her blaster. "Open that one up," she says, "or I blast it off."

Nixon hesitates then flicks his wrist. The orbs fly out a few feet then form a rectangle that hangs in the air. It shimmers black in the middle. Nixon turns to dive through.

"Stop!" It's Aldius. "Make another move toward that portal and I'll shoot you dead right here."

Nixon freezes in a half stoop. He stands back up straight.

"Now the real case, please, Mr. Shaine."

"I don't have it."

The woman gestures to the portal. "Then go get it."

"Are you sure?" Aldius asks. "He goes through there and he can get away."

"Nah, he wouldn't do that. He wants these credits too bad."

She's right. He does. Nixon hasn't yet considered just walking away from this. There's too much on the line. And with Aldius out of the picture now, he's not splitting this take three ways. If he can save this deal, he will.

"Let me go through, and I'll come back. Trust me."

"Says the guy who tried to pass off a fake as the real thing." She tosses Aldius' case over her shoulder and it bounces off the steps behind her.

"You're right," Nixon says. "I want the credits. I'll give you the case."

"Leave the portal open," she says. "You have until I count to fifteen to be back. If you're not then I send Aldius through after you."

"You won't have to."

She starts counting and gets to three before Nixon gets through the portal.

"What's going on?" Laana asks as he emerges from the inky black hole floating in the middle of EHL's main deck.

Nixon hears the woman counting from the other side of the portal, but it's a muffled garble of words, like she has a mouth full of rocks.

Nixon grabs the Tychon case off the dash and holds it tight in his clenched fist. He starts running through ways to get out of this, but his mind is slow to spin up any idea that feels feasible. This may just come down to who's the best shot.

"Under my bunk in the crew quarters. Go get your gun."

"What?"

"I may need help."

FOURTEEN

Nixon emerges back through the portal just as the woman counts fifteen.

"Just in time," she says. Her blaster is still drawn. It's still pointed at him, and it follows him as he walks back to where he'd been standing before.

Aldius has dropped his blaster, and Nixon looks at it. It's old. It's dinged and scuffed. The metal's clearly aged. Nixon doesn't know that it will fire, at least not reliably. He's also not convinced that Aldius has the instincts and timing to beat him on the draw. Too out of practice. So that's an advantage. It's not much, admittedly, but he'll take anything he can get.

"Where's my case?" she asks.

"Where are my credits?"

"You think we're still doing that?"

"We are if you want the case."

"I think you're mistaken. I'm not giving you any credits at this point. I'm giving you something that's a lot more valuable. I'm giving you the ability to walk away from here still breathing."

"Aww. We are?" Aldius asks, a smile on his face that shows off his jagged yellow teeth.

"Well, I was. But what do you think?"

"I don't think you're getting that case from him voluntarily if you aren't giving him credits."

"Good point. Maybe we just shoot him now."

Nixon looks to Aldius and then to the woman then over to the portal.

"Don't give me another reason to shoot you, Nixon," Aldius says. His blaster is up and aimed at Nixon again.

"Sorry, I'm late to the party, boss." They all turn to the portal and see Laana stepping through. Her gun is up and shouldered, ready to fire.

"You too?" Aldius asks.

"I don't want to hear a word from you. I thought we were friends. I had to convince him to trust you."

"We were acquaintances. At the very best."

Nixon stares at the Tychon woman. She keeps her blaster trained but runs her other hand down her face. She's either tired or she's frustrated. Either one can work to Nixon's advantage.

"Come on," she says. "Make this easy. Give me the case." She puts a hand up and gestures with her fingers for Nixon to pass the case over. Her fingernails are intricately decorated, and her hands are smooth.

"Walk away," she says. "Leave with your life."

Nixon shakes his head, but he doesn't say anything. He just stares at her. Without the ability to draw his own blaster, intimidation is all he has at this point. He's relying on irrational confidence to raise enough questions that it creates some kind of hesitation.

He looks at her blaster, the one that could leave him split open if all of this tips the wrong way. Hers isn't like Aldius'. Hers is new. It's thick through the middle. The barrel still looks shiny and bright. It's only been fired a few times, if at all. And that barrel is wide. Nixon thinks he might be able to squeeze his fist inside if he pushed hard enough. That thing fires a heavy shot.

All of this tells him that it's not her gun. It's too big for her. Not that she couldn't fire it. Anything can pull a trigger if it has fingers or something that's a close approximation. But she's a tall woman. And thin. She won't be able to control the blast once she does try to fire it. She'd use something just as deadly but smaller to preserve her accuracy.

This blaster. Those nails. This isn't the kind of work this woman does regularly. At least she doesn't anymore. Her talk about the credits and letting Nixon walk away alive, that was no joke. She's delivered those kinds of lines before. But Nixon doubts it's been recently. She was sent out here by someone. A favor maybe. And she grabbed a blaster as she came outside. Not thinking. Just something from a table. She never planned to fire it. She was counting on Nixon walking away. Now he hasn't, and she's had to draw that blaster. That heavy blaster that she's had trained on Nixon for a while now.

She has to be feeling the stress of keeping something that size out in front of her. It's starting to hurt, pain that Nixon figures is beginning to spiral up her arm. Starting near her wrist, slow walking across her forearm, resting for a moment in her elbow then settling for good in her shoulder. He's been there. He's felt it. He knows that his ability to fire a shot after this kind of standoff would have been non-existent. And that was with a blaster that he was familiar with.

That confidence is feeling a little less irrational now.

Laana to Alduis: "Acquaintances? How many jobs did we pull off together in the Urrutikoa Section?"

Aldius to Laana: "That was business. We were both hired hands. I wasn't looking to make friends."

Nixon looks to Laana. Aldius isn't firing shots from his blaster, but these verbal blows are stinging. She really did think of him as a friend, and Nixon could have sworn back on Otanzia that the feelings were mutual. So, this little performance—big orange and angry man—is for Aldius as much as it is for Laana. If he can convince himself that he never liked her, that they were just partners on a few jobs, then it's going to make what's beginning to feel like an inevitable gun fight a lot easier.

Nixon turns back to the blaster that's still pointing at his chest. The woman behind it is tiring. That barrel is dipping and swaying slightly. She's watching Aldius and Laana argue about their relationship, and Nixon sneaks his arm back inside his cloak. He puts a hand on his own blaster. He slips it from his waistband. His heart that had started to race begins to slow. This fight feels fair again.

"My reader is still in my pocket," Nixon tells the woman. She turns her attention back to him. "Send the credits. I'll feel it vibrate. When I do, I'll put the case on the ground, and we'll walk away."

She smiles and shakes her head. "We're past that now. You don't get the credits and you don't walk away. Tychon will get its case, and we'll get you and your friend too. I've already made sure of it."

Nixon asks the woman "What do you mean?"

She reaches into a pocket on her jacket and pulls out her own reader. She holds it up so Nixon and Laana can see it. "I'm tired of this. I've other things to do. This wasn't supposed to be this difficult. I've already signalled for help. It should be coming through those doors any second now."

Nixon: "OK, Laana. Now."

Laana pulls the trigger on her gun, and a thick bolt screams from the barrel. Nixon fires his own, and the bolt burns a hole in his cloak.

Laana's bolt hits Aldius in the waist. Doubles him over and leaves him without most of his critical insides.

The Tychon woman squeezes off a shot just before her chest blooms red because of Nixon's blast. Her shot splits Nixon and Laana and tears a chunk from the building across the street, turning a section of the wall into dust.

"Well, that was easier than I expec …"

Nixon is interrupted by shouts from Tychon's doors.

One voice: "Stop!"

Another: "Don't move."

Nixon doesn't shout back. He answers with blaster fire. Armored Tychon security agents charge down the steps. A shot catches one of them in the ankle, and he tumbles to the side. The others stop and return fire.

"Go!" Nixon shouts to Laana. "Back through the portal."

Blaster fire sizzles past Nixon's ear. He drops to the ground, getting low and shouts to Laana again as more agents exit the building and take up positions next to those already firing.

"If you don't get back to the ship now, then I'm going through and leaving you here to fend for yourself."

She fires one more shot at the gathering gang in front of them then lowers her gun and throws it through the portal then follows.

Nixon stands and starts firing indiscriminately as he runs toward the portal. He dives through backward and keeps firing as everything in front of him goes black then becomes the inside of EHL.

It's disorienting, changing locations like this, and it takes Nixon a moment to make sense of everything. The portal still shimmers in front of him, and voices getting louder from the other side snap him out of his confusion. He gathers the orbs with the swipe of his hand, and everything goes quiet. It's just Nixon and Laana and EHL.

Nixon stands and walks to the ramp. Once it opens he steps down. They are in the starport where they landed a few days ago. It worked. The case and the portal actually worked.

He walks back onto the ship, and Laana asks, "What now?"

"EHL?"

"Yes, sir."

"Get us off this damned planet."

FIFTEEN

EHL flies without direction.

It's been two days since Nixon and Laana left Azken. The case is closed and back in its spot on the dash. Nixon has finally stopped watching the ship's monitors, looking for Tychon security forces giving them chase. He's still not sure they aren't out there—in fact, he knows they must be—but he does know there wasn't a large fleet of them that blasted off of Azken to track them down and recover their case.

Nixon sits in the captain's seat, his cloak draped across his lap. He's using a needle and suture thread from the medkit to close the hole he's shot into it.

"Sorry about your cloak," Laana says. She's sitting in the navigator's seat looking at her reader, scrolling through job listings on a message board.

"It wasn't going to last forever."

"Still ..."

Nixon concentrates on the final few stitches. He pulls the thread through one last time and pulls the fabric tight together. It puckers like a scar, but he's happy with it. It should hold. He snaps the thread and ties it off.

"Yeah," he says, "still ..."

Laana turns her reader so the screen faces Nixon. "I think I found something."

Nixon stands and folds his cloak in half and then half again. He lays it across the back of his chair then sits back down.

"It's a job from a captain needing a small temporary crew. Not hauling anything, just some extra hands. Pays five thousand credits."

"Five thousand to be extra hands? Seem suspicious to you?"

Laana shrugs. "Maybe. But sometimes these captains don't know how to write these things. It's enough credits to make it worth checking out."

"Yeah, OK," Nixon says. "Where's it at?"

Laana scans the post for the coordinates. She enters them into the keyboard in front of her, and a spinning planet appears on the screen a second later.

"Planet called Ezola." Laana pushes a few keys on the keyboard in front of her and a galactic map appears on a larger screen between their seats.

Nixon studies the image then says "No. Too close to Azken."

"It's five thousand credits," Laana says again.

"But it's too close to Azken. Tychon likely has agents there."

"Tychon likely has agents everywhere. What's going to be far enough away?"

Nixon rests his heels on the bank of equipment in front of him. "What did you say the other day? Where you and Aldius pulled jobs?"

"The Urrutikoa Section?"

"How far is that?"

"Far enough that you aren't going to find a whole lot of Tychon."

"Good, then there."

"Really? That far?"

"Honestly, yes. Tychon. The Uzeks. Whoever the humans are who want this case. We've made too many enemies here. Nowhere is going to feel safe."

"Urrutikoa is tough. There's not many Tychon agents there, but there's not much of anything in the way of civilization. You go there, and it's all illegal mining operations, outlaws trying to hide, wildcatters looking to make a fortune."

"It sounds perfect.," Nixon says. "Let's go make some friends and earn some credits."

Laana enters new coordinates into EHL's systems, and the ship banks hard. It puts a big fire into its engines, and the force pushes Nixon and Laana deep into their seats.

Nixon looks at the screens in front of Laana. Urrutikoa isn't a short flight. He grabs his reader and starts looking at the message boards. He has plenty of time to find them work.

Continue Trevor Nixon's Galaxy-Hopping
Adventure With a Preview of Episode 7

07: Watchmen Waketh

ONE

Trevor Nixon dumps the contents of his bag onto his seat for a third time then immediately starts to repack it.

"Do you have the blaster?" Laana asks.

"Funny," Nixon says.

Laana laughs. "You'll get it all to fit. Just think of it as a puzzle."

"Sure," Nixon says. "A puzzle that if I don't get it right could get me killed."

"Don't be dramatic."

"I'm not being dramatic."

Laana pulls the small metal case off the dash in front of her and begins unfolding its sides. A moment later, when she's finished, a small keyboard and two-line monitor sits in front of her.

She begins typing into the keyboard.

"You *are* being dramatic. Not having a blaster on this jump isn't going to kill you," she says. "Tychon's going to do that once they catch you. Or the Uzeks."

"Shut up."

Laana laughs.

"All set," she tells Nixon and grabs the orbs from the dash and tosses them. They spread evenly to create a wide rectangle. The space between them fills with an inky black shimmer.

Nixon pours out the contents of his bag one more time, gear falling off the ship's pilot's seat and collecting at his feet. This whole thing wasn't supposed to be this hard.

His plan was simple. Foolproof in his own mind. Use this Tychon tech, this case and these orbs and the portal they open, to jump to all the highest paying jobs. He'd be able to get there first and increase his chances of picking up the work, but none of it had worked out like that.

Jumping wasn't as easy as he thought it would be. It wore him out, making it tough to jump right into a new job. But even if he wasn't getting wiped out by these jumps, he still wouldn't be at the front of every line. There are just too many others here in the Urrutikoa section looking for work. There are obviously Snapsits and Uzeks, but Nixon is seeing all kinds of species he never knew existed. But that just means more bodies to fill a limited number of jobs, so even if Nixon can be there first or close to it, there's no guarantee of getting a job.

Nixon puts a hand deep into his bag and pushes some of the contents around. Things shift and drop, and Nixon slips the blaster into the bag. He smiles a small smile.

"OK," he says and looks at the inky rectangle hovering next to him.

Laana reminds him of the same things she's told him the five other times he's jumped in the two weeks since they arrived in the Urrutikoa section of the galaxy hoping to pick up work while staying out of the view of Tychon.

"I'm here," she says. "If you're up, I'm up. If you need something, I'm here. Toss the orbs, and I can step through and join you."

Nixon nods as she speaks.

Laana continues. "If you get this job, you aren't there to be a hero. You're there to complete a task. I've lost too many friends who started doing things they weren't asked to do."

"Yes, mom."

"Stop it. Now go get us some credits."

Nixon takes a deep breath and puts a foot into the black. It disappears to the ankle. To the knee. To the hip. He ducks his head and steps the rest of the way into the portal.

When he steps out on the other side it's deep in a narrow alley. There's a slight hum and crackle of energy that he hasn't felt in weeks. There are others here.

His other jumps to jobs since he and Laana arrived in Urrutikoa have dropped him in the middle of an open field, in the storage unit on a farm planet, and twice have put him in waist deep water. This, though, is better.

He looks left then right and finds the light at the end of the alley and heads toward it. He's passing doors on his left and his right. His feet splash through small puddles, and the air is sticky.

"You there?" he asks Laana through the earpiece connected to his reader

"I am. How's it look?"

"Just stepped out of an alley."

"Give me a second."

Nixon waits for more directions from Laana. The road he's stepped out to is roughly paved. Traffic has cut deep and wide ruts into the street. He can hear voices to his right and sees lights glowing above the tops of the buildings. There's laughter and shouting. It sounds like a celebration, and Nixon would love something to celebrate right now. He'd love to be able to go toast himself and the landing of a job.

Laana cuts back in. "OK, I've got you on my reader. Head left. According to the posting for this job, it's a couple of blocks away."

Nixon looks to the lights. He listens to the voices. Then he turns and heads left, away from all the excitement.

Laana gives him an address then says, "I feel good about this one."

Any residual glow from the lights behind him is gone, and Nixon is walking in the dark, nearly black. He activates the screen on his reader and it lights up the area around him.

"What am I looking for? You have a description of the building?"

"Ummm …. Two stories. Big door on the side. Says it's number 13."

"Number 13? Great."

Nixon walks in silence for a few minutes. He hasn't seen anyone since he started walking down this street. Can't even hear the people he could hear before. The whole place feels dead, all of the energy he'd felt on his arrival is gone.

This is starting to feel like every other jump so far. A long walk that ends up with nothing.

"My map says you should be there by now."

Nixon sees it, a couple of building up. The only two story structure he's seen so far. There's a small light that shines a dim glow on a main door. A paper is tacked to the frame.

"There's something here," Nixon says to Laana.

He reads the paper out loud once he gets close enough. It's two words written with a fat marker and a shaky hand. "Job full."

Nixon screams and rips the paper from the door frame. He crumples it into a ball and throws it into the dark.

"I'm coming back," Nixon tells Laana then drops the connection between their readers.

Nixon sits in the captain's chair on EHL. His feet are up on the dash in front of him, and he's looking to the ceiling.

"Was it a bad plan?" he asks Laana.

"No, it's still not a bad plan." She's in the navigator's seat looking at her reader. "There are lots of jobs available."

"Then why aren't we able to catch any of them? Not one."

"Timing."

Nixon kicks a foot at the case but misses. "This dumb thing was supposed to be our answer to that. It was supposed to be our advantage."

"It will be," Laana says.

"I thought we'd be swimming in credits by now. What if we were wrong? What if I was wrong? What if ..."

Nixon doesn't finish his thought. Instead, he starts to push the buttons in front of him and pulls up a galactic star map.

"You know I can do that for you, right?" Laana asks.

"I need a drink," Nixon says.

"We can mix up something ..." Laana points over her shoulder to the galley.

"I need it not to be here. Not on this ship. I just need a planet that's close."

"And what credits are you going to use to buy these drinks?"

Nixon turns his work from finding a place to land to programming directions into the ship's auto-pilot systems. Then he stops and undoes all of the work he'd just done.

"Killjoy."

"I'm not. But I don't want you giving up. Your plan is good. It makes sense, you just have to give it time to work. Have you ever heard of the Rule of Seven?"

"Tell me."

"Jobs come in sets. You'll get nothing for a long time. So long that you're ready to give up. Ready to abandon the work altogether. Then something happens. Something pops. You get that big job. Then you get another and another and soon it feels like you'll never miss out on a job again. But you do, and then you start the whole process over again. That's why most of the bounty chasers run broken down ships and shoot common guns. They don't want to have to spend money at all if they can avoid it."

Nixon shakes his head. "You just made that all up"

"I didn't. Everyone goes through this. It's the dry spell. It follows the good spell."

"What good spell? If you hadn't noticed …"

"It'll come. I believe that down to my shoes. And the good thing is …"

"Good thing?"

"Yes. The good thing is that all we need is one good spell. We just need to land a handful of good paying jobs, and we cash out. We both make the number we need to retire, and we walk away."

Nixon thinks about that for a moment. If she's right about this Rule of Sevens then his jobs are just around the corner. He just needs the patience to wait for them, but that's not something he's ever been good at.

ABOUT THE AUTHOR

Sam Renner is a Texas-based writer of science fiction serials. He loves daring crews, hopeless missions, and gutsy captains. When he's not writing sci-fi stories, he's helping his wife raise their three kids near Dallas.